Dawn *of a* DEMON

NIGHTFLY · BOOK 1

CHRISTINE SCHULZ

Emma-
Stay Magical

1

"WHAT KIND OF MAGIC DO you think he has?" I squirmed uncomfortably in the hard wooden chair and chugged the rest of my beer from the oversized glass, slamming it on the table in victory when I finished. My tongue licked the fizzy foam coating my lips, the flavor-enhancing magic bubbles tickling my taste buds and sending enticing notes of citrus dancing across my tongue.

"I'll bet you the next round of drinks he's some kind of elemental. I'm thinking … water." Ryker, sitting next to me with an empty glass in need of a refill, curled a half smile in my direction.

"Water? Nah. Why would you say that?"

"Because he's slippery and cold. Just like water."

"Real clever," I intoned.

My brows lifted at my teammate. I rested a hand under my chin, then discreetly glanced the other way to detail the situation before I agreed to his challenge. With a quick sniff, I tried to catch our target's magic scent, but he was too far away and all I could pick up on was the malty aroma of beer mixed with copious amounts of cologne and perfume worn by all the business workers enjoying a drink at the bar.

Despite it being a Tuesday evening, bodies occupied almost every stool. With a friendly staff and cheap drinks, the watering hole was a popular place for working professionals to unwind and relax after an exhausting day at the office. As the evening went on, people piled in, loitering near the crowded bar. The upbeat music playing in the background drowned out the loud chatter amongst colleagues and friends. Ryker and I stayed huddled at our corner table, pretending to be two casual drinking buddies.

Unfortunately, our visit to this bar wasn't a social one.

After three years of rigorous training, both physically and mentally, I finally became a full-fledged military soldier six months ago. The mission this evening was supposed to be an easy one—to apprehend Davian Grymes, a man with a name perfectly befitting his dirty schemes. The military had received an anonymous tip that Davian would be here conducting an illegal transaction.

"Zulli?" Ryker's voice calling my name snapped me out of my trance. I peered up to a server batting her baby blue eyes adoringly at him as she slid a beer across the table.

"If you need anything else, just let me know." Her voice was smooth and feminine. The petite woman dipped her head and brushed a brown curl behind her ear, biting at the corner of her lip as she conjured a bashful smile.

"Thank you." He smiled warmly at her. "Actually, would you mind grabbing another one for my friend?"

The woman's expression went blank. "Oh. Sure." And then she stormed off.

I threw my head back and laughed at Ryker. "You'll never figure it out, will you?"

"Figure what out?" he replied, a look of bewilderment on his face.

"She was obviously flirting with you."

2

"What?" Ryker swiped a quick glance over to the brunette filling a pint glass behind the bar. "She was just being an attentive server, asking if we needed anything."

"And I supposed you *needed* her phone number?" I tapped on the cardboard coaster under his drink.

His eyes blinked at the numbers written in black ink. "Oh. *Oh.* I should apologize."

"Probably not necessary. I think she got the hint."

I took one look at Ryker and shook my head. He didn't exactly stand out in a crowd, with his cropped brown hair, amber eyes, and rosy skin, but he had this charisma that attracted people to him like lint on a dryer sheet. He was always smiling and going out of his way to make people happy. That he didn't know he had this effect on people made him even more alluring to others.

"Here, you can take my beer." Ryker slid over his glass. "This one's on me."

"Thanks." I flashed Ryker a grateful smile and pressed the cold pint glass to my lips.

"I still can't get used to your hair." Ryker tilted his head, scratching his own scalp.

"Me neither. But it beats getting my neck snapped in half next time some jerk decides to yank on my ponytail again."

I twisted my neck and ran my fingertips along the smooth shaved sides of my scalp. I rarely styled it, the longer forest green tips left sticking out in all directions. With a flick of my head, I attempted an overly dramatic hair flip but ended up giving myself whiplash instead.

"So how's the almighty CEO of NightFly Technologies holding up?" Ryker asked in a pretentious tone. "After fifteen years of working as your father's right-hand man, Davian goes rogue and is caught stealing sensitive data and equipment. Isn't Zavyr worried that Davian might be targeting him after what happened?"

3

My hand reached for the back of my neck and rubbed it. "My father's fine, I guess. He doesn't talk to me much about the family business. I know he has increased security on the building. I keep him updated on what the military finds out about Davian, but otherwise, he tends to keep me out of the loop on what he's doing."

A girly laugh heard from one end of the narrow establishment to the other caught my attention. It came from none other than my third teammate, Kasra.

She leaned in with a delicately placed hand on the nape of Davian's neck, grazing her fingers through his short, graying hair. Davian returned the gesture with a set of hairy fingers slowly gliding down Kasra's skin-tight pencil skirt. She pushed her blond hair off her shoulder, fanning herself as she unbuttoned the top button of her white blouse. Davian, and everyone else at the table, dropped a lascivious gaze to her chest.

Kasra had a gorgeous, curvy figure and could fake an infectious personality like a pro. She was an expert at playing to the whims of others, the perfect person for getting Davian alone so we could finally apprehend him and make him pay for his crimes. Most importantly, as a soldier in the Chitol army, she was trained to hold her own. She could take down this whole bar before anyone even knew what had hit them, no magic necessary.

"Uh oh. Looks like we have trouble." Ryker's hand dropped to a knife concealed under his loose-fitting hoodie.

I followed his gaze to a drunk man stumbling over to Kasra. His foot struck a table leg, causing a loud screech that was muffled under the noisy conversations going on around us. Leaning back in my chair, I adjusted my belt. To the average person, it appeared to be a decorative leather strap holding up my baggy pants, but the fake metal bullets that lined it each held a small amount of magic liquid or powder.

"Hey, beautiful!" The obnoxiously loud drunk slurred his words and swatted at Kasra's ponytail.

Kasra leaned out of his reach. With a lazy smile, she rose from her seat and attempted to steer him away in the opposite direction.

A disapproving growl came from Davian's mouth, his attention locked onto the imbecile bothering his pretty eye candy. He stood up from his chair to confront the man. Kasra gently touched her fingers to his forearm, hoping to calm him down before things got out of control.

Davian roughly pushed Kasra aside to take a swing at the drunk. Her hands braced the edge of the table as she collided into it. Pint glasses wobbled, beer and other liquids spilling over. With the reaction time of molasses, the unstable loudmouth let out a painful whimper as Davian's fist connected with his jaw. The intoxicated man stumbled backward into another half-drunk man, whose whiskey he was now wearing.

Davian whipped out a gun from a holster on his waist and pointed it at the drunk's head. Kasra jumped in to intervene. In one swift motion, she grabbed Davian's wrist and thrust it upward toward the ceiling, continuing to push his arm behind his back in an unnatural direction. With her free hand, she chopped at his knuckles. Losing his grip on the gun, it dropped and clattered at his feet.

The patrons in the busy bar began scrambling in all directions, screaming and knocking each other over like a bomb was about to go off in the building. The sober guests ran for the exit, while the intoxicated ones stuck around to cheer on Davian and join in on the fun. The excitement on their faces was alarming. With battle cries full of determination, they snatched anything within their grasp and launched it at whoever was nearby.

"I think that's our cue." Ryker nodded to me, and we both darted over to Kasra, diving into the chaos.

Rushing past our target, I activated my own magic to get a whiff of Davian's oozing from his body. I violently rubbed my nose, the smell of salty air burning past my nostrils. Water magic. Glad I didn't take Ryker up on his bet.

The tip of my boot nudged something soft on the floor. I looked down to see one of the drunks, who had fallen flat on his back. His poor balance made it look like he was trying to stand up on a patch of black ice, his flailing arms knocking over everything in his way.

"I'll get you for this!" The incoherent words babbling out of his mouth took me a moment to decipher.

"Doubt it." I kicked him over with my boot, and he was officially down for the count.

Returning my gaze to the room, I watched as half the bar had joined in on the fight. The noise intensified to eardrum-rupturing levels. The three other men who had been sitting at the table with Kasra circled her, taking turns with their knives and magic, trying to take her down. She ducked and dodged their attacks, smacking the men around with her bare hands. One of them snatched a pair of kitchen shears from behind the bar and sent it flying toward her face. She stepped to the side, narrowly avoiding it, but the blades now had another target.

"Watch out!" I dove at the brunette bartender about to be on the receiving end of the sharp object embedding itself into the back of her head. As I crashed into her, the pointed tip of the scissors pierced me in the arm, ripping open my skin before clattering to the floor. I seethed at the burning pain that radiated from the shallow puncture wound, warm blood soaking into my plaid button-down.

"You're welcome," I insinuated, although I was certain she was too in shock to hear my words. The woman froze, let out a high-pitched shriek, then ran out the front door and never looked back.

Ryker was battling his way through some angry patrons, using his magic to stab his knife through expertly placed portals while trying to prevent an angry mob from reaching Kasra. Glasses shattered across faces. Plates were thrown like deadly frisbees. Tables overturned and chairs flew across the room.

An overly confident man came charging at me with a fork. I picked up the scissors by my feet and chucked them at him. Missing my mark, sharpened cat claws shot out of my fingertips. I lunged in his direction, my body contorting as he swung his fist at my jaw. As I twisted around him, my claws cleanly sliced four gashes up his forearm. The man's eyes bulged open and he took a step back. The once fearless man dropped his utensil and scampered off in a different direction.

I winced as something heavy shattered against the back of my head. Whipping around, my foot crunched on broken glass from a liquor bottle. I skewered my next target with an unflinching stare and ripped a blue bullet from my belt.

"*Dormeo!*"

Sleep powder exploded across his chest, and the man dropped to the ground with a thud, eyes rolling to the back of his head.

"Show women some respect," I muttered to the unconscious man as I defied my own statement by grabbing a wooden chair and chucking it at a husky woman about to pounce on Ryker. Just beyond her, a man with dark-rimmed eyes and washed-out skin concealed himself with a trench coat while he pushed through the rowdy crowd.

"Ryker!" I cried, pointing at Davian attempting to make a run for it.

"Go get him!" Kasra insisted as she punched a pot-bellied hooligan in the gut. She still hadn't activated her magic. "I've got this."

Fighting the curiosity to watch Kasra in heels and a skin-tight skirt take down a horde of savage men, Ryker and I took off. We chased after Davian as he left through the hallway and out the back door in the kitchen.

Rounding a dumpster, I darted down the alley and abruptly stopped when I reached the main street. The sidewalks outside were bustling with people, noticing that half the pedestrians around me were wearing trench coats similar to Davian's. This was a business district and everyone was rushing to get home after a busy day at work.

"Can you smell his magic? Or hear him?" Ryker appeared beside me, scanning the street.

"Give me a second," I replied.

Closing my eyes, I engaged my magic and focused on targeting Davian's presence. Vibrations from cars whizzing down the street buzzed through my feet. The smell of rubber slipped past my nose as tires churned in a whirling motion around me. Mumbled conversations from those passing by offered no insight as to where Davian might have gone. I then tilted my head up toward the evening sky, inhaling a deep breath.

The salty stench of Davian's lingering magic stung my nostrils. My ears twitched at the slightest rattle of metal above me. I opened my eyes just in time to see our escapee's foot swinging over the ledge and onto the roof of the building adjacent to the bar.

"*Capto!*" My spelled boots stuck to the brick wall, while magic enveloped my hands. They became tacky, sticking to the brick just like a spider, as I climbed up the side of the three-story commercial building.

Although I couldn't see it, the presence of magic hummed directly above my head. Ryker's portal opened, and I crawled through skipping straight to the top floor. Without a clear picture of his destination, this was as close as he could get me to the roof where Davian had fled to.

My weak hands began slipping on the cold brick. They scraped down the side of the building a few feet before my magic completely gave out. A shriek flew out of my mouth, my stomach making its way up into my throat. Ryker's cinnamon scent mingled with the polluted city air. He appeared through a portal at the top of the fire escape, grabbing my wrist before I plummeted to the sidewalk below. He hoisted me up, and we stepped over the ledge onto the roof.

Ryker gave me a look, scrunching his brows and pressing his lips together. He didn't need to speak to remind me that, while I may have had two shifter powers inside me, I only had half the strength and abilities of each.

Fans and vents were scattered sporadically across the flat roof of the commercial space. The tall office buildings around us reflected the late evening sun setting over the city, casting sharp shadows that made for great hiding spots. Lucky for me, I didn't need to see to know where Davian was. I placed my palm on the ground, feeling the slightest vibration of footsteps to my right.

"Over there!" I called out, pointing to the man fleeing toward the rooftop's access door.

I couldn't see Ryker's portals opening. Magic energy was something only a few select people could physically see. However, with my heightened senses, I only needed to feel for the vibration of his magic to know where I needed to go.

My foot kicked through a small portal, tripping Davian and sending him flying face-first into a ventilation unit. As he scrambled to his feet, I ripped a bullet from my belt. Although our target was well over twenty feet away, I dropped the cylinder right at his feet.

"Demitto."

Bright green sticky goo erupted from the bullet, and like heavy duty bubblegum, it stuck him in place. Feet cemented to the ground, he tried to jerk free as I trotted over to him. Sharp pointed claws protruding from my fingertips aimed right at Davian's throat. I approached him warily, and he returned my frown with a smirk.

"Nice try," he sneered.

Water slipped down Davian's body, and the elastic substance securing him in place washed right off. He threw out his arms in front of him. A water cannon shot from his palms like a fire hose, the swirling cyclone plastering my face and pushing me back.

Despite popular belief, human cats do not always land on their feet.

My boots slipped, the gravity magic useless against the slick service. I slapped a hand onto something metal, but my sticky fingers were too wet to lock on.

I gulped down a mouthful of icy water, the saltiness burning my throat. Another blast of Davian's magic rushed at my chest. Rocks, twigs, and other debris caught in the vortex scraped across my skin. My body became numb as it was dragged across the rough concrete surface of the roof. I tumbled, somersaulting over myself until I rammed into a metal fan vent, flipped over it, and soared into the open air.

"Zulli!" Ryker rushed over to me just as I was hurtled over the ledge of the roof.

Before my body splattered across the pavement in the alleyway below, a warm pocket of magic subdued the icy water around me. The scenery suddenly changed. Instead of falling to the street below, I was dropped out of the sky about six feet directly above Davian.

A rush of adrenaline mixed with panic as I screamed, frantically waving my hands around. When my body crashed into his, he flattened to the ground like a pancake, air hissing through his lips like a deflated balloon. Ryker's portal closed, and the water flowing through it shut off like a faucet.

Davian threw me off his back. I flipped around, grabbing his pant leg. He kicked out his foot and caught me in the jaw. The pain throbbed through my skull. I spat out a wad of blood, reaching for another bullet on my belt before I noticed Davian remove something from a pocket in his trench coat.

"I hear water and electricity don't mix well." He threw a yellow marble at me, a cloud of magical powder exploding across my chest.

The current paralyzed my muscles. My whole body began contracting and twitching, and I watched helplessly as he lingered over me.

10

"Tell Zavyr I'm coming for him."

"Wha-what do you wa-want with my d-dad?" My chest burned with magic as I pushed out the words.

He turned on his heel and darted for the exit, disappearing into the shadowy stairwell. His heavy footsteps echoed down the stairs as he made his escape.

"Zulli! Are you okay?" Ryker sprinted over to my side and dropped to his knees in a puddle of water.

I pushed myself up onto my elbows. The military had trained its soldiers to endure a number of different magic attacks like these, allowing us to recover faster. This one, though, had really packed an extra punch.

"I'm okay. Just a couple cuts and bruises. His water mixed with the electricity magic really got me good, though." I threw my head back and clutched a hand to my chest, desperately panting. The electric current had fizzled out, but my body was still pulsing with pain.

Relief washed over Ryker, dimples forming on his cheeks as a smile tugged at his lips. He raked a hand through his short chestnut-colored hair. "Zulli, what would you ever do without me?"

"Pretty sure I'd be dead by now. Sorry you got stuck with me and …" I suddenly remembered. "Kasra! We have to go back for her!"

"Let's find her, head back to base, and then you should get those injuries looked at. Did you get … stabbed? When did that happen?" His finger traced the tear in my shirt, sopping wet with a dark red stain.

I shrugged at the hole in my arm, pretending I wasn't bothered by the throbbing pain. I ran a finger across the bumpy, bleeding surface of my skin, tenderness settling in. When Ryker turned away, I licked it and made a sour face. I watched as the bleeding began to stop, the burning pain starting to subside. It was common knowledge cat shifters had the ability to heal minor cuts and wounds with their tongues, but I wouldn't be caught dead letting anyone see me lick myself.

Ryker opened a portal, and less than a second later, we entered through the back door into the bar. Piles of unconscious bodies lay sprawled across chairs, tables, and the floor. A grunting sound came from behind the bar top. I peered over, and there was Kasra, holding the last stubborn thug in a choke hold. The man's mouth went slack, gasping for air that never came. He gave up trying to free himself and silently passed out.

"Took you guys long enough," Kasra chided. "The rest of Davian's bimbos are tied up over there in the corner. Did you get him?"

Kasra didn't come out of this ordeal unscathed. She picked tiny pieces of glass shards from cuts on her arms and neck and beer dripped from the hair sticking to her skin. A red welt had taken shape on her cheek, the likelihood it would turn into a nasty swollen bruise pretty high. At some point, she'd lost her heels, probably using them as a weapon to stab someone. Her black pencil skirt and white blouse looked like they had gone through a paper shredder.

"No. He got away." I looked to my feet, embarrassed at myself.

"Oh. Well that sucks." She scanned the bar and pursed her lips. Anyone who was lucky enough to escape had long since fled the building, and everyone else was either unconscious or almost unconscious, too drunk to move or understand what was going on. "Hmm. We should probably get out of here before anyone else shows up."

Kasra had done a number on Davian's henchmen, but unlike the rest of the people in the bar, they were still very conscious. And very pissed off.

The spicy scent of cinnamon cut through the musky atmosphere as Ryker used his magic to open a portal back to base. Kasra passed through first, shoving a stout man firmly in front of her.

12

I grabbed the bulkier of the two remaining men, leaving the remaining scrawny guy for Ryker. I smirked at him, and he just chuckled. I'd never felt like I had to prove anything to Ryker, but the two of us always had fun challenging each other to see who was stronger, faster, and smarter. Obviously, being a hybrid cat and spider shifter, that was me.

"Let's go, Baldy." The man was almost a full head taller than me, his biceps the size of my legs. I grasped one of his meaty arms, clasped it behind his back with magic-dampening hand-cuffs, and pushed him toward the portal. He abruptly stopped, firmly planted his feet on the ground, and head-butted me with the back of his skull. It packed such a punch that my vision van-ished momentarily and I fell backward onto my ass. "Son of a ..."

"Zulli!" Ryker took a step toward me but I waved him off.

I shook off the dizziness, jumping to my feet and throwing myself onto my prisoner escaping toward the exit. My arms wrapped around his neck and my legs around his waist, holding on with all my remaining strength. Since I was half his size, he just took me for a piggy-back ride through the bar.

For such a bulky man, he darted around the unconscious bodies like a rabid fox, grunting and seething. Baldy then twirled around with more finesse than I could have imagined. My legs lost their hold on his waist and swung out to my side. My foot swept across a table, taking out a group of martini glasses that shattered when they hit the ground.

My fingers started to slip, my limited magic of little use. My palms burned as they chafed against the scratchy fabric of his shirt. After a few minutes of struggling, my grip finally let go. My momentum carried me forward, and my head smacked against the sharp corner of a table. I barely had a moment to blink before I saw the plastic pitcher full of beer come crashing down onto my face.

The alcohol soaked into the scrapes and cuts on my skin. It burned my eyes, igniting an eruption of pain like a pot of boiling water was just dumped on me. I used the hem of my shirt, soaked with Davian's salty magic water, to try to wipe it away. Black dots danced around my vision, my ability to stand thwarted by dizziness. My sight returned when a thick leather boot was about to stomp down and crush my skull.

A blast of heat hit my face. A hand shot through a portal, grabbing onto the man's ankle from the side and yanking his leg out from under him.

Baldy let out a frustrated grunt as he lost his balance, toppling over and slamming his jaw shut when it hit the floor. Licking the tip of a pointed fang, I crawled on top of him and sunk my teeth into his neck.

For such a brute, I felt only a minimal presence of magic. I sucked it out, careful only to take enough to subdue him. Draining too much magic would likely kill him, but if I didn't take enough, he'd still be able to attack me.

Like a silky mouthful of chamomile tea, notes of honey and citrus mingled with a delicate floral aftertaste that glided down my throat. My insides warmed with his magic. While I wasn't able to take on his powers, the extra magic energy boost was just what I needed to replenish my own.

Having completed my fill, I retracted my fangs and pushed myself off Baldy's back. His feet slipped across the wet floor as he tried to stand, kicking over a chair that clattered loudly.

"I totally had him," I reprimanded Ryker, not angry at him for assisting me but more annoyed that he'd had to.

The tenacious fugitive no longer had the energy to stand, so I wrapped both my hands around one tree trunk arm and hoisted him up myself.

"I know you did," Ryker responded, grabbing the other beanstalk of a man, who was too scared to try anything after seeing what happened to his buddy. Ryker's portal reopened, and he led me through it back to base. "I saw an opportunity and wanted to help."

We surfaced at the Chitol military base in the hallway near the heavily guarded holding cells. The soldier on duty buzzed open the thick steel door that let us inside.

"How's it going, Private Haynes?" Ryker marched through like he was carrying a sack of feathers, while my knees were buckling underneath me as I tried to carry the weight of a horse over my shoulders.

"Slow night, so I can't complain." The soldier, a younger fellow whose newbie excitement hadn't worn off yet, grabbed Ryker's prisoner by the arm and led him down the hallway.

My foot squeaked against the tile floor, and I nearly flattened to the ground with a giant falling on top of me.

"You need some help, Zulli?" Ryker asked, holding out his hand to grab the man's waist before I could stop him. This time, I accepted his generosity because otherwise, he'd end up having to carry both of us.

Our footsteps echoed in the quiet corridor. Most of the cells on either side of us were empty, and those that were occupied had sleeping bodies in them. The soldier unlocked two adjacent cells, and hurried in our captives. They'd be kept here pending further investigation and, assuming they'd be found guilty of their crimes, transported to a more permanent prison facility.

On our way out, a burst of cheers and a round of enthusiastic applause rang out from the end of the hallway.

"What's going on over there?" I asked Private Haynes.

"Captain Myra Llama just successfully completed her twenty-fifth mission by capturing one of the country's most notorious terrorists! She's not only the youngest military captain we've ever had, she also has a solid track record of never failing. She told me the guy was like twice her size and had some super powerful strength magic. He took a hostage and was about to snap the woman's neck with his bare hands, but Myra used her ninja combat skills to not only free the hostage but also knock the guy out and bring him in! She's amazing, right?" The guard peered up at the ceiling, dark eyes gleaming and a smile creeping up his thin face.

"Fan boy," I muttered under my breath while rolling my eyes.

The soldier heard my comment, snapping his gaze at me and giving me a critical assessment. "You're soaked and you smell like garbage. Go take a shower." He waved me off and went back to his station.

As most people had gone home for the day or set out on other missions, the rest of the base was quieter than usual. Only a few night owls roamed the hallways and stuck around to get some extra work done.

I kept my chin up and shoulders stiff, stared straight ahead, and tried to avoid eye contact with Ryker and Kasra. I didn't fool anyone, though. Ryker always had a sixth sense when he knew something was bothering me.

"It was a team effort, Zulli," he spoke softly, patting a hand on my back. "We failed as a team."

"It's not that." I shook my head, scrubbing a hand through my damp hair. "Davian made this comment about my dad. He said he was coming for him. Maybe he was just playing with me. I don't know. A lot of people have strong feelings about my dad, since he makes money off people's illnesses, but given their history together, I can't help but to worry that Davian is planning something against him. I should check on my dad, make sure he's okay."

"*After* you get those wounds checked out. You look like a bloody swamp monster."

I could smell the stench of blood, beer, and saltwater wafting off me. My finger touched the side of my head, a thick coating of warm liquid coating it. My head was still spinning, and my ripped clothes were stuck fast to my skin.

Ryker headed off to the locker room in the other direction. Kasra followed alongside me as we made our way toward the infirmary. The small medical space had six exam tables sectioned off by curtains. Fluorescent tube lights ran the length of the room, its stark white plastered walls, white furniture, and white tile floor almost blinding.

"What trouble did you get into this time?" My favorite nurse, Lana, approached me, hands on hips in disapproval.

"Got stabbed, blasted with a water cannon, almost fell off a roof, and lost a battle with the side of a table. The usual." My half grin was accompanied by a raise of my eyebrows.

Lana's short auburn hair fell in flat waves just above her shoulders, the fringe pinned up and out of her face with a clip. Her blue-gray eyes were dulled by the black bags under them. She wore with pride, a sign that she tirelessly labored to attend to her patients no matter what time of day, forgoing precious sleep to ensure they were treated properly. Not bothering with a typical white lab coat, she wore a pair of black slacks and a neatly pressed patterned blouse.

She picked at every limb on my body, checking for injuries and determining how she should treat them. She slathered a variety of different gels all over the cuts and burns on my skin. The magic infused in them burned more than the wounds themselves, proof that they were working. After a few minutes, it looked less like I had been skinned alive and more like a nasty sunburn from a long day at the beach.

"You're lucky, Zulli," Lana told me as she listened to my breathing through a stethoscope. "I know you're trained to endure magic, but had that energy spell been more powerful, it would have likely stopped your heart."

"Well, I *am* half cat shifter. Don't I get nine lives?"

The nurse smiled and quietly laughed, adjusting her metal-rimmed glasses to get a better look at my injuries. "You're also half spider. A lot of those buggers only live a few days, and that's if no one squashes them first. Besides, with the number of times I've seen you in here, I'd say you're long past nine lives! Be careful will you?"

17

"Sure thing, Doc. Thanks." I hopped off the examination chair and strolled out the door.

Kasra was waiting for me outside the infirmary, leaning against the cinder block wall with her arms folded across her chest.

"Aren't you going in to get checked out?" I asked her.

"I'm fine. All I really want to do right now is go home, take a shower, and sleep. You ready?" She picked at a crusty piece of hair, saturated with dried blood and beer.

"Where's Ryker?" My head twisted to scan the hallway.

"He said he had to do something and not to wait for him."

Kasra jiggled her car keys in her hand, and I responded with a lazy smile. She happened to live in the same apartment complex as I did, so I hitched a ride back home with her. Private Haynes would have to alert the proper authorities about the three men we brought in. After that, we still had to meet with the colonel for a debrief and there was a mountain of paperwork ahead of us before we'd be allowed to question them. There was no point in any of us sticking around for the rest of the night. We'd come back tomorrow re-energized and with clear minds to get our answers.

2

ON THE CAR RIDE BACK to my apartment, I tried to call my dad. He didn't pick up, so I left him a voicemail recounting what had happened. Either he was too engrossed in his work to bother answering his phone or he was actually sleeping for once. When I woke the following morning, I had several missed calls from him. I was about to return them when someone knocked on my front door.

"Kasra? What are you doing here?" I asked, bleary eyed, as the door creaked open.

She tapped her wrist. "It's ten in the morning. We have to head over to base for a debrief and to see if the interrogators got any information out of Davian's men."

I waved Kasra into my apartment and she sat down on the flat-cushioned couch, pulling at the frayed edges of the fabric. She waited impatiently, tapping her foot, while I went to change out of my pajamas.

My apartment was nothing special, but the small studio was one of the few places I could unwind and be myself. A small kitchen took up a corner of the apartment as you walked in. In front of the couch, lining the wall to the left, was a scuffed up wooden coffee table. Across from it was my full-sized bed on a cheap metal frame. Darkness usually overwhelmed the space, given that my view of the city through the two small windows was the drab concrete side of the office building next door. The place had my own personal touch, though, with a few family photos and other items I had brought from home.

I yawned, flattening the wrinkles out of my oversized t-shirt, then clipped my bullet belt around the waist of my ripped jeans.

"All right, I'm ready."

Kasra snorted at me. "The colonel isn't going to be happy with *that*." She circled a finger at my outfit. "Don't you ever wear your uniform?"

Somehow, Kasra had made the boring military uniform look fashionable with her snugly fit black t-shirt and khaki cargo pants that hugged her long legs. A leather belt with a shiny silver buckle was wrapped around her waist. Her blond hair was neatly braided, swung over her shoulder with a glittery hair tie at the end. She had just enough makeup on her face that her hazel eyes popped against the golden glow of her skin.

As I pondered her question, I slipped on my worn-out motor-cycle boots and a leather jacket. "The colonel already dislikes me. Besides, my uniform is still covered in mud and I ripped my pants on our last mission. I'm wearing a camo t-shirt with skulls on it, though. Does that count?"

"It also has more wrinkles than a crumpled up used tissue. What's that red stain on it? I hope that's not blood."

I rubbed the stain with my thumb, then licked my shirt. "Nope, just tomato sauce. Let's go."

We stepped out of the apartment building and onto the side-walk. While we could have driven, the sunny spring day in the city Chitol was perfect for a stroll to our favorite coffee shop just around the corner. At that point, we were only a few more blocks from Ryker's place, so we decided to meet up and take the shortcut to base using his magic.

A crisp spring breeze swept through the streets, and I drew in a deep breath of polluted city air. The sulfuric smell of car fumes mingled with the delectable aroma of freshly baked bread as we continued to our destination. Tall skyscrapers formed the city grid around us, the bright late morning sun that reflected off the rows of glass windows above us. It didn't matter the time of day, though. The city sidewalks were always packed with busy pedestrians and the roads were crowded with vehicles weaving their way through traffic.

We entered the coffee shop and waited in the long line that nearly reached the door. My heightened senses went into overdrive, the nutty smell of freshly brewed coffee tingling my nose. I had to stop myself from drooling when someone passed by me, holding a cup of my favorite magic-infused brew. I could taste its magic through the steam lingering in the air, subtle notes of cherry vanilla passing my lips and teasing my tongue.

"Good morning, Zulli! What can I get you today?" the barista chimed, his toothy grin too big for his narrow face and his overly excessive enthusiasm ringing in my ears.

"Morning, Briyan. The usual please. We still hanging out on Saturday?"

Briyan's smile lit up the room. "Of course! You won our last five games of World Domination. I can't let you do it again! I'll bring the pizza and beer." He reached behind the counter to grab a paper bag. "I saved this for you. Our baker is testing a new recipe for crumb cake muffins. I just …"

Briyan stopped moving, his face locked in a stony expression, his eyes staring off into the distance. It was like someone had turned off his power button and all the energy drained from his body.

"Briyan? You okay?" I waved my hand in front of his face, but he had completely zoned out.

His body swayed slightly, then his legs gave out. His head smacked against the counter on his way down. Gasps erupted from guests as the staff behind the counter rushed over to him.

My heart jumped into my throat and instinct kicked in. I braced a hand on the counter and slid over it to attend to Briyan on the other side.

"Briyan!" A female employee dropped to her knees and pressed a hand to his face. "He's burning up!"

My hands were shaking, my pulse pounding so loud in my ears that it was all I could hear. I was trained to give basic first aid, but everything I learned had been tossed out of my mind as I stared at Briyan's disabled body in front of me.

"W-what's wrong with him?" My voice quavered. Not surprisingly, no one gave an answer. I turned to the guests watching us with curious worry. Some were actually taking pictures and recording with their phones. "You think this is a joke? Someone call an ambulance!"

A woman fumbled with her phone before lifting it to her ear.

Blood seeped out from a deep gash on Briyan's forehead. He was shaking so much that his teeth chattered, and only the whites of his eyes were visible. His limbs twitched and jerked uncontrollably. I crouched down next to him. He slapped my arm as I tried to hold him down to prevent him from further injuring himself. He started gurgling and choking as four other employees came to our aid.

"Roll him over onto his side so he can breathe." Kasra had joined me to help, pushing on Briyan's shoulder to roll him over. With a quick glance over to the brunette employee next to her, she commanded, "Give me your apron."

The brunette immediately complied, handing it over to Kasra with shaking hands. Kasra balled it up and placed it under Briyan's head. Regaining my focus, I grabbed a wad of napkins and pressed it against his head wound. Blood soaked right through it.

"Where's the ambulance!" I screamed, sweeping my gaze around the cafe. A woman warily raised her hand.

"I just called. They're five minutes away."

There was nothing else we could do but wait.

Briyan's foot kicked out to the side, knocking over a plastic waste bin full of coffee grounds. White foam bubbled from his mouth, and his thrashing became more violent. It took every staff member to hold him down. He was gasping for air, barely breathing. We didn't have five minutes.

A final choke came from his mouth, a wad of blood-speckled foam spraying out. His movements began to calm, his consciousness fading. Kasra checked for a pulse and immediately began chest compressions.

"Briyan, come on. Stay with me, bud," I spoke to him as calmly as I could, but the panic was obvious in my unstable voice. I wasn't sure if he could hear anything I was saying, but I kept speaking anyway. "I never got a chance to thank you for that free slice of pound cake you slipped into my bag last week. It was delicious. And I have a confession to make. I sometimes cheat at World Domination. You would have won last time. Let's have a fair rematch, okay?"

The front door crashed open, and a uniformed woman carrying an industrial-sized medical kit hurried inside. "Out of the way! Everyone get back!"

The first responder rushed behind the counter and pushed us aside, taking over chest compressions and giving Briyan oxygen. She shot something into his arm with a syringe, then tried to speak to him.

"Hey, Briyan. My name's Trist. Are you still with us?"

Briyan gave her no response, not even so much as a blink.

Two female baristas behind me held each other, crying as the medic desperately tried to revive their friend and fellow colleague. Another responder joined, bringing more equipment with him.

With a sleeve, Trist wiped off the sweat that had formed on her shiny forehead. She leaned back on her knees, raking a hand through her long jet-black hair. She closed her eyes and inhaled a deep breath.

"I'm sorry. He's … gone."

My heart sank to my toes, and my disbelieving eyes stared at Briyan's lifeless body on the floor. For the past six months, Briyan had been here at this cafe almost every morning to greet Kasra and me with his charming smile and cheerful laugh. We'd become good friends, binge eating junk food and playing board games on the weekends. He'd always ask how we were doing, sneak us free samples when new recipes were used. Briyan was a good man. He didn't deserve this.

The first responders wheeled Briyan's body out of a gurney and into the back of an ambulance, then drove off down the street. The siren was never turned on.

Kasra and I stuck around outside until the police showed up. We were about to go back into the cafe when a distressed grunt caught my attention. The brunette barista from earlier was pacing back and forth on the sidewalk. A shaking hand wiped away the tears streaming from her face. Her sorrow transformed into anger as she kicked a crumpled soda can littering the street.

"Go on inside," I told Kasra. "I'll check on her."

With a worried glance in my direction, Kasra left us while I strolled over to the brunette.

"I'm sorry for your loss," I said as I cautiously approached the woman. Comforting people was usually Ryker's job, but this woman had just seen someone die, a friend and fellow coworker. *Somebody* had to be there for her. "I'm Zulli."

"I know who you are. I'm Ambyr," she responded through trembling lips. "Briyan spoke about you all the time. You're a soldier in the military?"

"Yeah. Kasra and I are—"

"I should have known this would happen," she sniffled, rubbing her watery eyes. "I should have done more to stop it!"

"This isn't your fault, Ambyr. There's no way you could have—"

"He was using Bliss," she stated, cutting me off again. "Briyan and I had been dating for about three years. He was always a cheerful guy, but about a year ago, everything changed. His

24

younger sister called one night while we were out drinking at a bar. Said she needed him to come pick her up from a party that had gotten out of hand. I told him not to go, to call her a cab, because he wasn't in any condition to drive. He insisted he was fine." She paused to sniffle, her fingers fidgeting with her long ponytail.

"Well, he got there but something happened on the way back. A truck cut him off, and he couldn't react in time to swerve out of the way. The car overturned. He survived, but … his sister didn't. It came down really hard on him, and he couldn't stop blaming himself for her death. Recently, that spark of life came back in his smile. I didn't question it. I was just happy to see him no longer suffering. I didn't find out it was Bliss until a few weeks ago. I begged him to stop taking it, but he was already too reliant on it. Every time the memory of his sister would come back, he'd take another hit of Bliss to forget it."

Tears glistened in her eyes, and she slapped her hands to her face to hide her distress. I didn't know what to say. Thankfully, I didn't have to try. The police had arrived and requested to speak with both Kasra and me.

"What happened here?" the officer asked in a flat tone. He didn't even look at us, scribbling something down in his notepad instead.

"Um … I … he …" I knew exactly what had happened, but my throat clenched tightly every time I tried to speak the words.

Kasra took over, recounting the situation with every precise detail. "He started convulsing, then went unconscious. That's when the paramedics showed up and took over."

Satisfied with our statement, Kasra provided her phone number to the police officer.

"Come on. We gotta get over to Ryker's place." Kasra began walking down the sidewalk, right past a lonely Ambyr leaning against the storefront window.

"Hold up a minute." I stopped in front of Ambyr. "Um, I know you don't know me that well but, if you need anything,

I'm around. The military is trying to find the person responsible for distributing Bliss, and I'm helping them do it. We're gonna get this guy so no one else suffers. Promise."

A twitch of a smile barely reached her lips as we exchanged phone numbers. Hopefully, I would be able to keep that promise.

The busy city around us was bustling with life and energy, but Kasra and I were caught in a disbelieving trance, our heads hanging low and feet dragging.

We were about halfway to Ryker's apartment when Kasra spoke. "This Bliss drug is getting out of hand. I heard on the news this morning that over a hundred reported cases have been filed about addicts frying their brains in the last few weeks alone."

"I really don't get its allure. Why would anyone do something so irrational that it might end up frying their brain in the process?"

Kasra shrugged. "Why does anyone do drugs? The high. Bliss helps you leave the past behind. Completely forget your troubles and what's bothering you. Think about it. Don't you wish you could forget what you just saw?"

I shook away the mental image of the paramedics taking away Briyan's dead body. Then I remembered what Ambyr had told me. How he had been so traumatized about his sister's death that he'd rather completely forget she ever existed than deal with his guilt.

"I guess I can understand, but facing your problems is what helps you move on, not pretending like it never happened. It changes what makes you *you*. I just can't believe Davian would do something like this. After fifteen years of working with my dad to *save* lives, he decides to start *destroying* them? The guy's got a screw loose." My fingers rubbed the palm of my hand, flecks of Briyan's dried blood still coating it.

Kasra scratched her arm, staring up into the clear sky. "Money. Power. Greed. Maybe even revenge. Zavyr fired Davian from NightFly Technologies for stealing, right? It's like the ultimate bitch slap to your dad's face. The same drugs Zavyr uses to save lives are now being used to kill people. Not to mention anything NightFly Technologies produces from now on will be put under a microscope. Davian isn't just killing people, he's also killing your dad's business."

In the distance, I could just make out the tallest building in the city—the headquarters of my father's magiceutical company, NightFly Technologies. He was probably there right now in his office on the top floor filing through a mountain of paperwork. I pulled out my phone from my back pocket to return my dad's calls. Once again, it went straight to voicemail.

We approached Ryker's apartment complex, a much larger, much nicer building than where Kasra and I lived. A woman, whose designer heels probably cost more than my entire year's salary, strolled by me in the lobby. She scoffed at my ripped jeans, then gasped at my wild haircut, clearly offended that someone so lowly would dare enter her sanctuary. I hid my face behind the collar of my leather jacket and kept my gaze forward.

"Why does Ryker even live here?" I grumbled to Kasra. "He's not like these high-maintenance people."

"What I'd like to know is how he can afford it." Kasra pushed the elevator button. "Because there's no way any low-level soldier like us could afford living here with the measly salaries we get. If it weren't for Ryker's generosity and always offering to buy our meals, I'd be dying of starvation. You think his parents are loaded? Maybe he won the lottery and never told us."

We rode the elevator up to his bachelor pad on the fourteenth floor, a single bedroom condo with top-of-the-line appliances, sleek furniture, and a beautiful view of the city through a wall of windows.

"After you, ladies." Ryker fanned out his hand toward the portal he had created in his foyer. A gentle heat caressed my skin. The spicy smell of his cinnamon magic warmed my insides as I passed through the invisible opening to the side entrance of the military base. The guard on duty acknowledged us and waved us inside.

The military base had become my second home, and I spent just as much time here training as I did at my apartment sleeping. The large concrete block building wasn't much for the eyes, and the vast open parking lot with a few sturdy vehicles parked in it seemed like a waste of space, but it was the people inside and the mission they were dedicated to that really counted.

Ryker started massaging his hands, pressing his thumb into his palm and flexing his fingers.

"You okay?" I asked skeptically. Kasra briefly glanced over but ignored my conversation with Ryker. "Does it hurt?"

I'd known Ryker since I'd officially become a soldier. After our very first mission together, I found myself fascinated with his portal magic and the way he used it. Most people envied transporters like Ryker, who could go anywhere they wanted in a blink of an eye. But ripping open a hole in the universe didn't come without consequences. It wasn't just taxing on the mind, having to clearly concentrate on his destination. It was physically painful as well.

"I'll be okay. The smaller portals are usually bearable ... but the bigger ones are a bit much sometimes. It feels like I'm punching through a thick window. Like bits of jagged glass are scraping across my knuckles, pressing deep into my skin. Sometimes it's so bad my hand goes completely numb, but the side effects usually pass in an hour or two, as long as I don't overdo it."

I felt a familiar rush of selfishness for taking advantage of Ryker's abilities and asking him to transport us to base. Not to mention all the other times I had begged him to stop by my apartment when I was running late. He never once complained, always willing to help out either me or Kasra when we needed it. Never once did he ask for anything in return.

"How about I bake you some of my famous snickerdoodle cookies? And I will personally drop them off at your place so you don't have to come get them."

"Mmm. I could live off those things. Deal." His warm smile formed crinkles at the corners of his dimpled cheeks, his rosy skin brightening with joy.

"Privates! With me!" The three of us whirled around in the other direction, following a muscled giant down the hall until he disappeared through a doorway.

The empty office wasn't Colonel Buckner's, but was used for visiting personnel. A single floor lamp stood in the corner, the bookshelves completely bare, and not a single piece of paperwork cluttered the desk.

I straightened my spine, placing myself between Kasra and Ryker. Colonel Buckner opted not to sit, instead positioning himself behind the cheap metal desk. He leaned forward, pressing his fingertips against it. His shadow stretched across the fake wooden work surface and stopped right at our toes.

"Officers," he addressed the group, but his gaze was pinned on me. "Where is your uniform, Private Taracula?"

"Um, it's at the dry cleaner's, sir."

Kasra bit her lip, faking a cough to hide her laugh.

"The next time you come in here without your uniform, Private Taracula, there will be consequences," the colonel growled. He let out a deep sigh and continued. "I commend you all for bringing in three of Davian's men, but you let our most valued target escape. We *need* Davian Grymes."

"I know, sir, but—"

Ryker cut me off. "But we slipped a tracking spell on him, sir. It only lasts twenty-four hours, but we thought tracking him would lead us to more valuable intel." Ryker kept his stony gaze straight ahead. He could be sneaky with his portal magic, but when the hell had he managed that last night? I shifted my gaze toward Kasra, and judging from the crinkle of her eyebrows, she didn't know either.

Colonel Buckner stared at us with his cold, gray eyes. Being intimidating came with the role of running this military base. From his strong, sharp jawline to his impeccable buzzcut, each strand of silver hair exactly the same length, he oozed power and authority.

"I see." He rubbed the tip of his bushy mustache between two fingers. "Have the trackers found anything?"

"I informed them right after we dropped off Davian's men. The tracking dogs should be out sniffing around the area for suspicious magic, but I haven't heard anything yet," Ryker assured him.

"Good. In the meantime, I will fill you in on the others you brought back last night."

The colonel stiffened his posture, clasped his hands behind his back, and marched out of the room. He never said a word, but we knew to follow. We tagged behind him until he turned into a small observation room, stopping in front of a one-way mirror. On the other side, Baldy was being questioned by our most accomplished interrogator, Lieutenant Velveteen. She must have been verbally abusing her victim for a while since sweat was dripping from his shiny dome, down his face and neck. His eyes were dark and sunken in, his shaking hands causing the metal cuffs on his wrists to clatter against the table.

"This is Shayn Dalton," the colonel informed us. "We don't know much about him, but we do know he's an associate of the Black Mark, the criminal organization Davian is working with to distribute Bliss. A team sent to Earth a few months back was investigating the presence of the Black Mark organization there and recognized his face. The black crosshairs tattoo on his knuckle confirms his membership, but we believe he's just a lackey."

"Earth?" Kasra scoffed. "Why would they go to Earth when magic on Iradel is so much more advanced?"

The colonel grabbed a paper cup and filled it from the water cooler behind him. "That's exactly the reason why they should, Private Klein. There is no competition. But we have reason to believe there's been a disagreement among Black Mark members. Those criminals who fled to Earth are tied to a different mission we have yet to figure out. That faction is likely being led by someone else, and at least right now, they aren't our top concern."

There was a brief moment of silence until Kasra spoke. "So, has Shayn said anything yet? Can we confirm what Davian was doing at the bar?" She narrowed her eyes, leaning in toward the window until the tip of her nose nearly touched it.

"No." Colonel Buckner sucked in a deep breath. "Because he took this."

In the colonel's burly hand was a small plastic bag with two white capsules in it. My hands clenched into tight fists, my heart skipping a beat when I realized what it was.

"He took Bliss." It was more of a statement than a question. The signature crosshair symbol stamped on the outside of the pill indicated exactly what it was.

"Indeed, Private Taracula," the colonel responded, returning his steely gaze to the prisoner. "And the other two you brought in took it as well. They don't remember a thing, and according to Lieutenant Velveteen, they're telling the truth. Her lie detector magic isn't picking up any deception."

"The effects of Bliss only last a day or two," Kasra pointed out, leaning back from the window and drumming her fingertips across her bicep. "Can't we just ask them again when it wears off?"

"If it wears off in time. We can only hold them another day before—"

Shayn's head shot up toward the ceiling and his eyes rolled into the back of his head. He puckered his lips. The corners of his mouth twitched, his jaw jerking. He pitched to the side, but the metal cuffs securing him to the table stopped him from falling to the floor.

A stream of Ryker's cinnamon-scented magic formed in front of him. He darted through the portal into the interrogation room next to Lieutenant Velveteen. The colonel, Kasra, and I trailed behind him.

"Grab a medic!" Colonel Buckner demanded, his voice booming inside the small room. Ryker had disappeared before he finished his words.

White frothy saliva speckled with blood started fizzing around Shayn's pale lips. His chest thrust out as he gasped for air that would never reach his lungs. My stomach wanted to roll up into my throat, out of my mouth, and onto the floor. The blood rushed from my brain. Still fresh in my mind was the emotional wound of seeing Briyan suffer the same consequences of Bliss.

My gaze focused only on Shayn, my limbs paralyzed in fear as the flashback replayed in my head. I forced my legs to move and ran out of the room into the hallway, pressing my back against the cool cinder block wall and sliding down until my butt hit the floor. A sudden explosion of intense fear felt like hands squeezing around my heart. My hand clasped my chest, gripping my shirt and pulling it away from my body. A cold sweat shivered through me, my muscles tensing. My eyes squeezed shut, a numbness taking over as I lost all sense of my surroundings.

"Zulli?" The voice didn't register at first, but I was brought back to reality the second time. "Zulli? It's okay. Calm down."

The sensitive touch of a hand pressed against my shoulder. My eyes slowly opened to see Ryker's gaze flickering over me, his mouth flat and worry carved into the dimples on his cheeks.

He helped me to my feet, and I inhaled a few deep breaths to relax my spasming lungs. "Sorry. I didn't mean to run out like that. I'll be fine."

"The medic gave Shayn a sedative. He should be okay for now, but the brain damage from Bliss could be permanent. Soldiers are going to keep an eye on the others." Ryker paused as I looked up at him. "Kasra told me what happened at the cafe this morning. I'm sorry you had to see that. Maybe you should ask for a few days off?"

"No!" My sharp words caused a few soldiers in the hallway to stop and look my way. "The longer we wait around, the more people will die. I want to put an end to this. To Davian. To give my father some peace of mind."

Ryker nodded, and Kasra's head popped out of the interrogation room. "You okay, Zulli?"

"Fine." My phone buzzed. Speak of the devil. The screen lit up with a message from my dad.

Don't forget dinner tonight! Someone will come to pick you up at seven.

"I have an idea." Ryker's amber eyes lit up and his dimples deepened.

"Does it involve lunch? Because I … I didn't get a chance to eat breakfast this morning." My fingers occupied themselves by tugging on a loose thread of my leather jacket.

"Come on, Zulli. Let's go to the cafeteria. I'm buying."

Kasra coughed behind us.

"You, too, Kasra."

The three of us slowly made our way to the cafeteria. The noise that rushed into my ears rivaled a rowdy stadium full of sports fans. The rows of cheap white plastic tables were occupied with starving soldiers chatting and shoveling food down their throats. This morning's events meant that our meeting with the colonel had ended later than we'd expected, so we were caught right in the middle of the lunch rush.

Kasra and I pushed through the busy crowds until we found a cramped spot over by the bathrooms. Ryker waited in line for food. He came back about twenty minutes later juggling three beige trays with enough food to feed a small army.

"Milkshakes weren't on the menu, but I charmed one of the staff into making one especially for you." Ryker slid over a tall cardboard cup with a straw, along with a cheeseburger, a double serving of fries, onion rings, a chef's salad, and a fruit parfait.

"I think these are yours." I handed over the leafy greens and yogurt to Kasra.

Ryker took a granola bar for himself and watched as Kasra and I devoured our meals. I pushed over my second helping of fries in front of him.

"You don't want it?" Ryker frowned, almost like he was hurt that I declined the food he'd purchased for me.

"I'm getting full. You can have some."

Ryker knew my stomach was a bottomless pit that never filled, but he graciously accepted and began picking at the fries. We took our time eating, none of us bothering to speak.

Just as we were finishing up, a brunette with a short brown bob appeared out of thin air next to us. My hair stood on end, and I jumped right out of my seat like the frightened cat I was.

"*Gah!* Someone needs to put a bell on you!"

I didn't recognize the female transporter, but she had the last name "Stacks" embroidered on her uniform. She was bouncing up and down, her deep blue eyes nearly popping out of her head and her mouth twisting into a grin. "You're needed in the communications room immediately! The trackers picked something up on Davian!"

She spoke like she had a megaphone in front of her, partly because it was hard to hear anything among the noise but also because she seemed overly excited about something.

The three of us leapt directly in front of Private Stacks, waiting for her to lead the way.

3

---◇---

SOME TRANSPORTERS LIKE RYKER RELIED on creating portals to their destination by visualizing a place in their head. Others could teleport based on their connections to people and places, allowing anyone in contact with them to go along for the ride. Private Stack's must have been the latter, seeing as she slapped both her hands on me and Kasra, then shoved her hip up against Ryker and winked at him. The warmth of her magic enveloped me, a delightful taste of blueberries tickling my taste buds. My vision went black, and for a brief moment, I felt weightless until my feet hit solid ground in the communications room.

Soldiers were scrambling around desks and chairs like busy worker ants. Their chatter intensified as they attempted to decipher Davian's next move. Rows of monitors displayed camera visuals and data on several targets being tracked, including Davian. Sweat started beading down my forehead. The amount of computer equipment and magic output in the room was throwing off enough heat to roast me alive.

"What's going on?" Ryker rushed over to a giant flat screen television displaying a live feed from a drone near the shipping docks on the other side of the city. Kasra and I joined him.

A scrawny soldier with the structural integrity of a leaf answered Ryker in a squeaky voice. "Private Lara Sims. Pleasure to meet you, Private Stone. I'm currently tracking Davian Grymes. He's at Yarwell Port, and it looks like he and some of his crew are up to no good. They seem to be eyeing that shipping container." She pointed to a blue rectangle on the screen.

I checked the clock hanging above the door.

"It's two in the afternoon," I concluded. "They must be on a deadline if they're moving this quickly and in the middle of the day." Unfortunately for them, I was on my own deadline. As long as we didn't run into trouble, I'd have more than enough time to take down Davian and make my family dinner tonight.

"Not necessarily." The gangly soldier swiveled around in her chair to face me. "Shipping docks are typically busiest early in the morning and late at night. So right now is actually the most convenient time to strike. Although, there should still be some dock workers hanging around. I'm not really sure where they went. Maybe Davian scared them off?"

For about an hour, we continued watching the monitor feed. A continuous stream of orders came from Davian bossing around a bunch of men. There was no audio, so we couldn't hear what he was saying, but our analysts were trying to figure out what he was instructing based on everyone's movements.

"I think we have enough information." Ryker placed a hand on the officer's shoulder. "Thank you, Private Sims. Your tracking skills are superb. This has been extremely helpful."

The woman blushed under his compliment. I crossed my arms and gave Ryker a dramatic eye roll.

Someone handed Ryker a printed photo of a commercial warehouse, and his eyes began rapidly scanning it to analyze every detail. For his portal magic to work, he needed to have a clear vision of where he wanted to go. It could be from a memory or a detailed picture. In fact, he kept his wallet full of photos specifically for that purpose, along with a bunch more on his phone just in case.

While Ryker was studying the photo, Kasra and I raided the equipment room across the hall, loading up on gear and weapons. I strapped on a tactical vest, leaving my leather jacket behind. Guns weren't typically my thing, so I secured a leg holster for a knife and a few paralysis daggers instead.

"Here, take this." I handed Ryker a set of the same equipment I had. He slipped on a vest over his polo shirt before he explained the plan to us.

"I can get us to the freight yard on the roof of the warehouse. Make sure to crouch down so they don't see us. We'll stay there and observe. If Davian gives us an opening to attack, we'll jump him. Hopefully we can catch him off guard with a strategically placed portal. But we only go after him if it's safe! Got it? If the situation appears to be too dangerous, we pull out and come back or wait for reinforcements."

"Sounds like a plan." I sloppily tucked in my t-shirt so I had access to my belt and the magic bullets attached to it. Behind me, Kasra grunted her approval.

Ryker inhaled a deep breath and focused. The air around me began to thrum with magic, but it was the cinnamon scent it gave off that entranced me. His magic permeated the air like a warm sticky bun, fresh out of the oven.

The slight tremble of Ryker's hands didn't slip past me unnoticed. For me, traveling through his portal was simply like passing through a doorway into a different room, but I knew Ryker's experience was on a completely different level.

He ushered us through his portal, and immediately we dropped onto our bellies when we reached the flat concrete roof on the other side. The salty breeze that swept off the water ruffled my short hair, the chilly spring breeze sending shivers down my bare arms. It wasn't yet evening, but the low hanging sun descending in the sky reflected a warm orange glow across the harbor. The picturesque view with the city skyline in the background would have been much more appreciated had we not been here risking our lives to stop a criminal.

The flat roof offered no ledge to hide behind, but it wasn't completely level. We crawled our way over to a raised section on our right, hiding behind a part of the roof that was a whole story taller than the rest of the building.

"Can you home in on anything?" Kasra asked me as she flattened her back against the metal siding.

"They're too far away for me to smell anything, but I might be able to hear them," I replied.

I shuffled as close to the edge of the building as I could get without revealing myself and quickly peered around the corner to scan the area. Rows upon rows of colorful shipping containers lined the wharf. Just as Private Sims had stated, it was odd that at three thirty in the afternoon, the wharf seemed to be completely vacant and all the machinery had been shut down. Thankfully, it allowed me to better focus my hearing. I immersed myself into the scenery around me and let my heightened senses take over.

"What are you hearing?" Kasra's impatience was taking over.

"*Shhhh!*" I hissed through my teeth. "I'm trying to concentrate. All I can hear is your yammering and fingers anxiously tapping your gun."

She glowered at me, folding her arms across her chest and tucking her hands under her armpits to stop herself from fidgeting.

Seagulls were squawking in circles above me, car horns blared off the main road nearby, and waves gently lapped up against the port's sea walls. I shut them all out, trying to extend the range of my magic. And then I heard it.

"If I can get closer, I might be able to tell what they're saying. All I hear are muffled voices over there." I pointed off into the distance. "It sounds like maybe four people? One of them is definitely Davian."

"Then we have to get closer." Ryker cracked his knuckles. "Let me scour the area. I'll be right back."

He opened a portal and vanished through it. I saw him reappear behind a shipping container on the ground below us. He cautiously opened one portal at a time, searching for the safest place for three people to not only conceal themselves but also spy on Davian.

About ten minutes later, his head popped through a portal without a body. "Hurry up and be quiet."

We swept through the portal and ended up behind a semi-trailer that had been attached to a loading dock. I dropped to my stomach to look underneath the truck and make out what was happening on the other side.

"I see feet," I whispered, crawling a little bit closer.

"But what are they saying?" Kasra began to whine. "We need to figure out what they're doing before we can move in. Technically, right now they're not doing anything illegal. Just loitering around."

"I can't make out what they're saying. They're all talking over each other, and they're moving so much stuff around I'm having trouble isolating the voices. I have an idea." I started crawling my way under the truck.

"Zulli, I know what you're thinking. That is a terrible idea." Ryker, the practical one of the group who always stopped me or Kasra from doing something stupid, grabbed a strap on my vest and stopped me from going any farther. I jumped up to my feet, brushing the dirt off my vest.

"I'll be fine, Ryker. It's the only way we can get close enough without being noticed."

"But we won't be able to communicate with you." He tugged on the neck of his shirt, his voice heavy with worry.

"I appreciate your concern, but I can handle myself. Just give me five minutes and I'll come crawling right back. Promise."

"Let her go, Ryker." Kasra's eagerness was shining through.

Ryker scratched a finger under his chin, then his gaze shot to me. He studied me for a few seconds before making his decision. "Fine. Five minutes or we're coming to get you."

"Yeah, yeah. Understood. I can't hold my form much longer than that anyway." I patted him on the chest. "Can you guys, um, look away for a second?"

Without question, they both turned their attention elsewhere. They knew about my ability to turn myself into a spider, but there was something about it that put people on edge and made me a little insecure. Most people hated the creatures, and I turned into an ugly, black, hairy arachnid. I'd lost track of how many times people had tried to squash me. It was too bad I couldn't completely shift into a cat. They were much more likable animals.

My magic activated, and it coursed through my veins. The warmth was like a magic high, tingling my senses as my body shifted into an eight-legged, inch-long creepy crawly.

I scuttled under the tractor trailer toward the voices. My spider body, half the size of other spider shifters, pushed my tiny legs to cover as much ground as quickly as they could.

On the other side of the trailer, I could see Davian and two of his men. They were hauling pallets of something from a bright blue shipping container into a delivery truck.

"Hurry it up, boys!" Davian's slick voice called out to his men.

"We're almost done, boss," one of his workers answered as he loaded the truck, his blond beard longer than the hair on his head.

"Good, keep it going."

I crawled closer, determined to get a better look at what they were moving. My sticky legs climbed up the dull metal siding of the shipping container. The jagged hole in the side appeared to have been recently created by a blast of Davian's water magic, a recent downpour having targeted that one specific spot.

I jumped onto a palette and continued investigating, eventually crawling my way up to the ceiling so I could get a better look from above. One benefit of being a shifter was that we didn't take on the mental state of the particular animal. I could

40

still hear, see, and feel like the human I truly was but with the added benefit of my heightened senses and reflexes.

My spider body lowered down on a silky thread directly above a wooden pallet, cardboard boxes stacked on top of it. Inside were packages of cylindrical vials filled with a transparent orange liquid. I couldn't read the tiny print on the red caps, but the words stamped on the side of the box were very clear. Night-Fly Technologies.

"*Eeeek!*" A high-pitched squeal that should never have come from any man caught me off guard, and a meaty hand came swinging my way.

A rush of magic overcame me, and my body transformed back into its human shape to avoid his hand of death. Crashing into a stack of boxes, I kicked out my legs into the man's broad chest. He let out a grunt, then smashed up against the interior wall of the metal container.

Maybe next time he'll think twice about killing a spider.

He regained his balance and ran out the opening into the shipping yard screaming. "Boss! Boss!"

With my quick reflexes, I wasn't too far behind. Ryker and Kasra had already jumped into action to chase after Davian and the others trying to flee.

I kept my focus on Blondie, letting Kasra and Ryker deal with the others. My target rounded another shipping container before he approached the transport truck and frantically tried to open the driver's side door.

"*Demitto!*" My feet scraped against the asphalt as I tossed a bullet into the air, sticking the nervous man's hand firmly to the door handle.

"What is this stuff?" I snatched the vial of transparent orange liquid he clenched in his other hand and tucked it into my vest pocket. Leaning in, I wiggled my cat claws under his nose for some extra encouragement.

"Like I'd ever tell you." A wad of his frothy saliva splattered against my cheek.

I untucked a part of my shirt, wiping off his spit, although the feeling of disgust never went away. "All right. I tried asking nicely. Now we do this the hard way."

I flashed him a toothy grin, my pointed spider fangs digging into my bottom lip.

"What are you doing?" He tried to yank his hand free, but the thick elastic magic kept snapping his arm back in place.

My claws dug into his free arm, and he wailed as I sunk my teeth into his wrist. I drew out his magic. A bland, starchy taste, like popcorn, coated my tongue and slipped down my throat. His magic energy flowed through me, my insides warming with his power.

His arm turned an icy cold. "You bitch! Stop it! You're going to kill me!"

I raised my head, along with an eyebrow, pulling away. "Are you gonna tell me what you're doing here then?"

He started breathing erratically, sweat dripping down his face and soaking into his beard. His anxious dark eyes darted back and forth as if he was expecting someone to show up and save him.

"Time's up." My fangs grazed his broken skin.

A gunshot rang out nearby, and Kasra's shrill cry stopped my heart from beating.

"Heh. Looks like *your* friend's time is up."

I unleashed my frustration into the man's gut with a feisty punch, then left him stuck to the truck.

"Hey! Let me go!"

Ignoring his plea, I bounded off in the direction of Kasra's voice at lightning speed. For as long as I had known her, Kasra had always managed to fight through every challenge that came her way. If she was in trouble, then I could be certain I was too.

4

KASRA'S CHILLING CRY BOUNCED OFF every metal surface around me. My heart raced faster, thumping rapidly inside my chest. With a running start, I used my feet to pounce on a bright yellow safety guard and spring forward. My arms stretched out before me, fingers latching onto a cable hook hanging from a crane. I swung high above the ground before I let go and launched myself into the air. A loud boom rumbling like thunder as I landed in a practiced roll on the top of a cargo container.

"Kasra? Where are you?" I came to my feet and scanned the shipping yard. Rows upon rows of colorful containers were stacked high and spread out like building blocks around me. Commercial machinery lined the docks, a few vehicles in the parking lot, but there was no sign of Kasra or Ryker.

Shock registered like a heavy knot in my stomach, and I narrowly dodged the path of a water cannon. Jumping off the side of the container, I landed in a crouch ten feet below on the pavement.

A middle-aged man in a black trench coat approached me, his hands casually tucked inside his pockets. Dark shadows cast across him, catching in the pockmarks of his dull skin and accentuating the predatory smile he flashed me as he spoke.

"You know, I always wondered … do human cat shifters hate water as much as their animal counterparts?"

A ferocious growl tore from my throat, and I sprinted toward Davian. Claws ready for action. I took a couple steps before a burst of his watery magic slammed into my chest. My feet slipped out from under me, the force of his water cannon tipping me backward. I waved my arms frantically. Torrents of water dragged me across the pavement, the raw flesh on my arms burning with infuriating pain. I didn't stop moving until my back collided into a ladder propped up against a storage shed.

I squinted, trying to shake off the dizziness and tunnel vision creeping in. My heartbeat was pounding in my ears, my bare arms red and bleeding from the tender flesh being ripped away. My head jerked to the right at the sound of Davian's voice.

"Don't be so hasty, little spider. Don't you want to know why I'm here, stealing from your father?" Davian's voice was as slick as the water magic he used.

"Don't call me that," I revolted, using the hem of my t-shirt to wipe away the saltwater stinging my eyes. It came back sticky with blood.

"You know, I worked with your father for fifteen years and that nickname was the only thing he ever mentioned about you. That and, of course, your weak half-shifter abilities. He was always worried about you. And when you joined the military … boy, he went off the deep end. He was certain you were going to get yourself killed. You still might." He arched an eyebrow at me.

"You don't know a thing about my family. Leave them alone." I rose to my feet, fingers ready to grab one of the paralysis daggers strapped to my leg.

A self-satisfied grin stretched across Davian's face. "Oh really? I know *everything* your father has ever done at NightFly Technologies. What about you? Has he ever told you anything?"

"Is this payback because you're mad my teammate tricked you at the bar? Did you really think a pretty young woman like Kasra would be interested in scum like you? You fell for our trick and ran away like a coward."

"How about a rematch, then?" He pointed behind his shoulder and toward the evening sky. Kasra was trapped in a magical sphere of turbulent water. About twenty feet below her, the shallow tide revealed waves crashing against jagged rocks. Fear swelled in my stomach, and I held the air in my lungs so long my eyes throbbed in my skull.

"Let her go," I snarled.

"And where's the fun in that? Make your father proud. Save the day and take me down! If you can ..." He pushed up the sleeves of his trench coat, readying himself for a fight.

My eyes ping-ponged back and forth between Kasra and Davian. She was desperately trying to keep herself afloat with one arm, the other drifting freely at her side with a swirl of red around it.

Glancing to my left, Ryker came into view from the shadows. I was about to yell at him to get Kasra out of there when I noticed he wasn't alone. Another of Davian's men had a gun shoved up against his head.

Ryker held up his hands, his wide eyes sending me a warning to be careful of my next move.

"My portals aren't faster than bullets, Zulli." There was a slight tremor in his hands, but his voice was absolute. "If I try anything, the gun goes off and Davian releases his magic. I can't guarantee I'll be fast enough to save Kasra before she crashes into the rocks." He completely disregarded the fact that the bullet would go straight through his brain. He couldn't save her because he'd be dead.

I closed my eyes and filled my lungs with air, giving myself the one second I could spare to clear my mind. My magic searched the docks, making sure Davian had no other hidden surprises. I thought I had heard four voices before. Maybe I was wrong. I couldn't sense anyone, but I did hear the faint hum of a military surveillance drone. I just needed to stall Davian and his men long enough until backup arrived.

The young man holding Ryker was probably in his late twenties, a white scar running down his cheek. He stood close to my teammate, pushing him forward with a jab of his left hand. Although he cackled with savage delight, there was a slight waver in his voice—a diversion from the fact that his sweaty hand holding the gun was trembling.

Davian's impatience was growing. "I'm on schedule here, Zulli. What's it going to be? Save your teammates or be a hero and stop me from escaping … again?"

The transport truck rolled up a mere ten feet away, driven by none other than the man I had previously stuck to the door. Davian confidently turned his back to me and walked toward it. "I'll just be over here loading up the remaining vials in the truck. Karter, please deal with the situation so we can get out of here quickly."

My sight left Davian and glued to the man pointing the barrel of his gun to the side of Ryker's head. Ryker's amber eyes widened with warning. He knew me better than I liked to admit, and judging from the subtle shake of his head, he knew what I was about to do.

"Hey, buddy," I spoke calmly to Karter, slowly inching my way toward him. "Have you ever killed a guy before?"

"What? Yeah, of course I have. Don't come any closer!" He jerked Ryker in front of him as a shield and reinforced the fact that a gun was aimed at his head.

"Uh huh. I don't mean *shot* a guy. I mean ended a life. That gun goes off and my friend's brains are going to rain down on us like chunky, fleshy confetti."

"I don't think you're helping the situation, Zulli," Ryker admonished. I held out my palm, kindly gesturing for him to shut up.

46

As I delicately crept closer, my sensitive hearing picked up the man's labored breathing.

"You try to kill me, and I kill him!" There was hesitation in Karter's voice, and his finger twitched slightly on the trigger.

I held up my hands to show him I wasn't planning on grabbing a weapon. "Can't say I've killed anyone before, and I'd like to keep it that way. But I can tell you from experience that blood stains are pretty damn difficult to get out of clothes. You don't wanna ruin those pretty leather boots of yours, now do you?"

He glanced down at his feet, and my opening appeared. I ripped a bullet from my belt and dove at the man.

"*Demitto!*" I had hoped to jam the barrel. Instead, the sticky magic glued his hand directly to the gun. A shot rang out, and my ears started ringing. The acrid smell of the gunpowder lingered in the air, and as I inhaled it, I could taste its bitterness coating my throat.

My hand grabbed the pistol, thrusting it down and away from Ryker, but the damage had already been done. My teammate dropped to the ground. His terrifying cry of pain sent a surge of panic through my chest. He rolled around, groaning and clutching his lower leg. Blood gushed down his pant leg into a pool by his feet.

The second I took my eyes off my target, he pistol-whipped me with the gun. Shock swept through me as I swayed off balance. My vision instantly went black in my left eye, and the throbbing felt like a ticking time bomb about to detonate in my head. A slight shift in the air came from my right, and I blindly threw out a pointed elbow into Karter's shoulder.

Before Karter could fire off another shot, I clapped the pistol between both my hands and dragged his arm across my chest. The elastic magic stretched as he tried to pull away, his hand still attached to the weapon. The joint of his index finger caught in the trigger guard made a loud pop. It was followed by a grinding, crunching noise, like fracturing glass under a hammer. He wailed in pain as I kept driving my full strength against the magic. Eventually, his grip released and the gun slingshotted across the asphalt out of reach.

"*Dormeo.*" Ryker, even in his jumbled state of mind, threw a sleep spell against Karter's chest. Blue powder exploded against his chest. His knees weakened and he dropped to the ground. Ryker was clutching his leg, hissing through grinding teeth. While I was concerned for him, I knew what Davian's next move would be.

"You won't make it," Davian provoked, mocking me as I bolted toward Kasra.

Water completely filled her bubble, and she was barely moving. As if taunting me, Davian waited to release his magic until I was just out of her reach, knowing there was absolutely nothing I could do to catch her from dropping twenty feet into the shallow, rocky harbor below.

A gun appeared in front of me, floating midair and pointed directly at my chest. A female body took shape behind it. The fourth man I had failed to locate was actually a woman, her invisibility magic concealing her presence.

With fingertips forming claws, I sliced through the air, catching her firing arm. With my other hand, I flicked a paralysis dagger at her shoulder.

"*Torpens!*"

The numbing magic took over and her arm flopped to her side. She raised her other fist but never got the punch in. I steamrolled right into her. She fell down like a falling tree, hitting her head against a raised safety curb that warned my runway was about to end.

I leapt into the air toward Kasra's falling body, hoping to use my momentum to propel her away from the rocks and into deeper water.

Latching onto her vest, I pulled her close and offered my body as a cushion. Ten feet away from impact. Sharp, fragmented rocks offered the promise of serious injury, maybe death. I closed my eyes, not wanting to see what happened next.

A pocket of warmth brushed against my face. My eyes shot open, a ripple of magic opening up a portal beneath us. My back snapped against the edge of the invisible opening. We somersaulted over each other, ending up on the wrong side of Ryker's portal and hitting the rocky shore.

The jolt shook my bones as my own body collided on top of Kasra's. I squeezed my eyes shut, thinking for sure that she was dead. Air rushed past my ears, a cool breeze gliding over my arms. She had hit the rocks ... then bounced right back up. The evening sky welcomed my vision. This time, Ryker's magic was perfectly placed, and we were transported back onto solid ground.

"Damn it, Zulli!" Kasra breathed out heavily, coughing up some water in the process. "You know I can turn my body into rubber with my magic. You didn't think that was going to take me down, did you?"

"It *would* have if you were unconscious and couldn't use your magic! Your arm ... you were shot."

"I'll be fine. The invisible bastard caught me off guard. Never saw her coming. Thankfully, her aim sucks." She cupped a hand around the wound on her upper arm. A steady stream of thick blood trickled down and dripped onto the pavement.

The rumbling sound of a vehicle's engine roared to life nearby. Tires squealed on the pavement, and a minute later, the noise vanished.

"Well, there goes Davian. Again," I pointed out.

Kasra peered over my shoulder at Ryker limping his way over to us. He smiled at the sight of the both of us, let out an exasperated sigh, then collapsed into my arms.

"Woah, Ryker. Let's sit down." I carefully lowered him to the ground, not letting him go in case he passed out. "Help will be here soon. I heard a surveillance drone in the area earlier."

"Looks like the bullet went right through his leg. We have to stop the bleeding." Kasra removed a piece of cloth from a pouch on her vest, but it was completely soaked and therefore useless. Tossing it aside, she then dug out a thin piece of string that she tied around his leg to stop the flow of blood.

I bit the tip of my tongue at the urge to use my magic ability to lick his injury. Even if I had, it would have done very little to heal a gunshot wound.

"Are you both okay?" Ryker's head rolled on his shoulders, and he was speaking into the direction of a forklift.

"We'll survive." I smacked him gently on the cheek. "Stay with me, pal. You're not gonna pass out from a measly bullet wound to the leg, are you? Look at Kasra over here. She got shot and she's doing just fine."

The bullet wound wasn't fatal, but Ryker had definitely lost a lot of blood. His entire pant leg was soaked red and a small puddle was forming under him. I handed Kasra a white metal cylinder from my belt. "Healing ointment. Won't help much, but it's all I have."

She activated the magic, delicately smearing the gel around his pant leg and into the bullet wound. Ryker winced, jerking his leg, but managed to stay mostly still as Kasra treated the wound as best she could.

It took about fifteen minutes for reinforcements to arrive. A paramedic immediately tended to Ryker, properly cleaning and bandaging his injury.

"Keep taking these pills and let the magic do its work. You should be all healed up in a few days." The medic, a stout fellow with a man-bun knotted on the top of his head, handed Ryker a plastic container that rattled with pills inside it.

When he was finished with Ryker, he turned his focus to Kasra, then finally to me. I shrugged him off. Other than some healing ointment, which I already had, there wasn't much he could do about a black eye and asphalt burns.

Leaving behind the racket of agents investigating the scene, I leaned against a shipping container and peered out into the city skyline across the harbor. Davian's words still rattled me. He probably did know more about my own family than I did. My dad had spent more time with him, conducting business day in and out, than he had with his own children.

My fingertips ran across the bumpy surface of my skin, and I stuck out my tongue to give it a lick.

"What are you doing?" Ryker found my hiding spot and hobbled over, leaning against the metal side of a shipping container for support.

My tongue quickly retreated into my mouth. "Uh, nothing! It's just … my throat is a little dry. Davian's magic is salty." I licked my lips to cover up any suspicion.

Ryker tossed me over his half empty bottle of water. "Don't you have a family dinner in like … an hour? Why are you hiding out over here?"

"And why are you even walking? Go sit down."

"I came to make sure you were okay. Judging from that pouty face you have going on, I can sense there's something wrong."

"Nope," I lied. There was no need to complain to him about my family drama. "Just pissed. Davian got away again, and this time with some of my father's property."

"Well, look at the bright side." He shifted from leaning against his shoulder to his back. "If we weren't here, he could have gotten away with all of it. We're getting closer each time. We'll get him eventually."

"Yeah, I guess. I should call my dad. Let him know what's going on."

As per usual, the call went right to voicemail, so I left a message telling him I might be a few minutes late.

"Do you need a ride?" Ryker reached for the wallet he kept in his back pocket. When he opened it up, an accordion of photos unfolded and fluttered past his waist. "I still have that photo you gave me of your dad's place in case of emergencies. I can take you right there."

"No, that's fine. I'm gonna catch a cab back to my apartment. My dad's sending someone to pick me up there. Plus, he gets all twitchy when unwelcome guests show up at the front door to his home."

"Oh, right." He shoved his wallet back into his pocket. "Forgot you mentioned that the last time I asked."

I started to head toward the main street when Ryker grasped my shirt sleeve, twirled me around, and pulled me into his chest. He plucked a white bullet from my belt. "You're not going to show up to dinner with *that* on your face, are you?"

Adrenaline had buried the pain of my black eye, but upon Ryker's reminder of my injury, it all came rushing back.

"*Sana.*"

His delicate fingertips rubbed the ointment in circular motions around my eye. His focus was absolute, concentrating on reaching every bump and crease around the injured area. Even though he wasn't pressing firmly, it sent a deep radiating pain pounding through my skull. A warmth ran through me as the magic took effect, beginning to heal the bruise and reduce the swelling.

"There. Now you can go. Enjoy your dinner." He rubbed the rest of the ointment into a cut on his arm.

"Call me if anything changes?" I gave him a friendly punch to the chest.

"Will do."

As I turned around to leave, I reached into my back pocket to grab my phone, hoping to be able to reach one of my brothers instead. With my head down and locked on the screen, I furiously tapped a text message. I didn't immediately realize that the gray asphalt below me had turned into an ugly green carpet. The cool, salty breeze rolling off the harbor transformed into the warm, dank smell of my apartment hallway.

A smile crept up my lips, and I picked up a hop in my step as I skipped to my front door. That stupid lovable bastard. He'd brought me home anyway.

5

---◇---

AFTER A QUICK SHOWER, I changed into leggings and an over-sized striped tunic that fell right above my knees. With a sweep of my hand through my longer hair, I gave myself a messy style with a bit of gel. I finished just as a well-dressed gentleman wearing freshly ironed black dress pants paired with a pale blue polo showed up at my front door.

Rich people hired their own drivers. Filthy rich people who had more money than they knew what to do with, like my father, employed their own personal human transporters. Having your own personal transporter, someone like Ryker who could use portals, was the ultimate status symbol among the rich and famous. Not all transportation magic was created equal. Some types were more useful than others, and if you could afford such a convenient mode of transportation, then you were no doubt someone with wealth and authority who should be admired and respected.

I slipped on a pair of red high tops. "Okay. I'm ready."

The man placed his white-gloved hand firmly on my shoulder, the warmth of his earthy scented magic slithering over my skin. A haze clouded my vision, and I was whisked away from the comfort of my cozy apartment to my childhood home, a twenty-room mansion with a separate guest house for all the staff my father employed to manage the property. It was located about fifty miles outside the city of Chitol in a gated community where all the high-class business tycoons lived.

It took me a moment to catch my balance and my breath. My knees buckled when my feet hit solid ground, the experience of being dumped out in a random location much rougher than what I was used to when I simply walked through Ryker's portals.

The dining room I walked into was twice the size of my studio apartment, dimly lit crystal chandeliers hanging from the ceiling and impeccably polished marble floors under my sneakers. The transporter disappeared, and I was left staring at my two older brothers sitting at the far end of the exquisite oak table, big enough to seat about twenty people. Maeck flashed his fork in front of Brodin to grab the last frog leg, but he wasn't quick enough.

"Hey! Leave some for me!" I yelled at Brodin, the eldest brother.

"Get here earlier next time." Brodin crunched down on the crispy delicacy and flicked his gaze at me. His jet-black hair, thick and well-coiffed, was just long enough for a strand to fall across his forehead. His eyes closed as he slowly chewed with extreme satisfaction.

My dad strolled in from the hallway through the double arched doors. He loosened his tie and draped his pinstripe suit jacket over the back of the chair at the head of the table. His black hair had a single silver streak running from front to back, and while it was usually slick with gel, it had lost its shape and fell messily to one side. The rims of his deep set eyes shadowed the silver irises in the middle.

"I'll have the kitchen start making dinner. Any special requests, Zulli?" My father pressed his hands to the top of the chair, his posture like a distinguished king addressing his people.

I thought about his offer as I pulled out a heavy chair and sat down next to my other older brother, Maeck.

"Chicken pot fly," I responded.

"Good choice," Maeck confirmed with a sharp nod. He shrugged off his white lab coat, revealing his khaki pants and argyle sweater vest underneath. My dad stepped aside to flag down one of the kitchen staff, then took his place at the head of the table.

It wasn't uncommon for shifters to enjoy eating cuisine that their animals often ate. I enjoyed seafood and other meats in a cat's diet, but I couldn't deny myself a good meal seasoned with flies.

A full glass of red wine appeared in front of me, and I swirled it around before taking a big sip. My stomach rumbled, my eyelids feeling heavy. The drowsiness that overtook me could have been from either being whacked in the face earlier or due to the alcohol going straight to my head.

"Hey Sis, what the hell happened to your eye? That looks nasty." Maeck leaned in closer, narrowing his silver eyes to take a closer look.

I touched a finger to my cheek right below my left eye. The swelling had gone down significantly thanks to the healing ointment, my vision fully restored, but the area was still tender.

"Oh, it's nothing. I just dove in front of a guy holding a gun to my teammate's head to save him from having his brains splattered all over the asphalt. The guy ended up whacking me with his gun in the process." A devilish smirk creased my lips.

"Nice!" he exclaimed. "I bet you returned the favor and got that guy good!"

"Sounds irresponsible," Brodin added to the conversation. He pulled in his chair, a brown leather jacket hanging over the back of it slipping off and falling to the floor. Within a fraction of a second, one of the house staff had come rushing over to pick it up and offered to hang it up in a closet for him.

My dad shook his head at me. "You have to be more careful, Zulli. You may have the magic abilities of two shifters, but seeing as neither of them are fully developed, you need to understand your limits." His voice lacked compassion but had a special tone that commanded respect—a strong, authoritative strength, expertly honed from years of being a powerful CEO at one of the world's most renowned magiceutical companies.

A forced cough came from my mouth as I uncomfortably drew in my chair, thankful that the long sleeves of my tunic top hid the scrapes and burns on my arms. Maeck and Brodin hadn't inherited a single drop of cat shifter magic, making them both powerful spider shifters with complete control over their abilities, just like my dad. "I know. This had nothing to do with my magic. It was just an unfortunate circumstance."

I had conveniently left out the part of the story where I'd accidentally glued the gun to my opponent's hand and he'd managed to shoot Ryker in the leg.

"I have something you can use to clear that right up. Remind me after dinner to get it for you." My dad paused, but continued staring at me, exhaling a loud sigh. "Are you sure joining the military was a wise decision? It seems these missions are becoming increasingly dangerous. You can still join me and your brothers in running the family business at NightFly Technologies."

"Yeah, it would be fun! We really miss having you around," Maeck exclaimed, slapping me on the back so hard I nearly spat out my wine.

"I find that hard to believe," I scowled at him. "But this is *my* way of saving the world. You guys can go on developing your life-changing magic medical devices and drugs, and I'll do my part by taking down the bad guys that want to steal them. Speaking of bad guys, Davian Grymes is on the move again. You know, he said something to me before he got away." I rubbed my fingertips over the white cloth napkin on my lap.

The kitchen attendant walked through the door, placing a steaming plate of food in front of me. I gave her my thanks with a smile.

My dad picked up his fork and broke into the flakey crust. "I'm sure the man has a lot to say about me and my business. We worked together for nearly my entire career as CEO."

"Will you take this seriously, Dad?" I slapped a hand down on the table, the china clanking against the wood. "He said he was coming for you!"

"I'd like to see him try," Maeck snorted, flicking a short, wavy curl off his forehead. "NightFly Technologies is impenetrable. Even the employees who have access to the labs have trouble getting into them because they can't figure out all the security protocols."

I threw my head back in frustration, grunting with annoyance. Every time I updated my father about what was going on with Davian and his plan with Bliss, he'd brush me off like he was untouchable. I wasn't sure whether he truly felt that way or if he was just trying to prevent me from worrying more about it than I already was. But Davian's attempt to steal from my dad earlier today proved that he was just as vulnerable as everyone else.

"Were you expecting a shipment of something at Yarwell Port?" The sharp words rolled off my tongue in a condescending tone.

"We're always getting shipments. Why do you ask?" My dad picked up his napkin and wiped a splatter of sauce from his chin.

"Because Davian broke into one of your shipping containers and stole something. This injury?" I pointed to my eye. "It came from one of his men. What was he after?"

"I'm not sure how to answer that," he responded calmly. "Davian probably received word from one of his minions that, earlier today, I met with our mayor, Ethin Henderson, about receiving a grant for a confidential project. I wouldn't be surprised if he was trying to steal my supplies to set me back."

"What's the project about?" I narrowed my eyes.

"Confidential, sweetheart. I can't provide details." He swiveled his head to address my brothers on either side of the table. "Do either of you happen to know anything about this shipment that Zulli is speaking about?"

Brodin shrugged, his broad shoulders barely flinching. "That shipment was just a bunch of chemical additives we use to increase the bonding compatibility of different magic medicines. They're useless unless you mix a catalyst with it, and even then, you need the correct formula for it to work properly."

The room grew silent. Maeck eyed the doorway like he wanted to make a run for it. Brodin turned away from me and poured himself a glass of water from a porcelain carafe. My father quietly chewed on his meal, avoiding eye contact with everyone. Before I could demand more answers, my father spoke.

"Thank you for your continued support, little spider." I cringed at the nickname. I could only hear Davian's voice inside my head repeating it. "You protected my assets, and I appreciate your dedication to bringing my former colleague to justice. But why don't you focus on your own mission and I'll continue with mine?"

I rolled my eyes at his attempt to change the subject.

"You know, you remind me a lot of your mother." His smile softened, but his sharp facial features didn't offer much warmth. "The green streaks in your hair match your emerald eyes, the same color as hers. She was always the rebel, you know. Never let anyone stand in her way or tell her what to do."

My gaze got lost in the intricate dark wood grain of the table, and I scratched at it with my fingernail. My two older brothers were both spitting images of my dad in his earlier years, with their tanned skin, thick black hair, and silver eyes. They'd even inherited his mind for magic. But me? I was different. While I had inherited my father's midnight black hair and dusky skin, my emerald green eyes and half-cat shifter capabilities had been a gift from my mother that only I could claim.

"You still think Mom's coming back, don't you?" I remarked. "She disappeared eleven years ago when I was fifteen. I think it's safe to assume she's not coming back."

"You don't know that!" Maeck called out, slamming a fist down on the table. "The investigators never found a body or any leads that led them to believe she was dead. She could still be out there."

It was definitely a possibility, but my dad had hired the best private investigators to find her and they'd all come up empty. If she really was still out there, she didn't want to be found. That was almost worse than being dead. That meant she had abandoned her family, and I didn't want to believe that.

I finished up my meal and gulped down my wine. Our plates were cleared away by the kitchen staff. The awkwardness between us stretched on until Maeck broke the silence.

"Who's ready for dessert?" he exclaimed, gleefully rubbing his hands together.

"You know what? It's late. My head hurts and I'm really tired. Can someone bring me home?" I propped an elbow on the table and massaged my temples with my fingertips.

"Of course," my father replied. "Let me make a call and go grab something for that eye of yours."

I met my father in the hallway, Maeck appearing by his side and Brodin, a few inches taller, standing next to him. A warm rush of air brushed across my skin, and the same nicely dressed transporter appeared out of thin air with a pop of magic.

"Here." My father handed me a plastic bottle with a few round pills inside. "Take one tonight and by tomorrow morning you'll be as good as new. Good night, little spider." He kissed me on the forehead. The silver gleam in his eyes and his expressionless face vanished as I disappeared into darkness.

6

---◈---

THE RAIN PATTERING AGAINST THE windows was a rhythmic tapping, sending me into a relaxed state of tranquility. I lay in bed, staring at a drifting cobweb floating down from the ceiling in my apartment. Dark shadows were cast across the small studio, but the clock across the room informed me it was late morning. After the incident at the Yarwell Port, the colonel had decided to give my team the day off. However, later this evening it was back to work. Colonel Buckner wanted to go over what we discovered at the wharf and needed a full debrief of what exactly had happened.

I tossed the warm comforter off my shoulders, a cold rush of air sending shivers up my arms as I slumped out of bed. Just as my dad promised, the pills worked overnight to heal my injured eye, along with what remained of the burns on my skin. The swelling and bruising were so faint it was barely noticeable, the tenderness completely gone. The rough, scabrous skin on my arms and legs had returned to its original unblemished olive color.

With not much planned for the day, I shuffled my way into the kitchen on my own personal mission—to bake a double batch of snickerdoodle cookies for Ryker. It was a small token of my appreciation, even though Ryker wasn't the type to expect anything in return for his good deeds.

Upbeat music cranked out of a speaker and I danced around my tiny kitchen as I mixed the batter, scooped it into balls onto a sheet pan, and baked them in the oven. By the time they were ready, the sweet and spicy aroma of cinnamon filled my entire apartment. I bit into a warm cookie and found myself smiling. Its smell reminded me exactly of Ryker's magic.

The cookies cooled on a wire rack, then I bagged them up and put them in my backpack. I planned on stopping by his place to drop them off before heading to the military base later on.

The rain had picked up by late afternoon, now pounding against the windows in thick sheets that completely obscured the view of the concrete walls they faced. Unfortunately, I was starting to get hungry and I wasn't in the mood for cereal or stale pizza. Something juicy, greasy, and fried was calling my name. I slipped on my rubber boots and shrugged on a nylon coat, grabbing my worn, green umbrella to venture off to my favorite burger joint a few blocks away.

I stood on the stone steps under the flapping fabric canopy of my apartment building entrance. A woman across the street scrambled out of a cab and rushed for cover. The narrow brick building she ran up to was like a fragile skeleton, cracking and crumbling with age. White paint was chipping off the windowsills, and the metal railings that lined the small balconies were orange with corroding rust.

My dad had insisted many times that he pay my rent so that I could live in an upscale apartment downtown. I had refused his offer, choosing to depend on myself rather than his handouts. Having grown up in a wealthy household, it took some getting used to, but eventually I realized I didn't need a penthouse suite outfitted with all the latest amenities to make me happy. I had my job, my friends, and my family, and that was more than enough to put a smile on my face every day.

I zipped up my jacket. The wind was an icy chill that ran the length of my spine, numbing my fingers. Waterfalls of rainwater hammered against the metal roofs of cars and puddles splashed high into the air each time a pothole was hit. Pedestrians were scrambling on the sidewalks, those without magic umbrellas uselessly covering their heads with purses or briefcases and clutching their hoods whenever the wind blasted into them.

"*Obvolo.*" The umbrella snapped open and enveloped me in a bubble of magic that shielded against the sideways rain slamming into the protective barrier. The mouthwatering smell of freshly charred meat grew stronger and beckoned me down the street. I would have eaten at the restaurant, but all five tables in the cramped joint were occupied. I grabbed my burger and milkshake and hurried home, salivating every step of the way.

Fighting the turbulent winds, I trotted up the steps to my apartment building, shook out the umbrella, and waited for the elevator to take me to the fifth floor. The door rolled open to Kasra pacing back and forth down the hallway, her wounded arm no longer in a sling. Ryker was leaning up against the peeling plastered wall, hands in his pockets and eyes closed like he was fighting the urge to grab Kasra and force her to stand still. Both were wearing black pants and their tactical vests over black, long-sleeve thermal shirts.

"What are you two doing here?" I fumbled to fish out the key in my pocket with my hands full.

"We tried calling. Thought we could grab an early dinner together before work. Looks like you beat us to it, though." Ryker removed his hands from his pockets and folded them across his chest.

"Whoops. Must have forgotten my phone when I went out. You're welcome to the leftover pizza in my fridge." I swung the door open to my apartment and they followed behind me into the living room.

"Pizza?" Kasra spat out. "As in the pizza we ate for dinner *over a week ago?*"

I neither confirmed nor denied her statement, but she knew the truth.

I hung my completely dry nylon coat on the wobbly rack by the door. The umbrella fell to the floor with a slap just as a boom crackled in the sky. It was so fierce that I felt a slight vibration under my feet. The short percussive bang was over in an instant. But it wasn't a rumble like thunder, and no lightning flashed through my windows. If it had been right next to me, I might have related it to a gunshot. But since this had come from a distance ...

My heart threatened to shatter my ribcage. I dropped my dinner on the floor, thick strawberry milkshake coating my boots. Heading out the door, I sprinted down the hallway. Without a second thought, Kasra and Ryker trailed behind me, our stomping feet echoing in the stairwell as we raced to the roof.

"Zulli, wait!" Ryker huffed out. Magic had mostly healed the worst of his bullet wound, but there was still a slight limp to his gait. Kasra zoomed past him to match my speed.

I stepped out onto the rooftop deck, weaving around the few plastic chairs blown over by the angry wind. I ran straight for the iron railing, clenching it with white knuckles, and peered out into the city skyline.

"I can't see anything in this rain. What was that?" Kasra was beside me, flattening her hand to shield her eyes as she scanned the hazy horizon.

"There's only one place you need to look." I pointed to my left at the top half of a skyscraper towering above the smaller buildings surrounding it. On a normal evening, the setting sun would be reflecting vibrant orange hues off its rows of glass windows soaring into the sky. But today, the tallest building in the city, NightFly Technologies, had a different glow: a fiery golden burst of light that lashed out from about halfway down the building. A cloud of billowing smoke trailed up and disappeared into the overcast sky. Although it was difficult to hear over the pounding rain, my keen senses picked up on car alarms and horns blaring in the area.

"We have to get over there. Right now." I turned to my teammates and wiped the dripping rain out of my eyes.

"I'm calling the colonel." Ryker shuffled his way over to us, pulling out his phone to make a call. Rain flattened his hair and soaked into his shirt.

I tugged on his sleeve, my eyes pleading with urgency. My lips parted to say something, but Ryker held out his free hand in front of him to prevent me. He turned to walk back into the stairwell while he discussed plans with the colonel on the end of the line. Kasra and I followed, eager to learn any information on what happened.

A wave of spicy warmth filled the stairwell, and I jumped through Ryker's portal back to my front door. Kasra was right behind me, and Ryker followed last. Bolting over to my bed, I rummaging through my pile of clothes in the corner of the room. I secured the tactical vest over my wet shaggy plaid shirt and clasped my bullet belt around my hips. I spent all of five seconds looking for the leg holster with my daggers, but gave up and left it behind.

"Come on. What are you waiting for?" I stared at Kasra and Ryker, their worried faces averting eye contact.

"The colonel's orders are to stay put. We are under no circumstances to go over there." Ryker never raised his voice, remaining perfectly calm despite the circumstances. Still, his words stabbed me like a knife in the chest.

"What do you mean stay put? That's my father's company! What if Davian is there stealing something right now? What if my dad is actually there? Or my brothers? I'm sure as hell not going to stand here and let Davian get away again!"

"It was a direct order from the colonel. If this was an attack directly on Zavyr ... you're too close to this, Zulli. He wants someone else to handle it." His fingers grazed my shoulder blades. He tried to steer me toward the couch to sit down, but I shrugged him off.

"I'm going with or without you." I pulled out my phone and dialed my dad. Just like every other time I had called him, it went straight to voicemail. My brothers didn't pick up either. My heart raced with urgency, the need to get over to NightFly Technologies and make sure my family was safe rushing through me. I needed to know that anyone who might have been there had made it out okay.

Storming out of the apartment and down the stairs, I had reached the lobby when Ryker and Kasra caught up to me.

"Zulli, wait! Just listen for a minute." Kasra jumped in front of me to cut me off, but I elbowed her out of my way.

"We've been chasing Davian for months now," I spat at her. "I figured you two would understand how important this is to me. Davian made this personal by stealing from my father, and now he has attacked NightFly Technologies. I'm not letting him get away with this any longer. I'm ending this with or without your help." I tried to storm out the front entrance, but a portal deposited me right back where I came from. I growled at Ryker, but the sincere gleam in his eyes turned my anger level down a notch.

Kasra broke my staring contest with him. "We don't even know if it *was* Davian, and you know we can't just go barreling in there without a plan."

I made a second attempt to walk out the door but crashed into Ryker's chest, a brick wall that had appeared out of nowhere.

"Get out of my way, Ryker." I threw out my arm, but he caught my wrist and gently lowered it to my side.

"Will you calm down, Zulli? The colonel doesn't want us to go, but I never said we *wouldn't*."

The heavy rain had flattened Ryker's short hair. Wet clumps of reddish-brown strands stuck to his forehead and droplets of water rolled down his face. His warm smile cut right through the bitter cold gust of wind that lashed at me. An apartment tenant gave us a sideways glance as he hurried through the entrance.

"I estimate we have maybe twenty minutes before the police or military show up." Kasra must have applied a little magic to her ensemble when she was getting ready this morning. While Ryker and I were completely drenched from standing outside, there wasn't a single flyaway on her head or smear of mascara running down her face. "If we hurry up, we can get in and out before anyone sees us. We could at least do a quick round to make sure no one's hurt."

Ryker wiped away a drop of water from his nose. "All right. Let's get in and out as quickly as we can before anyone notices us there. If you see Davian or anyone else suspicious, *do not engage*." Ryker's fierce amber eyes gave me goosebumps.

A slight nod confirmed my understanding, and Ryker removed his wallet from his back pocket. An accordion of photos protected in plastic unfolded. He found one of the lobby at Night-Fly Technologies, studied it for a moment, and hurried us through the portal before closing it.

I immediately clasped my palms to my ears. The security alarm was blaring, the high-pitched siren repeating a squalling *meep, meep, meep*. With the explosion occurring about twenty stories up, the lobby appeared untouched. A few decorative chairs were out of place and a light disturbance of dust drifted down from the ceiling and onto the white marble floors.

Thankfully, the normally bustling human traffic that occupied the building was minimal. If there had been anyone in the lobby, they'd already escaped to safety.

"The elevator probably isn't a good idea. The explosion might have damaged something." I peered over to Ryker, rubbing a hand against his injured leg. "Are you going to make it up twenty flights of stairs?"

"Now is hardly the time for a challenge, Zulli." He squinted his eyes at me and smirked.

I rolled my eyes, my feet already heading toward the stairs. "Come on. We don't have much time."

Ryker used a portal to create an opening at the top of each flight of stairs. After about ten floors, I noticed he was no longer favoring his leg but kept massaging his hands.

"We can walk the rest of the way up," I assured him, yelling over the blaring alarm that was echoing even louder in the stairwell. Kasra and I slowed our pace to match his, but Ryker just shook his head.

"You don't need to wait for me. Go on ahead. I'll catch up."

Kasra took off, her long legs dominating the remaining ten flights of stairs. My heart stammered in my chest, my hesitation to leave Ryker behind causing me to trip over my shoe. My fingers tightened around the railing, but Ryker steadied me before I fell. His nudge forward gave me the reassurance I needed that he'd be right behind me.

The stairs spat me out on the twenty-first floor located in a wide, central hallway that opened up into community space. Obscured by a cloud of smoke, I noted that to my right was a lounge area with a few tables and chairs and to my left was an office kitchen. Soot was coating the laminate countertops and sticking to the light gray walls. Kasra had arrived before me and was searching the cabinets for something we could use to cover our mouths. She grabbed a roll of paper towels from under the sink and threw it at me. I promptly crumpled up a few sheets and covered my face.

The alarm finally shut off, although the ringing in my ears continued. I couldn't even hear the words come out of my mouth when I spoke to Kasra. "I'm gonna go search around. Wait here for Ryker?"

She must have heard me because she nodded.

I didn't know every specific detail of this building, but I did know each floor that housed administrative personnel had the same exact office layout. I left the hallway, passing the elevators, bathrooms, and a storage closet, until the communal space opened up into rows of cramped cubicles that circled the perimeter.

The overhead lights were flickering, and the smoke grew denser as I turned a corner, getting closer to where the explosion had taken place. The sprinklers had been set off and were spewing out magic-infused water to dampen both fire and magic explosions. The air was warm, but I didn't notice a fire anywhere in sight. Carefully, I searched under the jungle of overturned furniture. A tornado of papers whirled around from the stormy wind blowing in through a section of shattered windows.

The sprinkler system shut off, but my clothes had absorbed so much of the water that I felt like they had been dipped in wet concrete.

"Hello? Is anyone here?" I called out, closing my eyes and crouching to the floor. My hand spread out on the wet carpet, feeling for vibrations, my hearing tuned in to any movement nearby.

A stifled cough came from my left. I whirled around to see a man covered head to toe with wet streams of black ash. Soot dripped down his face and arms. He took one look at me and bolted for the emergency exit sign, glowing a neon red through the midst of the smoke.

"Hey! Wait!" I chased after him, leaping over a small filing cabinet and a waste basket that he kicked in front of me. Ryker had been firm in his orders that we were not to engage with anyone suspicious, but if this trespasser did in fact work for Davian, or whoever was behind this attack, he might be injured and an easy catch. I couldn't just let him go.

The runaway grunted, tripping over a tangle of cords in his way and giving me just enough time to catch up. I reached out my hand, my claws raking through his arm. Crimson blood pooled out of his wounds but he didn't seem to be affected by pain. He spun around, slashing a knife directly at my chest. It ripped across my tactical vest, too close for comfort. I froze, my pulse racing, patting my chest to make sure nothing had been torn. Had he aimed just a little higher, that would have been my throat.

The man took advantage of my shock, turning to scramble for the door. I shook myself out of my daze. Leaping at him, I tackled him to the ground before he could escape. On the back of his back was a black, crosshair tattoo—a member of the Black Mark. No doubt one of Davian's men, here to steal something from my father.

I reached for a dagger on my leg, remembering too late that it wasn't there. His blackened fist struck me in the jaw. He kicked free, scrambling to flee. Stars danced in my blurry vision, my entire head throbbing. In a last-ditch effort, I thrust out my hand, managing to snag a claw across his pant leg. It wasn't enough to stop him. The stairwell door clicked shut behind him, and he was gone.

"Damn it." I pounded my fist right on top of a crumpled piece of paper, absorbing some of the water that had soaked into the damp carpet. I picked it up and fanned it out, noticing a small tear at the corner from where I had slashed the man's pant leg. Carefully, I unfolded it, reading a printed list of names out in my head.

Cullin Maddox. Abril Penton. Ethin Henderson. The list had ten different names on it. The ones I recognized were well known authority figures including government officials, celebrities, and business owners.

There was another name scribbled in blue ink at the bottom. Water had made the ink bleed, and I couldn't make out what it said other than that both the first and last name started with a "T."

I folded the paper back up and slipped it into my vest pocket for further investigation later. Deep in my pocket I felt a cold, round glass tube and was reminded of the vial I stashed there when I'd fought Davian at the shipping yard. My hands began to shake, disjointed thoughts running through my mind. I didn't want to jump to conclusions, but I had a sinking feeling that my dad was in trouble. I wouldn't sit around and wait to find out what would happen next.

My ears twitched at the sound of movement. With my thoughts of Davian disappearing, my gaze snapped to a broken cubicle desk. With my claws out, ready for action, I crouched and tiptoed my way over to the noise. Again, the debris rumbled.

"Hello? Can someone help me?" the trapped voice called out. Despite the man's predicament, his words showed no signs of fear or panic. My stomach churned in knots and my limbs started moving on their own before my brain had a chance to catch up.

"Dad!" I darted over and began digging through the piles of plastic boxes, computer equipment, and tacky desk decorations. My muscles strained to push against a heavy piece of metal that lay on top of him. Enhanced strength was not one of the spider shifter traits I'd inherited.

My dad's worn face finally surfaced, black ash caught in the creases of his dusky skin and in his jet-black hair. There was a small cut on his cheek, blood rolling down and dripping off his chin.

"Dad, are you okay?"

"Zulli? What are you doing here?" He ignored my question, engaging his magic to use his strength to toss the rest of the rubble off him. He sat up, then flapped open a blue pocket square from his suit jacket and patted at the dust sticking to his face like it would do any good.

"I should be asking you that, Dad. It's late. You should be at home." I held out my hand to help him up.

"I *was* at home. But I received a security alert on my phone, so I had someone immediately bring me here to investigate. I was just about to leave when the explosion went off."

I picked up an office chair and set it upright. "Sit for a minute. I'll go see if I can find a bottle of water from the kitchen and grab both Kasra and Ryker."

"Oh?" The whites of his silver eyes stuck out against the soot coating his face. "Your teammates are here too? Anyone else?"

"No one else. Why?"

"It may look like a mess here at the moment, but confidential information is still kept here. I'd just like to know who's snooping around in my business. That's all."

I barely turned around before I glimpsed two figures rushing through the smoky haze. "Hey! I'm over here!"

"We heard the commotion. Everything okay?" Ryker made a quick assessment of my well-being.

"I found my dad. He's a little rattled but seems fine. I'm gonna go grab a bottle of water and some paper towels from the kitchen. Be right back."

I returned a few minutes later just as Kasra was introducing herself to my dad. "I'm Kasra, by the way," she said in a casual manner, waving at him.

"Hello, Kasra," my father nodded to her.

Ryker stood up straight and puffed out his chest. He snapped one arm to his side, the fingers on his other hand spread wide ready for a firm handshake. "Nice to meet you, Mr. Taracula. I'm Ryker Stone."

"Please, call me Zavyr. Zulli has told me much about you, Ryker. I presume you are keeping my daughter safe?"

"Dad!" I cried out, heat warming my cheeks.

"Of course!" Ryker glanced over at me and smiled. "Although she actually saved my ass the other night."

"I see."

Kasra rejoined the conversation. "Do you know if anything was stolen, Mr. Taracula?"

My father stalled the conversation by crossing his legs in the chair, dusting off some dirt on his suit pants. His gaze lazily drifted around the office.

"She's just trying to help, Dad. All the labs are on the lower levels. Do you know what they would even want here?"

He sighed, and his reluctance to tell us anything was clear in his snappy tone. "This floor houses the records department. If they were after anything, it was information on our trial patients, the blueprints for our medical devices, or patented formulas for all our medicines. But there's no way of knowing what they stole or if they even stole anything. This place is in shambles. There's paperwork flying everywhere."

"We'll figure it out, sir." Ryker, always the optimist, reassured my dad with a quick nod of his head.

Marching footsteps and the clattering of equipment came from close by.

"We have to go," Ryker's gaze flickered over toward the noise.

I cast a nervous glance at my dad.

"I'll be fine, little spider. I presume that means you aren't supposed to be here, so leave while you still can. I will handle this."

Ryker held out his hand, the vibrations of his magic buzzing through me, warmth caressing my skin. Just as we were leaving, my dad spoke his farewell.

"It was a pleasure to meet you Kasra, Ryker. Have a pleasant rest of your evening."

7

---◈---

IT DIDN'T COME AS A surprise to me that after the previous night's attack on NightFly Technologies, that my team would be permanently removed from any future assignments connected to Davian. The unit that responded to the security breach found no evidence the attack was linked to Davian, and it didn't fit his typical way of doing things. Davian was usually methodical, working in the shadows to avoid being seen. It wasn't like him to call attention to himself.

I knew for certain he was behind the explosion, though. The man I'd attacked had a black crosshair tattoo that linked him to the Black Mark, the gang working with Davian to distribute Bliss. Unfortunately, that piece of information, along with the list of names I'd found, would have to stay with me for the time being.

Until a new mission came my way, I had the foreseeable future to myself. That meant I had way too much time to run countless scenarios of Davian's next move in my head. What was the list of names for? Why did he need that bonding agent in the vial? What the hell was he planning and how did it involve my dad?

74

My heart sank into despair. I went digging in my pile of clothes on the floor next to my bed, removing the crumpled list and finding the red cap of the vial of the bonding agent poking out of my tactical vest. I pinched it between my fingers and swirled it around, the transparent orange liquid sloshing inside.

My brothers had never been secretive people until they'd begun working alongside my dad. My oldest brother, Brodin, was often strict and by the books. I would never be able to get him to speak. But Maeck and I had a special connection. He always stuck up for me, boasting about my accomplishments to Dad. If I could get anyone to tell me what was going on, it would be him. I pulled out my phone and dialed.

"Hello?" It was early in the afternoon and I could hear people chatting and machines humming in the background. Despite the explosion, NightFly Technologies was still in business and it sounded like Maeck was working in one of the labs.

"It's me. Got a minute?"

"Yeah, sure. What's up?" The sound of a door clicked shut and the background noise died down.

"I want to know more about this special project Dad's working on." There was complete silence for a solid minute. "Maeck? You there?"

"Yeah, I'm here."

"So?"

"Zulli ..." I couldn't see his face, but I could picture him cradling his head in his palm as he dragged out a long sigh directly into the speaker, making it crackle. "Why do you always have to go snooping around in everyone's business?"

"I'm not snooping. I'm worried Dad isn't taking this situation seriously. The attack on NightFly Technologies was definitely Davian. I know it was. The bastard made a show to warn Dad that he's not untouchable, and I worry he might be in trouble. Can't you give me any information about what's going on? Maybe I can do something to help protect him." I started pacing in circles around my coffee table.

"I …" He paused as if second guessing what he was about to say next. "Look, Zulli, I can't go into details, but I can tell you this new drug is going to be a game changer. In light of all these negative side effects caused by Bliss, there's been an increased interest by the board members in finding ways to preserve the mind. That's really all I can say, Sis."

"Wow. That sounds intense. You think Davian is trying to steal this formula for something?"

Maeck's tone didn't match the eagerness in my words. "Zulli, you have to leave this alone. It's a sensitive project, and we don't want any information leaking out. We have enough on our plates with Davian to worry about. And don't you dare tell Dad I said anything to you about this!" His stern warning blared through the phone speaker.

"I won't. Thanks, Maeck. I appreciate you telling me this. Let's do lunch sometime?"

"Yeah, sure. Sounds good."

The call ended and I stopped pacing, gripping my phone firmly in my hand. Was Davian trying to enhance Bliss some-how? Maybe it had something to do with whatever he sent that Black Mark member to steal from NightFly Technologies.

There was still something nagging at me that gave me a sour feeling in my stomach. The list. Were those people in danger? I had a sneaking suspicion there was more to the story, and I knew just the person who could help me put the rest of the pieces to-gether.

I dialed another number. The phone rang twice before a voice on the other line screamed out of the speaker. I had to pull the phone away before my eardrums ruptured.

"Zulli! Where have you been, hun? You didn't return my calls last week. We were supposed to make plans to hang out!"

"I know. I'm sorry, Catilda. I was on a mission. Are you free today?"

"What? Today?" She paused. "What's going on?" There was a sly curiosity in her voice.

"I have a favor to ask. I'll tell you more when I get there."

"A favor? Well, now I'm intrigued. Are you really going to keep me in suspense all day without even a hint? It's going to drive me downright mad."

"Yeah," I swallowed the shakiness in my voice, hoping it still sounded calm and casual. "There's just a lot to explain. Best to do it in person."

"Okay, hun! Meet me at the shop, because now I *really* need to know what's going on and it can't wait until I get home."

"Great. I can be there around five."

"You better not be late!"

The phone went silent, and I put both the vial and list of names in my backpack by the front door to take with me later. The smell of cinnamon tickled my senses, a reminder that I never dropped off Ryker's cookies.

Ryker and I were close, but Catilda and I were even closer. I had known her my entire life, our mothers having been good friends who shared a bond over their cat shifter magic. The time I spent with Catilda's family had blossomed into some of the happiest memories of my childhood, and for my own selfish reasons, I didn't want to share them with anyone else. After my mother's disappearance, I had never told anyone I still kept in contact with her. She was my little secret—a memory of my mom only I had, and I wanted to keep it that way. Not even Kasra or Ryker knew about her.

I threw on my leather jacket and a pair of ripped black jeans. The bullet belt was replenished and clasped around my waist. I never went anywhere without it.

It was a beautiful spring day in the city of Chitol. The cool dampness in the air from yesterday's rain had disappeared and turned into a bright, sunny afternoon. I decided to take a stroll over to Ryker's apartment and enjoy the fine weather.

The front of his apartment building had a shiny golden awning, complete with thick glass doors trimmed in matching gold metal. The doorman greeted me, and I held my head down as I uncomfortably crept inside the swanky lobby, the glossy white furniture sleek and modern without a speck of dust. The front desk attendant gave me a questionable glare, as if some homeless person off the street had snuck into the building and needed to be led out. Ignoring her, I took the elevator up fourteen stories to Ryker's place, knocking furiously on his door until he opened up.

"Zulli? What are you doing here? Everything okay?" He panted out his words, heavy and full of effort. His gym shorts fell to his knees and his sweat-soaked tank top clung to his chest. He grabbed a towel draped over his shoulder to wipe the perspiration running down his forehead, then used it to blot his glistening, damp hair.

"You always assume I have a problem every time I come to you. Actually, I just wanted to drop something off." I opened up the backpack and pulled out the cookies. "Here. A double batch of snickerdoodle cookies just for you."

Ryker's eyebrows shot into his hairline and he ran along his lips at the sight of the bag. He immediately ripped it open and shoved a cookie in his mouth, throwing his head back and moaning. "Mmm. Just what I needed after an intense workout. Thanks, Zulli. How you feeling after … everything?"

My gaze averted his and I rubbed the back of my neck. Being taken off this mission had made me feel like a failure, but I wouldn't burden Ryker with that. I wasn't looking for sympathy. "I'm fine."

He sighed, knowing it was a total lie. "We did the best we could, Zulli. We prevented Davian's deal from going down at the bar, and who knows what else he could have gotten away with if we weren't at Yarwell Port to stop him."

I forced myself to look up at Ryker. His eyes, lips, and kindhearted spirit all smiled at me at once. I couldn't help but smile back.

He opened his door wider, inviting me inside. "Hey, since you're here, you want some coffee or something? There's a nice cafe down the street if you want to grab a late afternoon snack. I hear they have shoofly pie. With real flies."

"That sounds amazing, but I actually have to get going. I'm taking advantage of the time off. Lots of stuff to do."

"Like what?" His smile turned into a frown. "Promise me it has nothing to do with Davian Grymes."

I shoved my hands into my pockets to keep myself from fidgeting. My teammates had already stuck their necks out for me at NightFly Technologies. What I was planning violated military rules and could get anyone involved in serious trouble. That wasn't a position I wanted to put either Kasra or Ryker in.

"I promise." My throat tightened, and I felt a sharp pang in my stomach as the lie came out of my mouth.

Ryker stared at something on the floor. "Hey, what's that?"

My gaze followed his to the glass vial that had rolled right next to my feet. My heart jumped into my throat. I must have jostled it loose when I grabbed the cookies out of my backpack. I quickly swiped it up, shoving it back inside my bag before Ryker could see. "It's nothing …"

"Zulli …"

"It's just something the medic gave me for my injuries the other day. Hey, I gotta go. Raincheck on that pie?"

"Of course. Anytime."

My palms started to sweat and my heart pounded wildly in my chest. I clutched the strap of the backpack so tight my fingernails dug into my palm. Although I tried to walk calmly down the hallway, I found myself picking up speed to get out of there as quickly as I could.

8

---◈---

MY SWIFT PACE CONTINUED ALL the way to the nearest bus stop, where I stood on the busy sidewalk waiting anxiously for the next bus to arrive. Beside me on a bench sat an elderly woman with several bags of groceries. As time drew closer for the scheduled arrival, more passengers crowded the busy area. A few businessmen and women heading home from work stood by the curb. A couple of rowdy teenagers chased each other around, and a man with a thick black hoodie pulled up over his head leaned against the shelter wall off to the side behind me. We all boarded the bus, and an hour later, the claustrophobic skyscrapers in the city opened up into single family dwellings in the suburbs.

It was the last stop on the route, and the bus emptied when it came to a halt in the center of town. The remaining passengers left the bus in single file, including the hooded man who'd got on with me, helping the elderly woman down the steps with her groceries.

I found myself standing in the center of town next to a charming little cafe, the sidewalk seamlessly blending with the stone patio. A few weary pedestrians sat at wooden tables drinking a late day pick-me-up.

The area where Catilda lived was known to be one of those hot spots where all the city-dwellers flocked to when they became responsible adults. It was close enough to the city for an easy commute but far enough away that you could leave it all behind at the end of the day. It wasn't so much a town as it was a community—a neighborhood where you'd find a group of mothers chatting their way through garden paths, and residents supported small local businesses as opposed to corporate conglomerates.

I crossed the street and entered the small public park nestled in the middle of the town square. It had been a while since I'd ambled through its spacious pathways and breathed in the fresh, earthy air. Swelling red and yellow flower buds filled the gardens along the path, promising to soon ignite spring into a vibrancy of life and sweet floral scents. The trees that lined the stone trails were lithe but strong. They were shedding their winter layers and whispering in the crisp spring breeze that grew colder as the sun started to set in the sky.

At the edge of the town center a quaint little shop was sandwiched between a hairdresser and a bank. The narrow brick building had a black iron sign dangling out front that read "Harper's Treasure Chest." The large display window showcased a variety of unique spelled objects and magic gadgets to attract anyone who passed by.

I was about to open the door when someone else beat me to it. My nose smashed into the glass pane, and I was knocked backward. Bicycles toppled over and created a loud racket when I stumbled into the rack.

"Zulli!" A flash of pink too fast for my eyes to see darted toward me, and a pair of freckled arms wrapped around my neck. "I missed you, hun! Six months is way too long without seeing your adorable face!" She leaned back and gasped. "Your hair! It's gone!"

"You like it?" I twisted my head from side to side, running my fingertips along the fuzzy short hairs above my ear.

She studied me for a moment, picking at the green strands on top of my head. "It's very … you."

A snort escaped me. "Ah, I missed you too, Catilda. So, how was your visit to Earth?"

Catilda clapped her hands and jumped. "Fantastic! My internship ended a couple weeks ago. Another certification under my belt to add to my ten others and two advanced degrees. One step closer to becoming a fully-fledged magic archaeologist!"

A delightful smile curled my lips. Catilda came from a family of brilliant minds, and she was no exception. At twenty-three, she'd accomplished more than what most people could in a lifetime. Even her two younger brothers were budding geniuses.

"Why didn't you come visit me on Earth?" she whined. "It would have been so fun!"

"I would have, but I've been dealing with my own problems here."

"Oh yeah? Is it that Ryker guy again?" She clasped her hands together and batted her glittery eyes at me. "Every time I tried calling you, you were always with him. Are you two a thing?"

My smile disappeared and my lips pressed into a thin line. What Catilda lacked in tact, she made up for with her fun-loving, adorable girliness. She had so many freckles you couldn't tell she actually *had* freckles. Along with her short ginger curls that bounced with every exuberant step, she gave off a child-like playfulness that made most people want to pinch her cheeks and coo baby noises at her.

"We're teammates, Catilda." I narrowed my gaze on her. "Being around each other comes with the job."

"Oh yeah? Well, I don't ever hear you talk about that other lass. I can't even remember her name. Kassy? Kara?" She scrunched her nose up and made a judging face at me.

"Kasra," I corrected. "And I hang out with her too." Catilda was always high energy, always inserting herself in conversations and needing to know all the latest gossip.

"Yeah, yeah, whatever." She pressed a perfectly manicured hand against her cocked hip. "Anyway, I seem to have picked up a new thing or two about Earth's primitive magic, along with this hideous sunburn. My skin is peeling, Zulli! It's absolutely disgusting!"

Her slinky pink polka-dot sweater slid off her shoulder, exposing her slightly reddish skin peeling underneath. It was normally so pale a single ray of sun would catch her on fire.

"Come on inside, hun." She waved at me. "It's getting chilly out here, and I have to close up the shop for the day."

She sashayed her way back into the shop, shiny black leggings hugging her feminine curves. Catilda and I were polar opposites in the dress department, but we had a lot of other interests in common. For one, we shared a bond over our cat shifter magic, even if mine was limited. And neither of us was ever known to pass up a good adventure.

I followed behind her, but not before noticing the black hooded man who had boarded the bus with me sitting on a metal bench a few stores down. He stared straight ahead across the street like he might be waiting to meet someone, but he seemed oddly out of place just sitting there doing nothing. It only made me wary of his presence.

A bell jingled as the door to the shop opened, and a pleasant floral scent reached my nose upon stepping inside. The place was clean, with glossy oak floors and exposed brick walls that matched the outside of the building, but the disorganization gave it a bit of a messy feel. Catilda guided me through the narrow, cluttered aisles to where the register was. Guitars and animal heads hung from the walls, trinkets were stacked on unorganized shelves. The more valuable items, like jewelry, were secured behind glass display cases. The inventory may not have looked like it, but each item had a rare or highly sought after magic quality to it.

I picked up a ball of yarn and ogled it with curious eyes, giving Catilda a smirk. "Is this a special toy for cat shifters?"

"Zulli ... put that down ... very carefully." She held out her hands like she wanted to snatch it away from me but was too afraid to touch it. "That's a never-ending ball of yarn. If you drop it and it unravels, we'll never be able to roll it back up again."

Delicately, I placed it back on the shelf like I was handling a highly unstable bomb that would go off if I so much as sneezed on it.

"So, what's this favor you have to ask me, hun? Tell me! I can't wait any longer!" Catilda balled her hands into fists and vibrated with excitement.

"I need you to look into something for me." I swung my backpack around and pulled out the glass vial. "Can you tell me what this is? What is it made of and what can it be used for?"

Catilda took the vial and pouted as she read the small print stamped on the red cap. "NightFly Technologies? Zulli, what are you doing with this?"

The suspicion emanating from her striking baby blue eyes was more curiosity than anything. I had known Catilda and her family since I could walk. She knew more about me than my own family. I trusted her completely and knew I could always count on her.

"I think something might be going on. I know you've been gone for a while, but you've heard about Bliss, right? It's this memory drug that's destroying minds and killing people who become addicted to it." Her loose curls bounced with her nod. "Well, the man behind it, Davian Grymes, used to work for my dad. He attacked NightFly Technologies last night, and I'm worried that was just the beginning. Someone trying to escape dropped a list of names, big names like government officials, business owners, and celebrities. And before that, Davian tried to steal a shipping container full of this transparent orange liquid. My brother Brodin said it's just some ordinary bonding agent they use in the lab, and I want to trust him, but I'm having a hard time believing Davian would go to such great lengths to steal some ordinary magic chemical. I know I'm asking a lot from you, Catilda, but I didn't know who else to go to. I need to figure out why Davian wants this stuff so badly and if my family is in trouble."

Catilda narrowed her eyes on me. "Why not go to the military with this? They have more resources than I do."

My hand reached for the back of my neck and I scratched it. "I was actually taken off the mission. No one knows I'm still looking into Davian, and I doubt the military will take my suspicions as seriously as I am. But I know you use those special machines to test magic when new items come into the shop. Can it analyze something like this?"

Before she could answer, the bell above the front entrance chimed and an unexpected guest slipped inside. My heart stuttered before slightly relaxing. Our visitor was tall and stylish, with boot cut jeans and polished dress shoes. His brown leather jacket creaked with the motion of his arms. While he wasn't the same hooded man from the bus stop, a deep hood from the sweatshirt under his jacket concealed his shadowed face. He kept his head down, hands in his pockets, and aimlessly strolled over to a display case filled with jewelry along the far wall.

Catilda started walking over to him. "Sorry, sir, but we're closed for the day. We open up again at—"

His hand whipped out of his pocket faster than a bolt of lightning, and Catilda disappeared into an explosion of magical navy powder.

"Catilda!" I cried, my heart threatening to burst from my chest.

Sharpened claws formed on my fingertips. I lunged into the cloud of sleep powder, careful not to breathe it in. Thrusting my arm forward, I aimed for the man's neck. His forceful grip squeezed my wrist before I could reach. With his other hand, he formed a "V" and struck me in the throat.

I dropped to my knees, gasping as I desperately tried to inhale air. My hands pressed into the floor, and I shook my head. Forcing myself to get it together, I swept out a leg and to take out the man's feet. He stumbled backward into the wall, knocking over a shelf of academic textbooks.

Rebounding to my feet, I ripped a yellow bullet from my belt. *"Fo—"*

A fist like an iron brick sent a crippling punch into my chest. The bullet clattered to the floor before I had a chance to activate the magic. My hip collided into a metal shelf, the delicate ceramic trinkets resting on it smashing into a million pieces. My attacker's hand chopped into my torso. A sharp crack produced a radiating pain that shot outwards from the center of impact. I gritted my teeth, wheezing as I clutched at the pain. I toppled backward, my body tense. Glass shattered, fracturing into sharp, tiny razor blades as my back landed hard on a display case.

I lay there, feeling like I had just been hammered into a bed of nails. Small beads of blood bubbled from my skin. Every time I tried to breathe, my vision swirled in blurred circles and a sharp pain stabbed me in the chest.

"Demitto," I rasped out. The bullet rolled on the floor and bumped against the man's shiny dress shoe. The elastic magic exploded into an amorphous substance that clung to the lower part of his legs, sticking him in place.

"Meow."

A shimmering calico cat with bright blue eyes bounded off a bookcase. With outstretched paws, she leapt straight for the man's head. Catilda raked her nails down the back of his neck, then hooked them into his leather jacket. The man bellowed in range. His feet were stuck in place, but his arms swayed from side to side with each jerking movement. Catilda's body slammed into a bookcase. He shrugged off his jacket and hurled it, along with Catilda's delicate feline body, against the wall. A terrifying smack vibrated against the unforgiving brick. A strangled howl came from Catilda, but then she went silent.

I got to my knees but collapsed onto my side. The pain in my chest grew angrier with every slight movement and my lungs struggled to fill with air. I bit my lip, trying to focus on a different pain. Catilda could hold her own, but she wasn't a trained fighter. I needed to help her.

The man roared in frustration, and the magic binding his feet stretched. With his powerful strength, he tugged against each elastic strand until it became so thin it snapped. He picked up the vial Catilda had dropped on the floor, then marched over to me.

"Consider this your only warning. Stay away." His throaty voice was a sinister growl that piqued my interest. It was almost like he was forcing himself to sound menacing, lacking the conviction of someone who truly meant harm. I attempted to get a better look at the face under the hood, but a plasticky scent poured off it. The magic emanating from the fabric concealing his identity.

"Who are you?" I felt compelled to ask, not that I was expecting an answer. If he knew I had the vial, then he must have been one of Davian's men.

A guttural scream, raging with both power and malice, resonated throughout the shop. The black hooded figure from the bus had passed right through the front window as if it wasn't even there. He rushed down a narrow aisle straight for my attacker. The black blur rammed his shoulder into my enemy's sternum, the forceful assault shoving him off balance. The glass vial dropped to the floor, the liquid splattering everywhere as a dress shoe stepped on it. The two hooded assailants continued pursuing each other, slashing knives and dodging magic.

I let them distract each other while I rolled myself over onto my hands and knees. I winced as a ceramic vase exploded against the wood floor, fragments flying in all directions. It was followed by the scratchy resonating sound of a guitar being smashed to pieces and then the bell jingling above the door. A few seconds later, a shadow darkened over me.

"You can hurt me, but if you hurt my friend, I will crawl out of my grave and kill you myself." The words wheezed out of my mouth, hardly threatening.

"I would never hurt you, Zulli. Or your friend."

My mysterious savior pushed back his hood, revealing a head of messy, short chestnut-colored hair and worried amber eyes. His florid face was several different shades of red.

"Ryker? I *knew* I was being followed!" I tried to push myself up to my feet. Ryker crouched down to my level instead.

"You seemed worried. Mind telling me what's going on? What are you doing here?"

"I didn't realize I needed to run my plans by you every time I went out." I pushed through the pain, rolling myself up into a sitting position. My fingers picked out the tiny shards of glass stuck in my skin like porcupine quills. It must have hurt, but the only pain my mind was registering was in the side of my chest.

"You don't need to," Ryker shook his head. "But lately it seems like every building you step into somehow gets destroyed. I just want to make sure you're safe, given everything going on."

"I'm not a child, Ryker. You don't need to supervise me."

My blood boiled, and if it got any hotter I'd be breathing out fire. The inferno extinguished when I realized Catilda wasn't anywhere in sight.

"Where is she? Cat—" I coughed, clutching my stomach and unable to complete her name.

"You mean that calico feline intensely staring at me with distrusting eyes over there in the corner? She seems fine."

My head turned toward the sound of an aggressive hiss. Catilda, still in her cat form, was watching Ryker's every move from her perch on top of a shelf. Her ears were flattened to the back of her head and her tail flicked, ready to attack her prey. She jumped down from the shelf and slunk her way over to sit next to me. Her glossy coat was mostly orange and white patches with little dots of black covering her sinuous body. It bore a striking similarity to her pale freckled skin and fiery copper hair in her human form. The only exception was the solid black circle that surrounded one of her blue eyes.

"Come on out, Catilda. Time to meet Ryker."

The air around me hummed with magic, a cloud of warmth overtaking the vicinity and the smell of fresh cut grass heavy in the air. Catilda's padded front paws morphed into two human hands, her arms with smooth skin. She rose upright on two feet as her hind legs grew back into their shapely form clothed in black leggings. Her pointed ears disappeared, but she kept her claws out and pointed at Ryker.

"What are you waiting for, dummy?" She flicked a string on his hoodie with her claw. "Help her."

Ryker didn't hesitate. "Of course. But I have to get something first."

The smell of his cinnamon magic tickled my nose as he stepped back into a portal. A few minutes later he reappeared with a first aid bag. He dug through it and handed me two pills along with a bottle of water.

"Take these."

I rolled the small white pills around in my palm, noticing the initials of my father's company stamped on them. "This is the same stuff my father gave me for my eye. How did you get your hands on it?"

"You're not the only one who gets hurt, Zulli. Your favorite nurse, Lana, gave them to me for my leg injury."

I tossed back the pills, taking a big swig of water to wash them down. The cool liquid felt refreshing slipping down my dry throat. Ryker started carefully removing the rest of the tiny pieces of glass that dug into my skin.

"Catilda first," I demanded.

He swiped a quick glance at Catilda. She sat down beside me in a pile of debris. Her makeup was smeared like war paint across her face and her glittery eyelids were drooping, likely a side effect of whatever sleep magic she had breathed in. She had a deep cut on her forehead, blood drying in a thin streak past her right eye. She rolled her shoulder in circles, rubbing her neck as she did.

A delightful chuckle rolled off her painted lips. "I'm fine, hun. Can't take me down that easily! Who would have thought I'd be thrown into a pile of the world's fluffiest pillows that never flatten?"

Ryker cleaned her wound, then pressed a gauze pad to the cut on her head and secured it with a long piece of medical tape. "You're lucky. A cat's body is more delicate than a human's. If you'd actually hit your head against the brick wall, it could have killed you."

He twisted the cap off a white tube. Returning his attention to me, he activated the magic-infused healing ointment and began gently slathering it over my arm. I swatted his hand away, grabbing the tube from his hands.

"I can apply it myself."

Ryker let me be, focusing instead on Catilda. "Is there somewhere more comfortable we can move Zulli to?"

"There's a couch in the break room. Follow me."

Ryker delicately slid an arm under mine and lifted me up, then used his other arm to sweep my legs out from under me. He held me close against his warm body as he carried me down the hallway toward the back of the shop. With every slight jostle, I hissed at the pain coursing through me.

"Put me down, Ryker. My legs work just fine." I half-heartedly smacked his shoulder.

"I think you might have bruised a rib. Maybe even fractured it. Best you don't move that much." His strong hands gripped me a little tighter.

Catilda turned into a doorway and flipped on the lights. A sharp reflection bounced off the shiny checkered tile floors and temporarily blinded me. Black dots flashed before my eyes. I blinked them away and a circular wooden table with four plastic chairs appeared before me. To one side of the table was a small kitchenette, a variety of mismatched mugs and dishes scattered across the spotless beige laminate countertop. To the other side, a large couch was pushed up against a peeling floral wallpapered wall.

"Don't think I'm letting you off the hook," Ryker said as he lowered me down onto the couch, an overstuffed light blue monstrosity that I remembered used to be in Catilda's living room. "Why did you feel you had to hide this from me?"

The emotional hurt that ruptured inside me left behind a feeling of brokenness, an intense pain much worse than the stabbing sensation on the left side of my chest whenever I breathed. I glimpsed the anguish in Ryker's eyes before he turned his back to me and slumped toward the other side of the room.

Catilda appeared beside me with some blankets draped over one arm and a bag of potato chips in the other, sparing me from the conversation with Ryker I knew I'd eventually have to have.

"Those for me? You're the best, Catilda." I reached out to grab the snack when she placed it on the floor next to her feet. Yearning, she then snapped out the blanket and flattened it next to the couch. As she got comfortable in her makeshift bed, she replied, "No. These are for me. I'm tired, hungry, and I need a nap."

She munched on a handful of chips until she could no longer keep her eyes open. Her soft snores sounded like the gentle murmur of a cat purring.

I snuck my hand in for a few chips. With a strenuous effort, I turned myself over and nuzzled my face into the back of the couch, not wanting Ryker's disappointing gaze watching over me to be the last thing I saw before I fell asleep.

The light touch of a blanket covered my shoulders. It was followed by a miserable sigh and a warm, masculine hand sweeping away the short hair covering my forehead, picking out a tiny crystal of glass caught in it. My eyelids fluttered closed and I melted into the sofa, but I struggled to let go of the thoughts concerning the mysterious man going after the vial. Eventually, I drifted off, welcoming a peaceful darkness that settled over me.

The sound of Catilda raising her voice startled me awake a few hours later. There were no windows in the break room, but the wall clock hanging above the doorway confirmed it was well into the night.

I watched Catilda inch closer into Ryker's personal space just outside the door in the hallway. Half curious to eavesdrop on their conversation and half afraid to make any sudden movements due to my injuries, I didn't shift from my position on the couch. I could feel the medication kicking in, but the severity of the trauma meant it would take at least a few days to completely heal, even with magic aiding me.

I pulled the blanket up to my eyes, squinting them so it appeared I was still asleep.

"I think you need to go." Catilda crossed her arms, thrusting out her chin and narrowing her eyes. Her tense, high-pitched voice was loud but hardly threatening.

"Who are you again?" Ryker stood with his hands inside his single oversized hoodie pocket and leaned his back against the doorframe. There was a small cut on his cheek, a rainbow of magic powders from the earlier flight clinging to his skin and staining his clothes.

"Catilda Harper. Best friend and fellow cat shifter. Now *go*! Get out of my shop! Zulli doesn't want you here." She leaned in closer to Ryker, the bounce normally in her voice had a hint of venom in it.

"You don't know what she wants. Zulli is my friend, too, you know." Ryker dropped his shoulders, his head hanging low. "I'm just trying to protect her. Something seemed off, and I thought she might be in trouble."

Catilda bopped him on the head and he winced. "You dummy. Zulli doesn't need a knight in shining armor to come rescue her at the first sign of danger. Trouble will always find her. She needs someone to support her, have her back when trouble arrives."

"How do you know what she needs?" Ryker's voice grumbled, a muscle in his jaw ticking. He pushed off the doorframe and leaned in toward Catilda. An unfamiliar anger I had never seen before started to bubble inside him. "She's determined, but reckless. She could end up getting into serious trouble one day, and I want to make sure that never happens."

Catilda curled her fingers, and I watched, expecting the claws to come out. "I've known Zulli my entire life. She's going to do what she wants to do. And if you're going to stand in her way rather than stand by her side, then you need to leave."

As curious as I was to see how this conversation would play out, a fight between my two best friends wasn't something I wanted to encourage.

I flung the blanket off and stretched out my arms, yawning obnoxiously loud.

"What's going on?" I asked, rubbing the bleariness from my eyes and sitting up on the couch. It was followed by a terrible yelp of pain as I clutched my rib.

Ryker opened his mouth first but Catilda cut him off. "Sorry, Zulli. I can't do that favor for you anymore. The … *stuff* you asked me to look at before spilled onto the floor."

She shot a bitter glower at Ryker.

"It's fine, Catilda. He'll just keep following me around until he figures out what we're up to, anyway."

A complacent smile flashed across Ryker's face, and Catilda scowled like she wanted to slash it right off him with her sharp claws.

"In that case …" Catilda flicked her hair back from her face. "While your creepy babysitter was watching you sleep, I ran into my parents' research room and got a magic sponge. It soaked up the remaining liquid on the floor. I reversed the magic so it expelled the bonding agent into a test tube. It should be a large enough sample to test."

Ryker leaned against the arm of the couch, keeping one eye on Catilda, the other one on me. "So is someone going to tell me what's going on? Why was that man in the leather jacket attacking Zulli?"

"No idea," I dragged a hand down my face. "I'm guessing one of Davian's men knew I had that vial and wanted it back before I could do anything with it."

My feet barely complied with the will to walk as I stood and shuffled over to the kitchen table. I slid my backpack closer, unzipped it, and took out the crumpled up piece of paper.

"There's also this. From what I can tell, it's a list of high-profile names. A member of the Black Mark dropped it the night NightFly Technologies was attacked. I think it might be a list of targets."

Ryker swiped the list from my fingers and sagged his shoulders. "Mayor Ethin Henderson is on this list. Along with several other big names. And what's this handwritten name at the bottom? I can't make it out." He looked up to gauge my reaction, but I had no answers. "What would Davian even want with these people? And why didn't you tell me you had this list, Zulli? Did you steal that vial from the crime scene?"

"Not on purpose." I dipped my chin and averted my gaze from Ryker.

Catilda read the list next, humming in disagreement. "Hmm. I'm not an expert detective or anything, Zulli. But I'd say this is more a list of potential business partners. There's never a shortage of corrupt politicians and business owners, and celebrities are always looking for a way to bring attention to themselves. There are some names on this list I don't recognize though. Maybe whatever Davian is planning, stealing all this tech and the drugs, these people want in on it?"

I sucked in a deep breath and threw my head back. "Well, until we gather more info all we have is a sample of magic liquid and a crumpled up list of random names. How long does it take to analyze that magic chemical?"

"Not long. I'll get started now." Catilda scampered out of the room, and I trailed behind her, using an exhausting amount of effort to keep up so that I wouldn't be left behind with Ryker.

Catilda stopped in front of a heavy door that looked oddly out of place compared to the rest of the moderately accessorized shop. The thick steel slab was painted a dull gray with a silver lever, kept locked with a high-tech looking keypad. She punched in a few numbers, using a bit of magic to confirm her identity, and the door clicked open.

The lights came on automatically when we entered, illuminating the clean white walls, shiny steel machinery, and a cheap workstation decorated with stains, chips, and peeling plastic. A few worn black leather stools were scattered around and an office chair was tucked under a metal desk. The smell of bleach and old plastic lingered in the air.

"What the hell is all this stuff?" I asked, eyeing several cylindrical tanks labeled with various aerosolized magic particles.

"Do *not* touch anything," Catilda admonished as she sat down on a stool. "This is where my parents do all their research on magic objects. My dad travels around the world, trying to locate specific artifacts for clients or rare finds for the shop, and my mom does all the testing and validation of the objects once they arrive."

Ryker stood next to me, his gaze staring straight ahead at Catilda. She pressed a few buttons and turned on some alien-looking machine that roared to life like an airplane ready for takeoff. Using a dropper, she sucked out the liquid and piped a few drops into a small compartment on the side of the machine. A few seconds later, she started typing away on the keyboard, letting the contraption do its thing.

I knew better than to bother Catilda while she worked, so I silently stood in place, rocking back and forth on my heels until she was finished.

"Hmm." A bewildered look appeared on Catilda's tilted head. "The analysis says it's a bonding spell. Just like you said, Zulli."

Ryker and I leaned in closer, our shoulders brushing up against each other. He stepped around me to the other side of Catilda.

A quick, exasperated sigh exhaled out of my nose. "Well, that was a waste of time. I shouldn't have bothered you, Catilda. Guess I'm just paranoid after all."

"As you should be, hun. Look." She pointed to two identical pictures on the computer monitor.

"What am I looking at?"

Ryker's voice answering my question startled me. "The molecular structure of the magic in the bonding agent. One is what it *should* be. The other is what it actually is. Both images are similar, but not quite the same."

Catilda shot an irritated glare at him.

"I have no idea what that means," I admitted. "I'm not a magic technician."

"Neither am I." Catilda shrugged. "You'd have to ask my mom. All I can tell you is that whatever was in that vial was changed somehow. What it was altered to do is anyone's guess. You'd have to get it analyzed by a real lab."

A troubling thought popped into my head. "Could the military figure it out? If they examine any of the evidence from the shipping container?"

Catilda twirled her finger around a curl. "They could, but unless they're specifically looking for something out of place like I was then probably not."

I skeptically peered over at Ryker, his eyes scanning the data on the screen. While I couldn't be certain, I had a hunch this new spell had something to do with the secret Maeck had warned me against telling anyone about. If Ryker went to the military with this data, as any loyal soldier should do, it could set my father's plans back by months, maybe even years. Or put an end to the testing all together.

"Please don't tell anyone about this, Ryker. Not even Kasra. Not yet."

"Because you don't want her help? Like you didn't want mine?"

"I told you I can handle this, Ryker!" I tried to hide the sting of his words behind my anger. It wasn't that I didn't want his help. I knew he would offer it no matter what I asked, even if it meant going on a rogue mission without the military backing us up. But getting caught would destroy his career.

"I won't tell her, Zulli. She needs to hear this from you. But you should really consider leaving this alone. You no longer have the support of the military behind you." Ryker's hand fell to my shoulder. A sense of overwhelming compassion returned to his voice, but his brown eyes were empty, lacking his kindhearted soul. "Let Zavyr and your brothers do what they do best. I'm sure it's just a new, enhanced version of something. Nothing to risk your life over."

I jerked my shoulder away from Ryker. "Davian not only went after my father and his company, but he destroyed the lives of so many people with Bliss—people like Briyan who didn't deserve what happened to him. I'm not sitting back and waiting for the military to have some miracle breakthrough. Davian has to be stopped, and that drug needs to be taken off the streets."

"I will support you, Zulli!" Catilda jumped up from her stool and stood alongside me with a pompous grin on her pink lips. "I have your back. Always."

"Great." I matched her smile, slinging an arm around her neck, then turned to Ryker. "Your concern has been noted and ignored. If my dad or my brothers are in trouble, then I'm obligated to do something about it. And I don't need people sneaking around behind my back while I do it."

Catilda and I shoved Ryker out of the research room and into the hallway. He didn't fight us, and he could have used a portal to make his way back inside, but he respected our need for privacy.

"I'm not leaving," he said as he slid down the paint-chipped wall in the hallway and sat on the dirty carpet, hugging his legs.

"And I'm not letting you back in." I curled an evil grin at him and slammed the thick steel door in his face, resulting in a satisfying thunder rattling the walls.

9

CATILDA RAN A FEW MORE tests on the magic liquid before we decided to call it a night. Out in the hallway, Ryker had fallen asleep, having removed his hoodie and shoved it under his head as a pillow. After grabbing my backpack, I left a blanket next to him. Catilda and I decided to leave him there, proceeding to slip out the back door and lock up.

Catilda offered me her family's guest room for the night. The buses had stopped running until morning, and without Ryker's magic I had no way to get home.

The room was a small but comfortable space with a twin bed, complete with fluffy pillows and silky sheets in an elegant midnight blue. I snuggled under the warm comforter, but the stabbing pain every time I moved didn't allow me the luxury of rest.

After hours of tossing and turning, I gave up on trying to sleep. At the sight of golden light peeking in through the blinds, I dragged my feet out of bed and down the hallway toward the bathroom. My sluggishness meant I wasn't in any rush to get ready for the long day of cleaning up the mess we'd left behind at Harper's Treasure Chest, but I knew Catilda had probably worried all night about the shop. Until everything was fixed and back in place, she had to keep the place closed, and her parents wouldn't be happy about that.

A cold shower gave me life and felt good on my aching, burning skin. Most of the pinpricks from the glass had healed overnight, thanks to the magic healing ointment. My throat still felt tight and dry. The garish yellow and purple streak that wrapped around the side of my left breastbone was tender to the touch but not as painful as it was yesterday. I could raise my arms and breathe with only moderate discomfort.

I hadn't planned on the sleepover, but I always kept a few necessities in my backpack. I threw on a thin, long-sleeve sweater, big enough to fit both me and Catilda at the same time. Next came a pair of stretchy yellow and black plaid pants. My fingers gave my hair a quick comb. Finally, I snapped on my belt and slipped on my boots, then met Catilda downstairs in the kitchen.

"What the hell are you wearing?" were the first words out of Catilda's mouth. With the help of the same magic healing gel, the cut above her eye was just a faint white mark now. She had covered up what was left of it with excessive makeup. Otherwise she looked straight out of a fashion magazine with her tousled curls, skinny jeans, sequin tank top, and pink blazer. I, on the other hand, looked like I had picked my clothes out of a lost and found bin.

"Morning to you, too," I croaked, shuffling my way over to the platter of chocolate chip muffins on the counter. Taking a quick sniff, my eyes lit up at the realization that the nutty scent wasn't chocolate chips.

"Black flies …" I humored myself.

My teeth sunk into the sweet treat. I threw my head back and moaned, savoring the rich earthy taste of the insects. Catilda's eyes twinkled with enjoyment watching me eat.

"I made them just for you, hun!" This morning, Catilda displayed the liveliness of a butterfly, fluttering around the kitchen in a gentle breeze, brewing some coffee, and grabbing herself an apple from the fruit bowl on the counter.

The bright kitchen was a colorful reflection of the Harper family personality. The walls were painted a glossy sunshine yellow, with clean white wooden cabinets wrapping around the outer wall in an "L" shape. The backsplash was a fun display of turquoise and orange decorative tiles that brightened up the cozy space. I lazily made my way over to the corner by the back door, where a square table was squished into an alcove and bordered by bench seating.

My fingers ran over the padded cloth cushion as I scooted in. In the Harper household, breakfast was the most important meal of the day, and with everyone's busy schedules, sometimes it was the only meal they shared together. I had so many memories of gathering here, smiling, laughing, and sharing stories together as part of their family. Today, however, it was oddly quiet.

"Where is everyone?" I asked.

"My parents left yesterday to meet up with someone and check out a new potential magic object for the shop. My brothers took advantage of the lack of parental supervision and stayed at a friend's house."

She slid into the booth on the other side of me, two steaming mugs of coffee in hand. She pushed one over to me.

"So, do you and that big genius brain of yours have a plan?" I tilted the mug to my lips.

"I was thinking about it last night. We sometimes reach out to this contact when we're in desperate need of help identifying something at the shop."

"Well, I don't know about you, but I think this qualifies as a desperate need."

Catilda twirled a ginger curl around her finger as she spoke. "This guy calls himself the Breaker, because, well, his magic ability is to break things. In a good way. He can look at something and use his magic to break down its composition and run countless scenarios in his head on what it might be used for, how it can be modified. He's basically a human research lab, and the best part is there's no paper trail. No records will tie us to anything he does."

Catilda paused, her mouth open like she was going to say something, but she quickly snapped it shut.

I scraped the muffin crumbs from the table and cleaned my hands with a napkin. "I sense there's a catch to all this …"

"My parents only go to him as a last resort. What he does isn't exactly, um, legal. And it comes at a price. Neither of us has anything of value to offer him. If he chooses to help us, we'll be in his debt."

"One problem at a time." I rubbed my forehead. "Give him a call and let's see if we can make a deal."

"You got it, hun!" She firmly nodded. "I have to go find his contact information in my dad's office. But after, let's head on over to the shop. We need to start cleaning up before my parents get back and figure out what happened. They'll never trust me to run the place on my own again otherwise."

Catilda left the kitchen, and the patter of light footsteps disappeared up the stairs. I cleaned up our dishes then followed her, heading toward the bedroom to grab my things. The door to her father's office was shut, but I heard Catilda's lively voice arguing with someone. I pressed an ear to the door, activating my magic to listen in. She hung up before I could decipher any of the conversation. Catilda swung open the door, catching me as I scrambled toward the bedroom.

"The guy I spoke to, the Breaker's assistant, said he'll relay the message to his boss and give us an answer later today." Catilda slumped her shoulders, a tinge of frustration growing in her eyes. "Come on, hun. We have work to do at the shop."

I tidied up the bedroom, then grabbed my backpack and met Catilda outside, hopping into her purple coupe. Most modern vehicles were powered by a special magic battery and included more magic technology inside them than drivers knew how to work properly. Catilda's ancient relic, however, ran on a less efficient magic-infused fuel and had the bare minimum necessities. It turned on, had a steering wheel, and got her from point A to point B. Most of the time.

She turned the key a few times before the motor sputtered to life. Just as we were pulling out of the driveway, my phone started vibrating in my pocket. I pulled it out and answered my brother's call.

"Hey, Brodin. What's up?"

"Hey, what are you doing today? I thought maybe we could grab Maeck and the three of us could go out for dinner later on. There's a new gourmet burger place that opened up right by NightFly Technologies."

"Sounds great, but now's not really a good time. I'm … needed on base today. I won't be around." It was a good thing he couldn't see me because my nervous scratching and trembling lips would have been a dead giveaway I was lying.

Brodin's silence was infuriating, making the heat trapped in the car feel like a burning furnace.

"Okay. Maybe another time, then."

And then he hung up.

I shook my head at the phone then looked over to Catilda. "That was weird. Brodin called me to go out for dinner. He never calls me. Ever."

Catilda shrugged as she bobbed her head to a song on the radio. "Eh, stop complaining. You always say they're too busy with work to spend time with you. Give him credit for trying."

She cranked the music up so loud that the car shook. She proceeded to tap her hands against the steering wheel and belt out the lyrics to the upbeat song playing on the radio.

"Come on, Zulli! I know you know the words!"

I couldn't leave her hanging, so I joined in as her backup. My voice squeaked with every high note and rasped with every low one.

Rolling down the window let the chilly morning breeze brush over my warm face. The sun rose as a canopy of gold, bright amid the blue, clear sky. Its shimmering rays basked the quaint suburban streets with an orange glow. The stately trees lining the professionally manicured front yards cast long shadows in our path. The closer we drove toward the town center, the livelier the activity became. The small cafe near the bus stop had a queue out the door of nicely dressed businessmen and women trying to snag some breakfast before boarding the bus into the city.

The short twenty-minute drive was over in a flash, and Catilda pulled the car into a parking lot shared with the other shop owners downtown. As we circled around and passed the back entrance to the store, I noticed a man sitting on the back steps, black hoodie over his head and hands hidden inside his single large pocket.

Catilda parked the car and turned off the engine, but she just sat there in the driver's seat, staring at Ryker from afar.

"You gotta talk to him, hun." Catilda's sweet voice was serious but not angry.

"I know. But what could I possibly say? He's just ... too damn nice all the time. I feel like a terrible person even being mad at him, but he can't keep following me around! I don't need a babysitter." I sunk into my seat and sighed.

Catilda let out a taunting laugh. "Did you know, back at the shop while you were still sleeping, he apologized to *me*? He said he was sorry everything got destroyed. Like it was his fault that some jackass attacked us."

"That definitely sounds like him. So why the hell didn't he apologize to *me*, then?" I scoffed at her.

"Because he doesn't want forgiveness, Zulli. He wants your acceptance. Even having just met him, I can tell he really does care about you." She puckered her lips and smacked them together, batting her eyes adoringly at me.

"Oh, please. It's not like that between us, Catilda. Besides, Ryker acts that way toward everyone. Always putting others

104

first. He would have done the same thing for anyone else." I paused. "Any ideas on how I can fix this that don't end in you planning our wedding?"

Catilda sat in the driver's seat twirling a curl of hair around her finger. She was the perfect mix of both beauty and brains. Sometimes, I envied her life. She had a loving family, good friends, and a promising career. My family kept things from me, I was one mistake away from being kicked out of the military, and I might be about to lose one of my best friends if I couldn't muster up the courage to confront him.

The sunlight peering in through the windshield caught Catilda's shimmering lip gloss when she spoke. "I don't agree with what he did, secretly following you, I mean, but you can't fault him for wanting to be there for someone he cares about. And you're not perfect either, Zulli!" She jabbed her finger into my arm. "You hid something important from him. How would you feel if he did that to you?"

Frustration consumed my groan. "I'll think about it. My way with words usually involves cursing and yelling at people, and I'm guessing that's exactly what I should avoid doing."

I climbed out the car and slammed the door shut behind me. Slinging my backpack over my shoulder, I strolled up to Ryker who was sitting on the concrete steps leading into the back of the shop. Catilda followed behind me.

Ryker pulled down his hood, revealing wild chestnut-colored hair and dark bags under his normally gleaming eyes. He must have washed up as best he could in the bathroom, but a light dusting of magical powders still stained his hoodie and remnants had caught in his dimples as he smiled.

"I told you I wasn't going to leave," he said as he stood up from the back steps to let us pass. "I stayed the night and kept an eye out just in case the intruder came back. I think there's a family of raccoons living in the dumpster, but otherwise it was a peaceful night."

Catilda fished out the keys from her purse and unlocked the back door to the shop. "Good to know, hun. Since you're here, you can help us clean up."

The lights flickered on and we made our way down the hallway to the front of the shop. I was expecting to see the warzone we'd left behind yesterday. Instead, the shelves were erected upright, the floor swept and washed clean, and everything was neatly put back in place or packed away in boxes. In fact, it looked much cleaner and organized than it had before it was destroyed.

"Oh, about that ..." Ryker hustled over beside me and Catilda. "Since I was here the whole night, I figured I'd at least be of some help. Some things I couldn't repair, like the glass display cases and the broken ceramics, but I did the best I could with the rest."

"Wow! Thanks, Ryker!" Catilda's voice boomed with over-exaggerated excitement, her sparkling eyes turning to me and narrowing. "I'm just gonna take this box of stuff here and go into the back room. For a very long time."

Catilda grabbed a cardboard box from the floor. Her perfectly pruned eyebrows shot up and her eyes widened as she gently elbowed me in the arm, gesturing toward Ryker. She then made her way down the hallway humming a cheery tune, leaving me and Ryker alone.

"You feeling any better this morning, Zulli?" Ryker's gaze traveled to the injury along my chest, and I hugged myself with my arms.

"Still hurts, but those pills are helping a lot."

"Glad to hear." His response was flat, spoken softly. He flashed me a quick smile, more of a twitch that caught his lips, then picked up a bucket full of cleaning supplies on the floor.

I grabbed a broom and started mindlessly sweeping, fixated on the dark oak floor, glossy and already impeccably clean. My mouth opened, then snapped shut again. I did this a few more times, my throat constricting. Like a fish out of water, I was choking on the words I wanted to say. I couldn't force a single sound past my lips.

Ryker had his back facing me as he wiped a rag in slow, circular motions over a blotch of blue powder coating the front door. He was crouched down, shoulders drooping and head low, and doing his best to keep up his charming persona despite the overwhelming hurt I could tell he was keeping bottled up inside. Ryker was no stranger to my temper tantrums, but he always knew what to say to make things better. The fact that he wasn't saying anything right now made me think I might have finally broken him.

A deep and painful breath filled my lungs, and I remembered what Catilda had said in the car. If Ryker had run off on his own secret mission without me, would I have been mad at him? He had every right to do whatever he wanted, and he didn't need to include me if he didn't want to. Just like I had chosen not to include him. But there would still be a part of me that would wonder *why* he didn't include me.

"Hey, Ryker?" I managed to rasp out, my voice low and scratchy.

"Huh?" He stopped cleaning and turned to face me, the whites of his eyes growing as they widened.

My heart jumped and I completely froze. The words were on the tip of my tongue, but I swallowed them back down. The job of being a military soldier didn't come without danger. In the past six months, I'd had every muscle and organ in my body paralyzed. I'd been stabbed more times than I could count, and I'd ingested my fair share of poisons to last a lifetime. So what was it about standing in front of Ryker trying to speak a few simple words that had made me so utterly terrified?

"You need any help?" I finally squeaked out.

A bright, curvy smile creased his cheeks, but it didn't reach his eyes. "I'm good, thanks."

He went back to cleaning, grabbing a bottle from the bucket and spraying the solution on the mat by the front door. He scrubbed furiously, trying to get the blue stain out.

We tidied up in silence until Catilda returned.

"You," she pointed at Ryker. "I had to get some display cases shipped overnight to the shop. I need some help bringing them in and setting them up."

"What should I do?" I asked Catilda before she disappeared.

"Hmm. You're still injured, so you shouldn't push yourself too hard. Why don't you keep trying to get that stain out of the mat? It's going to take Ryker and I a few hours to finish setting up the new furniture and rearranging everything in the new display cases. Then you can pick out some place for us to eat lunch! Ryker here offered to treat us!"

"I did?" Ryker looked genuinely bewildered.

Catilda scowled at him. "Zulli told me about that fancy apartment of yours. I'm sure you can afford to treat two very nice, attractive ladies to a decent lunch."

I rubbed my hands together and licked my lips. It was late morning and I was already starving. "Lunch. Now *that* is a task I can handle. You can count on me."

10

---◈---

NOT SURPRISING TO ANYONE, I settled on a burger joint about a half mile away. Their menu listed an enormous selection of specialty milkshakes, a build-your-own burger bar, and, of course, leafy greens for Catilda, whose weekly portion of fat had come from the handful of potato chips she had scoffed down last night.

"I can't believe I ate those greasy things! What deranged magic spell was I under that compelled me to eat that crap?" She continued to criticize herself as she locked up the front door to the shop.

"You're lucky you didn't eat a whole slice of pizza! Imagine the consequences!" I teased in a friendly tone.

Catilda responded with a wry smirk, then the three of us set out to fill our bellies.

Pacing ahead, I led the way down the paved sidewalk. The sun was high in the afternoon sky, the chill of morning replaced with a subtle warmth that felt pleasant on my skin. We passed a cluster of buildings that stood confidently together in the town center, bordering the public garden nestled in the middle. The shops, mostly small family-owned businesses, each had their own unique characteristics setting them apart from the next.

Some were rusty-colored brick, others brown and gray uneven stones. My favorite was the candy shop, a colorful combination of purple grape and bubblegum pink painted wood combined with the tantalizing smell of so many variations of sugary goodness creeping out the open door.

I was about to make a detour for some gummy bears when Catilda leapt up next to me, wrapped her arm around mine, and whispered into my ear. "You didn't talk to him, did you?"

Without thinking, I peered over my shoulder at Ryker, strolling casually with his hands in his jean pockets. His shoulders drooped at his sides, his gaze fixated on the laid-back atmosphere of the delightful town around him. He often walked behind me and Kasra, always on high alert and surveying the area for danger. I couldn't help but wonder if, this time, he was doing it to avoid me.

"I tried. I think I'm just gonna let this one ride out. Ryker doesn't dwell on the past. He'll get over it in a day or two, and everything will go back to normal."

Catilda's lovely face turned bitter, her nose scrunching in disagreement, and she made some kind of indiscernible grumble. "Do what you want, hun! But it ain't gonna work. You'll never find a man if you keep pushing them away!"

"Who ever said I was looking for a man?" I argued, a little louder than I had anticipated.

"Everything okay?" Ryker caught up to us, his eyes darting back and forth between me and Catilda.

"Oh, we're just talking about cat shifter stuff!" Catilda flapped her hands about in a disregarding manner. "Dealing with people constantly trying to pet you, fur stuck everywhere to everything, keeping our coats glossy. Nothing that would interest you." She gave him the cold shoulder and kept walking.

"But none of that pertains to Zulli. She can't actually shift into a cat."

Catilda whipped around and beat his chest with her purse. "How rude!"

110

"*Ow!* Gee, what the hell do you carry in there? Bricks?" Ryker pressed his fingers over his stomach where Catilda had hit him.

"Among other things," she smirked, a mischievous grin spreading across her mouth.

It was then that my stomach began to rumble, and I realized we had been walking for way longer than we should have been. The charming shops in the town center had vanished and opened up into a nature landscape. We were the only people wandering through the quiet park. A canopy of bare trees hung above our path. The branches swayed in the gentle breeze, the shadows they cast moving like slithering snakes at our feet.

"Where are we?" Ryker's hand hovered near the knife on his waist, his instincts on high alert.

I adjusted my belt, the bullets being the only magic objects I had on me. Catilda opened her purse, took out a travel-sized spray bottle of something, and started sweeping her arm back and forth in front of her like she was brandishing a gun.

A low, unfamiliar male voice hit my ears and made them twitch. "I thought cats were supposed to have an excellent sense of direction."

The three of us whirled around to see a trio of unexpected visitors standing on the gravel path. They had definitely not been there a minute ago.

"Look, we don't want any trouble. We just—" Ryker didn't get a chance to finish his plea.

"Neither do we," the ringleader replied. He was a tall and lanky man, early forties maybe, with a pinched face that made him look like he was permanently sucking on a lemon. His bald head was shiny but dented and misshapen, giving the impression that his skull might have been hit one too many times with a baseball bat.

"What do you want?" Confusion twisted my voice. They didn't seem to fit the persona of Davian's typical goons. The three of them looked about as threatening as a group of carnival clowns.

The man stood there casually with his hands clasped behind his back, making no indication that he might attack. I discreetly snagged a navy blue bullet from my belt, but kept my hand at my side.

"Allow me to introduce myself. I'm Jax. My friends here are Gavin and Kora. We already know who you three are."

The female to his left was equally as tall but more toned. She was wearing a soccer mom ensemble with running shoes and tight yoga pants. The other man was wearing what I'd describe as a shiny plastic trash bag that doubled as a coat, his body so round and oversized he could have had his own orbit. Either these misfits grossly underestimated our fighting abilities or maybe they really weren't here to pick a fight.

"Don't shoot the messengers," Kora joked with a hint of mockery in her laugh. "We're just here to inform you that the Breaker has accepted your request for help. *You* will meet him at the skating rink tonight at nineteen hundred sharp."

She was pointing her finger directly at me. I twisted my head side to side to check if she was mistaken. To my right, Catilda stood completely still, spray bottle in hand and eyes glued to the female target. On my left, Ryker knitted his eyebrows, cautiously inching his way closer to me.

"Me? Why me?"

"Our boss has some words to say to you. Alone," Jax answered, his beady eyes blinking in their narrow sockets. "If anyone is seen following you, make no mistake, Ms. Taracula, your life will end before you step foot inside the door. Our boss takes his meetings seriously."

"Whatever he has to say, it can be said in front of these two. Come on, at least let me bring Catilda. Look at her. She's harmless, and she already knows the guy."

I glanced over to Catilda, her finger pressing down on the pump of her bottle that released a mist around her like a magical barrier of bug spray. She then let out a horrific screech as a slight breeze sent the magic aerosol directly into her eyes.

"It stings!" she wailed, trying to rub away the discomfort.

Jax shook his head, a sliver of sunshine reflecting off his shiny dome. "Fine. But you will come without magic."

"*Excuse me?*" I shrieked.

A cool gust of wind swept past me, a faceless blur too quick for even my superior reflexes to detect. A minty scent wafted off the magic left behind. I let go of the bullet I was holding in my hand. "*Dormeo!*"

The cloud of sparkling blue dust was sucked into the current. I held my breath, hoping to avoid the effects of my own spell. My long, slouchy sweater lifted up and flapped around me like a plastic bag caught in a burst of wind. A slight pressure pushed against my waist, cold fingertips, then a weight was lifted.

I thrust my claws down, catching nothing but air. I looked up to see Kora standing in the exact same spot she had been a mere fraction of a second ago, her blond ponytail a frizzy mess. My belt dangled from a single finger.

The whirlwind weakened, the sleep powder dispersed, and Ryker, now standing next to my shoulder, handed over his knife. "Zulli ..."

"I know."

Without my belt, I had little in the way of offensive tactics. My claws would get nowhere near close enough to take out someone with speed magic, my sticky hands weren't strong enough to hold on to her, and the other two messengers were still a mystery. I realized now that I was the one who had underestimated them.

Catilda stepped back behind me and Ryker, no shame in using us as a shield if she needed to. She dug out something new from her purse and stood there with her claws out, ready to defend herself.

"If you don't want me to bring the belt, I won't. But give it back." I held out my hand as if Kora might decide to have a change of heart and return it.

"You'll get it back after the meeting." She secured the cracked leather belt around her waist, adjusting it around her slender hips. "It's not really my style, anyway."

My feet launched me forward, a ferocious growl seething past my teeth. A ripple of magic opened, the warmth brushing against my skin for the slightest second. Ryker's portal positioned right behind the speedster. My sticky fingers ripped a clump of hair from her head, the knife in my other hand ripping a small tear in her jacket. A frantic cry poured out of her mouth before she disappeared from my sight. Her magic was vibrating at a frequency so fast that a high-pitched hiss surrounded her. A layer of static electricity danced on her skin. I focused on it, tracking her footsteps, her minty smell, anticipating her next move.

"Catilda! Watch out!"

No portal would be fast enough to get me to Catilda in time.

"*Lapsus!*" Catilda dropped the tube of lip balm in her hand, the wax spilling out into a slippery puddle flowing before her feet. There was a yelp, followed by a grating sound as skin hit the gravel path. Long legs barreled into Catilda like a bowling ball, taking out her feet as she crashed hard on top of Kora. They went sliding together, limbs tangled and reaching for hair or clothes.

My reflexes kicked in, and I sped to Catilda's aid. A loud voice rang in my ears and caused me to stagger before I got too far. "*Where are you going?*"

The disembodied voice rippled through me. The sound wave was amplified by my own enhanced senses and made my hair stand on end. The vibration traveled through my ears, my brain sloshing around inside my head. I threw out my hands for balance, stumbling on my feet like a drunk.

Ryker's lips were moving, his hands pressed against his ears, but I couldn't make out the words. He started toward me, eyes wide and mouth parted. He stopped, hesitating with the slightest twitch, then turned around to rush toward Catilda instead.

I dropped the knife and clutched my palms to my ears. With every slight movement, I anticipated my liquid brain pouring out of the holes on my face.

"What's happening?" The words that rolled off my tongue had no sound. I hunched over, squeezing my head tighter. My gaze traveled past Jax to Gavin, the round blob of a man hovering behind him. He was standing there like a solid stone statue, not a single flinch at the fight going on around him. I wasn't sure he actually *could* move.

"Sound waves are a bitch when your hearing is so good." Jax's eyes crinkled with amusement, a dangerous grin barely noticeable forming across his thin lips.

The world spun around me. I pitched sideways, catching a glimpse of Ryker locking his arms around the speedster and Catilda taking a swing at Kora with her purse.

My voice cried out for help, but I wasn't sure what sounds actually came out.

"*Stop!*" Jax's voice tore through me like a thousand nails hammering into my brain. My knees wobbled, then buckled. I hit the ground, as did Ryker and Catilda. I gritted my teeth, squeezing my eyes shut and trying to will away the pain before my head exploded.

"I said you'd come without magic. That includes your own." Jax's voice was garbled, distorted, like he was speaking underwater. I forced my eyes open to watch his lips move as he spoke something to Gavin.

In a single exhale, a cloud of neon green powder was forced out of Gavin's mouth and he deflated like a rubber balloon. He hissed and wheezed every last particle from his lungs, the roundness of his body shrinking as the air escaped.

The magic blasted me in the face. A cold numbness washed over me. It traveled into my nose and down my throat, spreading like an icy river toward every limb until it reached my toes. The magic powder left behind a feeling of emptiness, like my soul had been ripped from my body. The warmth of my own magic disappeared. I wiggled my fingertips, no claws forming. My chest ached, throbbing steadily from my previous injuries not quite fully healed. The pressure in my ears was replaced with a persistent ringing.

Jax's shadow loomed over me with a warning. "Tonight. Nineteen hundred at the skating rink."

He disappeared from my view, along with the rest of his team, and I lay there staring up at the bright sun through the bare tree branches.

"Zulli!" The faint noise sounded like my name. "Zulli!" I heard it again, this time a little more clearly. It was still barely audible over the ringing. My hands left my ears, a thin smear of blood on my palms.

"Zulli! Get up!" Ryker was kneeling a few feet away from me cradling Catilda in his arms. She was shaking violently, her breathing erratic. I blinked a few times, returning my senses to reality. The magic inhibitor Gavin poured out of his mouth had removed all of my magic, but it also erased the effects from Jax's. The ringing in my ears began to soften, and my liquid brain solidified until I could hear properly again. I immediately crawled over to Catilda, the gravel on the dusty path scraping against my palms.

"Her hearing is even sharper than yours, Zulli. It really did some damage to her." Ryker gently lowered her onto the ground, pressing a hand to either side of her head to stop her shivers.

"Hey, Catilda! Focus on me!" I clasped her hand in mine. "It's okay. Everything's going to be fine. Bear with me just a little longer and the wave of throbbing pressure will pass. I swear."

Catilda blinked her agreement.

116

"You need to breathe. Deep breaths in. And out." I emphasized the action in case she couldn't process my words. She mimicked my movements, her chest rising and falling with each breath falling back into rhythm.

"Where did you learn that?" Ryker asked, a stunned expression on his face.

"My mom taught it to me when I was a kid. She would always remind me to breathe when I overreacted to things I didn't like."

"Well, I think you should use it yourself more often. It works." Ryker glanced down at Catilda. She had stopped shaking, her breathing returning to normal. She blinked a few times before sitting up and rubbing the back of her head.

"Damn, is this what you guys deal with all the time?" She paused to let out a cough. "That was absolutely terrifying."

"This? This was nothing," I snorted at her. "One time, a guy surrounded me in quicksand and I slowly sank into the earth until it reached my eyes. I was suffocating. *That* was terrifying. Knowing you're dying and can't do a thing about it."

A slight heat rushed to my cheeks and the faintest smile curled my lips. The only reason I'd survived that day was because Ryker had risked his life to save me. He dove right into the sand pit along with me, shoving me through a portal just in the nick of time.

Ryker, however, didn't share my sentiment. His bleak expression warned me that he was growing increasingly irritated.

"Are you going to tell me what you're up to with this Breaker person or am I going to have to find out by myself?"

I sighed, letting go of the fond memory. "Fine. But burgers and milkshakes first. I'm starving."

11

---◈---

THE WALK TOWARD THE BURGER joint was something similar to a funeral march. My body, tired and battered, felt heavy without magic to support it. It was a numbing feeling, like I was a zombie without a soul, mindlessly dragging myself around without a purpose. It was a feeling of defenselessness, knowing that if someone attacked us, I'd be helpless to protect myself or my friends.

The three of us chose a bright red booth in the back corner of the restaurant. We stared up at the chalkboard menu that ran the entire length of the wall. An upbeat tune blared out of the speaker above us, but our weary faces didn't reflect its happy rhythm. The lunch rush was over, and only a few diners were left enjoying a late meal.

I explained everything to Ryker while we ate. "So, Catilda gave the Breaker a call and his assistant said he'd give us an answer later today. I just didn't expect his response to be so ... flashy." My hands hugged the cardboard cup and I took a huge slurp of my extra-large strawberry milkshake. I pressed a hand to my side when I inhaled, the deep radiating pain returning to the side of my chest.

"My family has done business with him before. He's never done anything this drastic," Catilda added as she picked out the croutons in her salad. "Is our magic really going to return? What if it doesn't?"

Ryker stared down at his basket, containing a thin cheeseburger on a soggy bun. His curly fries were untouched and getting cold. He rubbed his chin, stubble starting to form on his round jaw. His amber eyes had lost their shine, taking on a dull, distant, and lifeless aura.

"It'll return, Catilda," he answered her with a polite smile. "The dust works only to suppress magic for a limited time. It doesn't actually remove it or we'd be dead."

"It better come back," she stabbed angrily at her salad but didn't eat it.

With my own basket having been picked clean, I snatched a handful of Ryker's fries. Unlike Ryker and Catilda, I had a nasty habit of overeating when I was stressed or angry. He pushed his basket over and stared at me. There was the slightest twitch in Ryker's jaw.

"Everything okay, Ryker?" I garbled through a mouthful of fries.

"Is everything okay, Zulli?" he repeated in tone more worried than with anger. "We were attacked today and lost our magic. Someone could have been seriously hurt. And then you tell me you made a deal with this sleazy man called the Breaker? Did you even ask what he wanted from you in return?"

Catilda shrugged, her lack of words confirming an answer.

"You act like you know the guy. Do you?" I dipped a fry in some cheese sauce.

"Not personally. I know his name and I've heard stories. He'll do you a favor and expect the world from you in return. Did you ever think about what this could mean for your family, Zulli? I know you want to protect them and get to the bottom of this mess with Davian, but what if this man asks you to do something for him that could destroy NightFly Technologies?"

119

I stopped chewing and got lost in Ryker's uneasy gaze. "I …
I hadn't thought of that."

"Exactly! You don't think about the consequences of your actions … for yourself or others. Why didn't you come to me
first?"

Catilda chimed in to defend me, wagging her finger in
Ryker's face. "Look here, Mr. Not So Perfect. You were the one
who told her to back off. Nothing would have changed if she had
come to you first. You would have told her it's a bad idea, not to
get involved, and she would have done it anyway."

"You're right." He sunk into the booth, resting his head
against the back. "I know I wouldn't have been able to talk her
out of it but I would have offered my help regardless. The fact
that I'm still here with you despite everything that's happened
should be proof that you can trust me. I don't understand …"

"Ryker …" I reached my hand a few inches across the table
before changing course and grabbing my milkshake.

Ryker threw some cash on the table and slid out of the booth.
"It's okay, Zulli. I may not fully understand but I respect that
you have your own way of doing things. I hope you ladies enjoy
the rest of your lunch."

He navigated his way around several tables and left through
the front door.

"Move!" I shoved Catilda out of the booth to run after him,
but by the time I got to the sidewalk Ryker was already gone.

Catilda caught up to me, threading her arms through mine and
leaning her head against my shoulder. "Still think he's going to
get over this in a few days?" She let go of her embrace and
tapped me on the elbow. "Come on, hun. I gotta go back to the
shop."

The shine in her copper curls glimmered in the early evening
sunset as we puttered our way back to the shop. I allowed myself
to become absorbed in the sounds around me—birds squawking
in the streets, cars whizzing by in a hurry to get home, and the

overall gentle energy of the town residents returning from the city.

With a few hours before we had to meet the Breaker, we spent our remaining time resting on the plush couch in the break room and catching up on lost time.

"How do you do it, Catilda?" I melted into the soft cushions, kicking off my boots and lacing my hands over my stomach as I stared at the ceiling.

"Do what?" Catilda splayed herself across the length of the couch, her bare feet, toenails painted a romantic red, resting on my lap.

"Speak your mind like that. You're not afraid to tell anyone what you're thinking."

Catilda wiggled, getting comfortable with a pillow behind her back. "Simple, really. I don't want to live with any regrets. I'm young, way younger than most people with my skill set. The people I study with treat me like I'm a privileged phony, like I'm too young to understand such complex subject matters. Most think I only got to where I am because my dad just happened to have a contact who could squeeze me into a program."

"Seriously? Invite them to trivia night. We'll show them who's smarter." I tried to laugh, but the pain in my ribs throbbed with the movement.

"Hell yeah, we would!" She flicked a curl off her face, and her striking baby blue eyes fixated on me. "My point, Zulli, is you have to ask yourself the same question. If you lost Ryker as a friend and teammate, would you have any regrets that you didn't try harder to do something about it? You have no problem talking to me. What's so different about Ryker?"

I scratched the side of my head, my mouth dropping in awe. "Huh. You're right. I guess it's because I've known you forever. I've only known Ryker for about six months. And he's only offering his help because he's so damn selfless. I don't want to drag him into this because he feels obligated to be a part of it."

"Hun, now you're just making excuses. Ryker's a big boy. If he wants to help, let him help. We could use someone like him in our corner, anyway."

I checked the clock that hung above the doorway. "We have about an hour before we need to be at the skating rink."

"We should get going soon." Catilda jumped up from the couch, brushing out the wrinkles in her sequin top and straightening up her pink blazer. She grabbed her purse on the table and picked out a makeup compact, dabbing some powder on her face.

I glanced down at my own outfit and the mismatched assortment of clothes I was wearing, now with a few added dirt smudges and small rips from our encounter at the park earlier. My reflection in the glossy surface of the kitchen counter confirmed that my hair looked like I had stuck a finger into an electrical outlet. "Do we have time to stop by your place? I feel grossly underdressed for this fine occasion."

Catilda's eyes gleamed with excitement and an evil grin crept up her perfectly plump lips. I instantly regretted asking.

"Of course, hun! I'll fix you right up!"

We grabbed our things and left out the back door. Catilda locked up behind me, while I meandered over to her car. Leaning against it on the hood was a clean shaven man with a blemished face. His clean, loose fitting t-shirt peeked out from under his black canvas jacket. He held his head like a concrete block, too heavy for his neck to support. Familiar amber eyes stared back at me.

"Ryker? What are you doing here?" I stopped a good six feet in front of him, adjusting my backpack on my shoulder.

"Well, I can't exactly leave without my magic so I found a hotel room nearby. But I came because I wanted to let you know that I won't be following you." He pushed himself off the hood, his warm breath creating a fleeting, misty cloud that rose into the cool evening air.

"Well, good. Because Jax made it very clear we'd be dead if anyone else came with us." I shifted uncomfortably, Ryker's body inching closer to mine. He then leaned in and wrapped his arms around me in a gentle embrace. His hands shifted slightly lower down my torso. I jumped before realizing he was only trying to avoid my injured ribs. His warmth sent my heart thumping in my chest, my own hands hesitating to return the uncomfortable gesture. I pressed them up against his back, but didn't fully accept the hug.

"Don't do anything stupid. Please." He offered one of those forced smiles meant to hide his worry.

Catilda crept up behind me and winked as she slipped by. The car unlocked with a beep from her key fob. She crawled inside, slamming the door behind her and blaring the horn at me to wrap things up.

Ryker turned away, presumably to go back to his hotel room and worry all night about both me and Catilda.

"Hey, Ryker ..." I called out to him before he got too far.

His head twisted over his shoulder.

"Come back tomorrow morning? I'll let you know how things went."

The bright smile that curled his lips and lit up his eyes was almost blinding.

"Sure thing. I'll be waiting."

He continued away from the parking lot, and I watched as his figure disappeared around the corner of a building.

It wasn't an apology, but it was certainly a start. I'd be back at the shop first thing tomorrow morning to greet Ryker. Of course, that was assuming Catilda and I survived the night.

12

---◈---

"I CAN'T BELIEVE I LET YOU TALK ME INTO WEARING THIS. What the hell is this thing? I can barely breathe!" The black, lacy corset was a little too revealing for my taste. Combined with the fact that Catilda was a size smaller than me meant it was even tighter than it should have been. My chest was pushed up to my chin, the unforgiving steel boning pinching my waist. My only saving grace was the cropped faux-snakeskin jacket that covered my bare skin.

"That's the point, hun. Your ribs are still injured. It'll offer you some support until your magic comes back and you can continue with the medicine. Besides, you look absolutely *adorable*!" Catilda bounced alongside me as we approached the entrance to the skating rink. A concrete canopy slab, dimly lit with most of the light bulbs having burned out, covered the walkway into the building.

She was strutting like a supermodel in her slim-fitting black leather pants tucked into her knee high lace up boots with just enough heel to be both practical and stylish. She adjusted the collar of her cherry red leather jacket and tugged on the bottom of her top to straighten it out, pulling the plunging V-neck down even farther.

"We're heading into a skating rink, Catilda. Not a strip club. The guy's gonna be more focused on using his magic to break down what's under our clothes than what's in the vial." My hips swayed side to side as I poorly attempted to copy Catilda's swagger. My hand awkwardly reached behind me to pick out the wedgie caused by my too-skinny dark wash jeans. Thankfully, I was able to avoid the five inch stilettos in favor of my own motorcycle boots. Even though they were spelled with magic, the magic inhibitor would make it difficult for me to use anyway. Hopefully the Breaker wouldn't notice.

A group of casually dressed bystanders loitered outside the automatic sliding doors by the entrance. The five of them twisted their heads in unison, flashing me and Catilda an icy death glare. I wasn't sure if they were the Breaker's bodyguards assessing us or if they were just generally intrigued by our inappropriate attire.

There was a cool bite in the air as we stepped inside the skating rink. The smell of chemicals on the freshly smoothed ice caused me to itch my nose.

"I don't suppose you know where we're supposed to meet?" I asked Catilda.

"After what happened at the park, I reckon he's going to find us."

We started patrolling the perimeter of the rink, the rubber floor squishing under my feet. The sturdy white and red plastic boards that surrounded the ice were scuffed up, the plexiglass attached to it scratched and wet with droplets of water. The arena was moderately packed for the youth hockey game currently being played. Overly aggressive parents screamed at the referees and teens sipped hot chocolate while they watched their friends compete.

"Isn't this place a little too public? What if someone over-hears us?" Acid gurgled in response to the queasy feeling settling in my stomach.

Catilda clutched her purse closer to her chest, protecting our most prized asset, the vial. "It was meant to be this way. It's noisy, but not loud. And the fact that it's populated reduces the risk of either party trying to do something that draws attention."

We looped around the rink a few times, the glass rattling whenever a player was slammed against it. I peered up into the vast open arena. The domed ceiling was bright with fluorescent fixtures, illuminating the glassy ice but leaving the stacked rows of bleachers shadowed in the dark.

A gloved hand touched my shoulder. "Keep walking. Do *not* look behind you."

The male voice was almost robotic, showing no signs of evil but not exactly welcoming either. The hand guided us up a set of stairs to the very top of the bleachers behind the visiting team's goal cage.

"Sit here." He gave us a shove toward the second to last row while he shuffled across the top to sit behind us. I squirmed as I sat, the corset keeping my back straight and the tight pants cutting off the circulation in my thighs.

A soft chuckle came from behind us. "Your misguided ward-robe was gathering some unwanted attention. I needed to wait until people lost their interest."

Catilda flashed me a sheepish grin, her cheeks flushing.

"The vial please." His hand slipped between me and Catilda. The black leather glove concealed what looked to be fat, stubby sausage fingers. "Don't turn around."

Any confidence Catilda had coming into this meeting had completely fled her body. Her lips and hands were trembling, and she kept fidgeting with the zipper on her jacket. "It's in my purse. Is it okay if I take it out?"

He grunted an approval. The button on Catilda's rosy red shoulder bag snapped open. She took out a small glass tube with

126

a few drops of orange liquid in it. The man behind us swiped it from her hand.

Anxiety crept down my spine. I listened to the chorus of intriguing, curious mumbles and groans coming from behind me. I assumed he was examining the contents inside the vial.

"Tell me about this magnificent specimen you brought to me today."

My throat constricted, my mouth went dry. There was something about the darkness in his voice that set me on edge. "It's some kind of bonding spell. We'd like to know what it was designed for and what other magic might be required to use it."

"I see. Stealing from your father, are we, Ms. Taracula? I guess the spider doesn't crawl too far from the web. You are very much the daughter of Zavyr Taracula." The rustle of a nylon jacket sounded in unison with a creak from the metal bleacher.

"What's that supposed to mean? Is that what you wanted to talk to me about? My dad?" Sweat moistened my palms, and I wiped them along my jeans.

His distasteful snort caused me to clench my teeth. "You have no idea the war you just threw yourself into, Ms. Taracula. Your stubbornness intrigues me, though. Not many people would seek my assistance on a mere hunch."

My body started moving on its own. Feet stomping on the floor, I yearned to twist around and use my tightened fist to right hook this jackass in the face.

Catilda's hand slapped down on my thigh, eyes widened in alarm, and I settled back down.

"Think about it, Ms. Taracula. I suspect I wasn't your first choice for finding out what was in this vial. There is a perfectly logical reason why Zavyr won't give you any information."

My breathing came in short bursts and fingernails dug into my jeans.

"The information. Please," Catilda asked politely, trying to steer us back on topic.

"Of course. But I'm not sure you can handle what I'm about to say." His words sent a storm of rage gathering inside me, begging me to unleash my fury.

"Just tell me what it is." My teeth clenched so hard my jaw hurt.

"This liquid here is very special. Unique. Meant to bond with blood."

"Blood?" My muscles tensed but then slightly relaxed. "But … a lot of medical drugs are designed to use magic that bonds to certain cells. What's so bad about bonding it to blood?"

His bellowing laugh echoed in the cavernous arena, causing the few onlookers scattered around us to turn around and glower at us. "I presume you have heard of a drug called Bliss?"

My mouth dropped open. My throat tightened and the words I was trying to speak died on my tongue. Briyan's face as he took his last breath was still clearly etched in my memory.

Catilda fired back an answer. "Sure. It's that memory drug sweeping the streets. People take it to escape reality, forget their bad memories."

"Very good, Ms. Harper." The sound of his slow-clap was dulled by his gloves. "This right here is the base for creating that drug. It's not meant to bond with just anyone's blood, but a magic-infused blood. Mix one drop of this special blood with this bonding agent and you get an orange liquid that's then filled inside the white capsule stamped with the Black Mark symbol we know as Bliss. Swallow it and you have all you need for a wild night down memory lane."

Disbelief swelled in my stomach. "Are there any other ways it could be used? To maybe *heal* someone from the effects from overdosing on Bliss?" My brother's conversation replayed in my mind, and I wondered if any part of what Maeck said had been true.

"Perhaps." He paused to dwell on the possibility. "But I highly doubt it, Ms. Taracula. This is Zavyr Taracula we're talking about. The man is a genius, yes, but how do you think he got

128

to be so powerful? By crossing every line drawn out in front of him."

My hands slapped down on the metal bleacher and I shot to my feet, not caring about the attention I was drawing to myself. I was fuming like a bull, trying to keep my temper and voice under control. With a quick count to three, I was able to clear my mind before I did something I'd regret. "I don't know what you're suggesting, but my dad would *never* go so far as to create something like Bliss. He ... his work *saves* lives! It doesn't destroy them! Davian Grymes ... this must have been Davian's doing before he left the company."

"I'm sure he had some part in this as well," he huffed, sounding uninterested. "Now, I gave you what you came for. Let's talk about my payment."

My spine stiffened and the color drained from Catilda's face.

"We can get you money," Catilda's normally energetic feminine voice squeaked. "We just need—"

"Money?" the Breaker scoffed. "I don't want cash. It's traceable and boring. So much work to secretly exchange it for something useful."

"So, what do you want?" I asked hesitantly, dreading his answer.

"You stole something that belongs to me, Ms. Taracula. I would like it back."

"What? I don't even know you!" I dared myself to turn around. My eyes locked onto a scruffy looking man, slightly overweight, with a baseball cap shadowing his hazel eyes. The collar of his navy blue polo was popped, sticking up over his gray nylon windbreaker. His brown wiry hair formed a nicely trimmed goatee under his hooked nose and hid his double chin and round cheeks.

"Ozcar Thorne. I should have known I'd see your slimy face again. How's the Sixth Scents bakery doing? I hear someone stole the magic spatula you were using to illegally mix magic drugs. Oh right, that was me." I curled a half smile at him.

"I have taken on a new venture, using my magic ability to break apart spells and gather intel within criminal organizations around the world. Much more lucrative business, actually. But I still have use for that spatula, and it's time it's returned to its rightful owner. Me." He tucked the glass vial with the remaining liquid into his jacket pocket.

A predatory growl rumbled from my throat. "You're lucky I don't rip your head off right now for snapping my neck and burning the tips of my ponytail."

"Still bitter about that? I don't particularly enjoy hurting women, but you left me no choice. Your new hairstyle is very becoming, though, I must say." A false smirk crept up his face.

"You're delusional if you think I'm giving you back that spatula." My boot smacked down on the bleacher, and I was about to tackle the man before Catilda held out her arm to stop me. Her entire body was shaking, but she held her voice together with a strong confidence.

"I know you have done my family a great service in the past by helping us out, Mr. Thorne. I mean no disrespect to you and your business, but perhaps we can make a different arrangement? Is there something else maybe we can find for you?"

Ozcar snorted at Catilda's request. "I respect your tenacity, Ms. Harper, but you are not your parents. There is nothing *you* could possibly find for me. Except the spatula."

Dark thoughts danced at the edge of my awareness. Flames of anger licked through me, heat rushing to my skin despite the cold, damp air. My curled fingertips scraped helplessly across Ozcar's chest.

He stifled a half-hearted laugh. "Did you forget you don't have your magic?"

"Zulli, come on. We should go." Catilda's face had turned a steamy red. She grabbed my forearm, yanking me away from Ozcar.

"Oh, you forgot something!" Ozcar called out. We both froze and my heart shot into my throat. "You can have this back now."

He handed me my belt, completely emptied of its magic bullets. I buckled it around my waist anyway.

"Also, I may have bragged to a few of my business contacts about our meeting tonight," he added casually. "They seemed very eager to kidnap the daughter of the powerful NightFly Technologies CEO Zavyr Taracula and trade her in exchange for a few company secrets. I suggest you start running."

A woman wearing a knitted beanie and scarf about six rows ahead of us shoved her phone in her pocket and jumped to her feet. From the opposite end of our row, an athletic man in a track jacket snuck toward us.

"Catilda, go!" I shoved her into the aisle. Her light feet sped down the concrete steps. I side saddled the railing that ran down the middle and slid my way down to the ground floor.

My hands swung out, clearing a path through hockey moms and teen fanatics. Catilda followed in my wake, darting and dodging the chaos. We were almost at the front door when a man holding a hot chocolate backed into me. The scalding liquid splashed onto my neck, burning as it dripped down the corset and stung my chest.

The man, padded in a puffy winter coat, dug his elbow into my cheek. My head snapped sideways, feet stumbling as I tripped over myself.

"Oh, I'm so sorry." He pressed his hands against my shoulders as if to help steady me, then drove his knee directly into my chest. All the air rushed out of my lungs. My hand clutched my stomach, grasping at the pain blossoming from my injured rib.

"Zulli!" Catilda launched herself at our cold-hearted attacker, arms and legs splayed out in starfish formation. She ensnared him like an octopus, her human limbs like tentacles wrapping around his body in a violent entanglement. He hit the ground with a bounce on the rubber floor, taking Catilda with him.

"Get off me!" he grumbled, hands grabbing at Catilda's wrists as she balled up her fists. He overpowered her easily, rolling onto his side and pinning Catilda under him. She writhed and twitched under his weight. Then her leg kicked up. In a perfect display of her scrappy fighting style, she kneed him in the nuts.

While whimpering and rocking on the floor with his legs clamped shut, Catilda managed to scramble to her feet. She was almost free when his fingers caught hold of her purse. He yanked on the strap, ripping it right off her shoulder. Everything inside spilled out onto the floor. With a swift strike of her foot, Catilda nearly crushed the guy's skull. He immediately dropped his hold, his angry growl replaced with painful whining.

"You okay?" Catilda didn't wait for an answer because it didn't matter. Leaving behind the purse, she took my hand and together we ran through the sliding door and into the parking lot.

With heavy breaths, we scurried past the crosswalk and leapt over a curb, crouching in the narrow space between two parked cars. I flexed my fingers and a nervous prickle ran through me. Without my magic, my limbs were heavy and unresponsive. Neither my claws nor my enhanced senses were available to me, which meant I couldn't protect my friend. The realization that I had put Catilda in this dangerous situation sent a pang of guilt burning in my chest. "You gotta get out of here, Catilda. They're after me, not you. Take the car and go."

"Like that chivalry is gonna work on me, hun. Besides, the keys were in my purse. I'm just as stuck as you are."

Carefully avoiding our pursuers, we slithered through the parking lot. The jungle of motorized metal had at least a dozen rows of SUVs, sedans, and trucks. Every rattle of a soda can was like a warning call, alerting the hunters to our location. Every car was like a shrub hiding a hungry predator. The only advantage we had was the darkness of night, and even that was thwarted by the glow of floodlights casting harsh shadows over the asphalt.

We bent down and sandwiched ourselves in between a red pickup truck and gray sedan parked near the edge of the parking lot. My jeans stuck to me like plastic wrap, and my corset kept my spine ramrod straight.

"We should head toward the trees over there," Catilda whispered, pointing to the wooded area just beyond the parking lot.

I shook my head. "I think we're better off heading for the main road. We could easily get separated in the woods."

Catilda gnawed on the corner of her lip. "I don't know. It's well lit, but this late at night most of the shops are closed and it's probably not that busy. We'll just be putting ourselves out in the open for them to see."

"Check over there!" The male growl was too close for my comfort. "They're around here somewhere. They couldn't have gotten far."

I pressed a finger to my lips, then pointed it upwards toward the bed of the pickup truck.

She nodded, knowing exactly what I was going to do.

My hands firmly grasped the top of the tailgate. With my foot on the bumper for support, I launched myself up and over into the bed of the truck. A clatter of metal sounded when my boot rolled on something round.

"What's that? Over there!" Heavy footsteps started marching in our direction and my heart fluttered inside my aching chest.

"Uh, Zulli …" Catilda whispered as she yanked repeatedly on all the nearby door handles, hoping one may have been left unlocked.

I dropped to my knees, crawling around the bed of the truck. Whoever owned it must have been a contractor. A rusty metal toolbox was tucked into the corner behind some plastic tarps. I snapped open the spring loaded latch. The loud clank of metal striking metal would have been easily heard by anyone nearby.

"Zulli …" Catilda whispered again, this time a little louder.

"Get under the truck and hide." My arm swung over the side of the vehicle to hand her a wrench but she was frozen in place.

"I … I can't. I can't move!" A man, more of a silhouette under the cloak of night, had her pinned up against the side of the truck. Both his hands were clasped around Catilda's wrists, and he leaned his strong body against hers to keep her from moving.

A second figure slipped out from the darkness, the faint yellow glow of a floodlight casting ominous shadows across his face. His unsettling gaze held a certain heartless quality. Along with his wild black hair and brooding sense of evil rolling off his muscled body, he appeared like a demon straight out of a fairy tale.

Our pursuer had shed his puffy winter jacket, leaving behind a fitted brown turtleneck and dark washed jeans. A bright red mark from Catilda's boot marred the side of his face. He dipped his chin low and spread his hands out wide.

"Where you gonna run to now, little lady?" A smirk creased his lips, amusement burning in every deep wrinkle. "You have no chance against me without your magic. My boss is gonna *flip* when I return with the daughter of Zavyr Taracula and … you."

Dark, lecherous eyes closed in on Catilda. The man overpowered her, squeezed his grip tighter. She twisted her head away from his gaze, unable to do much else.

"Get your damn hands off her!" My voice vibrated with indignation, adrenaline saturating my veins. Magic or not, I wasn't going down without a fight.

The wrench went flying at the skull in front of me. With a quick tilt to the side, he dodged my attack. The metal tool crashed into the gray sedan with a thundering clunk, creating a crater in the passenger door.

My other hand wrapped around the first thing my fingers touched—a long, thin piece of steel rebar. With one hand braced on the lip of the truck bed, I bounded over the side panel. Shock waves rippled through my feet as they pounded onto the asphalt, shooting upwards toward my aching chest. My anger pushed aside the pain, replacing it with a ferocious need to help my friend.

The steel connected with the backbone of the man gripping Catilda's wrists. He froze in place for a split second, then turned his face toward me. My mouth dropped open at the sight of an exact duplicate of the man we had just encountered, except this one lacked any form of expression. He was a mindless drone, a magic duplicate of the real thing.

I clenched my teeth. The heaviness of swinging my limbs was exhausting without magic to support me. The body double carelessly threw Catilda to the ground. Her abrupt scream ceased when a loud smack signaled her head colliding with a side mirror.

Her attacker then lunged at me, a solid, realistic embodiment of the real thing and equally as dangerous. His right hook grazed my jaw as I jumped back. The driver's side window of the pickup truck shattered as his fist went through it. A left jab came for my nose next. I ducked, swiping the piece of the rebar into his ankle. With a loud grunt, he hopped on one foot, stumbling off balance. He dropped to his knees, his hands scraping at the side of the truck attempting to hoist himself back up. His body slowly faded in a haze of wispy smoke.

"Catilda!" No reply came from my friend, her lifeless body sprawled out next to my feet. Before I could make sure she was still alive, another body double slithered his arms through mine and pulled me away.

"*Capto!*" My boots scraped across the ground, the magic failing to activate. My feet kicked up high into the air. I pushed them off a tire, thrusting my weight into the man. His body slammed in between mine and the nearest vehicle.

"How long can you keep this up? I can create hundreds of duplicates of myself." His chilling laugh sent shivers to my bones. "Let's finish this before someone else comes along to snatch you up."

He fanned out his hands and five more duplicates crammed into the narrow space between the two cars. Both escape paths were blocked. I swung the rebar at one of figures, the steel rod scraping against plastic instead. The car alarm started blaring.

A strained moan made its way through the grunting of men surrounding me.

"Catilda? Is that you? Get up and run! I'll hold them off as long as I can."

"But Zulli …" came her groggy voice.

"Catilda, go! I got this!" A set of hands grabbed at my corset, fingers hooking around the low-cut hem crossing my chest. The rebar came down hard on his knuckles, but that didn't stop another set of hands from slithering in and trying again.

Fake magical bodies reeking of dirt, blood, and malicious intent, tackled me to the ground and piled on top of me. Fingernails scraped at my face and neck. I couldn't see Catilda, but I definitely heard her.

"Jackass. You won't get away with this." She must have found the wrench, because the sound of resonating metal rang in my ears as something collided with the lamp post. "Hold on, Zulli! I'll find help!" Her boots scraping against the asphalt slowly disappeared.

"Well, at least I still have the main prize." The man sighed, but didn't seem too upset at letting Catilda go.

Even with my magic, taking on five men at once would be a challenge. If I somehow did manage to defeat them, more duplicate bodies would keep appearing. I kicked, screamed, and cried but it did me no good.

My skull cracked against the asphalt. Stars danced in my vision and my heart thumped inside my chest, unable to pump blood fast enough to my brain. Hands kept grabbing at me, but I lacked the strength to fight back.

In a single flash, the body on top of me was ripped away. The starry night sky above opened up in my vision. My eyes widened at the sound of bone connecting with hard metal. The pressure on my chest lifted and another body disappeared. The hands squeezing my neck faded into a ghostly apparition.

"Zulli!" A familiar voice made my ears tingle with excitement and gave me a second wind.

My fist tenderized the nearest face, my boots punching into his gut.

136

A broad-shouldered man wearing fitted boot-cut jeans and a green zip up hoodie approached me. The yellow gleam of the parking lot lights reflected in his familiar silver eyes and shadowed his strong jawline. "Brodin? What … how …?" I was too caught up in the moment to care why or how he got here, just glad that he was.

"Zulli, are you okay?" He focused on his attacks rather than me, taking out the remaining three men. I hadn't known Brodin to be a violent man, but his enhanced spider strength certainly gave him the power to be one. After taking out all the duplicates, his hand reached out to me. I clasped it, flying to my feet. It took a moment for the wave of lightheadedness to pass.

"I'm better than how that guy's gonna be when you get done with him." I dusted off some dirt from my pants, nodding to the coward trembling over by the light post. I leaned casually against a parked car to keep myself upright.

My brother's gaze shifted to the last remaining body—the original. Brodin grumbled, huffing his way toward him. "What do you think you're doing here?"

"Hey, now. I'm just following orders." No longer confident, the man continued to step back until he was bent over the hood of the sedan.

Brodin flicked out his hand. Silky threads shot out of his fingertips, wrapping his prey in a thick, sticky cocoon. His prisoner squirmed and writhed against the webbing, unable to break free from the magic strings holding him tight. With little effort, Brodin hurled him over the pickup truck. Several painful thuds later, the duplicator's mangled body landed in the open road between parking rows.

I moved to sit lazily on the bumper of the pickup truck and watch Brodin kick some ass. Anyone in their right mind would have taken note of what was happening and promptly given up on chasing me if they knew what was best for them.

My pulse beat like a ticking time bomb, my legs uncontrollably shaking. I rubbed my forehead with the back of my hand and a few streaks of blood stained my skin, the sweat stinging my cuts. Catilda's corset was ripped at the neckline, exposing the edge of my bra underneath. I pulled the faux-snakeskin jacket across my chest to cover myself up.

Brodin ripped off a windshield wiper before marching over to this victim holding his shoulder and whimpering in pain. "I'm going to shove this so far down your throat it'll come out your ass."

A wave of nausea began dragging my consciousness along with it. The sound of flesh against crunching bone and crumpling plastic echoed in the darkness. There was something in the terrifying, tortured scream that followed that made me feel bad for the guy getting his ass kicked, and I winced at his misfortune.

My legs collapsed under me. I slipped down the back of the truck and dropped to the pavement.

"Get up. We need to get out of here." Brodin's rough hands jostled my shoulders and the world began to spin.

"Ca-Catilda …" I stuttered out in a near silent mumble.

"Catilda?" Brodin straightened his posture, casting a worried glance around him. "She was with you? I didn't see her. She must have escaped. I'm sure she's fine, but you're not. You need medical attention."

I was worried for my life and the debt I owed Ozcar. I feared for Catilda's safety, wondering if she'd successfully escaped. But with my last ounce of energy before I succumbed to the exhaustion overtaking me, there was only one thought that crossed my mind: *Ryker is gonna be SO pissed when he finds out what happened tonight.*

13

---◇---

THE ROOM SPUN LIKE MY brain was churning in a blender. I knew I wasn't moving, but it felt like everything around me was. The sweet sound of chirping birds that reached my ears might have been pleasant under other circumstances, but with this pounding headache, it reminded me more of a horde of squawking seagulls.

My heart thumped inside my chest, pulse racing when I realized I had no idea where I was. I rolled over onto my stomach ... then right off the bed.

Tangled in the sheets, I swung out my arm trying to soften the fall. A lamp rolled off the nightstand. The loud crash of ceramic onto the wood floor resulted in footsteps rushing to investigate and someone barreling in through the door.

"Zulli, sweetheart, you have to be more careful." My dad crouched down beside me, gently helping me up off the floor and back onto the bed.

"I'm fine." I pressed a hand to my ribs, surprised that no pain resulted from it. The room was still a blur, and a wave of light-headedness overcame me. I blinked rapidly, trying to clear my focus. "Where am I?"

"You're in your bedroom, my little spider. I gave you some strong medication to heal your injuries, so you might want to take it easy for a while. I also resupplied you with magic for your belt." He sat down on the mattress beside me, meticulously picking off a piece of lint from his neatly creased dress pants. Along with his light blue checkered shirt, shiny slicked back gelled hair, and cleanly shaved face, I figured he was about to head off to work before my accident had stopped him.

My childhood bedroom was just how I had left it the day I moved out five years ago. I sunk into the pillow-top mattress, a gently worn blue and purple striped comforter covering it. The reach-in closet and mirrored dresser were brimming with the clothes I didn't have room for in my tiny apartment. Despite the walls being a muted gray, my personality still shone through the gallery of family photos and maps of all the places I wanted to visit someday.

The thick curtains were pushed back, letting the diffused morning light obscured by the trees outside trickle in from the double windows. One of them was slightly ajar, allowing a strong floral scent to drift throughout the room.

"How did I get here?"

"You don't remember?" My father's comforting hand settled on top of my knee. "Zulli, you were attacked in a parking lot last night on your way home from dinner with your brothers. Brodin heard you scream and came to help. Can you recall anything about the man who attacked you? Where you were when it happened?"

My fingertips massaged my throbbing temples, straining to recall the last thing my brain had registered. My limbs were heavy, my stomach rumbled, and my mouth was drier than sand.

"No ... I don't. I can't remember anything."

The last few days came flowing back to me. Davian had attacked Yarwell Port, attempting to steal a shipment of magic-filled vials that belonged to my father. He also caused an explosion at NightFly Technologies, where one of his men dropped a list of names as he was trying to escape. The last thing I remembered was Catilda running an analysis on the liquid that Davian wanted to get his hands on and discovering that it had been altered. I'd decided to stay the night at her place, but the entire day yesterday was a complete blur.

The gears continued churning in my brain. From the deepest, darkest corner, I dusted off some cobwebs and pulled out a fuzzy memory of having a conversation with Brodin about dinner.

Bile rose in the back of my mouth, my throat tightening. I could barely breathe when an image sparked of a man punching and kicking me in a parking lot and Brodin rushing to my rescue. It was only a fragment of the night's events, the rest blank holes in my mind's eye. But an unsettling feeling kept tugging at the edge of my awareness. Like one of those missing holes was something important that I needed to dig up.

"Is Brodin okay?"

There was a light knock on the bedroom door, and one of the kitchen staff strolled in with a plate of buttered toast and eggs. She offered me a tight-lipped smile, placed the wooden tray on the nightstand, and left without saying a single word.

"Brodin is fine." My dad rose from the mattress, his shoulders straight and confident, but the concern flickering in his silver eyes hadn't gone unnoticed. "Eat up and get changed. I want to show you something."

The bedroom door clicked shut behind him as he left, leaving me in the silence of my own scrambled thoughts. My head continued throbbing like the worst hangover. I massaged my forehead for a moment, then shoved the buttered toast into my mouth and chugged down the orange juice. After a quick shower, I pulled out a pair of faded jeans and a long sleeve shirt decorated with silver zippers and rivets. I wrapped my belt around my waist, running a finger across one of the magic bullets my dad had replaced for me.

My hands felt for the duffle bag I kept stashed under my bed. I stuffed my dirty clothes, ripped and destroyed, into it and frowned at the black lacy corset with one broken strap. It was Catilda's. That much I knew because I would never be caught dead owning such a skimpy, uncomfortable piece of impractical clothing. Which then raised the question as to why I had been wearing it last night in the first place. What was I missing?

In the hallway, magic hummed to life with an abundance of smells around me. A colorful collection of exotic foliage in decorative pots was strategically placed throughout the wide walkway. Their existence in such an unnatural environment was made possible by a magic fertilizer mixed into the soil. There were no windows nearby allowing in sunlight, but the sconces and low-hanging chandeliers basked the dark wooden floor in a warm magical glow as if there was a glass ceiling above.

My father usually dealt with medical-related magic, but some of his failed experiments became helpful in other ways. The fertilizer, which had originally been intended as a way to provide nutrients to humans, was adapted to help struggling communities grow food in rough climates. In an attempt to create a cleansing treatment to neutralize poisons from venomous animals and plants, he'd stumbled on a way to purify contaminated water. Those weren't the accomplishments he was most proud of, though. There wasn't much profit to be made in aiding the less fortunate, but they were the experiments my mom had always said my dad should pay more attention to.

I continued following the beige floral carpet runner that stretched down the grand staircase and into the main living area.

"Good morning, Ms. Taracula. How was your breakfast?" The familiar face of the woman standing at the bottom of the stairs had aged slightly since I'd last seen it. Deep wrinkles creased her mouth and crows feet were etched into her eyes from always smiling. Her blond, thinning hair had faded into more of a beige, her waistline a little rounder than I remembered. She dressed casually but professionally, with a pair of black wide-legged trousers, a light pink blouse, and a loose purple cardigan that fell just past her hips.

142

"Lorina!" I jumped into her open arms, squeezing a hug so tight she gasped. "I told you to stop calling me that. It's Zulli."

"Of course, Zulli. I haven't seen you since you moved out. How are you feeling? I heard about what happened to you last night." She rubbed a lock of my short, green-tipped hair between her slender fingers, nodding a somewhat approving look at the new style.

"I'm feeling better, just a little headache. I've actually been working with the military to track down Davian Grymes and stop Bliss from taking over the city." It was only a half lie. I *had* been working with the military up until recently.

Lorina's honey-colored eyes softened, a grim expression deepening her wrinkles. "I see."

"What's wrong?"

"I'm sorry, Zulli. I don't know how to tell you this, but … your childhood friend, Catilda Harper? Your father said he received a phone call last night that she … passed away unexpectedly. They think she was addicted to Bliss and overdosed on the drug."

My limbs locked in place, the only movement coming from my blinking eyes as I fought back the tears. Briyan's face flashed before my eyes, a painful memory of how good people could get caught up in bad situations. It took me a moment to process the meaning of Lorina's words. An empty feeling twisted knots in my stomach. I couldn't imagine a world without my best friend. Catilda couldn't be gone, could she?

The disbelief rose to anger. "No. I don't believe you." I violently shook my head at Lorina. "She would *never* take a drug like that!"

"I'm so sorry, Zulli. I know you two stopped talking after your mom's disappearance, but people change. The last time you saw her you were both teenagers." She held out her arms and pulled me in for a hug, gently stroking my hair with her fingers.

What Lorina didn't know was that I had kept in touch with Catilda and I had seen her not more than two days ago. Were those sparkling eyes and bright smile a result of her using Bliss? Catilda always told me everything, but she had been studying on Earth for the past several months. Did something happen there that she hadn't told me about?

There was no point in fighting back the tears. They streamed down my face. Lorina kept her arms wrapped around me and I squeezed her waist, my fingers tugging on the fabric of her cardigan. I pressed my head into her chest and sobbed. Lorina held me for as long as I needed, continuing to stroke her fingers through my hair until I was ready to push her away.

"Damn it, I need to get out there and do something. This needs to stop before more people get hurt." I balled my hands into fists and felt the need to pound something.

"Oh, Zulli," Lorina chuckled, trying to lighten the mood and steer the subject in another direction. "You haven't changed one bit from when I took care of you growing up, have you? Always running off on some adventure, wanting to save the world. Remember that time I took you to that carnival and you found a lost cat wandering around in the parking lot? We never actually made it into the park because we spent the whole afternoon running around town, looking for the cat's owner."

"You mean the trip that my dad was supposed to take me on but ditched me because he apparently got stuck in a 'very important work meeting'?" I pouted at her, and Lorina's solemn gaze softened with remorse.

"You know he did his best, Zulli. He really does care about you and your brothers. It's just ... well, between you and me ... let's just say I'm happy you decided to join the military. I've seen the things his job has done to him. It may not have seemed like it, but your father has sacrificed a lot. Deep down, he knew he couldn't be the father you wanted him to be, so he did everything he could to make sure you and your brothers didn't have to suffer because of it."

"Well, he could have at least *tried* to do a better job at parenting," I scoffed at her. Growing up in a wealthy household with

144

everything I could have ever wanted would have been a dream come true for most kids, but I'd never wanted to be showered with toys and fancy gifts. All I wanted was to spend time with my family.

"All things considered, you grew up to be a fine young lady, Zulli. Now you just need to find a charming young man to—"

"Ugh, okay Lorina." My eye roll was accompanied by a hand wiping away my tears to hide my embarrassment. "Thanks for saying that, though. It means a lot."

"I meant every word. It was great to see you again, Zulli. I'm usually kept pretty busy around here trying to manage all the staff, but I hope we bump into each other again soon. You'd better get going. Zavyr is in his office, and I think he's waiting for you."

I gave her another hug, then she headed off to continue her work. I wandered down another hallway, passing a library full of textbooks on magic, a music room with a shiny grand piano that my mother used to play, and a sitting room that served no purpose other than to have a place to sit. Through the arched windows that lined the outer edge of the hallway, I could see the beautiful, serene gardens surrounding the acres of land that the house sat on. It was one the thing I missed most about being here—the sweet floral breeze suffused with the smell of blossoming flowers all year long, elegant birds chirping from the top of the pine trees. Stopping for a moment to collect my thoughts, I relished in the vibrant colors of all the different exotic plant life that painted a breathtaking canvas, like something out of a picture book.

I knocked on the closed door to my dad's office.

"Come in." My father's voice was barely audible through the thick wooden barrier between us.

The door swung open on silent hinges, and I took a few steps inside but didn't go any further. My father's home office was about the size of my entire studio apartment. In the center of the room was a three-inch-thick slab of mahogany. It wasn't one of those mass-produced desks with veneers over compressed fiber boards, but real, solid wood the entire way through. Where my dad sat, the glossy surface had turned dull with age and constant usage, a byproduct of many late nights on conference calls and typing for hours a day on his computer. The bay window behind him overlooked a flower bed full of blooming red roses despite the early spring weather.

"I assume Lorina told you about your friend? I'm terribly sorry, Zulli. You should reach out to her family to ask about the funeral arrangements." If he felt remorse for me, he didn't show it. His lack of interest was something I'd become accustomed to over the years. Someone with his status wasn't allowed the luxury of showing compassion as it would be perceived as vulnerability.

"Funeral?" My head hung low and my gaze got lost in the intricate geometric design of the rug under my feet. My heart stuttered, and there was this falling, spinning-down feeling when the realization set in. Funeral. Catilda truly was gone. "Yeah, I'll do that. I miss her. I wish I could have at least said goodbye."

"Are you still up for this, Zulli?" My dad rose from his executive chair, the leather-bound notebook on his desk thumping shut under his heavy hand. He pulled out a drawer and tucked it away inside.

"Up for what? Where are we going?" It was too late for my dad to start making up for all the time he'd missed during my childhood years, but a part of me still secretly wished for it.

"To NightFly Technologies, of course. I think it's about time someone explains to you what's really going on." He ran a hand across his button-down shirt to smooth out some wrinkles, then picked at his hair while looking directly into the massive, antique floor mirror positioned in the far corner of the office.

With a touch of his finger on the reflective glass and a single word, the mirror began to ripple with magic. Most people used mirrors for transportation, spelled to go back and forth between two set points. In this case, the mirror in my father's home office

146

was connected to somewhere at NightFly Technologies. He kept it handy in the event his personal transporter couldn't be reached or when it was more convenient than waiting for his ride to arrive.

My father grabbed a brown leather satchel from beside his desk and stepped through the mirror first. I grasped my duffle bag in front of me and followed behind him, the buzzing magic alive and tingling on my skin. One moment I was standing in my childhood home out in the suburbs and the next I was transported fifty miles away, staring out into the city of Chitol through the panel of windows lining the top floor of NightFly Technologies.

I canvassed the executive office, trying to remember the last time I had visited my dad at work. It was even larger than his office at home, with contemporary furniture that was more in line with the corporate, professional work culture most were familiar with.

"Come on, now. Stay close and follow me." My father dropped his satchel on top of his desk chair. He then slipped past the seating area, where two black leather sofas flanked a glass coffee table. A red and white houndstooth chair was set to the side, adding a touch of flair and boldness to the minimalist designs everywhere else.

My feet hurried to catch up to him by the elevator, my brain still pounding inside my head with each press of my foot. We waited in silence for a few minutes until the elevator arrived, then shuffled in to be taken down to the fourth floor.

The doors chimed open and we both stepped out into another hallway, one side of it a long glass partition that overlooked an elaborate medical lab. The overly bright clean space was busy with traffic this morning. Technicians hustled around in their white lab coats and goggles, checking tablets or holding glass jars filled with magic samples. Even though there was a sheet of glass between us, I could still hear the humming of machinery and chatter of employees on the other side.

Eventually, we reached a closed metal door that I presumed led into another lab. My dad punched a few digits into the keypad, then placed his hand on a scanner.

"Zulli, what I'm about to show you is top secret. You understand that, right? This isn't something you can go around sharing with others, especially the military."

I nodded. "Of course."

The door buzzed and my dad pushed it open. The smell of bleach and latex instantly slapped me in the face. The small waiting room had a few cheap plastic chairs scattered around, old magazines spread out on a folding table in the middle, and a water cooler tucked in the corner. We hurried through a set of double doors that led into a long, wide corridor similar to a hospital. The harsh glow of fluorescent lights shone down onto the glossy tile floor. About every ten feet was a medical rolling cart parked outside of each exam room. Most of them appeared empty, but a few were occupied with patients.

"Remember at dinner when I mentioned my meeting with the mayor, Ethin Henderson?" my father said as we continued walking.

"Sure. What does that have to do with anything?"

"For the longest time, we have focused on the physical aspect of our health. Replacing limbs. Curing illnesses that break down our physical bodies. But so little time has been spent understanding the mind and the diseases that plague our brains." He paused and nodded to a lab assistant rolling a medical cart full of machinery out of one of the rooms. Unlike the lab we'd passed by the elevator, this testing facility was relatively quiet. The only sounds I could hear were the beeping of equipment and, every once in a while, the movement of an attendant shuffling around to check on a patient.

"The mayor and I had a private meeting to discuss how Night-Fly Technologies can help those suffering from the effects of Bliss, but there's a secret component of this project. Most people who take Bliss are running away from something, trying to forget the past, but what if we could harness the magical power of Bliss to actually *cure* mental conditions like PTSD or dementia? Help their minds process tragedy in a different light or enable them remember their loved ones despite memory loss?" The lines around the corners of his eyes intensified.

"Makes sense, but how could you possibly do that?" I replied, remembering the conversation I'd had with my brother, Maeck. "A mental condition could be brought on by anything—a chemical imbalance, brain injury, or a traumatic experience. It's hard to pinpoint what actually needs to be treated."

"Very good, Zulli!" My father beamed a smile at me. "I knew you'd catch on."

We rounded a corner, and I peered into one of the exam rooms. The lights were on, and I saw an older man wearing a medical gown, resting in his bed. He wasn't moving, his eyes were closed, but seeing as he was frequently on the evening news most days I immediately recognized him.

"Isn't that ... Ethin Henderson?" My eyes widened with amusement. Not only was my father treating him for something, Ethin's name was on the list I'd found the night of the attack on NightFly Technologies. It couldn't be a coincidence.

"The mayor of the city of Chitol. Yes. And I bet you had no idea he suffers from psychosis. You would never know since it's still in its beginning stages, but he has difficulty discerning what's real and what isn't. Not the most desired quality in a leader, now, is it?"

I stepped inside the exam room, watching curiously as a young female technician piped two magic liquids into a single vial. She capped it, shook it up, and drew out the mixed liquid into the syringe. With a quick tap of her fingertip to remove the air bubbles, she whispered a word even my keen hearing couldn't pick up on to activate the magic, then expelled it into an IV that was inserted into a vein.

My father stopped at the foot of the bed, looking down on the comatose body with a mysterious gleam in his eyes. "It's quite simple, really. It's like surgery with magic words. Once the magic has run through his system, we speak a very specific command to the magic and it sends a message to the brain, informing it that it has a task to do."

The magical cocktail snaked through a long, thin tube before disappearing into Ethin's body. I took a step closer, following the transparent orange liquid along its path. An uneasy sensation stirred in my stomach. "Dad, that liquid—"

"We should let the technician do her job." My father cut me off before I could ask my question. He placed his hand along the small of my back and encouraged me to leave the room. "It's very important we don't disrupt the process, Zulli. If the command is interpreted by his brain as something else or we don't give precise orders, the magic may not do what it was intended to do."

The female technician ignored me, pressing the bridge of her round metal glasses up her nose. Her eyes were locked onto a monitor, writing down every little fluctuation in data. I left her to her work and met my father in the corridor.

"So now you understand why I've been so secretive. Many of our patients are public figures, and we need to keep their names and conditions from leaking out." We retraced our steps back toward the waiting room when my father finally stopped.

"We've been working to find the right ratio of magic to make the serum more effective, and there is still much more testing that needs to be done. But we can't have our competitors catching wind of this project and beating us to market, or worse, having a man like Davian Grymes take the information and sell it to criminals. I regret to say that someone must have found out and came after you last night to get to me. You must be cautious, Zulli. Stay diligent."

150

I nodded my agreement, dropped my duffle bag to the floor, then squeezed my arms around my dad in the tightest bear hug I could muster. "Thanks, Dad."

The side of my head pressed against his chest, my gaze eyeing the double doors that led into the hallway we'd just left. A heaviness weighed down my shoulders, nausea churning in my stomach. I let go of the hug, looking up at my dad just in time to see a flicker of apprehension cross his stern features.

As we were about to leave, the main door buzzed open. Brodin walked in with a ratty looking man. His companion had black hair that was a wild mess. Dirt mixed with dried blood was smeared all over his mangled face. Underneath his unzipped black hoodie I glimpsed a frayed brown turtleneck.

My gaze met the man's darkened eyes and I instantly froze. A memory flashed in my head of Brodin wrapping his magic around this man, tossing him clear across a parking lot. This must have been my attacker from last night. Why was he here with my brother?

"Zulli? What the hell are you doing here?" Brodin shoved the man to his side and stepped in front of him.

"Just hanging out with Dad. Thanks for being there last night. You okay?" I tried to peer around his broad shoulders to take a second look at the mysterious man, but my brother shifted his body to block me.

"Yeah, I'm fine. That idiot was no match for my spider magic."

A disgruntled snort came from behind him.

"I have to get to work with a trial patient. Maybe we should stick to having family dinners at home from now on." He flashed a hurried smile, a twitch pulling at the corner of his lips. Brodin twisted around to grab the man's arm and ushered him along.

"That man—" The double doors swished and Brodin was gone, the unknown man with him out of sight. "Dad, who was that? I think I know him."

"I'm sure you don't, little spider. Besides, I can't tell you that. Confidential, remember? Come on. Let me walk you out."

I picked up the duffle bag and slung it over my shoulder, following my dad to the downstairs lobby. So many questions scrambled my brain, but I knew better than to think he'd answer a single one.

We passed through the rotating entrance doors and outside into the busy plaza. The toasty afternoon sunlight was hotter than it had been the past few days but was a pleasant reminder that summer was just around the corner.

In the center was a flower garden that dominated the open area. A few NightFly Technologies employees in lab coats sat around the benches enjoying an early lunch. A fuzzy feeling warmed my stomach at the sight of the fully blooming rose bushes—the same roses outside my dad's home office kept alive year-round by the magic fertilizer. The vibrant pinks and reds of their delicate petals brightened up the otherwise dull browns and grays throughout the rest of the business district.

"I can have someone take you back to your apartment." My dad's voice slightly wavered, and if I hadn't known better I'd think he might have been a touch concerned for my safety.

I sucked in a deep breath, inhaling all the mixed smells the city had to offer. "It's such a nice day out. I think I'll walk back home and get some fresh air."

"Very well." My dad leaned in and kissed me on the forehead, then reached into his pocket to pull out a bottle of pills. "Take one of these for the next few days to help with the lingering pain and headaches. I'll check on you later. See you again soon."

14

---◈---

KASRA'S OBNOXIOUS SCREAMING COULD BE heard even before the elevator door slid open.

"Zulli! Are you in there? Open up!" Her fist was pounding so forcefully on the front door to my apartment that the walls rattled along with it.

"Would you mind keeping it down? I think the neighbors already hate me. And I'm not in the best mood right now."

"Zulli, where have you been?" Kasra stepped aside so I could unlock the door.

It had been a couple days since I'd been home, but the smell of spicy cinnamon from the snickerdoodle cookies I'd baked still lingered in the apartment. After tossing the duffle bag on the floor next to a pile of shoes, I flipped on the lights. Ignoring Kasra's question, I dragged my feet like heavy concrete blocks into the kitchen and filled up a glass of water from the tap, then plopped myself down on the sofa.

Kasra followed, crashing onto the flattened cushion next to me and eyeing me with a vicious gaze. "You had everyone worried. No one knew where you were, and you haven't been answering our calls or messages."

The cold water was refreshing as I gulped down every last drop. My throat was still dry, but the long walk back to my apartment was exhausting and I was too tired to get up for a refill. "Someone attacked me last night. I … I must have lost my phone at some point."

I didn't care about losing my phone, and I wasn't even upset about being attacked. I was alive. My best friend, Catilda, wasn't.

Kasra flipped her braid behind her shoulder. Her bare skin was flawless, even without makeup to make it glow. I wanted to steal the comfy fleece sweatshirt she was wearing and snuggle up in it like a warm blanket. She crossed her legs, her bouncing foot showing off her fuzzy bunny slippers.

"Yeah. I know," she snapped. "Ryker called me in the middle of the night in a fit of panic and told me something had happened. The worry in his voice had me terrified. I've never known him to overreact like that. He told me you were attacked and he had no idea where you were, so I came rushing down here hoping you might be home. Tell me what happened. Are you okay?"

My lips parted, wondering what to tell her. She probably knew just about as much as I did. "I went out for dinner with my brothers and someone jumped me in the parking lot on my way out. Brodin put the guy in his place, though. Beat the crap out of him. He took me to my dad who fixed me up. I'm a little tired but I feel fine."

"Well, it's a good thing he was there. I'm gonna call Ryker and let him know you're home. Are you hungry? I can run up to my apartment and grab us something to eat, since I'm guessing there's absolutely nothing edible in your kitchen."

Kasra stood up from the couch and fondled her phone in her hand.

"I could go for a grilled cheese sandwich. And maybe an entire bag of potato chips. Also a gallon of ice cream."

"I think that can be arranged." Her approving smile brought a touch of radiance to her face.

She called Ryker, and before she'd even hung up the phone, someone was knocking at my door. Without waiting for anyone to answer, Ryker and a feisty redhead with tousled curls burst in and rushed over to me. Disbelief swelled inside my chest, my heart dropping to my toes. It couldn't be …

"Zulli! I'm so sorry! I shouldn't have left you like that!" Catilda tackled me on the couch and squeezed her twig-like arms around my neck as hard as she could. She may have weighed about as much as a bag of feathers, but she was still cutting off my air supply.

"Catilda?" I choked out. "You … you're alive?"

She pulled away from her embrace, pushing an unruly curl behind her ear. Black eyeshadow was smeared around her red-rimmed eyes, and when she wiped away a tear, the makeup streaked across her cheek.

"Can I trust you guys to stay put for a few while I go upstairs and grab something to eat?" Kasra interrupted, narrowing her gaze on Catilda. The two had never met, and I had no doubt Kasra was curious as to who this strange woman was that had arrived with Ryker. "Anyone else want anything?"

Catilda and Ryker declined her request, and Kasra disappeared in search of food.

"Zulli, do you remember what happened to you last night?" Ryker waved his hand at Catilda, and she crawled over to make room for him next to me on the couch. He had heavy bags under his eyes, but he wore them like a badge of honor. The dark shadows were a sign that he hadn't slept all night, and I knew it was because he wouldn't rest until he was sure I was safe.

When his tired gaze settled on me, he smiled and all the tension he had been holding in washed away. His shoulders relaxed, his amber eyes softened, and he let out a whisper of a sigh in relief.

"I went out for dinner with my brothers. Someone attacked me in the parking lot, and Brodin came to help me." I repeated the same story I had told Kasra. "But … Catilda, my father said that you … you died? I thought I'd lost you!"

At the sight of Catilda's freckled face, a happy warmth swept through me and butterflies fluttered in my stomach. Joyful tears streamed down my face. My heart started beating faster than humanly possible, trying to compensate for the relief of seeing her alive.

Catilda brought me in for another hug and we rocked back and forth, refusing to let go. "They tried, hun. After I ran off, someone captured me, put a bag over my head, and shoved me into a car. I was injected with a needle of something, but the idiots who tried to drug me must not have realized I was still under the influence of that magic inhibitor. They kept yelling at me, saying that I needed to forget everything that had happened from the moment I woke up that day and that I needed to forget you ever existed! It had absolutely no effect on me, so I just played along. When they were satisfied with their results, they dumped me on the side of a road with a little baggie of five white capsules stamped with the signature Black Mark symbol. They wanted me to overdose on Bliss."

My gaze bounced back and forth between Ryker and Catilda on either side of me. Both had grim expressions plastered to their faces, concern flickering across their features.

"I'm not sure I'm following. Did you come with me to dinner last night? Were you attacked too? Why would my dad say you were dead?"

"Zulli …" Catilda scooched closer to me and lowered her voice into a gentle purr. "You were with *me* last night, hun. Do you remember our meeting with Ozcar Thorne at the skating rink? He told us about the magic liquid in the vial that came from NightFly Technologies. That it was used to make Bliss."

Catilda went on to explain everything that had happened yesterday, from the encounter in the park when we lost our magic to meeting with Ozcar and the details about my father's involvement with Bliss, along with our daring escape from the ice rink after we learned he'd sold us out to his cohorts.

Catilda squeezed my arm. "I'm really sorry, Zulli. I only left you because I thought I'd just be in your way. If I had known this would happen …"

The ball of disbelief and foreboding twisted in my stomach like a fist trying to bury itself into my ribcage. I wiped the beads of cold sweat forming on my forehead. Bile burned in the back of my throat and I inhaled deeply against it.

"There's something wrong here. This can't be right!" I jumped to my feet and turned to face them. "Why should we believe Ozcar? He's a criminal. Maybe he's trying to turn me against my dad …"

The room and everyone in it disappeared around me and dizziness overwhelmed my senses. I gasped harshly against the turbulent force of cold fear that ran through my icy veins. Tightness squeezed at my chest, an aching, dull feeling of doubt.

Catilda reached out to grab my hand. "You really don't remember? Ozcar wants that spatula you stole from him. On our way out, that guy with a puffy jacket and brown turtleneck attacked us with his duplication magic. Think, Zulli! You have to remember!"

Brown turtleneck? The same man with Brodin this morning? He was the one who had come after me, attacked Catilda. A dam broke in my mind, drowning me with a rush of memories from last night all at once. My soul screamed with rage, but the only indication of the torture I was holding onto inside was the tears streaming down my face and my bottom lip trembling. Firm hands caught me as the world folded in on itself.

"Zulli, you need to sit back down." Ryker lowered me back onto the couch. Catilda was holding out a fresh glass of water in front of me. I took it from her with shaking hands and sipped it.

I remembered everything, but a part of me wished I didn't. "After Catilda left, Brodin showed up," I recalled. "I don't know how, but he must have found out I was planning to meet with Ozcar and followed me to … I don't know? Stop the meeting? Protect me from Ozcar? When he was too late, he took both me and my attacker back to NightFly Technologies."

That wasn't the worst part.

"I remember … being brought into an exam room and placed on a bed. My dad and Brodin treated some of my wounds but …" Through my resurfaced memory, I saw a tube connected to my arm, the transparent orange liquid snaking through it. I tried to swallow, but the tightness felt like rocks scraping my throat.

"My own father drugged me and altered my memories, and Brodin stood right by his side as he did it." The words that rolled off my tongue didn't sound real. "This must be Davian's doing. It's got to be! Maybe he's blackmailing my dad. Or he's controlling my family using Bliss to make them forget the memories of their involvement."

"I don't understand, though." Catilda paused and peered up at the ceiling. "The drug is only temporary. Unless he was trying to kill you too, Zulli, what good would drugging you do if its effects wore off a day or two later and your original memories came back?"

I explained to both of them what I saw at the lab. "My dad told me he's trying to find a way to fight mental illness. Those people on the list? I think he's drugging them with Bliss, injecting them with a stronger, modified version of it, then giving them small doses through the pills to help sustain the false memories until he finds a way to make it permanent."

"Or they die …" Catilda muttered.

I ran over to my duffle bag and dug out the bottle of pills my dad had given me. There was no telltale stamp of the Black Mark and their crosshairs symbol, but the capsules were the same white color and oblong round shape. I pinched one of them open and a transparent orange liquid oozed out.

Ryker remained suspiciously calm, thoughtfully scratching his chin while he stared off into the distance. "I suppose it makes

158

sense. The drug is being tested illegally on the market to see how people react to it, and the people on the list have been selected as targets for more in-depth testing."

"But why would Davian attack NightFly Technologies?" Catilda's eyes narrowed on Ryker. "If Zavyr is under Davian's control, why send someone from the Black Mark to blow up the place? If he was looking for something, why not just ask Zavyr to hand it over?"

"A diversion?" Ryker dropped his head to his chest, his exhaustion apparent as he rubbed his eyes. "The two of them have history. By attacking NightFly Technologies, no one's going to suspect they're still working together. Your father never reported anything stolen, did he, Zulli?"

I shook my head. "A lot of the paperwork was destroyed. He said it would be impossible to figure out if they'd walked off with any copies that had been filed away in the records office."

Ryker and Catilda continued to speak. The words reached me, but their meaning was lost to deaf ears. A dull cloud of poisonous confusion blurred my senses and distorted my perception. I sat there on the couch, staring down at the worn out rug under my feet.

"This can't be happening," I muttered out loud, although the thought was more to myself than to Ryker or Catilda.

My sweaty fists shook furiously and my fingernails dug into my palms, sending a dull pain throbbing through my hands. I huffed like an angry bull, sharp breaths in and out of my nose. A flood of emotions hammered into me. I wanted to storm out of the apartment and hunt down Davian. I felt the urge to march right back to NightFly Technologies and demand answers from my dad. I tried to convince myself this was all a dream—a horrific, nightmarish dream world that was crumbling down around me, suffocating and burning me alive with no way to escape.

"Zulli?" My eyes blinked the room back into focus at the sound of my name. Kasra stood in front of me with a platter of grilled cheese sandwiches and two bags of chips tucked under each arm. "Ice cream is in the freezer. I've seen how much your stomach can hold, so I brought extra sandwiches."

Catilda clutched my hand in hers, but it was Ryker next to me that I gravitated toward. My head collided with his chest, and a wail of blubbering cries tore from my throat. My magic rose inside me, hot and heavy, a turbulent force responding to both the fear and anger twisting knots in my stomach. Air couldn't enter my lungs fast enough between the continuous screams and sobbing. My pulse pounded so fast, the fire racing inside me like someone had lit a match beneath my center, deep in the pit of my stomach.

My arms crushed around him, my fingertips digging into his shirt as I clenched the fabric tightly in my grip. He wrapped his own arms around me, stroking one hand gently down my back and pulling me in closer.

"It's okay, Zulli. We'll figure this out."

The warmth of his words enveloped me like a security blanket. He never spoke empty promises simply to comfort me. I had no doubt he meant what he said, and that he would go to the ends of the world to find a way to make this right.

The grief that tore through me felt like hot needles pushing to break free from every pore on my body. My insides were broken, shattered and ripped apart from the raging storm of fear, regret, anger, and sadness rising inside me.

I pressed my face into Ryker's chest, my rage threatening to rip his shirt into pieces when my claws sprung out. I kept this up for a good ten minutes until I had nothing left to give. Gathering my remaining sanity, I pulled away. Ryker didn't utter a single sound, instead grabbing a tissue from the end table.

"I was only gone for twenty minutes but I feel like I missed something really important. Zulli, are you okay? What's wrong?" Kasra still stood in front of me but had placed the platter of sandwiches on the coffee table. She glared at the three of us sitting on the couch. Maybe she was trying to shift the subject to something more pleasant, or it could have been her impatience getting the best of her, but when no one offered an explanation, she turned her attention to Catilda.

"I'm Kasra. Who are you?" She held her gaze on the woman who'd arrived with Ryker.

Catilda rose from the couch to greet her. Despite the disheveled appearance of her face, she stood proud in her olive green knitted sweater dress and chunky boots.

Smiling at Kasra, Catilda introduced herself with a familiar energy returning to her voice. "Catilda Harper! Best friend and—"

"Wait ..." Kasra cut her off. "Harper? As in the owner of the famous Harper's Treasure Chest?"

Catilda's freckled skin turned a rosy pink. "Well, it's technically owned by my parents, but yes. Have you done business with us before?"

"Yes!" Kasra's hazel eyes grew twice their size and she grabbed Catilda's hand, shaking it violently like she had just come face-to-face with a celebrity. "Last year, you helped me find this rare fabric that's unrippable! I had it made into a stylish halter top."

All eyes trained on Kasra, who was excitedly bouncing up and down on her rubber heels. "What? My clothes get ruined all the time on missions. I wanted something that was both pretty and practical."

A restrained silence filled the room for a brief moment. I bit the bottom of my lip. Ryker coughed to cover his laugh. Catilda burst out giggling uncontrollably.

No longer trying to hide it, Ryker and I joined in, as did Kasra. I snatched a grilled cheese sandwich from the platter. The cheese was no longer gooey, the toasty bread gone cold, but it was the best thing I had ever tasted because Kasra had made it just for me.

"I think I need a drink. Or five," I said as I shoved the second grilled cheese into my mouth and reached for the bag of potato chips.

161

"Coming right up!" Ryker disappeared through a portal, leaving behind his spicy cinnamon scent to fill my apartment. Fifteen minutes later, he came back with a case of beer and a bottle of rum. Plus a strawberry milkshake.

It was even better than the grilled cheese.

"I thought maybe you'd want to use some of that rum to add into your milkshake." He twisted the cap off the bottle and handed it to me.

"Brilliant thinking, Ryker." I poured a little bit of the vanilla flavored alcohol into the creamy drink and mixed it together with my straw, not so much that it'd overpower the sugary strawberry goodness, but enough to take the edge off.

We all stayed in my apartment for the rest of the day and well into the night, drinking, eating, and laughing. At some point, we left to buy me a new phone. I hadn't forgotten that I still owed Ozcar that spatula. Several times, Ryker had to stop me from storming off and pursuing my revenge against Davian. My skin itched to learn the truth from my dad, but I wasn't sure I wanted to hear it. If he really was under the influence of Bliss, could I even believe him?

Catilda yawned, looking out the window into darkness. "I gotta get back home. Ryker, do you mind taking me back, hun?"

"Sure thing."

Kasra was nodding off on the couch, arms stuffed under her head in what looked to be a very uncomfortable position. "I should get going too. It's going to be a long walk up three flights of stairs back to my apartment if I have any more to drink."

I hugged each of them goodbye before they left. The absence of our chatter gave the apartment an eerie silence, but their laughing voices still echoed inside my head. I stood in the middle of the gloomy living area, my rampant thoughts overtaking me. There had to be something I was missing. What was Davian's end goal? And why did he need my father to achieve it?

There was no way I would be able to sleep, so I shoved a few necessities into my backpack and had my hand on the door knob

162

when the smell of cinnamon alerted me to the fact I was no longer alone.

"Where do you think you're going?" Ryker's voice came from behind me. I kept my hand on the doorknob, my eyes locked straight ahead.

"I have to talk to my dad. I need answers." My fingers squeezed on the cold metal and began to turn.

"Zulli, stop. Please? It's the middle of the night. I can't begin to imagine how difficult this must be for you, but this isn't the way to get the answers you're looking for."

I spun around, tears welling at the corners of my eyes. "Oh, yeah? Then tell me how to get those answers, Ryker. My family could be in serious trouble. We have no idea what Davian is up to, and I don't want to wait around to find out what happens next. Catilda almost died last night. My own dad *drugged* me, and my brother watched him do it. Not to mention Ozcar still wants that spatula. I need to see my dad. Now."

Ryker placed a hand on top of my shoulder, a sparkle in his gaze igniting something inside me.

"I have a plan and I'll come back first thing tomorrow morning to explain it. But first, you need to get some sleep, Zulli. We'll find a way to fix this. I promise."

"Right," I responded dryly.

My uncomfortable gaze averted from Ryker and heat flushed my face. My pulse spiked, blood pumping steadily toward my fingers and toes. There was something else I still needed to tell him. And thanks to a little liquid courage, it seemed like a good time to finally get it out. I inhaled a deep breath and counted to three, then let it out along with the words, "Ryker, I'm sorry."

But he would never hear my apology. When I looked up, he was already gone.

15

MY NEW PHONE VIBRATED ON my nightstand, but I was too comfortably tucked in my sheets to roll over and answer it. After listening to it go off for about ten minutes, the buzzing turned into a knocking at my front door.

"All right, I'm coming," I muttered loudly. Flipping off the covers let in a rush of cold air that sent shivers down my arms and legs. Checking the phone, I saw it was late morning. Still in somewhat of a haze, I stumbled over toward the door.

"What do you want? It's too early for this." For some reason, I had expected to see Kasra. But then I remembered Ryker was coming back to check on me in the morning. He stood there in his military khakis, t-shirt, and vest, his trusty knife strapped to his leg.

Ryker gasped, his cheeks reddening like hot iron. The shock that registered on his face transferred to mine, and I knew something was wrong. That's when I realized I may have had a little too much to drink last night and never put on pants before I went to bed.

"I … um … uh …" I pulled down the oversized t-shirt as far as it would go, thankfully just enough to cover anything I preferred to keep private. My incoherent mumbling turned into a high pitched shriek. Ryker's eyes snapped shut and he winced. In a sheer fit of panic, I kicked the door shut with my foot, slamming it in Ryker's face.

Scampering over to my bed, I picked up the first pair of pants I could find. After slipping on the dirty gym sweats, I rushed back to open the front door. Ryker hadn't moved an inch.

Slowly, he pried open one eye, then the other.

"I brought breakfast?" His smile never wavered, but his voice did.

"Good. I'm hungry." I snatched the bag from his hand and moved out of his way to let him inside. Grease saturated the bottom of the paper bag, which meant whatever was inside it was automatically going to be delicious.

The only place to sit in my apartment was the couch, so we stood in the kitchen as I ate. My teeth sank into the egg sandwich. A juicy crunch of bacon sent a drop of grease down my chin that I wiped off with my shirt.

"Did you tell Kasra yet?" Ryker asked, searching through my refrigerator for something to drink.

"No."

"Zulli … you gotta tell her."

"Yeah, I know. It's just …" My gaze fixated on the counter where I scratched at a mysterious substance that had dried into a crusty stain.

"Just what?" A cabinet door slammed shut. "You don't think she'll understand?"

My silence was the only answer he needed.

"Zulli, whatever your father or brothers do has no reflection on you. You're a good person. She knows that. I'm sure she wants to help just as much as I do."

"I know. But that's the problem. Look what happened to you and Catilda? Her shop was attacked, we all lost our magic … I don't want to drag her into my mess if I don't have to. The longer she stays out of this the better off she'll be."

Ryker grabbed a cup from the shelf and filled it with water from the faucet. He then tore open a packet of magic powder, dumping it into the glass and swirling it around. The clear water turned a fizzy brown, bubbles hissing and popping on the surface. Instant root beer. As he took a long, slurping sip from the glass, I glanced up to notice his icy stare freezing the blood pumping through my veins.

"Why are you in your uniform?" I asked as I licked a piece of melted cheese off my finger. "Are we needed back on base?"

"No. But I reached out to some of my contacts," he began, putting his glass down on the counter to massage his palms as he spoke. "I have an idea."

"Contacts?" I stopped chewing to glower at him. "What contacts?"

"As a military soldier, I've acquired some contacts over the past few months. Don't you have any?"

About a dozen names popped into my head. "None that actually like me."

"Well, I have good news and bad news. The bad news is we have to get that magic spatula for Ozcar or he will make our lives a living hell."

"*That's* your plan? We can't give him back that spatula, Ryker! He was using it to mix illegal drugs before. What if he uses it to mix Bliss?" Pain shot up my arm as it slammed down on the counter.

"The guy can break down magic. He doesn't need the spatula to figure out the spell, only if he wants to mass produce it quickly and effectively, but I don't think that's his plan. When you stole the spatula from Ozcar the first time, he told us he wasn't interested in Bliss."

"And there's good news somewhere in this mess?"

"We can use the spatula to our advantage. But we have to go see Catilda. Hurry up and get changed into your uniform."

My eyes narrowed on Ryker, who was showing no hint as to what he was thinking. "Why? Tell me what you're planning."

"I'll explain when we get there. Just hurry up. We don't have a lot of time."

A quick shower washed away the sticky booze I had spilled on myself last night, then I changed into a pair of olive khakis, a black t-shirt, and a tactical vest. Helpful magic objects filled the pockets and hidden compartments. My belt hung loosely around my waist, and a leg holster equipped with paralysis daggers wrapped around my thigh.

I left the steamy bathroom, shaking out my damp hair like a wet dog. Ryker was standing in the middle of the living room, pacing as he swiped through his phone and searched his stash of pictures. "You ready?"

"To do something you refuse to explain to me? Sure, why not?"

He studied a photo he'd taken of Catilda's shop to refresh his memory, then closed his eyes and held out his hand. A warm pocket of magic gathered in my living room as his portal opened. I stepped through, inhaling its spicy cinnamon scent as I did.

We found ourselves near the back steps of Harper's Treasure Chest. Since it was the middle of a work day and open for business, we looped around and entered through the front door, hoping to find Catilda working.

The bell above the door jingled. A pleasant floral scent permeated the shop, mixing with the musty smell of old leather and decaying paperbacks. Just as we had left it, organized rows of magic gadgets and other contraptions lined the shelves of the narrow aisles. A short fiery redhead with freckles painted all over his pale face sat behind the counter playing a game on his phone. Sounds of explosions blared through his headphones. A series of grunts and insults came out of his mouth as his fingers furiously smashed on the screen.

I pressed a finger to my lips and shushed Ryker. "Watch this."

Magic wrapped around me, heat swirling inside as my body transformed into its spider shape. My eight elongated legs crawled up the brick wall, across the ceiling, and descended on a trail of silk inches away from the kid's nose.

The shrill noise of his scream ripped through me like a shock wave. A claw swatted at my swinging body, slicing through my magic thread. My tiny spider body went sailing through the air. Dizziness caused my brain to spin as I simultaneously reversed my magic, transforming myself back into my human form. My human legs skidded across the wooden floor, and I threw out a hand for balance.

Chuckling, I walked over and leaned on the glass counter. "You know, Saimon, it's not very professional to be playing games on the job. We could have walked out with half the store."

"That is *so* not cool, Zulli." Catilda's brother, the youngest of the two, swiped a wavy curl off his forehead and wheezed as he got his erratic breathing under control. Even though he was in his mid-teens, he had that cute boyish face that hadn't yet matured into a man's, with chubby cheeks and not a hint of stubble. His thick clear-plastic glasses hid the terror in his expressive blue eyes.

"Is Catilda here? We need to talk to her." Ryker appeared next to me, his face serious and full of concern.

"Yeah, she's taking her fifteenth break of the day to reapply her makeup. She's probably in the back."

We found Catilda sitting at the wooden table in the break room, guiding a large bristled brush in smooth motions across her face while staring into a small compact mirror. She had her short hair straightened and tied back in a stubby ponytail, rogue strands dangling down her neck and covering her ears.

"Zulli? Everything okay? Why are you here in your uniform?" The chair screeched on the floor as she rose to greet us. Her golden bangles jingled on her wrists and her pretty cotton candy pink sundress swayed as she made her way over to me and Ryker.

168

"I asked Ryker the same question before we left. Are your parents around?" My neck craned toward the hallway like they might pop in at any moment.

"No. They'll be out the rest of the day. Why?"

"Good." I stepped aside so Ryker could take over.

"The baking spatula we confiscated from Ozcar is secured away in a vault on the military base. Zulli and I are going to steal it and give it back."

Catilda waved her hands in front of her and shook her head. "Hold on a minute. Back up. This has been bothering me ever since Ozcar mentioned it. I have to ask … a spatula? Is this for real? Are you planning to bake him a batch of cupcakes and beg for mercy?"

I snorted at her response, but Ryker kept his expression serious. "It's more dangerous than it looks, Catilda. Ozcar was using it to mix his drugs before we took it. It has a special magic power that helps mix together any ingredients to create a flawless magic spell. It's why his drugs were so effective and pure."

"Right. So now you're planning to break into a highly secured military vault to steal it back for him because … you feel bad that you destroyed his business?" Her condescending tone was drier than a saltine cracker. "Help me out here, Ryker. This seems a little irresponsible coming from the guy constantly trying to talk Zulli *out* of getting into trouble."

"I know, but we already have several samples of Bliss that were given to both you and Zulli. Perhaps we can find a way to use the spatula to mix a spell and reverse the effects of the drug. Give people back the control of their minds that they lost or protect them from being drugged in the first place." Ryker pursed his lips, his eyebrows shooting up. He was giving Catilda those puppy dog eyes that melted hearts.

Except Catilda's heart was made of stone. "I don't know if you heard me the first ten times, but I'm not a technician. I don't know anything about that stuff, and even if I did, I don't exactly have a lab with high tech machinery to work in. The only person who could *maybe* do this is my mom."

Ryker inspected my reaction before answering. "Then let's ask her. This is important."

"What about the rest of the ingredients?" A bitter tone wedged itself in between her words, and she threw her hands up in frustration, slapping them back down on her thighs. "Bliss is already mixed. To test anything, I'm going to need the individual components of the drug, and there's a good chance the same ingredients aren't used to reverse it. Ozcar said that someone's blood activated the bonding agent. We have no idea whose blood that is, and Ozcar took what little we had left of the bonding chemical. This brilliant plan of yours is off to a fantastic start, Ryker."

"Don't worry about that just yet. Will you help us?" He took her hand in his, and Catilda's wall completely crumbled. A lovely scarlet flush colored her cheeks, and I could practically feel the heat radiating off her face. She leaned a step backward and turned away from him when she spoke.

"Fine. I'll do my best, but I can't promise anything." She ripped her hand away before Ryker got her to agree to anything else.

"That's all we can ask for. Thank you."

Catilda shot a vicious look at me. I shrugged at her. I had yet to meet anyone who could completely resist Ryker's charm.

"Zulli, we have to go." Ryker was staring at the clock that hung above the door in the break room. "If we hurry up, we can catch the lunch rush on base. Most people will be in the cafeteria eating, so there'll be less prying eyes on us when we sneak in."

"Hey, Ryker!" Catilda snapped as we were leaving. She stomped over to him and shoved her finger into his chest. "I swear, if you let my Zulli get hurt, I will come after you and rip your heart out with my bare claws while you sleep."

Ryker studied the seriousness of her words, and Catilda kept her attention locked on him. "You have my word, Catilda. I promise I'll do whatever it takes to keep her safe."

My eyes rolled so hard I was surprised they didn't fall right out of their sockets. Despite his sappy comment, I knew he was telling the truth, and that scared me. He'd give up his life if it meant saving mine. An overwhelming sense of dread settled in the pit of my stomach.

As we left out the back door of the shop and into the parking lot, I turned around to face Ryker. "You don't have to do this, Ryker. If you get caught, your career is over. Not to mention we're trying to steal a magic object from a military base full of heavily armed soldiers that aren't afraid to shoot and ask questions later. Drop me off and let me do this alone."

"And face the wrath of Catilda if something happens to you? I'll take my chances with the military. Besides, I said we'd do this together, and I meant it." His expression tightened, his eyes glowing with the loyalty and determination I knew him for. He placed his hands firmly on my shoulders. "The plan is simple. Keep your head down and move straight toward the vault. The less people who see us the better. You'll crawl into the vent and open the vault from the inside. In and out. We can do this."

A smile slowly crept up my face. Ryker pulled me close and I smacked into his chest. A little rush of butterflies fluttered in my stomach, the warmth of his embrace offering comfort from the bitter cold reminder of the dangerous situation we were about to put ourselves in.

"Okay, okay. Don't make me regret letting you tag along." I pushed him away and backpedaled, nearly toppling over as I tripped over a curb.

Ryker closed his eyes and drew in a deep breath. A cool breeze cut through the warm rays of afternoon sun. The perfect spring day would have presented a welcomed opportunity to walk around town or maybe have a picnic in the park. But we had a job to do.

He took a moment to rub his palms and draw in a deep breath. His shoulders stiffened, his magic thrumming with a steady vibration as it gathered nearby and formed an invisible doorway right to base.

We stepped through the portal and into a brightly lit room with a white tiled floor. Marker doodles decorated the peeling paint on the walls. The men's bathroom wouldn't have been my first choice, but the lack of foot traffic meant fewer people around to notice us and it was the closest place Ryker could transport us to the vault.

The gurgling of a flushing toilet triggered Ryker's instincts.

"Crap!" He threw my back against the wall and I bounced against the cheaply constructed plaster. As the stall door opened, Ryker pressed up close against me, his forehead touching mine and his rapid breath brushing over my lips. His hand raised to gently caress my cheek.

My brain stuttered and my vision hazed over, every part of my body frozen while my thoughts tried to catch up. All I could do was stand there and hope I was still breathing. When I realized what he was doing, I threw my arms around him, burying my face into the hollow of his neck.

The man finished washing his hands and glared at the reflection of us in the mirror. "Ugh. Do you two have to do that here? Go find a storage closet to make out in."

Keeping my face hidden, I discreetly peered past Ryker's shoulder to see the man grab a paper towel. The soldier started to approach us when a lustful whimper escaped my lips. Not wanting to stick around for the show, he hurried right past us and out the door without so much as a glance our way.

"*Phew!* That was a close one." I loosened my grip on Ryker, but he barely moved a muscle. "Um, Ryker? You can let go now."

He stepped back, blinking rapidly without saying a word. His face had turned a nuclear red. He rubbed his eyes with the base of his palms, stopping to push them deep into his sockets. "Zulli, I'm so sorry! I didn't know what else to do ..."

"It worked, didn't it?" I punched him playfully in the shoulder, trying to conceal my own awkward embarrassment.

The deafening alarm blaring out in the hallway gave us something new to focus on. The noise pounded in my ears, my sensitive hearing intensifying the high pitched siren.

"Did we just set off a security alarm? How? What's going on?" Ryker didn't offer me an answer. Instead, he took my hand and pushed open the bathroom door.

In the corridor, a stampede of military personnel scrambled in organized chaos. The spinning alarm lights basked everything in a haunting red. Orders bellowed from superiors, barely audible over the wailing alarm, but it didn't matter. Fire drills were a normal part of military training. Sometimes they were real, but most of the time they were used as training. Everyone had a place to be and knew exactly where to go.

And that's just what we did.

We slipped into the stream of soldiers and turned left toward the vault.

"Stick close," Ryker kept one eye on me and another in front of him, jumping and dodging oncoming traffic. While the alarm had thrown us an unexpected curveball, we could use it to our advantage. Everyone was so focused on carrying out the required protocols that they wouldn't be paying attention to the fact we were about to break into the vault.

"It's right around the corner." Ryker guided me to a thick, solid steel door, much like something you'd see in a bank. It was bulletproof, fireproof, and worst of all, magic proof. Short of chopping someone's hand off to activate the magic signature keypad, we had no way in. But thanks to a strategically placed air vent, we weren't totally out of luck.

Our opportunity came when the last soldier rounded the corner and disappeared out of sight. There was no telling how long we'd have before someone else came our way, so I knew I had to do this quickly.

"You got this, Zulli," Ryker assured me with a subtle crease of his lips.

"Can you, um, look away for a second?"

Without question, he turned his back and kept watch down the hallway. My magic activated and it coursed through my veins with a newfound purpose. The warmth was like a magic high, tingling my senses as my body shifted into an eight-legged creepy crawly the size of a walnut.

Although I was moving as fast as my spindly legs would take me, it wasn't fast enough. A tiny portal of magic opened up in front of me, and Ryker transported me right up to the air vent on the ceiling next to the vault door. I easily slipped through the grate. A blast of heat nearly incinerated me, but I scuttled on through what seemed like an endless tunnel until I reached an opening that led to the inside of the vault. I lowered myself down on a silky thread, struggling to maintain my spider form. My magic seeped out of me, and I willed myself to draw it back in. It rushed out of me right before I could reach the floor. My arm shot out, catching a pointed edge of a sharp wooden crate.

"Damn it," I hissed, looking at the small cut on my arm. Before I opened the vault door, I gave my arm a lick. The magic healing ability heated my skin for a second before it started closing the cut. The wound still burned, but at least I wouldn't be trekking blood throughout the vault.

As far as I was aware, no one had ever tried to break *out* of a vault, so opening the door from the inside was as simple as pushing the lever. Ryker quickly snuck inside, pulling it shut behind him.

"Look for Ozcar Thorne's name on the ID tag," I reminded Ryker, who was trailing behind me down an aisle. "It's probably in some kind of black plastic case, protected with magic to prevent idiots like us from trying to steal and use it."

Ryker snorted at the statement, but carefully started rummaging through cardboard boxes, envelopes, and heavy duty cases, making sure to keep everything perfectly neat so no one would know someone had snuck in.

The vault was where the military kept all the classified magic objects that were considered to be extremely dangerous. The storage room was brimming with thousands of items confiscated from missions over the years. Rows upon rows of metal shelving housed everything from magic grenade launchers to a ball cap that turned you invisible. None of that was what we'd come for though.

"Yes! I found it!" My hand clasped around the black handle just as the scraping of metal made my ears twitch. As I ripped the case containing the spatula from the shelf, a streak of light illuminated the room as the vault door opened. My heart jumped into my throat.

"*Hello?* Is someone else in here?" The animated female voice sang out the words in a cheery voice. A disappointed sigh echoed loudly around us, bouncing off the cinder block walls. Footsteps grew louder as they crept toward us.

I took one look at Ryker, not daring to speak. He just shook his head, a stern command to stay put and avoid drawing attention unless absolutely necessary. Above us, the lights flickered on, exposing us to our intruder.

"Peek-a-boo!" The short female soldier appeared before us. A thick set of bangs crossed her forehead, settling just above her feisty turquoise eyes. She smiled as she reached for the knife sheathed on her thigh.

My arm went swinging, the black plastic case tight in my grip aiming directly at the side of her head. She held up her hands to block. The knife she was holding went skittering across the floor, along with the case. I lunged at her, and we wrestled on the cold concrete, tumbling over each other. Pointed fangs grazed my lips, and I sunk my teeth deep into her neck. She yelped, thrusting out her hands and wrapping them around my throat.

Ryker scrambled over, grabbing each of her arms and ripping them off me. I closed my eyes. I didn't want the reminder of the terrified look that was likely plastered to her face as I continued to draw out her magic.

It was a sweet, fruity flavor, gliding down my throat like a warm cherry syrup on top of a sundae, smooth and silky. The taste was at odds with the heavy fresh scent of clean cotton that delighted my nostrils. Its hypnotizing effect took over both my body and mind, my senses dulling to focus only on her magic. There was something strangely alluring about it. Its power was sending me a message to stop, to pull away, but my need to survive and leave this vault with the spatula wouldn't let me. My insides livened with her energy. Her power fed me, a fire in my belly that flowed down into my chest, coursing outwards toward my fingertips and toes. As I got lost in her power, her pale skin began to turn an icy cold, the color draining from her face.

"Zulli! Stop!" Ryker's voice snapped me out of my daze. He let go of the woman and shoved my shoulder.

My fangs retracted. My jaw slackened, and I heaved deep breaths in and out. In the split second I froze, my eyes locked onto hers. They widened as something mysterious flashed through them, a sense of nervous anger that had her momentarily confused about how to feel. Her hand slapped to her neck where two small bite marks pooled with beads of blood.

"What did you do?" she growled, a touch of fear in her voice.

And then I noticed the name embroidered on her vest.

Captain Myra Llama. Oh, crap.

"Ryker, run!"

The captain's high-pitched wail tore through me, and my sensitive hearing couldn't ignore the threat. Blood pounded in my ears, throbbing behind my eyes. Draining her magic didn't seem to slow her down one bit. She threw me off her, my back snapping against a wooden crate. Another crash came as a shelf toppled over, Ryker's body underneath it.

As she continued to scream, a dense magical fog came out of her mouth and blanketed the room with the clean scent of freshly laundered cotton. I searched for Ryker, but all I could see was a wall of white in front of me. The temperature dropped at least twenty degrees, the moisture in the air crystalizing on my skin. I shivered violently, unable to control my spasming muscles. My lips trembled, knees wobbled, and I bit down hard to keep my teeth from chattering. Furiously, I rubbed my arms, trying to bring sensation back to them before they completely froze and broke off.

Captain Myra Llama was known as the Ice Queen, and there was a good reason why she'd earned the nickname.

An icy fist punched into my gut and I caved in on myself. Spit sprayed out of my mouth. I clutched my vest, inhaling to relieve the tight cramp constricting my lungs. Claws protruded from my fingertips, growing into sharp-edged weapons. I swung them out in front of me, slicing through nothing but air. My head darted back and forth, trying to place where Myra was. A heavy boot sideswiped me, taking out my legs as I went crashing hard to the floor. My head thumped on the concrete.

Darkness crept around the edges of my vision, my perception scrambled. My arm reached for anything nearby but came up empty.

"Zulli! Where are you?" Ryker called out to me.

Ignoring him, I lay completely still on the floor. Closing my eyes, I sent out my magic to scan for the slightest shift of air around me. The magical energy boost from Myra allowed me to expand my range. I searched for a smell. A vibration. Anything that would tell me where she was.

A slight quiver reached my fingertips. Feather-like footsteps were rushing toward me, each step barely touching the ground. I tucked in my knees, and when I opened my eyes, I thrust out my legs in front of me. The white fog around me dispersed with a whoosh of air as her body flew backward. I rocked back, then used my momentum to reach my feet. My hands patted at the pockets on my vest, and unsnapped a flap to find a small sponge.

"*Devoro.*" The yellow sponge began absorbing the magic in the air. With the haze starting to lift, Myra stood a few feet in front of me. She steadied her feet, popped a tablet into her mouth, and blew out a puff of blue powder directly into my face.

"*Dormeo.*"

"Ryker!" I yelled out, hoping he was somewhere nearby.

Unable to avoid inhaling the sleep powder, my eyelids grew heavy and my consciousness started to drift. My feet moved underneath me but I had little control over where they went. I could hold off the magic effects, but not for very long.

I swiveled to bolt in the opposite direction, my sluggish movements making it difficult to move quickly. Drowsiness fought its way through. Unaware of my surroundings, I crashed right into Ryker and collapsed into his arms. The black plastic case he was holding dropped to the floor so he could catch me before I fell.

"Zulli! It's okay. It's me."

Pushing away from Ryker, I lazily threw myself at the case. My knees hit the ground hard and sent a shot of intense pain up my legs. I reached for the handle when a palm smacked down on top of the case. Ice froze over the black plastic, Myra's hand fusing directly to it.

"If you want the case, you'll have to take me with you." Myra's high-pitched, sweet-sounding voice didn't match the intimidation she was trying to exude.

My own sticky fingers slapped the case, my feet following Myra's movements as she stood up. "Not if I can take it from you first."

A bold smile curled her lips. "Oh, I love a good challenge! Let's fight!"

We both began tugging in opposite directions. My fingers stretched, the joints rolling and grinding in their sockets. I pulled against Myra's force, the only indication of her effort a slight grunt that passed her lips.

"It's not worth it, Zulli. Let's go." Ryker's words were drawn out, his energy fading. He wrapped his arms around my waist and tried to pull me away. My fingers began slipping across the wet, slippery ice. A tingling pain shot up my arm and my grip gave way. Myra was flung backward, landing on her ass with a shocked *oof.*

I reached for the case in Myra's hands as the warmth of Ryker's magic hit my back. His portal felt disjointed, the humming magic pulsing at different frequencies as we fell into it. Myra beamed me an eerily friendly smile, watching with intense satisfaction as she clutched the black case to her chest. She waved goodbye as Ryker and I made our exit through his portal.

A small cloud of her magic fog managed to pass through with us, Myra's fresh linen scent lingering. Wherever Ryker had transported us, the dark space was confined, lit only by a sliver of light shining through a space between the bottom of the door and the floor. The strong smell of bleach not only burned my nose but my throat as well. Struggling to keep my eyes open, I used my hands to find a cold wall to prop myself up against. Ryker moved next to me and flopped to his side, his head directly on my shoulder.

"Hey. Where are we?" I smacked him across the face, the effort more exhausting than it should have been. "You can't fall asleep now. And don't you dare drool all over my uniform. It's dirty enough as it is."

He pushed himself up, wiping his mouth with the back of his hand.

"We're still on base. In a janitor's closet." His words slurred like a drunk, and his head rolled on his shoulders like it might fall off. He unsnapped a flap on his vest and dug out a small glass marble. He placed it on the floor and called out, "*Lumen.*"

A glow of soft light emanated from the sphere, dimly illuminating the space before us. A shelf of cleaning chemicals took up most of the closet, along with an assorted selection of brooms, mops, and other cleaning equipment.

Reaching into a vest pocket, I pulled out a pack of gum and handed a piece to Ryker. "Here. Chew this. Should help shake the effects of the sleep powder."

Ryker unwrapped the thin strip of gum and activated its magic. I did the same, letting spearmint flavor soothe the sting that had resulted from Myra's intense grip around my throat while also kicking the grogginess of the sleep spell from my system.

I nudged him with my elbow, catching a glimpse of the skin that had split open on his arm. "You're hurt. That looks nasty. Let me give you something for that." I searched my belt for a white bullet, but there was none.

"Oh, um …"

"It's fine. I'm fine. I just need a minute to regain my composure, then we can go back to see Catilda." He rested his head against the wall, his palm clasping tightly over his wound to stop the bleeding. His rosy face had turned pale, and he did his best to hide the discomfort through his heavy nasal breathing.

I sighed in resignation. "I can't believe I'm going to do this." I found a roll of toilet paper and used it to soak up the wet blood. Inhaling a deep breath, I took Ryker's hand in mine and stuck out my tongue, licking the underside of his arm. At the taste of his salty skin mixed with metallic blood, I shuddered at the unappetizing experience and immense embarrassment.

To my surprise, he didn't yank his arm away. I ran my tongue down his arm again, the bleeding slowing and the skin closing to seal the wound.

"I didn't know you could do that. You never cease to amaze me, Zulli." Ryker stared at the crusty scab that was starting to form on his arm.

"It only helps with minor injuries. It wouldn't do much for a gunshot wound or anything." I looked away from him, my fingers fidgeting with the foil gum wrapper. An awkward silence stretched between us before I spoke again. "Myra's magic had this … compelling effect on me. It was different from any other magic I've tasted. Like it had a mind of its own. It was trying to command me, trying to push me away, but I wouldn't let it. That's never happened to me before, Ryker."

Ryker turned to face me. "Sometimes our emotions can overpower us. You just got caught up in the moment. It happens."

"No, it was more than that. I saw the fear transfixed in her eyes. She was terrified of something I'd done. Do you … think she'll report us?" I flicked the crumpled-up ball of foil across the room.

"Why wouldn't she?" Ryker's voice was beginning to regain its strength, but he spoke the words softly. "We broke into a secured military vault and tried to steal a classified magic item previously used by a drug lord. We need to prepare ourselves for the worst."

The long sigh I exhaled was amplified as it bounced off the concrete walls. My eyes squeezed shut, and I used the back of my hand to rub them and rid myself of the panicked thoughts forming in my mind.

"This doesn't look good for us, Ryker, especially considering our connection to Ozcar and Davian. We withheld important information from the military about Bliss. I made a deal with a known criminal. And we just broke into a secured vault, attempting to steal a dangerous magic item."

"You're right, Zulli. We're screwed … but only if they catch us." He winked at me. "I suggest we keep our minds focused on the mission we set out to finish, because finding out the truth is the only way we're getting out of this. Let's forget about the spatula for now and move on to phase two of my plan." His even tone garnered no hesitation, the confidence of his words igniting a determined spark inside me.

"And what's the second half of this plan?" I asked hesitantly. The first one hadn't gone over so well.

"Operation 'infiltrate your father's lab to steal illegal drugs'. You in?"

Ryker rose to his feet and held out his hand to help me up. "You know I am," I replied. "Let's do this."

16

BEFORE MEETING UP WITH CATILDA to fill her in on the bad news, Ryker and I hurried back to our apartments to change out of our uniforms. While we were there, we shoved whatever we could into travel bags. Once Myra reported the incident, there was no telling what would happen, but there was a one hundred percent chance it wouldn't be good.

Whatever clothes were on the floor next to my bed found their way into my military travel bag. With a furious punch, I pushed them down so they'd fit inside. I struggled to close the zipper, my hand trembling with fear and uncertainty. I sighed as I ran a finger over my name embroidered on the side pocket. *Private Zulli Taracula.*

I joined the military to travel the world and do my part to make it a better place to live, to protect others from people like Davian Grymes. For the last six months, the military had been my home. Would it still be when all this was over? Would Ryker and Kasra still fight alongside me?

Another bag was loaded up with whatever weapons and magic objects I kept stashed in my closet. Just as I was finishing up, Ryker approached behind me. With my back turned toward him, I wiped the tears welling in my eyes before he had a chance to see them.

"Everything okay, Zulli?" He crept closer but respectfully kept his distance.

I turned around and plopped down on the bed, raking my hands through my hair. "No. Everything's not okay, Ryker! Ozcar's going to come after us. Davian already is. And now we have to deal with Myra. I don't want to keep doing this ... to you, to Catilda, to Kasra ..."

Ryker sat down next to me, the dent he made in the mattress causing me to lean into him. He placed his arm around my shoulder. "Trust me, Zulli. Let me help. I'll find a way to fix this. I don't know what Myra is planning, but maybe it'll work to our advantage."

"*Planning?*" I shot up from the bed and filled my lungs with air, taking in a slow, deep breath to calm my racing heart. "Myra is the poster child for the Chitol military. She's likable but fierce, super talented, and has a perfect track record of taking down every one of her targets. The only thing she's *planning*, Ryker, is an all out assault on us to make us pay for our crimes."

"You never know." Ryker stood up and reached into the back pocket of his faded jeans to pull out his phone. "People will surprise you. We've all done things we aren't proud of at some point. Maybe she's trying to figure out what we were up to, see things from our point of view before condemning us."

"You're always way too accepting of people, Ryker. Not everyone is good, even if they act like it." My gaze fell to the floor, my hand rubbing the back of my neck.

"I know what you're thinking, Zulli." He sifted through a few pictures, then returned his phone to his back pocket and adjusted the strap of his duffle bag on his shoulder. "Whether Zavyr is under Davian's influence or not, he's the CEO of a powerful magiceutical company that's saving millions of lives on a daily basis. He may not have been there for you growing up, but he

184

will always be your father whether you like it or not. He will always love you."

My eyes refused to stop blinking, and my head twitched in short, jerking movements. "I don't remember ever telling you anything about my childhood, Ryker."

"You didn't have to. It's obvious by the way you're always trying to prove yourself to him. Now, if you're done packing, we should really hurry up and get out of here in case we have any unexpected visitors."

Ryker lowered his head and closed his eyes. He dug his thumbs into his palms for a quick rub, a slight tremble in his hands as he pictured our destination in his mind. Heat gathered in his magic, and I could hear its steady rhythm as it took its invisible shape into a portal that would bring us back to Harper's Treasure Chest.

With an overstuffed bag on each shoulder, I followed Ryker's outstretched arm and passed through the portal. He stepped in behind me, traveling light with his single bag. We reappeared near the same place we'd left just a few hours ago, in the back parking lot of the Harper's Treasure Chest.

"You sure it's a good idea to be here right now?" Given that I had already destroyed Ryker's career, I didn't want to ruin another's if the military found out Catilda was involved too.

"I already asked her. She wants to see this through. Although I think she also wants to murder me." A teasing smile beamed across his face, and his amber eyes twinkled with laughter.

As if sensing our presence, Catilda burst out the back door, dropping the garbage bag she was dragging behind her, and rushed to greet us.

"What happened?" she asked, her vexing gaze locked directly on Ryker and ignored me. "You were supposed to be back here an hour ago."

"We ran into a little trouble and didn't get the spatula." Ryker's steady voice held no hint of frustration, but rather a strong sense of perseverance that he'd try again. He filled Catilda in on what had happened, and as the story progressed, so did Catilda's anger.

Claws lengthened from her fingertips, but instead of slicing his shirt to shreds, she grabbed it and pulled him in until their noses were touching. "I warned you to take care of my Zulli."

I waved my hand to get her attention. "I'm right here, Catilda. I'm fine."

"No, you're not! Your eyes are all red! Ryker, you made her cry!" She let go of his shirt, giving him a shove backward. Ryker stumbled on his feet to steady his balance.

"Catilda, come on. It's not his fault!" I cried out, slapping a hand to my forehead to hide my embarrassment. Intense heat warmed my cheeks.

Ryker gave me an apologetic look, remorse etched in the dimples on his face for failing me.

"I … I will fix this," he promised. Being so close to Ryker, my keen sense of hearing picked up on his racing pulse. The calm tone of his voice hid his frustration, but whether he was more concerned about upsetting me or failing the mission, I couldn't tell.

Gripping the ends of my hair, I threw my head back and grunted. "Ugh. Can we *please* just put this behind us right now and go inside, figure out what our next move is? We might not have much time before things go from bad to worse."

The two of them agreed to finish their argument later.

"Let me get that trash bag for you," Ryker offered, grabbing the plastic handles of the garbage bag Catilda dropped by the steps. "I'll meet you two inside in a minute."

I followed Catilda to the break room. She snatched a couple bottles of water from the fridge and placed them on the round wooden table. We sat there waiting for Ryker, the tension hanging heavy in the air.

"You were right, hun," Catilda said as she twisted open the cap to take a sip of water. "It's hard to be mad at that guy. I yell at him for putting you in danger and all he does is want to make it right. Then he offers to take out my trash. What an oddly loveable guy." Her childish giggle put a smile on my weary face.

Ryker walked in and took a bottle of water for himself.

"Okay. So we didn't get the spatula. And we still don't have the bonding agent or the blood," I summarized. "What do we do now, Ryker?"

Ryker pulled back, stuttering a few mumbles as if surprised I even wanted his help. The truth was I didn't. Not because I was angry at him. It wasn't because I didn't trust his judgment, but it was because I felt like I was digging him further into his own grave. I wanted to give him a way out, but I knew Ryker wouldn't back down now.

The confusion that clouded his eyes lasted only a moment, then a fire sparked inside him and the gears started churning inside his brain.

"Grestor Island," he said, finishing off his bottle of water and heading toward the fridge for another.

"Grestor Island?" Catilda asked. "The tourist destination? This isn't really the time for a vacation."

Ryker placed the new bottle down on the table, then pulled out a chair to sit beside me. "The city of Estine, to be specific. I had one of my contacts look into something, and he tells me there's an undocumented warehouse there where Zavyr stores a lot of his supplies. It'll be much easier to get inside there to steal the blood and the bonding agent than break into NightFly Technologies."

My arms crossed over my chest, and suspicion oozed from my voice. "Another contact? Where are you finding all these people?"

"I make a lot of friends. Some of them want to help me out every now and then."

I didn't argue it because it was true, although I was still curious who these "friends" of his actually were. Criminals? Undercover agents? Random people he'd come across in a bar restroom? Knowing Ryker, the options were wide open.

187

"Are you positive that what we need will be at this ware-house?" Catilda's hardened gaze could break through stone. She stood from her seat, the golden bangles on her wrists jingling as leaned over the table and glowered at Ryker.

"Yes. But we have to act on this now. The longer we wait, the more we risk losing this opportunity."

Catilda's expression slackened, the sweetness in her voice returning. "Great! I need to go pack a bag."

Ryker and I shot each other a nervous look, but he threw up his palms, indicating he was staying out of this.

"Catilda," I said. "I don't think you should go. This could get really dangerous."

"Nonsense, hun!" She flapped a dismissive hand at me. "I actually have a friend there who owns a magic shop. I want to pick his brain about something. I'll even crash at his place. I promise I'll stay out of your way unless you need me."

My stomach tightened into knots. A curl of apprehension knifed through me. "Fine. But if something happens to us, you run. You can't be involved with us."

"Got it. So, when do we leave?" She flattened out a wrinkle in her pink sundress.

"Well, Zulli and I already have our bags packed. Why don't we take a drive to your place so you can pack while I find a picture of Grestor Island that I can use to transport us there."

Catilda ran off to tell her brother she'd be gone for a while and to close up shop. Then we all piled into her purple coupe and took a twenty minute drive to the Harper household.

Unfortunately, Catilda packing wasn't a quick ten-minute activity. I had to hurry her along, reminding her that she would only be away a day or two and didn't need to bring sixteen bags full of clothes and accessories.

"But these yellow sunglasses don't go with my purple jacket. And these green ones will clash with my red heart necklace!" She held a pair of sunglasses in either hand, weighing them like a scale to decide which to take before I snatched one and tossed it into her purse.

"Come on, Catilda. We don't have time for this," I pleaded, making room for myself on her bed, which was piled high with clothes.

"Fine, fine." She zipped up her luggage case and carried it downstairs to the front door, where Ryker was snapping a picture of Catilda's living room with his phone. The Harpers were always on the go, but as we were inching closer to evening, they'd soon be returning.

"Are we all ready?" Ryker rubbed his hands together, wringing them and massaging his palms with the pads of his thumbs.

"Yup!" Catilda wheeled her suitcase into the entryway next to the vibrantly painted red front door.

Ryker let out a shaky breath, his eyelids fluttering shut like they were too heavy to keep open. With his shoulders sagging, he strained to hold up his hands. They tremored so slightly most wouldn't have noticed. The past few days I had been so focused on getting answers, I hadn't realized how much Ryker had been using his magic to help me find them. He wasn't just tired, he was in pain.

Catilda must have noticed him struggling as well, along with the aching expression that crossed my face, because she jabbed me hard with her elbow.

"Say something," she muttered softly through clenched teeth.

"I can't. We're low on time."

Ryker lowered his hands, catching me and Catilda mid-conversation. "Is something wrong?"

Another sharp elbow struck me, and I rubbed the soreness from my upper arm.

"Uhh ..."

Catilda rolled her eyes and stomped an impatient foot to the ground before speaking. "You see, the thing is, your portals make me feel sick. Every time I go through them, I feel nauseous afterward. I refuse to pass through one again!"

"But I've never actually transported you anywhere." He scratched his chin and peered up at the ceiling. "If you don't want to go, Catilda, it's okay. You don't have to. Zulli and I can handle this."

The spicy scent of cinnamon started to drift through the air.

"Wait!" I reached toward Ryker and grabbed his forearm, pushing it down before he could create a portal. "I know getting to Estine is top priority, but we can't just storm the castle once we get there, right?"

"I'm not sure I'm following, Zulli. That's the very definition of how you always do things."

I looked to Catilda for help, but she had none to offer. "Okay. That's true. But ... we're on a lot of people's radars right now. The military, Ozcar, my dad, Davian ... I know we're in a hurry, but I think it's worth the risk to lay low for a few days until we have a better idea of what's going on. Plus, it gives us extra time to recover and come up with a plan."

"Waiting only increases our risks of someone figuring out what we're up to." Ryker leaned against the front door, tossing his head back and raking his trembling fingers through his hair. "Zulli, what's wrong? Are you having second thoughts about this?"

"No!" The single word flew out of my mouth faster than my brain could think it. My eyes darted back and forth between Ryker and Catilda. "I just, uh ..."

The guilt twisted my stomach into knots, my head pounding from both exhaustion and confusion. The selfish part of me wanted to ignore his pain, focus on getting to the city of Estine as quickly as we could and find a way to save my family. But Ryker had already done so much for me, and he'd continue to push himself beyond his limits unless I put my foot down.

Catilda's lack of a verbal filter came to save the day.

"We all need a break, okay! If you want my help mixing this anti-Bliss drug of yours, I need my beauty sleep. I've been staying up late researching the past few days and taking care of the

190

shop, not to mention, you two can barely even stand on your own two feet. My family has a houseboat docked not too far from here. I say we use it and get to Grestor Island the old-fashioned way. It'll take two days tops with the magic-powered motors."

Ryker caught me glimpsing at his hands, and his cheeks dimpled when he smiled back at me. "Well, it's two against one, so I guess I'm outvoted. But setting out to sea in the evening isn't a good idea. We'll stock up on supplies now and leave bright and early tomorrow morning."

"Great!" She clapped her hands and rubbed them together. "Let's go shopping! I don't want my parents asking any questions when they get back tonight, so I'll drop you guys off at the marina afterward and you can sleep on the boat. It's only about a half hour drive from here."

We shoved our luggage into the back of Catilda's coupe, which happened to only fit four of Catilda's six bags. The rest we had to hold on our laps and cram into the back seat with Ryker.

Catilda slammed her door shut, turning the key to start the engine. Her ancient car wasn't powered by the latest magic and didn't have the fanciest gadgets inside it. But what it did have was a working radio, and it was turned up to full blast as she rolled down the windows and we pulled out of the driveway.

17

RYKER WENT BACK TO THE Harper household bright and early the next morning. He ended up having to drag Catilda out of bed then wait a good hour for her to get ready. We set out later than intended, but we pumped the magic engines full steam ahead, hoping to pick up some lost time. The best thing about magic powered boats? They drove themselves. All three of us got to sit back and relax.

"Where are the cheeseballs?" I asked Catilda as I dug out a bag of what looked like green potato chips. "And what the hell is this?"

She picked through the supplies we'd purchased last night and tossed the cheeseballs over to me.

"Kale chips! Are you familiar with what vegetables are?"

Ryker hooked a finger around one of the brown grocery bags on the counter, his hair wet and rosy skin glistening from his recent shower. "Did you guys get anything practical? Like, I don't know, water?"

"Of course we did!" I glanced warily over at Catilda.

She had a moment of indecision before she answered. "There's a case under the sink because the whole sheet cake Zulli absolutely had to have took up pretty much all the room in the tiny fridge."

Ryker gave us a glorious eye roll and left to catch some sun on the roof deck.

"I don't think he approves of our food choices," I told Catilda.

"Well then, he shouldn't have fallen asleep in the car before we got to the store!" she snapped, unpacking a bottle of vodka from the last of the bags that we'd been too tired to pack away last night. When she couldn't find a place for it, she unscrewed the cap and poured us each a drink instead.

"It's ten in the morning, Catilda."

She smiled, turned to open the refrigerator, and poured a splash of orange juice into our cups. "It's going to be a long few days. Cheers! Drink up, Zulli."

I took my breakfast of vanilla cake and boozy orange juice and joined Ryker on the roof deck. Catilda grabbed an apple and accompanied me.

"So, who's this friend of yours, Catilda? The one who owns the magic shop?" I took my spot on a beach chair. The sea vessel wasn't a luxury yacht and space was limited. It had two cramped bedrooms with the most uncomfortable paper thin mattresses along with a pull out sofa, a kitchen counter about the size of an ironing board, and one bathroom so small that I could sit down on the toilet and take a shower at the same time. The roof deck was the only place all three of us could fit somewhat comfortably.

"Someone I met from a volunteer program I joined a while ago. He has a fascination with herbal medicine. I thought I could pick his brain on a few things. He might know about some plant or something with mind altering effects that could be used to counteract Bliss." Catilda settled herself into the lounge chair, slathering sunscreen onto her pale freckled skin. She slipped on her sunglasses, holding onto her straw hat as her ginger curls flapped wildly in the ocean breeze.

"Don't give him too much information." Ryker leaned forward in his folding chair, eyeing Catilda warily. "The more people who know about what we're doing, the more likely we are to run into someone who will sell us out."

"Don't you worry about me, hun! If I didn't trust him, I wouldn't be asking for his help in the first place."

I was thankful that we had good weather the entire journey, and while I loved Catilda and Ryker, two days at sea were about all I could handle being constantly around them with no place to escape. By the time we reached Grestor Island, Catilda was bouncing off the walls with pent up energy, Ryker's rosy glow had returned to his face brighter than ever, and I wanted to find the nearest bar to order myself some greasy fries and a very strong alcoholic beverage since we finished off the bottle of vodka we had by the end of the first day.

We gathered our things and left the boat docked at one of the marinas.

"Say cheese!" Catilda snapped a photo of us in front of a "Welcome to Estine" tourist sign.

Ryker fit right in with the tourists, with his khaki cargo shorts and loose t-shirt. Catilda was stunning as always with her jean shorts and sparkly tank top. Sadly, I looked like a drunk who'd passed out in someone's bathtub. My hair was a mess, my clothes didn't match, and as much as she wanted to try, I had convinced Catilda there was no amount of makeup that could hide the black bags under my eyes from my inability to sleep on the flattened mattress.

"Here's the address where I'll be." Catilda handed me a business card. "If you need me for anything, hun, just give me a call. Otherwise, you two stay safe. I don't want a repeat of last time." She said the last words with as much malice as her chirpy voice would allow, her piercing stare stabbing Ryker.

I gave her a big hug, then she hopped into a cab and took off to see her friend. When I turned around, I saw Ryker flipping through images on his phone.

"What are you doing?" I asked.

"Trying to find a photo I snapped of a hotel the last time I was here."

He continued to swipe through images while I took in the beautiful scenery around me. The city of Estine was a fishing community at heart but also a tourist attraction, with some of the best beaches in the area. It stayed warm here all year around thanks to a unique combination of raw magic mixing together in the atmosphere, but today it was blistering hot. I decided to lose the leather jacket and began fanning out my t-shirt as the sweat started to soak in. Regretting the heavy jeans, I rolled up the cuffs to let in some air, not caring how ridiculous I looked with my motorcycle boots.

"Why don't we walk there? We can acquaint ourselves with the city." I had a feeling I would be regretting this decision in about fifteen minutes, but the guilt of making Ryker use his magic still lingered.

"Okay. It's about a one mile walk in that direction." Ryker pointed toward a cluster of buildings that sat on top of a giant hill, and we were all the way at the very bottom of it.

I forced a smile to my face that he saw right through. Exhaling a deep breath, I shrugged a bag on each shoulder. Steeling my posture, I readied myself to endure the brutal torture I'd signed myself up for.

We strolled through the busy streets on the main road that ran through the city. The rectangular buildings in Estine were much smaller and more spread out, and although they grew taller as we traveled inland toward the city center, I didn't feel as claustrophobic as I did in Chitol.

Right on cue, about fifteen minutes into our walk, my throat was parched and my stomach rumbling. The blazing afternoon sun beat down on me, searing my skin like a hot iron. A painful cramp was developing in my right leg, and I was constantly adjusting the strap from one of my bags to stop it from cutting into my neck.

"My feet are killing me and I need to shower. How much farther?" The words barely formed on my dry lips.

The smell of something smokey and charred drifted past my nose and sent me into a meat trance. Several tourists were enjoying themselves on the restaurant's patio. Ryker had to step in front of me, blocking me from jumping over the metal fence to devour a woman's meal and guzzle down her water.

"Not far. How about we stop for something to eat? My treat." He surveyed the street around him, paying extra attention to what was behind him. "Let's turn down that street. I bet we'll find a pub or something that sells milkshakes and burgers."

"But that's in the opposite direction of the hotel ..."

Ryker ignored my complaint and swiftened his pace. I struggled to keep up with my two oversized bags that weighed just about as much as I did.

"I can carry one of those for you." He wrapped his hand around the strap before I could even agree. I allowed myself to take advantage of his kindness.

"There are a million places to eat on the main road. I'm fine with just about anything. We don't need to go out of our way, Ryker."

"I know, but we're being followed. This way." Twisting his head, he tilted it in the direction of a narrow alleyway between a restaurant that appeared closed and a gift shop. As we walked further away from the main road, only a few pedestrians traveled along the sidewalks and the sounds of busy chatter and cars died down.

"What? Who's following us?" Terror screeched along my veins, and my already heavy panting became heavier as my heart squeezed in my chest. My natural instinct was to dart around and look then start bolting as fast as I could in the opposite direction.

Rounding the corner into the alley with Ryker, I immediately gagged at the scent of rotting food from the overflowing dumpster. Bile rose in the back of my throat, along with the taste of rancid flesh and decaying vegetables. I rubbed my burning eyes, blinking them rapidly to wash away the sting.

Ryker placed his bag down next to the side of the dumpster that faced away from the street. "I'm not sure who it is, but if they find out where we're staying, they'll no doubt make a scene. It's best we confront them now while we know they're following us. Crouch down and stay here."

Sandwiched in between two brick buildings, there was little else in the alleyway except for a ten-foot concrete wall at the end of it blocking any further advancement or a way to escape. I crouched down beside the dumpster that was shoved up next the staff exit of the restaurant. Empty soda cans clattered and pieces of cardboard fluttered as they were blown across the asphalt. At night, the alleyway would have been completely consumed in darkness, but in the middle of the afternoon, the space was still well lit and much less terrifying.

"Ryker, I'm not going to sit here and watch them attack you."

"*Shh!* Don't yell. I'm gonna draw their attention to me, and when you get the chance, attack them before they figure out you're still here."

Just as he finished his statement, I heard the crunching of shoes stop near the entrance to the alley—two pairs of feet from what I could decipher. Not wanting to risk giving away my location, I pressed up against the warm brick and closed my eyes tight.

My magic took control. Reaching past the smell of garbage, the magical scent of mint and wet paint stuck in my nose. When a male voice spoke, I knew exactly who the two figures were. Jax and Kora. Ozcar Thorne's messengers.

"Where's the green-haired woman?" Jax's squeaky voice echoed in the alley.

"I sent her away. She's not here."

Jax snorted. "Well, that's unfortunate. You left yourself wide open."

A mocking "*aww*" came from Kora, followed by the clicking of her tongue in disappointment.

While Ryker kept them busy with conversation, I carefully unzipped a pouch on one of my bags and pulled out a sponge. Normally, the object was used to absorb poisons and magical toxins, but the spell could absorb any magic, including Jax's sound waves. I ripped off two small pieces and stuffed them into my ears.

"*Devoro.*" It was barely a whisper, but that was all I needed to activate it.

Ryker stepped forward, slowly starting to disappear from my limited view.

"Tell Ozcar he'll get the spatula. We just need some time." Ryker slipped out the knife he kept on his belt, pointing it at Jax.

Daring a quick peek around the corner of the dumpster, I saw Jax crack his knuckles and roll his neck, a gesture that would have been much more intimidating on a man with solid muscle. "A very reputable source of ours informed the boss about your failed attempt at retrieving the spatula. Mr. Thorne sent us here to give you a little extra … encouragement."

A minty stream of magic overtook Ryker's cinnamon scent. With Kora's swift speed, she rammed into him before he could even flinch. The force knocked him into the opposite wall with a loud smack. Fighting the urge to leap from my hiding spot, I clenched my fists and stayed put.

"This is no fun, Jax. I wanted to fight the girl. She needs to pay for ripping out a clump of my hair." Kora ran her hands down her blond ponytail, sighing at the memory.

Her vicious cackle sent shivers down my spine, but the feminine yelp it turned into put a smile on my face. Kora motioned to stomp on Ryker's head, when a portal opened above him and she kicked herself in the ass.

"*Torpens.*" Ryker rolled sideways, and with a downward slicing motion, his knife disappeared through a small portal. She threw up her hands to block her chest, but the sharp edge reappeared to rip right through her thigh. The deep wound oozed thick crimson blood that soaked into her gray workout capris. It dripped down her leg, pooling into her stylish white running shoes.

Kora wailed in distress as she pressed her hand against the wound. She tried to speed off to safety, but the numbing agent released from the knife rendered her leg useless. She backpedaled away from Ryker, stumbling on her dead limb. I pressed myself into the wall, my pulse racing the closer she drew toward me.

Fearing my cover blown, I let my magic ripple through me. My human body turned into a tiny unassuming arachnid. In my spider form, I only had a few minutes before I exhausted my magic, so I had to act quickly. A silky string of webbing shot out toward the ledge of the dumpster, and I climbed my way up. From there, I leapt onto the brick wall to get a complete view of the alleyway.

Jax stood blocking the entrance to the main street, his bald head as shiny as ever in the glistening sun. He took a step back, his smug confidence turning into a worried look pinned onto his pinched face.

Ryker rose to his feet, lunging toward Kora with his knife in hand. With insane speed, she dodged his attack, his portal and the blade missing its mark. As Ryker flew past her, she chopped him across the throat. His neck snapped back, and he collapsed into our pile of duffle bags by the dumpster, his head rattling off the metal siding.

Kora sloppily kicked one of the duffle bags with her numb leg, flinching like an explosive might have been hidden inside. She tilted her head and her expression twisted. While Ryker was regaining his composure, she bent down to examine the duffle bag. Her finger rubbed over the embroidered patch of my name. She quickly swept her hand through the air and looked up at the brick wall, right at me.

My eight segmented legs pushed off the wall, and my feather light body flew toward Kora. Magic exploded out of me as I released my form, transforming back into my human figure. I fell on top of her, claws digging into her arms and fangs piercing the top of her shoulder through her spandex top.

"Get off me!" Kora wiggled under my weight. As I drew on her magic, she grew weaker. The intense vibration of her speed magic slowed to a steady rhythm.

"*Stop!*" Jax's voice bellowed. The magic entwined with it rippled through the air like the rise and fall of a tide, dissolving in my ears. The pieces of sponge absorbed the sound before it could affect me, but Ryker wasn't as lucky. He rolled over onto his side, slapping his hands to his ears and curling up into fetal position.

My fangs ripped out of Kora's skin and I screamed, "Ryker!"

The moment my focus wavered, my grip slackened. Kora tightened her fist and punched upwards against my lower jaw. My teeth clenched together, the pain radiating through my skull. Despite being partially drained of her magic, there was still a forceful power behind her hit. My head snapped back, stars dancing in my vision and blackness creeping in around the edges. The blow caused the sponges stuffed in my ears to fall out. She shoved me off her, and I landed on my ass next to a pile of recycled cardboard boxes.

Reaching for a bullet on my belt, I snatched a green cylinder and tossed it at Kora's chest.

"*Demitto.*" A green substance exploded from the bullet, consuming Kora's body and sticking it to the ground like a glob of sticky caramel beginning to harden. It stretched against her struggles, her screams muffled by the substance covering parts of her face.

"Jax!" she whined.

Jax's footsteps came rushing to help Kora, but before he could reach her, I tackled him to the ground. My clawed fingertips were after the thin t-shirt but raked against his leather jacket instead. Jax pushed his palms into my chest, his gangly frame stronger than it looked. My back bounced hard against the pavement. The world disappeared for a brief moment while the air rushed out of my lungs and I gasped to fill them. With my veins pumping adrenaline from Kora's magic boost, I growled my fury at Jax.

Rising to his feet, Jax stepped to my side as I propped myself up on a knee. Uncontrollable, psychotic laughter surged through him. The magic wrapped in his roar pounded in my brain.

"Let this be a warning. You have one week to retrieve Mr. Thorne's objects."

"*Objects?*" I scraped out through grinding teeth. "We only owe him the spatula."

"Interest. You not only need to hand over the spatula, but Ozcar is now requesting a sample of that special blood used to make Bliss." Jax sauntered over to Kora, who managed to snake an arm through the sticky goo holding her down. She clasped her hand in Jax's, and he yanked against the elastic until the weakening magic snapped and she was free.

Once they had delivered their message, they disappeared out of the shadowy alley. I scrambled toward Ryker, who went from screaming in agonizing pain to a silent comatose sleep curled up next to the brick wall.

"Ryker, wake up!" I jostled him gently, and when that didn't work, I slapped him across the face.

"Zulli? I … I can barely hear you. The ringing …" He blinked wildly, his palms rubbing against his ears.

"Hold on." I found my bag and pulled out the sponge. Tearing off a few pieces, I pressed them into Ryker's ears, as well as my own, and activated the magic. The warmth of the extracted magic burned the tips of my ears, rippling until it dispersed into the air.

"Thanks." Ryker plucked the sponge out of his ears.

"Feeling okay?" I slipped my arm under his and helped him up.

"I'm fine." He rubbed his forehead, a red welt forming on his head.

"Good. Because I'm officially taking you up on that offer to use a portal. Take me to the hotel. I am done with this crap."

18

RYKER ONLY KEPT A FEW important photos in his wallet for quick access. The hotel wasn't one of them. It took him half an hour to sort through about a thousand photos on his phone until he found what he was looking for. With a wave of his hand and a thrum of magic, we appeared right outside the front entrance of the hotel, a swanky downtown hotspot bustling with tourists.

"Um, Ryker? Can we afford to stay here? *Should* we be staying here? It looks awfully crowded." I knew he could afford to live lavishly, seeing as he lived in a condo in one of the most expensive complexes in Chitol, though I'd never questioned where the money actually came from.

"Let me handle it. In this case, the busier it is the better. So far, Ozcar's crew has only attacked us when we're alone. I don't think they'll risk being seen in a public area."

Inside the hotel lobby, a distinct, welcoming floral scent invited my lungs to expand, absorb the blossoming aromas, and relax. It was a type of magic aerosol circulating in the air that many businesses used to make guests feel comfortable, and it was doing a fantastic job. I had to fight the urge to kick up my aching feet and take a nap on one of the large luxurious sofas in the waiting area.

The lobby seemed to expand in infinite directions with no end in sight. It boasted sparkling chandeliers, plush furniture, and equally elegant guests, who glared at me as they passed. One woman cupped a hand over her mouth and nose, making an overly exaggerated gagging noise like a cat hacking up a hairball. I rolled my eyes, then surreptitiously sniffed an armpit to smell how bad my sweat-stained t-shirt really was.

I followed Ryker toward the front desk, a glossy white block of solid marble that was probably worth enough to buy me my own beach house on this island. Behind it was a professionally dressed desk clerk wearing a white button-down blouse under a black blazer and a matching pencil skirt.

"This is ridiculous! I want to speak to your manager!" A pot-bellied man wearing a polished business suit smashed his fist down on the desk.

"I'm sorry, sir. He's not available at the moment, but if—"

The man swatted a hand at her and stormed off.

I commended the woman for her dedication to the job, brushing off the man's outburst and beaming a courteous smile at Ryker as we approached. Ryker's dazzling dimpled cheeks reciprocated the greeting.

"Hello, how can I help you today?" She straightened her spine. Her loose auburn curls were tied back and away from her friendly face but fell in perfect coils that ran down the length of her shoulder blades.

"Hi there ..." Ryker leaned in to read the name tag on her blazer. "Caelia. It seems like you're pretty busy here, but I have a favor to ask you."

"Of course." Her smile never wavered, and she kept her expressive honey eyes trained on Ryker. I took a few steps behind him, embarrassed by my appearance. Ryker didn't fare much better, the hem of his shirt speckled with blood and dirt, but people were usually too captivated by his charming personality to ever notice or care about what he was wearing.

"My friend and I have traveled a very long, exhausting trip to get here." Ryker reached behind him, his hand grabbing my wrist and pulling me in next to him. "We just need a quiet place to stay and unwind for a few days. Preferably alone, in one of the more secluded areas of the hotel if possible. There's some business we need to attend to, and we'd like to remain undisturbed."

The heat rising in my cheeks was like a tea kettle steaming under pressure. I flashed the woman a cheap, plastic smile, doing my best to hide my discomfort.

"I see," the woman said, showing no signs of judgment. "Let me see what I can do."

While she was tapping away on her keyboard, I wiggled out of Ryker's hold and stood awkwardly beside him, my gaze becoming well-acquainted with the granite floor while we waited for an answer.

"I think I have something you'll both enjoy." Caelia's voice softened and dropped an octave, her smooth words sending an anxious shiver down my spine. "The suite is on its own floor. You'll have the entire place to yourselves. No one will bother you. May I have your I.D. for the reservation?"

"That sounds perfect, Caelia! Thank you." He pulled out his wallet and handed over a credit card. Matching her low voice, he added, "We're actually trying to keep our visit here a secret. Do you think you could put the reservation under a different name than what's on the card? And refrain from charging it until we leave?"

My chest caved, my chin disappearing into my neck. I gulped, tugging on the collar of my t-shirt like it was strangling me.

"Oh. Of course. Not a problem. Here's your key card, and I hope you don't mind, but I had the kitchen send up a special gift for the both of you. On the house. Enjoy yourselves … and your stay!"

Ryker slipped the card off the counter, smiling with more enthusiasm than he should have, given the woman's words.

Bags in hand, we rode the elevator up to the twentieth floor. The hallway was quiet, undisturbed by the hordes of guests we had just left behind in the lobby. At the very end of the hallway was a single door, the only room on the floor, just as the woman at the front desk had promised. Ryker swiped the keycard and the door clicked open.

"Ryker, what were you thinking?" I dropped my bags next to the entryway bench and slapped Ryker on the chest.

"I'm not sure I'm following …" He adjusted the strap on his shoulder and rubbed his chest with his palm.

I massaged my temples, exhaustion slowly consuming me. I sucked in a lungful of air and let my chest expand. Then I sharply exhaled my anger, letting it go in one invigorating breath. Speaking in a loud but concerning voice, I replied, "That woman thinks I'm your mistress!"

Ryker looked me straight in the eye, tilting his head slightly before abruptly letting out a laugh. When I didn't respond with equal enthusiasm, his expression flatlined. "Oh. You were serious. Why would you think that?"

"Uh, because you told her we wanted to be alone. Undisturbed. That no one could know we were here. You asked her to put the reservation under a fake name and to hide the charge. Do I need to keep explaining?"

"You're overreacting, Zulli. I told her you were my friend and we needed some privacy. The fewer people we come across, the less likely we'll bump into one of Ozcar's or Davien's men." Ryker turned around, leaving the walled off entryway that led into the main living area of the suite. His bag slid off his shoulder and dropped to the carpeted floor with a soft thud.

Dominating the living room was a white leather sectional decorated with rose petals and deep red throw pillows shaped like hearts. Opposite the couch was a cozy fireplace inlaid with a rustic stone facade, and lining the entire far wall was lined with windows that opened up into a wrap-around balcony overseeing the beautiful sunset along the coast. A small kitchenette was nestled in the corner.

Ryker darted into the bedroom, staring dumbfounded at the canopy bed. Its sheer white curtains flowed gracefully down to the floor and each corner tied back to a post. Placed at the foot of the bed was a set of towels shaped into two swans, their necks forming a heart. Beside them was a box of chocolates and a bucket stand with a bottle of champagne chilling in it.

I stepped up next to him, hands firmly on my hips, and watched as Ryker's jaw hit the floor. "Yeah. You get it now? We're in the honeymoon suite."

"Oh ..." Embarrassment consumed Ryker's face like a bright red balloon ready to burst, and his dark brown eyes pleaded with me for forgiveness.

My tension relaxed into a warm smile, and I slapped a hand on Ryker's shoulder. Sometimes, his ignorance of what was going on around him was frustrating, but I knew he never did it on purpose. "What's done is done. I guess it worked, didn't it? We got a room and we got our privacy. Now, if you don't mind, I'm going to take advantage of these amenities and enjoy a long hot soak in that fancy jetted bathtub I see in the bathroom. How about you make it up to me by finding something to eat? This bottle of champagne and box of chocolates won't hold me for long."

"You got it, Zulli. A five star meal for the lovely lady coming right up!"

I frowned at him.

"Right. Be right back." He left the bedroom, a blast of spicy scented heat making my nose twitch as he disappeared.

I grabbed one of the swan towels by the neck and made my way to the ensuite. Peeling off my sweaty clothes, they dropped down on the black and white marble floor with a heavy splat beside the tub. After a few minutes of fiddling with the buttons on a remote, a forest soundscape of chirping birds began playing through the built-in speakers above, and a rumble came from the jets submerged in the bubbling water. Steam rose in thick tendrils, creating a dense cloud of fog in the room that coated the mirror and window.

Satisfied with my achievement, I dipped a toe into the tub, nestled myself in a corner seat, and submerged myself, vowing to never leave the spot. Since I had left my childhood home and was on my own, the luxury of day spas wasn't an option for me. In fact, I didn't even have a bathtub in my apartment.

My eyes fluttered, barely able to stay open, until I startled myself awake by accidentally nudging a small silver tray with my elbow. I picked up one of the marble-sized colorful balls of packed powder and gave it a sniff—an invigorating smell of lemon and chamomile that warmed my insides. A word was scratched into it.

"*Dirimo.*" I tossed in the magic bath bomb and watched as a rainbow of glittery dust dissolved into the water. The smell erupted in the air like a stress-relief volcano.

My troubles drifted away, my senses lost to tranquility. I closed my eyes and tossed my head back, letting out a frazzled moan that melted all my tension away with it. Gliding down the side of the tub until my chin hit the blanket of foaming bubbles, I kicked out my feet and let the pressurized jets knead the stiff aching muscles in my soles. The pleasurable experience inflated my insides with happiness, the heaviness of my limbs vanishing and replaced with a weightless ecstasy. My breathing slowed, the deep exhales leaving my pursed lips in a gentle whistle.

"Is this helping?"

I yanked my foot back so fast I almost kneed myself in the jaw. My butt slipped off the seat, and my head completely submerged under the water. When I surfaced, I snorted out the water that had found its way up my nose and ran my hands through my short hair to stop it from dripping into my eyes. Through the steamy haze, Ryker looked like a ghostly apparition.

"W-what the hell are you doing, Ryker? Get out of the tub!" My heart was pounding so fast I felt dizzy. I hugged my arms across my chest and crossed my legs, thankful for the smoke screen and the colorful foaming bubbles that hid anything Ryker might have otherwise seen.

"You said your feet were hurting earlier. I thought I could help relieve some tension."

"You can't be in here, Ryker!" My voice was a high-pitched squeal, a nervous and frightened wreck. My fingertips dug deeper into my shoulders, my legs squeezing tighter together.

"What? It's not like I haven't seen you in your underwear before." He shifted his position, the water sloshing as he revealed his bare shoulders and part of his chest. The rest of his body was concealed by bubbles. I had only hoped he was still wearing something on his bottom half.

"A bathing suit is *not* underwear!" I snapped at him. "Besides I'm … I'm not …"

I choked on the words but Ryker easily figured it out. His eyes snapped shut, and, even though he could no longer see me, he turned his gaze away. "I'm sorry. I didn't realize …"

"Most people don't bathe with their clothes on, you know." With my cat-like reflexes, I swiped my sweaty t-shirt from next to the tub.

"Yeah, but … it's hot tub." Ryker tried desperately to explain himself.

"We're not at some party. We're in a private bathroom. It's not the same." I slipped on the t-shirt as quickly as I could, ensuring all the necessary parts were covered. Thankfully it was black, covering all the necessary parts, but it was also thin and wet, molding to my body like a second skin.

"I'm … I'm good now," I said, sinking back into the boiling water and keeping my arms crossed over my chest. I would have preferred to grab a towel and leave, but I was afraid my legs might fail me trying to get out of the tub.

Ryker cautiously blinked open his eyes, making certain that I wasn't going to gouge them out with my claws.

My muscles went from pliant rubber to hardened steel in a fraction of a second. I clenched my abs so tight there was no room for my lungs to expand. We both sat there in awkward silence, listening to the gurgling of the jets pounding out water and the pleasant sound of birds chirping through the music playing from the speakers.

"Aren't you going to leave?" I finally asked him.

"I don't see why I have to. You're clothed now."

I threw my head back and let out a tired, somewhat maniacal laugh. "Ryker, you are probably one of the smartest people I know. Aside from Catilda. But sometimes your ignorance just blows my mind."

I was about to command a second time that he leave when Ryker's face sagged, his shoulders hunched, and his heavy gaze fixated on the bubbles underneath his chin. The steam from the hot water blemished his skin. Even though he refused to look at me, I searched for the beauty and joy behind his amber eyes, but all I could sense was sadness and pain. He scratched his fingertips on his scalp, the water trickling down his face giving the illusion of tears.

"What's wrong?" I asked, cracking my neck and kneading a tight knot near my shoulder.

"Nothing important." He finally looked up at me, his brittle grin betraying his words. "Is your neck hurting you?" He reached out his hands toward me, water splashing as he did. I immediately jumped back, shielding him with my shoulder.

"Please? Let me help?" he pleaded.

The realization hit me like a frying pan across the head. This entire time, Ryker had only wanted to help me, yet up until now, he must have felt like he hadn't accomplished much of anything. He'd showed up after that man attacked me at Catilda's shop. He had failed to protect me against Ozcar and my dad when he'd wiped my memory, and we'd dropped the ball once again when we'd slipped up trying to acquire the spatula from the vault. I never once blamed him for any of it, but it was in his nature to blame himself when he felt helpless and couldn't follow through with his promises.

"Fine, you can help. Keep it above the shoulders, though, got it?"

He waded over next to me, lifting his hands out of the water, and began to knead the lump right above my shoulder blade. His wet fingertips had a smooth finesse, a precise pressure that was both sturdy but gentle. The slow, steady circular movements were like a lullaby singing me to sleep, washing away the tension between us as I leaned into the pressure, drawn in by the tenderness of his touch.

He hit a tender spot and I winced.

"Sorry." He paused for a moment until I recovered, then continued on a different spot.

The words came out of my mouth before I even realized I'd said them. "No, Ryker. I'm sorry."

The heaviness that had weighed me down for the past few days was let out in a whirlwind of relief. I hated myself for dragging him into my mess, and I realized that, no matter how much he appreciated me, a double batch of snickerdoodle cookies would never come close enough to returning his friendship.

"Sorry? For what?" Ryker removed his hands from my neck and sat next to me, his bare shoulder brushing up against mine. His gaze fixated on me, ears listening studiously to my next words.

"I'm sorry for everything. Back at the shop when I snapped at you, I know you were just concerned for me. I pushed you away because I was scared about what would happen if you stayed. But you didn't walk away, and I'm selfishly grateful that you stuck it out. I never properly thanked you for everything you do for me. So ... I'm sorry, and I promise it won't happen again. Forgive me?"

He didn't offer an answer, but when his face relaxed, I let out the breath I was holding. There was a faint outline of wrinkles around his eyes—eyes that sparkled again despite the emptiness I had seen in them earlier. The corners of his mouth slipped into a grin.

"So, is that a yes? You forgive me?"

Ryker leaned in, his lips, soft and light, brushing against my cheek. If it weren't for the wet puckering sound it gave, I would have thought I was imagining things.

My fingers ran down the side of my face, stopping on the area where he'd kissed me. Blood rushed from my brain, my thoughts a jumbled mess of indescribable static. Inside my chest my heart thumped sharply, a tingling sensation traveling through my veins.

"Zulli, you have nothing to be sorry for. Your actions speak louder than words. All this walking everywhere so I don't have to use my portals, the boat trip, and I'll never forget all those times you baked me cookies. Twenty two in fact."

"You're keeping track?" I blinked at him.

He shrugged. "I was wondering how long it would take until you just accepted the fact that I never wanted anything in return for helping you out. But you never did. Zulli, you don't give yourself enough credit. You're an amazing, sometimes stubborn, talented woman. And you always challenge me. Do you realize how aggravating it is when everyone always agrees with you and praises every little thing you do?"

An unexpected snort came out of my nose. I tried not to laugh at him, but he smiled and chuckled with me.

"Catilda disagrees with you all the time."

"Arguing and challenging are two very different things. I'm surprised she hasn't killed me yet." He wiped away a trail of water that dripped from my hair and down my cheek.

"Thanks for saying that, Ryker. It means a lot. Even if you act the same way toward every pretty girl who talks to you." I smirked at him.

212

"Not true!" He scratched his head and peered up at the ceiling like he was second guessing himself. "I'm extra nice to you."

"Ryker, you unknowingly flirt with everyone and feel the need to take care of every person who asks for help." I splashed him in the face with a flick of my hand.

Our smiles entwined, expressions softened. Something sparkled in his magnetic amber eyes, drawing me in with desire. The affectionate smile that crept up his lips wasn't lascivious, but gentle and full of fascination as he traced a line on my face with his fingertips.

He brushed away a couple strands of hair on my forehead, then ran his fingers across the shaved side of my head, cradling the back of my neck. Every hair on my scalp stood to attention, every skin cell tingled, every neuron fired. The room around me vanished and all I could focus on was Ryker.

My heart thumped faster in my chest, and an overwhelming urge fluttered in my stomach to pull him closer, to feel the warmth of his skin brush up against mine, to rake my fingers through his short hair.

He reached for my hand. Our fingers laced together and water cascaded like a waterfall as he lifted them to his lips. Another gentle kiss on my palm, and a sugary syrup of desire slid through my bones. I let a girlish giggle escape my mouth. He made his way up my arm, kissing the delicate skin on the inside of my wrist, the tiny ticklish hairs on my forearm, all the way up to my shoulder, stopping at the base of my neck. With every touch of his lips, my body pulsed with a slow, gentle pang.

Suddenly, Ryker stopped, his chin resting on my collarbone and his warm, heavy breath whispering in my ear. "Zulli? Did you put something in the water earlier?"

"Huh?" It took a moment for my brain to process his words.

"The silver tray. There's something missing."

"Oh. I threw in one of the magic bath bombs. It smelled really nice."

Ryker's grip let go as he swiped one of the remaining scented balls from the tray. His steady breath turned chaotic and rapid. "Zulli, that wasn't a normal bath bomb." He pulled away from me, amber eyes locked on mine. "We're in the honeymoon suite. There was definitely a little extra, um, magic in that bath bomb. You can't feel it?"

I shied away from him, and a wave of nauseous embarrassment stabbed through me. My mouth went dry, my throat tight.

Ryker reached to caress my face, stroking the pad of his thumb across my cheek. "What have I done? I can't do this to you." He squeezed his eyes shut to avoid looking at me and let out a sigh. "I still meant every word I said, Zulli. You are amazing, but I want you to know I would never take advantage of you."

He followed up his words with a squeeze of my hand. Water fell from him in sheets as he stood up, his plaid boxers covering any unmentionables, and grabbed a rolled up towel from a nearby shelf on the wall. After drying off his arms and chest, he then ruffled the towel through his hair and stepped over the ledge of the tub. Wrapping the towel around his waist, his wet feet slapped in hurried footsteps as he left the bathroom.

19

---◈---

EVEN THOUGH I HADN'T ACTUALLY gotten around to washing myself, there was a refreshing lemon scent infused into my shriveled up skin and a glossy shine that gave it a healthy glow thanks to the magic bath bomb. After thoroughly drying myself off, I wrapped the bath towel tightly around my chest and kept it tight under my armpits.

I paced around the damp bathroom for at least a half hour, the steam dissipating and a slippery mist coating the tile floor. I gnawed on my fingernails, the other hand furiously scratching the back of my neck until it burned from rawness. How could I face Ryker after ... *that*?

A rumble in my empty stomach gave me the extra encouragement I needed to steel my nerves. My hand tightened around the door handle and twisted. With a single prying eye I peeked through a tiny crack into the bedroom. Ryker was nowhere to be found, and the door that led into the living room was shut.

My two duffle bags were placed on the mattress, courtesy of Ryker. One bag was full of clothes, while the other was stuffed with whatever weapons, first aid, and other useful things I'd had time to gather in my apartment. My shaking hands rifled through the clothes until I settled on a comfortable pair of sweats decorated with cat paws and a lightweight matching tank top—a birthday gift last year from Catilda.

I removed my phone from the front pouch of my supply bag, a crumpled-up piece of paper falling out onto the bed along with it. Grabbing both in my hand, I inhaled a few deep breaths and thrust open the bedroom door with my chin up and chest out.

"*Oww.*" The door jarred to a stop, and Ryker stood in front of me, wincing and pinching the bridge of his nose.

"Ryker! You weren't spying on me, were you?" My hand reached for his and pulled it away to assess the damage. The simple gesture of our hands touching sent a tingle through my fingertips.

"Of course not! I was just about to knock on the door to see if you were ready for dinner. I placed an order earlier and just picked it up."

Looking past him, I noticed a small glass table over by the kitchenette. Two empty wine glasses were set at each seat, gold-rimmed plates beside them. Taking up most of the table top was a cardboard pizza box, the contents of which filled the room with a cheesy aroma.

"I know it's a little fancy for pizza, but that's all the dinnerware I could find in the cabinet." Having recovered from his nose being thwacked, Ryker wandered over to the table and pulled out a seat. He held out a hand for me to sit.

A part of me wanted to bark out some condescending remark, telling him he didn't need to be all chivalrous and that I was fully capable of sitting down in a chair myself, but I reminded myself to be more appreciative of all the things he did, big or small.

"Thanks, Ryker. This smells absolutely delicious." Greasy, cheesy goodness pleased my nose, a harmony of scents hitting every perfect note.

"You didn't actually drink that whole bottle of champagne, did you?"

I shook my head.

216

"Good. I'll go grab it."

While he stepped away, I glanced at my phone, the screen showing two missed calls from Brodin and thirty-two text messages along with a few voicemails from Kasra, ranging from a simple "*Just want to make sure you're okay,*" to "*Where the hell are you? I'm getting worried! Call me ASAP!*"

I fired off a quick text to her, saying everything was fine and that I just needed some time alone to deal with everything that had happened recently.

I skimmed my emails and did a quick search on my phone for any news, but there was nothing about our break into the vault. None of Kasra's messages hinted at anything wrong, either. Did Myra really not report us? Could we have finally caught a break?

"I couldn't find anything, either." Ryker returned with a chilled bottle in his hands, popping the cork and pouring the bubbling liquid into my glass. "I wish I knew what she was up to."

"Yeah, me too. I'm anxious and relieved at the same time. I wish she'd just make her move already." I took a long swig from the glass, then flipped open the pizza box. My eyes began to swell with happy tears.

"I knew you'd like it! Not many places cater to shifters. But this restaurant was apparently owned by one. I figured you'd take anchovy, black fly, earthworm pizza over burgers any day."

I could have dove across the table and kissed him right there. Instead, I removed a meaty slice, the stringy cheese stretching with creamy gooeyness. The taste overwhelmed my senses—the crunchy texture of the baked black flies, saltiness of the tender fish that melted on my tongue, and a surprisingly sweet aftertaste of earthworms. I bounced uncontrollably in my seat, overjoyed.

Ryker swiped a slice from his half, boring plain cheese, and placed it on his plate. "Is that the list of names?" he asked, staring at the crumpled-up paper next to my phone.

"Yeah, my father's—or maybe Davian's—test subjects. I think we should warn them about what's going on." I flattened out the parchment, scanning the list of printed names from top to bottom, most of them smudged from water damage but still legible.

"Too risky, Zulli. Besides, what are we going to tell them? Their potentially life-saving treatment could really be brainwashing them? Their memories could easily be erased again with Bliss, anyway. It doesn't matter what we tell them."

My gaze rested on the last name in the list, the only one handwritten in pen like it was added as an afterthought. The letters were beyond recognition except for the first and last initials. "Who do you think this is?" I handed the paper over to Ryker.

He hummed to himself for a moment, simultaneously chewing on a bite of pizza. "The initials are both 'T'. I can't read the rest. 'T-O' maybe? 'T-A'? No, it kinda looks like 'T-E.'" He shook his head at me and handed back the paper. "Sorry, I got nothing."

I folded the paper back up and placed my phone on top of it. "So, what's your evil genius plan for tomorrow? Did your contact give you a layout of this warehouse? We can't exactly just go knocking on the front door and ask, 'Pretty please can we have a sample of that special blood you're using to cook up drugs'?"

Ryker slipped me a mischievous grin, his lip turning up on one side and a wrinkle forming between his brow. "Actually, we can."

"I was just kidding."

"I know. But my source tells me that the people working at this warehouse are just grunt workers. They know the Taracula name, but they know nothing about the hierarchy of the business. If you show up, flaunting your name and demanding to be shown around, we won't need to sneak in and risk getting caught."

I leaned back in my chair, my belly overstuffed with pizza, and cautiously watched Ryker on the other side of me. "Who is this contact of yours, anyway? Someone on the inside?"

"You could say that," Ryker answered with a slight mysterious waver in his voice. "He's been approached by Zavyr himself once before. He's come through with valuable intel in the past, so I trust his judgment."

"Okay," I responded hesitantly. "Well, I trust you. And if you trust this contact of yours, then I'm in."

"Great. Let's head over in the morning, scope out the place first. If everything looks clear, we'll set the plan in motion by afternoon. I can play your faithful bodyguard and transporter, and we'll say we're there to check in on quality control and progress of shipments before they're sent out. I promise it'll work."

I nodded in confirmation, then rose from my seat to clean up our dirty plates while Ryker found a sponge to wipe the table.

A jaw-cracking yawn popped my ears, and I eyed the bedroom, realizing there was only one bed in the suite.

"Take the bed, Zulli. I'm fine with the couch."

"Really? Sleeping on a bed of nails looks more comfortable than *that* thing. Maybe we can call up the front desk and ask them to send up a cot or something."

"To the honeymoon suite?" Sarcasm dripped from his words. "I'm sure that'll go over well. Don't worry about it, Zulli. If I'm tired enough, I can sleep almost anywhere."

He let out a loud yawn himself, slumping over to an upholstered armchair in the living room where he put his bag. Digging through it, he pulled out a pair of plaid pajama bottoms and a faded t-shirt, the fabric worn so thin that light actually passed through it.

I left Ryker a couple of pillows and a spare blanket I found in a closet then dove face first into the monstrous mattress in the exquisite bedroom. The silky sheets were like creamy butter gliding against my skin, the scent of lavender inviting sweet dreams. After tossing about ten oversized throw pillows onto the floor, I snuggled up under the plush comforter embroidered with scarlet flowers.

Closing my eyes, I wished for sleep, but despite how exhausted I was, it never came. For two hours, I lay there trying to quiet my racing thoughts. I had never called Brodin back. Kasra had the right to know what was going on, but it wasn't something I wanted to explain over the phone. After we'd got everything we needed from the warehouse, I'd tell her everything.

In the quiet of the bedroom, I could hear my own pulse racing, my heart rapidly beating in my chest as all the worst possible scenarios played out in my head. What if Ryker's intel was wrong? What if we walked right into a trap?

I flung the comforter off me, left the bedroom, and silently made my way to the kitchenette to fill up a glass of water from the sink. On my way back, I stole a glance at Ryker. One arm hung off the side of the sectional, the other stretched out above him. The pillow I left him was on the floor, his head squished into the leather cushion. His tired eyes were wide open, staring right at me.

"Can't sleep either?" I asked him.

"Nope."

He pulled himself up from his awkward sleeping position, rubbing his neck and wincing. He threw his head back and let out an exhausted sigh.

"Come on, Ryker. Get up." I tugged on his hand and pulled him to his feet.

"What are you doing?" He dragged his feet behind me, my hand still clasped in his as I led him into the bedroom, then I shoved his butt down onto the mattress.

"I can't take the bed, Zulli. I swear, I'm fine on the couch." His kind words contradicted his fingers, which were smoothing out the silky sheets.

"I never said you could have the *whole* bed." Reaching for the throw pillows I had tossed on the floor, I began building a wall right down the middle of the bed. "This bed is huge. You stay on that side, I'll stay on this side."

"You sure?" He laughed at my childish gesture, then dug the heel of his hands into his eyes and rubbed them.

"No sense in me hogging the whole thing. Good night, Ryker."

"Night, Zulli."

Within about ten minutes, soft snores were coming from the other side of the bed. A throw pillow came tumbling down on my chest as Ryker tossed in his sleep. I gripped it by the corner, leaning over the pillow wall, aiming to hit Ryker across the head with it. I stopped when I saw him hugging his pillow, a peaceful smile embellishing his rosy face. The vulnerability of his presence, his loose limbs, his chest rising and falling with a soothing rhythm sent my heart aching with delight.

My hand ran down my cheek where Ryker had kissed me. Pushing past the initial shock, I realized his affection had made me feel strong and confident, like I could do anything as long as Ryker was by my side. I yearned again for the fragile touch of his fingertips stroking my skin and to have him tell me that everything would be okay.

When he tossed again, his arm went flying in an arc above him, smacking me right across the face.

My fingertips massaged the stinging skin from Ryker's slap. "Not quite the touch I had in mind, jackass," I muttered softly to myself.

With that, I rolled over onto my side and shrugged the covers up to my shoulders. I didn't know exactly when I fell asleep, but when the rising sun shining through the bedroom window woke me up the next morning, Ryker was gone.

Basking in the sun's radiance, I lay in bed for a few minutes, knowing I might never experience such serenity ever again. When I left the comfort of the bed, I searched through my duffle bag for something halfway decent to wear.

Unfortunately, playing dress up wasn't my style, and I hadn't exactly planned my outfits when I was frantically shoving whatever I could find into my bag. The black skinny jeans had a few rips, and they weren't the fashionable kind you'd pay extra for. The wrinkled white t-shirt was fitted but bunched up under the red plaid vest I zipped it up over it. I polished off the look with my bullet belt around my waist and said goodbye to the prestigious bedroom and all its luxuries.

Something was sizzling in a frying pan, and a thin layer of smoke filled the living room. "Morning!" Ryker called out through the haze.

I fanned my hand in front of me. "What are you doing?"

He held out a plate of burnt toast and dry scrambled eggs, their grayish color unappetizing. "Making you breakfast. Or at least trying to." Before I could take the plate, he retracted his hand and dumped the food in the trash. "On second thought, let's just grab something along the way."

I waited for Ryker by the door while he finished getting ready. It was supposed to be quite a hot day, and the poor guy was going to die from heat stroke in his entirely black outfit. His tapered jeans rested perfectly on his boots. A knife hung from a holster on his hip. He nailed the look of the unassuming bodyguard as he shrugged on his stylish shirt jacket over his black, collarless pullover.

"All you're missing is a pair of mirror-coated aviators." I laughed at him. Then he pulled out a pair of metal-rimmed sunglasses from his pocket and put them on, my face reflecting in the shiny lenses.

"Ladies first." He opened the hotel room door and stepped aside to let me pass.

He led me to the elevator, and when it pinged open, we both walked in together. My lips parted in an innocent grin as Ryker stood next to me, his shoulder brushing mine. I couldn't be certain what the future held for us, but I was glad it included Ryker.

20

---◈---

RYKER AND I POSITIONED OURSELVES on the roof of the storage facility adjacent to the warehouse entrance. The late morning sun was blazing down on us and would only get hotter as the day progressed. Ryker had taken off his jacket and laid it beside him while I guzzled my fourth bottle of water that we'd bought from the convenience store we'd stopped at along the way. Sweat was soaking into my white t-shirt and rolling down my forehead like a melted ice pop. I could only imagine the first impression I'd be making as the daughter of Zavyr Taracula.

"It's been two hours and we haven't seen a single person come in or out of the building. I'm roasting like a potato out here. How much longer?" I took a sip of water and ripped open my third granola bar since we'd arrived.

"It's almost lunch time. Let's give it a little longer, then we'll head in." Ryker leaned over the edge of the building as if something had piqued his interest, but no one was there.

The flat, featureless warehouse was constructed of corrugated steel, with a few loading docks to one side. Surrounding the premises of five buildings was a rusty chain link fence with a huge steel gate at the entrance of the industrial park. Apart from the few parked vehicles scattered around, the warehouse did in fact look abandoned. Not a single person so much as passed by a window or went outside for a smoke break, but I could just about make out the faintest of lights on inside.

We waited in silence for another hour before Ryker made his decision. "Let's do this."

After tossing our trash, Ryker shrugged on his shirt jacket and I zipped up my plaid vest over my sweaty shirt. I ran my fingers through my hair in an attempt to smooth it out. He opened a portal and we walked off the roof right to the side entrance of the warehouse.

"How do I look?" I asked him, almost certain it wasn't great.

He studied me for a moment, sweeping a finger across my forehead to brush a few short rogue hairs out of my face. "You look like the daughter of Zavyr Taracula."

"Is that supposed to be a compliment?" I tugged down on my vest and rolled my shoulders back.

"You look beautiful as always, Zulli."

If my cheeks weren't already radiating from the blistering sun, I would have flushed.

Ryker removed his sunglasses and stood a few feet behind me, clasping his hands together in front of him. The entrance was a simple frosted glass door with a push bar, but there was a potential roadblock.

"Ryker, there's a keypad. I don't know the code to open the door."

He scratched his chin thoughtfully, the gears inside his brain pumping full steam ahead.

"Maybe it's my dad's birthday." My shaking fingers pressed the buttons and the light flashed red. I then tried a few more combinations—my birthday, both my brothers', and even my mom's. None of them gave us the green light to enter.

Ryker stepped beside me. "Let me try something." He swiftly punched in the numbers, and the door clicked open.

"How the hell …" My jaw dropped and my eyes drooped.

224

"You're thinking too personally. None of the employees here are going to remember your dad's birthday. I tried the NightFly Technologies phone number for the shipping department, one that the employees would likely need to call all the time. That did the trick."

"So much for security," I griped, but I couldn't complain because it worked to our advantage.

Inside, a cold blast of arctic air instantly cooled down my baked skin. There was no lobby, just a hallway with a set of double doors at the end that led straight into what I assumed was the main warehouse. Getting into character, I straightened my spine so stiff it cracked. I thrust my chin out and held my head up high, arms hanging loosely at my sides.

I kept my gaze straight ahead like I knew exactly why I was there and what I had come to do. My swagger could have used a little help from Kasra, feeling more like an overexaggerated catwalk down the runway as opposed to the purposeful, confident stride I was aiming for.

With an arrogant shove, my hands pushed open the double doors like I owned the building, because, as far as all these people knew, I did.

A cacophony of noises hit my ears, and I instantly knew that Ryker's intel checked out. Busy employees, some wearing lab coats and others dressed casually in jeans and tees, were walking up and down the aisles, clipboards in hand. Large, steel support beams shot up toward the ceiling, at least two stories high. Forklifts zoomed by, transporting large barrels and crates either to the sturdy metal shelving units or to one of the loading docks. Bellowing voices echoed in the cavernous space, the sound of machines beeping and laboring along with it.

"Who are you?" A disgruntled man questioned me. His skeptical face was face wrinkled, weathered, and worn. "You new or something?"

"Uh—" All my confidence rushed out of me.

Ryker took a step beside me. He wasn't very tall, but when he leaned in, the man cowered under his shadow. "How dare you speak to Ms. Taracula that way!"

The man's demeanor completely transformed. He bowed to me like I was some sort of god, apologizing profusely for his rudeness. "I'm so, so sorry, Ms. Taracula. I didn't know anyone was coming today. I'll go get Dr. Keller and let her know you have arrived."

He scampered off in a hurry, sneakers squeaking against the concrete floor. Ryker stood next to me as I nervously tapped my foot while waiting for Dr. Keller to find us.

"I hope this Dr. Keller is as clueless as her employees are." I watched as a young female struggled with her hardhat, trying to get her ponytail to fit properly underneath it.

"Just … channel your inner Kasra and you'll be fine." I snorted at Ryker's remark. Kasra was always the one who did all the talking and mingling on our missions, and she was damn good at it too. I wished I had paid more attention to some of her tricks.

A few minutes later, a female lab technician emerged from an aisle and shuffled over to where Ryker and I were standing. Her long blond ponytail was swaying back and forth behind her, a pair of headphones resting around her neck on top of her white lab coat. Her high heels clicked on the concrete floor, her stride showing no signs of intimidation.

"Ms. Taracula! It's so nice to meet you." She clasped my hand firmly in both of hers and gently shook it. "I'm Dr. Kimbly Keller. I'm responsible for managing this facility, making sure the product is stored, handled, and shipped properly. I apologize for Jaymes. I'm not sure anyone here has ever met a member of the Taracula family. Even I have only met your father once. We didn't know you were coming today."

"It's—" Ryker coughed behind me, and I was reminded to put myself in Kasra's shoes. "It's unacceptable! I have never been treated with such disrespect in my life!"

"Of course, Ms. Taracula. I'll terminate him immediately."
The woman gave an affirmative nod, and I tried not to fight it
back. What happened to employees who were no longer welcome at secret facilities? Did being terminated mean the man
would be killed or simply fired from his job? It wasn't my intention to do either.

"Thank you, Dr. Keller."

"Please, call me Kimbly. That is, if you're okay with it." A
smile too big for her face accentuated her high cheekbones.

"Fine. Kimbly, I am here with my transporter and personal
bodyguard ..." I paused, realizing I couldn't use Ryker's real
name. "... Bob. My visit is unannounced because I want to see
how things are really run here on a day-to-day basis. Managers
tend to clean up when they know I'm on my way."

Dr. Keller glanced over my shoulder with a suspicious glare
at the man she now knew as Bob. Ryker kept his face carved in
stone, his only movement an occasional blink.

Kimbly shot me a forced smile. "Of course, Ms. Taracula. It
would be my pleasure to show you around. Right this way."

The second she turned away my heart stopped beating and I
held in a breath. She had a black crosshair tattoo etched on the
nape of her neck.

I followed, but slowed my pace to speak with Ryker. "Her
neck ..." I whispered to him.

"Yeah. A member of the Black Mark."

The thought sunk deep into my brain. Was my father aware
of this? One way or another, her presence in this facility could
only mean trouble, and I was certain Davian Grymes had something to do with it.

"These pallets here are all fresh batches of Nisotractin," Dr.
Keller informed. When a dumbfounded look crossed my face,
she explained. "It's the magic drug that helps cure autoimmune
diseases. It recalibrates the immune system so that the disease no
longer attacks healthy cells. It's one of our most popular drugs

…" She raised an eyebrow at me, and I simply waved a hand for her to move on.

The shelving was stacked high to the ceiling, full of packaged crates, barrels, and other equipment ready to be shipped. A horn honked at me from behind.

"Out of my way!" An employee whizzed by steering a pallet jack, and I had to jump out of the way to avoid getting run over. I glowered at Kimbly, ready to whip her with a nasty insult, but she began speaking before I could.

"And that would be our newest masterpiece! You know that venomous weed invading fields in tropical climates? Ivory Blade, they call it. Its white stem has tiny, highly toxic hairs that stick into your skin like blades. If ingested, it can kill you in minutes. Our first batch of antidote is ready to be shipped out today."

We continued strolling down the aisle, Kimbly pointing at different areas on the shelves, ensuring us that the cellophane-wrapped pallets were packaged and handled for shipment with the utmost care.

"Of course, we also have your standard magic powders and liquids. Sleep powder, water tablets, energy pills, and that kind of stuff. They're all packaged at the facility across from here, then brought over for shipment."

We stopped at the end of the aisle next to a large steel beam that ran up to the ceiling. Kimbly turned around to face me, clasping her hands and rocking on her feet like she was waiting for further direction from me.

"Right, right." I flapped my hand at her like I couldn't have cared any less. "This is all fantastic, Dr. Keller, but I think you know the real reason I'm here today." At least, I hoped she had known.

She peered past me, again looking at Ryker, but I didn't turn around to see the expression he returned to her.

"I was given strict orders not to show anybody the asset." Her pleasant voice turned guarded.

228

"By whom? My father? Surely that rule doesn't apply to other Taracula family members. Take me to see it. Right now." I stomped my boot down like a five-year-old being refused a candy bar.

"It?" She tilted her head at me, her brown eyes full of skepticism. "Are you referring to something else? I thought you meant … *her*."

A shiver crept down my spine, and I clenched my fists to stop myself from lunging at her and gouging her eyes out. "Yes. Of course. Her. I just don't consider *her* a person in this matter."

"Yes, ma'am. Please follow me."

The bright lights of the warehouse faded as we passed through a set of doors off to the side. The dimly lit corridor didn't seem well traveled by employees, the gray industrial carpet looking brand new and the smell of the freshly painted walls still damp in the air. We passed a few closed offices before Kimbly stopped in front of a solid metal door to a storage room. The sign slapped on the outside showed the "hazardous materials" symbol, with the words "Caution Danger" written under it.

The room was secured by another keypad. Ryker crept up behind me, widening his eyes to get a glimpse at the number pattern that allowed the door to swing open.

A cold push of air sent my hairs standing on end. Light from the hallway spilled in through the open door, inviting shadows to conceal the dark, empty shelves. What used to be a chemical storage room now held a small woman sprawled out on the floor. Her feet were bare, clothing tattered, and from what I could see, she had tattoos running along every inch of her body from neck to toes. Her long hair was matted, fanned out over her like a blanket. It could have been any color, but all I saw was the dried blood and dirt coating it. She barely moved other than to claw at the concrete floor like she was in agonizing pain but didn't have the energy to properly express it.

It took immense willpower not to run over to the suffering woman to help her. While Dr. Keller was occupied, conducting a quick check up on the prisoner, Ryker reached to squeeze my hand. The same rage I was feeling was written all over his fiery eyes.

Kimbly stood up to address me. "We have yet to conduct her daily purge, but we should have everything we need soon. Then we can get rid of her so no one else can synthesize her magic blood. We'll be able to purify Bliss to its full power."

Claws shot out from my fingertips, and I rushed to clasp them behind my back before Dr. Keller could see. As calmly as I could manage, I crouched beside the woman on the floor and turned her over onto her back, brushing the hair off her face. Cuts and bruises, both fresh and old, were a colorful canvas blemishing her skin. Her eyes were a striking turquoise, the intense color piercing through even the deepest shadows in the room. No sorrow shone inside them. There was no plea for help. Instead, they locked onto me like a heat-seeking missile bound to its target. She wouldn't stop fighting until the person who did this to her paid for it. And for all she knew, that person was now me.

My feet rocked on my heels as I pulled back, losing my balance. A sharp pang of shock hit me in the gut, fear firing on all cylinders. I had seen those same eyes before—eyes I had hoped I'd never see again. On Captain Myra Llama.

Regaining my stability, I quickly jumped to my feet and cleared my throat. "Give this woman some water and something to eat. She is no good to us if she's dead before we can get what we need."

Dr. Keller's face twisted with confusion, but she didn't argue with my demand. The cheery tune of her phone ringing made me flinch. She checked the name on the screen and told us, "I'll get right on that. My apologies, Ms. Taracula. I have to take this."

When she left the room, I turned sharply to Ryker. "We gotta do something, Ryker. We can't just leave her here. She's the source of the blood they're using to make Bliss. And … I think she's Myra's sister."

230

Shadows danced across Ryker's face as he studied the woman from a distance. "I've heard about a sister from others on base. The stories all say she's kind of an arrogant prick, but that's all I know. I've never heard of anyone with magic blood, though. If that's the case, her magic is either super rare, maybe even one-of-a-kind. In other words, valuable."

"Not to mention Ozcar wants his hands on it before he loses his chance." I ran a hand through my hair, pulling at the ends in frustration.

"Here, take a sample." Ryker held out his hand, a thin syringe with a long needle resting in his palm.

"You've got to be kidding me. Where did you get a syringe?"

Ryker shrugged. "Now's not the time for questions." He stormed over to the prisoner, inserted the needle into a vein, and took the sample himself.

"She's coming with us. Can't you use a portal and get us out of here?"

"We can't, Zulli. We already have Ozcar coming after us. If we steal from the Black Mark, too, we'll have even more trouble on our hands." He unscrewed the needle from the syringe, capped it, and tucked the barrel filled with blood into his jacket pocket. "Come on. Let's get out of here."

My boots were cemented to the floor, my feet refusing to move. Ryker stood by the door, shadows from the light in the hallway obscuring his features. At that moment, I saw a com-pletely different side of Ryker that I had never seen before. My friend, my teammate, the kind-hearted man who wore his heart on his sleeve would never refuse to help someone in trouble, no matter the cost.

"I promise I will fix this. *We* will fix this. But not right now." His hand clasped around mine, and my feet lurched into motion. Without a second to think, he hurried me down the hallway.

"I'm sorry, Ms. Taracula." Dr. Keller popped out of an office and spread her feet wide, blocking us from advancing any fur-ther. "You two aren't going anywhere."

Ryker's magic heated the back of my arms and legs. With my hand still clasped in his, he drew me back toward a portal.

"I can't let you do that ... Ryker Stone." Dr. Keller's arm came swinging down, stabbing Ryker with a syringe of her own. The needle had no trouble piercing through his jacket and into his shoulder, her thumb pressing down on the plunger to unleash a bubbling green concoction into his body. He ripped off the jacket, slapping his fingers over the injection area. Pain twisted his features, his face glowing red, eyes tightly squeezed shut. Beads of sweat rolled down his forehead. A violent hissing escaped through his grinding teeth as he threw his head back and dropped to his knees.

"Ryker!" I crouched beside him, cradling his sweaty head in my hands. "Ryker! Come on, snap out of it!" Fury ignited inside me, and I had to refrain from gripping him so tight that I'd crush his skull. I turned to Kimbly, my belligerent scowl challenging her and promising a world of pain for harming my friend. "What did you do to him?"

A male voice answered from behind me, a strong, confident sound that resonated down the hallway and commanded the attention of every cell in my body. The hairs on my arms stood on end, my muscles tense and quivering. "It's slowly draining his magic so you won't be able to portal out of here."

I drew in a stuttered gasp, my heart rapping against my chest. I didn't need to turn around to know who the voice belonged to, but as I did, I nearly collapsed under the weight of the world crashing down on me. "Dad ..."

"My little spider. How are you feeling? I presume you haven't taken your medicine."

"Dad ... it's Davian. He's ... he's controlling you and Brodin! With Bliss!"

His eyebrows arched with sudden interest. I expected to see some hint of fear or vulnerability, but the sense of amusement that came from his smirk sent shivers down my neck and spine.

232

"My little spider, you've got this all wrong. Davian is not controlling me, I am the one controlling him and everyone under him." He then turned to Ryker, an irritated look crossing his features. "And you, Mr. Stone, are no longer of need to me."

My eyes blinked wildly, darting back and forth between Ryker and my father. My heart thumped faster inside my chest, the blood rushing so fast my pulse was throbbing in my ears. A wave of sickening nausea overcame me, and I swallowed the burning bile rising in my throat. "Wh-what's going on here? Ryker, what's he talking about?"

Ryker rose to his feet, using the wall for support. "I won't let you hurt her." He hunched his shoulder. He was breathing erratically, but a fierce hunger burned in his amber eyes.

"That was never our intention," a young male voice responded. Two more figures had emerged through the door at the far end of the hallway. The older man had short graying hair, his skin dull and droopy due to years of stress and sleepless nights that were finally catching up to him. A khaki trench coat fell to his knees, and he kept his hands in his pockets.

The other standing next to him was a broad-shouldered man. The earthy scent of his brand new brown leather jacket reached my nose. Under it was a green zip up, the deep hood draping over his face and concealing his identity. As his hands reached to pull down the hood and reveal himself, a tanned young man stood before me with silver eyes and black wavy hair.

My voice trembled as I spoke to my brother, the pain of seeing him here eating away at my weak and brittle bones. "Brodin … you … *you* were the one who attacked me at Catilda's shop? Why?"

"I was trying to scare you so you'd stop pursuing Davian. You were never supposed to have gotten seriously hurt." There was a strong innocence in his shallow words. He *had* hurt me, along with both Catilda and Ryker.

A spreading numbness of disbelief filled my stomach, a devastating emptiness scrambling my brain. I couldn't figure out whether I wanted to scream or hold in the breath trapped in my lungs. "So … it's all true. What Ozcar told me is true. But … why? Dad, why would you do this?"

"I'm just gonna … check on something …" Dr. Keller threw up her hands and cautiously stepped backward until she was far enough away that she felt safe to turn and run. She disappeared down the hallway and through the doors back into the warehouse. I was left with my father and his accomplices, along with a slowly fading Ryker, who was being drained of his magic.

"People don't know what they need until they actually need it," my dad answered. "They want perfect skin, youthful joints that never age. It's always about having a strong physical appearance. I'm just giving society a little reminder of how dangerous the mind can be."

Ryker reached for the knife at his hip, a flickering portal forming as he slashed it down at my father. In retaliation, my dad snapped out his hand and a stream of woven spider webbing whipped Ryker in the face. His back smacked against the wall, his head bouncing against the plaster. He slid down to the floor and rolled onto his hands and knees, trembling like a fragile tree in a windstorm. Sweat soaked his hair, his face red and swollen. His amber eyes glazed over, the serum sealing away his magic.

"Zulli …" The way Ryker spoke my name sent a silky thread of dread down my spine. His eyes met mine in a look that wasn't so much mutual ambition but tragic acknowledgement that we had no chance to win this fight.

"This isn't over." I snatched a bullet from my belt and cried, "*Fumus!*"

A thick smoke hissed out of the bullet, erupting into a billowing cloud of white fog that consumed the hallway. A cough followed the strangled words from my dad. "Call the guards!"

I wrapped Ryker's hand around my neck and was about to slip away when he whispered, "The jacket."

Bending down to pick it up, I slung it over my shoulder and we hobbled as fast as we could to the end of the hallway. The

234

fog hadn't reached this far. To my left was an exit, the red sign above the door illuminating our freedom. All hope of escape vanished when a female guard, dressed in a green uniform similar to a military soldier, charged directly at us.

"Go right," Ryker rasped out. "Even if we make it into the parking lot, we won't get far like this."

When I peered to my right, another security guard wearing an armored vest and black dress pants came storming toward us. He lifted his gun and aimed right at my head.

"Trust me," Ryker wheezed.

Before pivoting, I reached for a navy bullet on my belt and rolled it down the hallway to my left.

"*Dormeo.*"

The sleep powder exploded, and I hoped it would slow down the female guard long enough for us to find a way out.

We stumbled to the right, and I let Ryker lean himself against the wall. "I can't hold you and fight this guy off. Sit tight for a moment."

Sharpened claws shot out of my fingertips and a raging growl of vicious fury ripped from my throat. The guard stopped running and backed away, lowering his gun. My claws caught the tip of his chin, trimming off the ends of his wiry beard. Reeling back my hands, I then slashed right across his vest. I leapt back, ready to pounce a second time, when a loud pop from his gun followed a direct punch to my chest.

The magic energy sizzled through me, paralyzing my limbs. Convulsions ensued, sending my muscles from tense to quivering to spasming. I fought against the magic, an intense heat that I was familiar with. My knee dropped to the floor, and I pushed against the bolts of magic searing my nerve endings. Fear swelled inside me, but it was quickly consumed by the pent up rage I was about to unleash.

"Zulli, watch out!"

Ryker's warning didn't come in time. As I whirled around, hundreds of thin needle-like strands of water struck me in the side. My arms crossed to protect my face, my eyes squeezing shut upon impact. The frigid water felt like a steady stream of bullets being shot into me, tearing through my clothes and ripping open my skin. With each hit, I was forced to take a step back. Blood dripped from open wounds over every inch of my body.

A panicked cry bellowed from behind me. The security guard shielded the water bullets with his hands. Doing little to protect him, he was knocked down, his head smacking hard against a decorative ceramic flower pot. He stopped moving.

Davian stood battle-ready before me, hands spread out and legs bent in attack mode. "Your father may not want to fight you, but I will."

With my magic engaged, Davian experienced the full brunt of my speed as I slammed into him, pushing him back and away from Ryker. Davian clutched his chest, stomping a boot to the floor for balance.

"Did you do this to my dad? To my brother? Did you force them into this? You coward!" My fangs grazed my lips, ready to suck his magic dry.

Davian chuckled, his gaze sliding over to Ryker, who was holding a knife in his hand with no strength left to wield it. "You still haven't told her, have you?"

Flinching for a fraction of a second was all it took. With a swift jerk, Davian's arm came swinging up to clock me in the jaw. As he did, I caught his wrist, digging my claws deep into his skin. I licked a fang and leaned in. I was about to break the skin when he decided to speak. "You heard your father, Zulli. This was all his doing. I just got dragged along for the ride. The man is such a genius it's driving him mad. He's never satisfied, always looking for something bigger, better, and more powerful. It wasn't enough to cure people; he wants to control them as well."

Davian shoved me away and slapped his hands together. A concussive blast of water slammed up against me on either side.

My brain rattled inside my head, the world spinning like a merry-go-round. My lungs burned with the sensation of drowning.

I choked out a mouthful of water, then ripped three red bullets from my belt.

"*Ignis.*" My voice was a throaty growl, seething with rage. All at once, a flaming magic exploded from the bullets. Fire crackled and snapped as heat swelled in the hallway. The carpet went up in flames, the inferno flaring out and snaked up the walls, rising to the ceiling.

"Magic fire isn't so easy to put out, even with your water magic. I dare you to try," I taunted Davian through the lashing flames between us.

Rushing over to Ryker, I let him lean against me. His waning grip barely held onto the jacket in his hand. "In there," he said, his head flopping toward a closed door about halfway down the hall. We hobbled over, but when I pushed on the door, it didn't budge.

"It's locked. Another keypad."

Ryker held out his shaking hand, and as he collapsed into the door, his portal landed us on the other side. I let go of Ryker, helping to prop himself up against the wall. I stacked a tower of boxes in front of the door, dragging over a sturdy metal table to barricade it. One of the flaps on the boxes opened up, revealing a case of glass vials, blue transparent liquid in them.

Confusion swarmed inside my brain, and I shook my head, unable to think clear thoughts.

"The bonding agent? But … how did you know it was in here?" I tucked a sample into my vest pocket.

Ryker licked his lips but couldn't get the words out. He tugged at the neckline of his shirt, then used it to wipe a trickle of blood dripping off his chin. "Zulli, you have to get out of here."

Tears welled in my eyes, my heart stuttering inside my chest. I dragged the heel of my palm across my face, wishing I could sweep away the distress along with it. "*We* have to get out of here, Ryker. Let me remove the magic sealing yours. With my fangs, I can—"

"Zulli, stop. Please. You have the blood, the bonding agent. Bring it to Catilda and let her mom figure out the spell."

"But the spatula … Ozcar still wants it."

"And he will get it," Ryker hissed, his words forming in short bursts. "But I have to do something first."

My voice turned cold and full of fear, and my throat tightened under the dread. "Davian said you still hadn't told me something. What aren't you telling me, Ryker?"

A wary smile stretched across Ryker's face. "I want you to know that I meant everything I said about you. And these past six months were the best time of my life."

"Ryker, this isn't funny." My blood pumped in rhythm with my heart, pulsing in my ears and behind my eyes.

Fists pounded on the door from the outside, and a box of glass vials tipped over. The bonding agent inside spilled out and pooled on the ground.

"I'm sorry, Zulli. I've wanted to tell you for so long."

"Tell me what, Ryker? Say it!" My hands clenched tight, nails digging into my palms. I crouched down next to Ryker, my shaking legs hardly able to keep me upright.

His lips quivered, his face sagged. "I work for your father."

The world stopped moving around me, all sense of perception lost. His words stole my strength, and I collapsed under my own weight. I searched Ryker's face for deception, like this was all some sick joke, but it held no malicious intent. All I saw was his familiar tender smile, working its way into my soul and warming me like patches of sunshine. A storm quickly swallowed it up and rained down on me with dread.

"Ryker, how could you …" I barely managed to choke out the words.

Heat hit my back, burning the lacerations on my skin. Ryker's portal was weak, flickering with unstable magic, but strong enough to send me through.

"I'm sorry, Zulli. I promise I will fix this."

The last thing I saw was the door being blasted open. A single fist, reinforced with the strength of a spider, had taken it down in one punch. In the doorway stood my father, his dark, unsettling gaze looking down upon me. A curl of anguish knifed through me, slicing my very soul wide open.

His gray eyes glittered with frenzied madness, wrinkles deepening as his ferocity intensified. Silent fury slid over his tense frame. He cut me a sideways glance, loaded with disapproval. I was hit full force with the cold vertigo of my splintered heart. Any fatherly affection I'd once had for him was lost to the brokenness I felt inside my aching heart.

The man looking back at me wasn't my father. It was the face of a monster, a demon hungry for power and willing to do whatever it took to get it. And I knew I had to stop him.

21

---◈---

RYKER'S PORTAL WAS ROUGH. THE magic fractured as I passed through it and scratched against my skin. It burned hotter than usual, but it did its job, tossing me out onto the living room floor of our hotel room.

I lay there, sprawled on my side, my brittle limbs hugging Ryker's jacket. My aching muscles lacked the strength to even twitch. Unable to hold in the heartbreak, a hot torrent of grief poured out of me in a flood of uncontrollable tears. My heart seized up, numbness overriding my soul as I gasped to fill my lungs with air through choking sobs. The emotional wound of Ryker's betrayal overwhelmed the physical wounds covering my body. A cold pain dragged me under like a rip current, drowning me no matter how hard I tried to climb back to the surface.

My head was flooded with a dizzy mix of confusing emotions. The despair in his amber eyes had been unmistakable, the burden he'd carried with him this entire time weighing down on him like a stone wall crushing his spirited soul. He had made his choice to work alongside my father, and for that, I wasn't sure I could forgive him.

Despite his betrayal, Ryker had stood by my side and protected me from Ozcar, from Davian, and even from my own family, who he had been working with all along. He continuously promised we would get through this together, and no matter how much hurt was pumping through my veins, how much my insides were tearing apart, I knew there was truth in his words.

I had to go back for him.

Taking a deep breath, I wiped the tears from my itchy eyes and rose to my feet. Charging into the bedroom, I changed out of my torn, bloody clothing and into a pair of black cargo pants, cropped at the knees and fraying at the edges. I licked a few of the smaller cuts to heal them then tore open a first aid kit, removing the tube of healing ointment.

"*Sana.*" Intense heat burned like someone was peeling the flesh off my skeleton. As the magic seeped into the wounds, the blood clotted, and the pain began to dull. None of the cuts had been very deep. In a few hours, most of them would disappear.

I plucked out a graphic t-shirt with a fire breathing dragon on it and tossed on a loose-fitting red plaid button-down over it. With what few bullets I had left, I restocked my belt, then I reached into the side pocket of my duffle bag to extract several bracelets and rings. The items were infused with magic, given to me by my father to protect me on missions. I had never worn them because I wasn't much into jewelry, but the time felt right to use them.

With a hardened sigh, I grabbed my phone and left the hotel room, trudged through the lobby, and began wandering aimlessly through the streets of Estine.

The late evening breeze was hot and humid, smelling of the salty coast nearby. The mugginess didn't deter the tourists, though. The streets were bombarded with pedestrians enjoying their evening strolls and filling restaurant patios with laughter. The thought of their happiness made my stomach lurch.

A crowd gathering on the sidewalk in a small plaza caught my attention. Through the wall of onlookers was a street performer, a sharply dressed gentleman whose magic smell reminded me of sunshine and rainbows. He held out his hands as butterflies and colorful birds flocked to him. With his magic, he communicated with the animals and they spiraled around the onlookers in a flutter of elegant beauty. A young woman in a sundress clapped with delight as a blue butterfly landed on her nose.

I stayed for a while to watch the man's performance, its mesmerizing display helping to clear my mind. My first instinct was to storm back to the warehouse on a crusade to rescue Ryker, but his voice of reason in the back of my head reminded me that doing so would end badly for the both of us. Instead, I held my phone in my hands and thought about who to dial first.

I needed more information on the woman being kept in the warehouse. If she really was Myra's sister, the military might already have an active mission set up to rescue her and I didn't want to get caught up in that. There was only one person I could trust to give me that information, and it was time to tell her the truth.

The line rang once before Kasra answered and snapped at me. "What the hell is going on, Zulli? Where are you? You haven't been at your apartment in days, you skipped out on several training sessions on base, and you aren't returning my messages."

"There's something I need to tell you, Kasra." I drew in a nervous breath and let it out slowly.

"I can't hear you, Zulli. It's too loud."

Dodging a group of beachgoers, drunk on sunshine and good times, I darted into an alley, away from traffic and the main road, and leaned against the sturdy brick wall of a building.

"That's better," Kasra confirmed. "So, you had something to tell me? Where are you and what's going on?"

The words poured out of my mouth, my voice becoming shakier with each thought. The palm of my hand rubbed against my forehead, my eyes squeezed shut as I spoke. I explained everything about my father's business, Myra, the female prisoner, and the debt I owed Ozcar.

"I'm so, so sorry Kasra! I've been meaning to tell you. I never meant it to be like this. But I really need your help right now."

She let out her disappointment in an extraordinarily loud, long exhale. "I can't believe you'd hide this from me, Zulli. We're teammates. We work together … as a *team*."

"I know. I was stupid. But I wasn't sure—"

"Wasn't sure about what, Zulli? If you could trust me?" There was a jolt in my heart at her sharp words. Ryker had given me the same speech not more than a week ago.

"I wasn't sure what I was getting into. I tried to make Ryker stay out of it, but he refused. And now look at what's happened. He was … he was … captured!"

"*Captured?* Zulli, who took him? What happened?" Kasra yelled so loud into the speaker it crackled in my ear.

"Davian and my dad have him. He stayed behind to protect me." I left out the part about Ryker working for my father. While I wanted to be truthful and honest with Kasra, I couldn't bring myself to say it.

Kasra grunted on the other end of the phone. "I will help you because I care about Ryker. You and me, though … we're going to have a long talk when you get back here. It's going to take a lot of work to regain my trust, Zulli. I hope you know that."

"I understand. And I'll do whatever it takes." I thought of Ryker's words, the ones he'd kept repeating to me. "I will fix this."

"You'd better," she spat. "So, what do you need from me? I won't be able to find someone to transport me to Estine without raising some flags on base."

"Can you look up someone for me? Does Captain Myra Llama have a sister? And what's her magic power?"

There was a short silence before Kasra spoke. "Are you serious? You don't know about Lizzy?"

I pushed myself off the wall I was leaning against, my attention perking up. "Tell me everything. I think she's somehow connected to Bliss."

"She has a rare blood magic with mind control powers. Most people who use mind control activate their magic using a personal object or by touching the subject. The bond can easily be broken by destroying the connection. But for Lizzy, she uses her blood. The liquid and her magic absorbs into your skin and there's no way to get rid of it. Once it's inside you, you're completely under her control. It makes sense why her blood is needed for Bliss. By extracting the magic in her blood and mixing it into a drug, it gives the user their own temporary mind control powers over themselves."

"That's pretty terrifying," I responded. "Have you ever met her?"

My hands were slick with sweat, the glass screen of the phone sticking to my face.

Kasra let out a disinterested mumble. "Few people will talk to her or even go near her because they're terrified of her magic. She's also a member of the Black Sheep elite military unit, and a lot of people question whether the only reason she's there is because Colonel Buckner is her uncle. She's not the nicest person in the world, either. She sounds like a stubborn, arrogant princess. I tried to say hi once and she just spat back an insult. She's the polar opposite of her super easy-going sister."

"There's one more thing I need to ask. Can you check if there's an active mission involving her rescue and if so, who's on it?"

There was a selection of curses followed by a clicking sound as she typed on a keyboard. She responded in an irritated tone, "A team set out a few days ago. And, just your luck, Captain Myra Llama is on it, along with two others, Blair and Eli. Have fun with that, Zulli. They're supposedly staying at the Coastline Motel."

"Fantastic. I gotta go. Thanks, Kasra. I appreciate your help. I'll call you as soon as I get Ryker out of there."

The line went dead and my fingers were already dialing another number. My voice cracked when I tried to speak her name. "Catilda."

"Woah. I can practically feel your tension resonating through the phone. What's wrong, Zulli?"

"Ryker's in trouble. Can you meet me at …" I searched around, trying to give her a destination as a reference. At the end of the alleyway was a rough patchwork door, stickers and other graffiti decorating it. A broken wooden sign hung above it. "The Tipsy Seagull?"

"I'm on it!" I heard fingers typing in the background. "Looks like that's across the city from where I am. Might take me a while to get there, but I'm leaving right now!" The call disconnected.

The creaky door brought no attention to my entrance into the bar, the chatter inside drowning it out. As soon as I stepped in, a magical cloud of noxious cigarette smoke latched onto me, swarming my head and seeping into my clothes. The bitter taste it left in my mouth left me choking on my tongue. Regular cigarettes were bad enough, but those infused with magic only made them more potent.

About ten tables and booths, all with dark worn wood and torn leather seats, were scattered around the room. Almost almost every one was occupied. Most bars that attracted tourists were decorated like the owner had spent an afternoon scouring each gift shop in the area, but this one was meant for the locals. On the walls hung several photos, both old and new, showcasing the generations of fishermen and business owners who kept this community alive. Their personal belongings—nets, aprons, and other fishing equipment—filled in the empty space around them.

My reflexes were put to the test as I danced around the patrons getting up to grab drinks at the bar, most of them reeking of fish or wearing festive floral shirts, cargo shorts, and flip flops. Finding an empty stool at the end of the bar, I sat down and glimpsed

245

the fully stocked shelves displaying rows of colorful liquor bottles.

A spirited woman darted back and forth from one end of the bar to the other, filling up beer mugs and mixing drinks that she placed near the server station. A single waitress shuffled around struggling to keep up with her guests. Eventually, when the bartender had a moment to breathe, she noticed me and came over. She held a wet bar towel in her hands, wiping the counter in front of me as she spoke. "Hi! What can I get you?"

Her friendly smile dominated her soft features, along with large freckles that looked like paint splatter covering her face. The bartender's exhaustion was apparent in her drooping eyes and the loose strands of butterscotch hair falling out of her low ponytail.

Snatching a laminated menu from the damp counter, I browsed the specials. My tongue licked my lips when my eyes stopped about halfway down the list. "Mai Fly, please."

"Shifter, huh?" She grabbed a highball glass from a stack of freshly washed barware, condensation still coating the outside. "The unique warm weather year-round attracts a lot of shifters to Estine, especially those affiliated with reptiles and birds."

The bartender poured about four different liquids into a shaker, shook the mixture, then emptied it into the glass, topping it off with a splash of pineapple juice and a squeeze of lime. Before serving it, she grabbed a dispenser full of what most would think was black pepper. Giving it a good shake, the tiny fruit flies came sprinkling out, sinking into the Mai Fly to give it that extra intense flavor that I could only describe as a tropical heaven. Notes of citrus mixed with a floral, earthy aftertaste that appealed to shifters who ate insects.

"Thanks." I dragged the glass closer toward me and took a sip, letting the surgery cocktail dance on my tongue and glide down my throat. Not really in the mood to chit-chat with the bartender, I pulled out my phone and began scouring through all my missed calls, emails, and text messages.

"I'll be around if you need me." With a tap of her hand on the counter, she left and went about her business serving other customers.

Sorrow and despair settled in, wondering how the hell I was going to rescue Ryker and stay off the military's radar. Over the next hour, I had a few more drinks before I realized I should have ordered something to eat. My limbs were starting to feel weightless, like floating puffs of clouds carrying me away through the sky. No one else in the bar had food in their hands, and I had to wonder if there was a reason for that.

My chin dug into my chest, sipping my drink as my eyes strained to make sense of the fuzzy words on the menu in an attempt to figure out what food was the safest choice to eat.

"… and whatever he's having." The uncertain male voice drifted across the bar, and I looked up to see his gaze wavering in my direction. *He?* I knew my short hair and messy clothes didn't scream glamorous female, but the guy must have been blind to think I was a man.

My near empty drink came with me as I stomped over and pulled out the stool next to him. I wouldn't say I was drunk. I knew exactly what I was doing. But I had enough liquor pumping through my bloodstream to build up just enough courage to approach him. Catilda still wasn't here and I was tired of drinking alone in the corner of the bar. The least I could do to entertain myself was have fun messing with the guy before she arrived.

"I don't think you want that," I warned him, simultaneously flagging down the bartender. Then I decided on my food order. "Get him a plate of fries and a whiskey on the rocks."

Intense curiosity widened his eyes as he peered down into my drink. "What is that?"

"Mai Fly." The ice clinked against the glass as I stirred my beverage with my plastic straw. He wrinkled his nose at the tiny black specs swirling around in a vortex of brownish-yellow liquid.

"As in, actual flies? Yeah, hard pass on that."

The pipsqueak must have been around the same age as me, perhaps in his mid-twenties, but with his scrawny frame, he could have easily passed for late teens. His mop of messy brown curls cast shadows on his pale face, and when I looked into his dark brown eyes, something unexpected flickered behind the exhaustion. There was a fire burning, hopeful determination that suggested he had also come to this bar on a very important mission.

I waved a dismissive hand at him. "They're fruit flies. Adds an extra sweetness to the drink."

The bartender eventually came back with a giant basket of soggy fries and a whiskey.

My fingers snatched a fry, glistening with grease. "Did I get it right?"

"Close. I'm more of a gin person. By the way, I'm Adrian." He pushed the basket so that it sat between us and took a generous gulp of his beverage. Despite his gin preference, he seemed to enjoy it.

"Zulli." Taking him up on his generous offer, I shoved a fistful of fries into my mouth and finished off my drink, slamming the glass on the counter in hopes of getting the bartender's attention for a refill.

"Uh, everything okay?" He put some space between us, leaning back on his stool.

"I'll be fine once I *get another drink!*" I searched around for the bartender, raising my glass and shaking the ice when she glanced over at me. She couldn't hear my yelling. I could barely hear it myself. The bar was growing increasingly louder as the evening drew in the after-work crowd. But my ears drowned out all the chatter when Adrian dropped an unexpected bomb on me.

"Hey, Zulli ... you don't happen to know someone named Lizzy Llama, do you? Short, tons of tattoos, pale skin, has—" he cut himself off. "She has strawberry blond hair. Or maybe you heard about someone who kidnapped a person with that description?"

Adrenaline saturated my veins, washing away all the cloudiness that came along with the booze. My heart thumped madly in my chest, my stomach clenching with trepidation. Who was this man and why was he questioning me about Lizzy?

I dialed back my eagerness to interrogate him with a thousand questions. While I held out hope that he was just searching for a lost friend, there was still a chance that he was working with my father or Davian, or maybe someone else was after her magic. I wasn't about to go dishing out the details without more information.

Remembering what both Kasra and Ryker had mentioned, I responded to him with a hint of smugness in my voice. "Lizzy? That princess is getting what she deserves."

Adrian's hands slammed down on the table, the basket of fries spilling all over the counter. He shot up from his stool, allowing me to get a full look at him. Definitely not a local, but not a tourist either. He wore baggy jeans with a black fanny pack clipped around his waist, a few daggers tucked in the straps to the side. What really had me worried was the military-issued pistol he thought he was doing a good job of concealing under his cheesy "I love Estine" t-shirt. A trained soldier, especially if he happened to be one traveling with Myra, wouldn't be so careless to brandish weapons like that in public or to spit out sensitive information about a kidnapping.

"So, you do know her? Where is she?" His voice was loud enough to garner some questionable looks from the nearby drinkers.

"Okay, sit back down, Adam. You're drawing unwanted attention." My hands guided him back down to his seat.

"It's Adrian," he spat back at me.

"Right. Adrian. Whatever." I chose my next words wisely. I couldn't tell him about the warehouse, but I needed him to believe that I really was acquainted with her if I was going to extract any information from him.

"I know Lizzy. We may have come across each other a few times at work. But I know *you* aren't a soldier. How did you get your hands on our equipment?" I nodded to the gun on his waist, and he instinctively motioned to draw it.

"I have … connections." It was clear by his guarded tone that he was just as skeptical of me as I was of him. As his cautious gaze assessed me in return, I concluded that he likely didn't work with my father or Ozcar. That left a burning question in my mind: what was he after from me? Was he simply looking for information or was he planning something else?

"Keep undressing me and I'll catch a cold." I waggled my eyebrows at him, trying to keep my cool.

"No, I'm not …" He squeezed his eyes shut and shook his head before looking at me again. "You know Lizzy was kidnapped, right? She's being tortured, drained of her magic. If I don't find her tonight, there's a good chance I never will."

I let out a deflated sigh, repeating what little I had been told about Lizzy. "Nobody likes that stubborn drama queen. She thinks she's all high and mighty, being a member of the Black Sheep, but everyone knows she only got to her position because her uncle is in charge. Some even speculate that she used her magic to manipulate her way to the top. If someone found a way to drain it from her, I say they're doing us all a favor."

The words felt like sharp barbs cutting into my tongue and my gaze dropped to my drink. The sentiment wasn't true, no one deserved to be treated like she had been, but I had to wonder what might have happened if someone had successfully removed her magic before it could have been weaponized. Maybe it was the alcohol talking, but without her magic, Lizzy would have never been captured in the first place. Bliss would never have existed. Ryker wouldn't have gotten himself captured, and I wouldn't have nearly lost Catilda. And my Dad? Maybe he wouldn't have taken the dark path of power.

"Okay, let's put our differences aside for a moment." Adrian regained his composure, his eyes now gleaming with distinct purpose. "Whatever you believe, that doesn't mean she deserves to *die*. Will you please help me?"

"Hmm." I tapped a finger to my lips, then took a long sip of the refilled drink that the bartender had placed in front of me. Perhaps there *was* a silver lining to all this. If I told him where Lizzy was, I could use him as a decoy while I went to rescue Ryker.

My nose picked up an intriguing scent and a deranged idea bubbled into my muddled mind. "Your magic smells delicious. Like … vanilla frosting with a hint of lemon and bourbon."

Adrian pinched his shirt and sniffed it. "I mean, you basically just described my entire diet. You sure it's my magic you're smelling?"

I curled back my lips, letting my tongue trace the outline of one of my pointed fangs. "Let me bite you and I'll take you to her. I want to taste your magic."

Adrian jumped back, nearly falling out of his chair. "Um, what? I don't think so. What the hell are you, anyway? A vampire?"

"Absolutely not!" I seethed at him, stiffening my spine and crossing my arms. "Bat shifters are gross and filthy. Do I look gross and filthy to you?"

That was probably not the most appropriate question to ask him considering I hadn't showered before I'd left the hotel and I had massive sweat stains under my armpits. Thankfully, he disregarded my appearance.

"Will you please just help me out? I'm here with some other members of the Black Sheep. They're nice people. I'll tell them to put in a good word for you. Maybe you'll get a promotion for helping?"

A snort huffed out my nose at the thought of a promotion considering how much Colonel Buckner despised me. "I doubt that option is on the table. Besides, I'm happy where I am. I just want to taste your magic."

A curious expression fixated on his childish face. "How do I know I can trust you?"

I rolled my eyes. "I took my military oath to protect and serve. I can be trusted to keep my word. She's being kept in what appears to be an abandoned warehouse right outside the city, but I assure you it's in full operation. It's both a storage facility and production plant for magic powders and liquids. I can take you there."

His hand clenched around his whiskey glass, fingers turning white. "How do you know this? Are you sure the information is accurate?"

"How I know is not relevant. But I am one hundred percent certain that's where she is."

Adrian sighed heavily and turned over his wrist, offering it to me. I swatted it away and pointed to his neck. "I want a taste of the good stuff."

"You really are a blood-sucking vampire, aren't you?"

It took a remarkable amount of effort not to use my claws as I slapped him across the face. "Say it again and see what happens next time."

He hooked a finger around the collar of his t-shirt, tilting his head to the side to make room for me to have an evening snack.

A quick glance around the bar told me that most people were too busy to notice us. While I didn't think Adrian would try anything funny, I didn't want to risk being alone with him just yet, so we stayed where we were.

I took no pride in what I was about to do, but my encounter with Davian earlier had drained more of my magic than I had hoped. If I was going up against Davian or my father, then I needed the extra magical boost.

With extreme apprehension, I slowly leaned in. My nose grazed against his skin and I inhaled a deep breath. An eager groan passed through my lips. My pulse was racing, my nerves running haywire like broken circuits throughout my body. The smell of sweet vanilla was like a blanket of sunshine teasing my nose, the hint of lemon and bourbon warming the insides of my nostrils. Before I realized what I was doing, I licked his skin with the tip of my tongue.

"This is really gross." Adrian's flesh heated under my touch. His vein throbbed in his neck and his breathing became unsteady. "Can you just get on with it already so we can go find Lizzy?"

My sharp fangs pierced his tender skin, his magic inviting my tastebuds to dance with excitement. The taste was equally as appetizing as the smell, the smooth texture like honey gliding down my throat. A rush of magical energy blazed through my body, igniting a fire inside my chest, sharpening my senses. His magic flowed outward to every muscle in my body, tingling my fingertips and toes.

My eyes darted to the side, watching as a trio of disgusted women gawked at me sucking on Adrian's neck. The bartender started making her way over, a stern look on her face as she prepared to ask us to leave.

With one last pull of his magic, strength saturated my veins, but this time something felt off. Amidst the candied warmth was a bitter cold. Something that didn't belong there. The magic latched onto my own and a shiver ran down my spine. The feeling was a swarm of bees attacking me from the inside, my skin buzzing and vibrating underneath.

Just as I ripped my fangs from his neck, two newcomers kicked down the door to the bar with an extravagant show of authority.

With a frantic gaze, I searched for an exit. The party crashers, one man and one woman, were both armed with a sling of bullets looped around their shoulders and guns half the size of my body pointing directly at my head. Their uniforms were neat and tailored, similar to a soldier in the military, but these uninvited guests were no officers. They were the hired help, and I recognized both of them from the warehouse.

"Oh, hello old friends!" I rose to my feet and greeted the male security guard that had attacked me in the hallway. My knees were shaking, my heart weak with fear, but I hid my terror behind stiff shoulders and an imposing glower. How did they find me? I wasn't about to stick around to ask. With a quick glance over to Adrian, I sputtered the first words that popped into my head before making a run for it. "I have business to attend to, so I'm just going to let my boyfriend here kick your asses today."

"What? No, I'm not ... she's lying!" He waved his hands up in the air, looking back and forth between me and the two attackers. Whatever magic Adrian possessed, its power was coursing through me like lightning. If he wanted to, he could probably blow this entire bar to smithereens. But judging from the panicked expression on his face, I sensed that wasn't going to happen.

With a hint of guilt for leaving him to deal with my own problems, I gave him my last remarks. "Thanks for the snack, Adrian! See you around!"

"Wait! You said you'd take me to Lizzy!" His hand shot out to grab me, but I was too quick.

It only took a split second for me to disappear. When the female guard charged at Adrian, I rolled over the bar top and crashed down on the other side behind it.

The drunk locals hooted and hollered, and with no idea what they were getting themselves into, started joining in on the fight. Glasses went flying above my head, cries of murderous rage and agonizing pain pierced my ears, and a mix of magical scents overtook the cigarette smoke I had finally come to peace with.

Digging out my phone, I immediately dialed Catilda. "You there?" I pressed a fingertip into my ear to dull the noise.

"I just got here as two very intimidating officers of some kind barreled into the bar. I'm waiting for you out back by the dumpster."

I peeked over the bar just enough for my eyes to see the male guard shoot off his gun at Adrian and a plume of yellow powder explode in the air. My eyes widened with shock and a pang of urgency shot through my heart, but the man's magic attack seemed to have had no effect on Adrian. He stumbled off balance, then thrust out his hands and released a stream of magic energy right back at his attacker. He then ripped his gun from its holder. Before he could shoot, he was tackled to the floor, the gun skittering out of his reach. The man jumped on top of him and brandished a knife in the air, about to plunge it into Adrian's heart.

My sweaty fingers clenched onto the lip of the wooden bar top, and as I was about to hurl myself over the bar and dive into the fight, the bartender lunged toward him. She took a swing at someone in her way, then dove in front of Adrian. The knife simply crumbled under her hardened skin, blanketed with magic.

Hoping Adrian had enough skill to survive, I snuck out from behind the bar and scrambled down the narrow hallway, past the bathrooms and the small kitchen, and out the back door.

Another armed guard was battling with a calico cat. He spun around in circles while Catilda dug her feline claws into his face.

"Get off me you annoying flea bag!" he cried out.

As he tried to rip Catilda off his face, her nails dragged across his dark skin. Lines of blood bubbled from the scratches.

Catilda opened her tiny mouth, hissing in a brusque snarl while baring her canines. With both hands, the man squeezed around her feline abdomen and launched her toward the brick wall.

"Catilda!" My reflexes engaged, Adrian's magic giving me an extra boost to my step. I lunged with lightning speed to grab Catilda in my arms before her delicate head cracked against the side of the building. I placed her down on the ground. Her earthy scent mingled in the air as her body morphed back into its human shape.

"I got this," I told her. "Go hide."

Without question, she scattered, hiding behind a recycling bin near a dumpster. The guard came storming toward me, a knife tight in his hand.

"*Viribus.*" A black ring on my index finger heated up, surrounding my fist with a solid coating of magic. My punch intensified under the strength spell. The impact flattened the side of the guard's jaw. His head jerked sideways, obscenities screaming out of his mouth as his knife soared in the air and right into the dumpster.

As he stumbled off balance, the guard swung around a gun that was hanging across his back. Not a second later, the long barrel of his rifle unleashed its fury against my chest. The muzzle flash was an orange-white glow. The tongue of the smoking magic rose into the air, sparks flying in all directions. A wave of pressure against my ears immediately caused them to pop. Although the only thing I was aware of was the deafening ring that ensued, I had enough sense to dodge out of the way of the speeding magic bullet.

My foot scraped against the asphalt, but the push off felt sluggish, like I had already exhausted my magic. That cold feeling inside my chest, the same one I had experienced in the bar, overcame me. The bullet grazed me right above my elbow and the magic energy scorched the muscle under my skin. Warm, fresh blood soaked into my shirt and coated my palms, dripping from my fingers as I clasped my hand around the wound.

A smirk appeared on the guard's hollow face, a wisp of his thinning hair falling across his manic eyes. "Your father really wanted to trust you. He told me to bring you back to him alive, but you've been nothing but a nuisance since you stuck your nose into his business. There's not much I can do to save you if a stray magic bullet 'accidentally' stops your heart."

My breath punched out of me in a terrifying scream. The fuming heat of the magic energy boiled under my skin as if my blood was replaced with lava. The fire was then extinguished by the bitter cold of death, shards of ice running through my veins until a numbness left my limbs weak and my bones brittle.

"Zulli!" Catilda darted out from behind her hiding spot as the security guard slung his rifle over his shoulder and bounded off down the alley.

I blinked repeatedly at Catilda. She slapped my face then began pounding on my chest to jumpstart my failing heart.

My eyes might have been deceiving me, but her skin was faintly glowing a shiny copper color, a glittery magical halo adorning her red bandana tied around her head. It shimmered against her leopard print tunic dress and black leggings, the sparkle lighting up the harsh shadows in the alley from the early evening sun. There was just enough energy left in me to raise my hand, a hazy neon green shine coating my own skin.

"Come on, Zulli. You're not dying on me!"

The tears she shed were stained with panic, a tremor taking over her lips. Gut wrenching sobs tore from her chest. She reached for her purse, dumping everything out and searching through it.

Catilda's frantic voice was a distant echo in my ears. The sound eventually faded, and I closed my eyes. The steady rhythm of my heart slowed until it beat one last time, and I surrendered to the magic taking my life.

22

———◈———

"ZULLI, COME BACK!" CATILDA'S PLEA reached my ears, her voice a disembodied murmur whisked away in the wind.

A faint spark of something latched onto my own magic, a small burst of heat that gave an electrifying jolt to my heart. The paralyzing numbness lifted like the calm after a storm. My fingers twitched, then my toes. Finally, my eyes shot wide open. I jerked upright from the pavement I was lying on, nearly headbutting Catilda in the process. Adrenaline ... no, it was magic ... blazed through me.

"Zulli? You're okay!" She fell on top of me, squeezing her arms tightly around my neck and choking me.

"What the hell just happened? What did you do to me?" I asked Catilda. She stopped suffocating me to wipe her face with a tissue that she had grabbed from her purse. Her eyes were puffy and red, mascara dripping down her cheeks like black tears.

"I ... I don't know. I didn't do anything. Your heart stopped beating. You were dead. And then ... you weren't. You were out for about five minutes."

I flexed my fingers, the green glow from my hands gone. Catilda's heavenly aura had vanished too. Bracing a hand on the ground for support, I pushed myself to my feet. I hopped from side to side, making circular movements with my shoulders.

"I feel absolutely fine. Like nothing happened." I checked the wound on my arm. My shirt sleeve was soaked with crimson blood, but the gunshot had completely vanished. How?

My gaze wandered over to the back door of the bar. My stomach dropped at the thought of Adrian, unsure if he was okay, but also genuinely curious about him. Extracting someone's magic had never affected me that way before. Exactly what kind of magic did Adrian have, and what had it just done to me?

"Catilda, can you do me a favor?"

"Of course, hun. What do you need?" She wiped the confusion from her face, replacing her expression with a more serious one.

My fingers were typing something on my phone as I spoke. "I met a guy named Adrian inside the bar. Looks like a scrawny teenager with curly brown hair. Whenever he's done dealing with the mess I threw at him, can you take him to this address?"

Catilda's phone chimed in her purse with my message. "Sure, but why?"

"It's the facility where they're packaging Bliss. They're holding Ryker there, but there's also someone else. Lizzy. This Adrian guy is looking for her. I told him I'd take him to her, but I have to do something first."

"And that would be …" Catilda narrowed her eyes on me.

"He's here with some soldiers trying to rescue his friend. I'm going to use them as a distraction so I can go rescue Ryker. But … he's definitely not a trained soldier, and I don't know if he can handle himself alone. I have to find his team and let them know where he's going."

A loud crash sounded from behind the closed back door and it shook as something—or maybe someone—bounced against it.

"You might want to stay in your cat form to conceal your identity. The less people who see your face the better," I added.

"How am I supposed to grab his attention as a cat?" She scowled at me with cherry lips.

I shrugged back at her. "You're pretty persuasive no matter what form you're in. I know you'll think of something."

The unease in her voice made it shake. "All right. But … are you sure you're okay?"

"Not really. But I *feel* normal, so I'm rolling with it. I gotta get Ryker out of there, no matter what it takes."

Her tight embrace squeezed the air out of my lungs, and I reciprocated with a hug that cracked her back. In a swirl of magic, she transformed into a slender calico cat and padded toward a wooden crate by the back door to wait for her guest.

Trusting Catilda would be able to get Adrian to where he needed to go, I darted around the corner and passed the entrance of the bar in the alleyway. Noise from inside drifted out, wooden chairs splintering and glass shattering, but I swept past it toward the main road.

Pedestrians casually strolled past me until I stepped off to the side of the walkway to search for the motel address on my phone. It was only a few blocks away, but I stalled before heading off. If Myra had been assigned to this mission, there was a good chance I'd come across her again. Fear sped up my pulse at the thought of what she and her teammates might do to me. Whatever it was, if it meant saving Ryker, I didn't care. He'd saved me more times than I could count. It was my chance to return the favor, and although the hurt of his betrayal was still coursing viciously through me, I needed to find out why he did it.

Each step felt slow and sluggish, like running with concrete blocks tied to my feet. With my swift cat-shifter abilities, I should have made it to the motel in record time, but something weighed down on my magic. I extracted my claws, the effort to keep them out straining my hands. What the hell had Adrian's magic done to me?

Taking the corner of my button-down shirt, I wiped down my face. My back arched as I bent over and braced my hands on my

260

knees, watching as more sweat dripped from my forehead onto the concrete sidewalk. Again, I looked at my hands in disbelief, wondering if I had imagined the green glow of my skin.

As I straightened my back, I inhaled a deep breath, determined to push forward despite whatever was going on with me. I took three steps before my feet froze in place, and I frantically started searching for a place to hide.

A petite female was strolling toward me, a heavy fringe covering her forehead. Her strawberry blond ponytail swayed from side to side with her exuberant step. She had a black plastic case strapped across her back and was flanked by two much taller soldiers, a male and female, both dressed casually in jeans and t-shirts with tactical vests protecting their chests. When her vibrant turquoise eyes locked onto mine, I knew it was too late to run.

Captain Myra Llama picked up her pace and jogged over to me, a mischievous but friendly smile plastered to her face. "You again? What are you doing here?"

Both soldiers on either side of Myra assumed attack positions. A crackling ball of lightning formed in the woman's hand while the male brandished a metal boomerang with a razor sharp edge. They looked ready to skin and roast me alive.

I threw up my hands in surrender and took a step back. "Look, I don't want any trouble."

To my surprise, it wasn't anger or hatred that came from Myra's words. Instead, happiness radiated off her, from her glowing creamy complexion to her cheery girlish giggle. "Good. Neither do we! Are you okay? There's blood on your shirt."

My hands slowly fell to my sides and I took another step back. My head tilted with confusion as I pondered Myra's unexpected kindness. Was she messing with me? "Uh, yeah. I'm fine. But … I know where Lizzy is! Your friend Adrian is on his way over to her right now."

The tall female, I assumed Blair from Kasra's information, stepped forward. Her golden hair was bunched up in a messy bun

261

and her imposing glare sent my pulse racing. Tendrils of lightning created dancing shadows across her face. "He ran off without telling us. What are you planning to do with him? Where is he?"

"Me? No! I'm trying to warn you! He ... he needs your help!" I backed out of the oncoming pedestrian traffic and tripped into a narrow alley between an ice cream shop and a salon. Behind me was a brick wall and in front of me were three elite military soldiers eager to jump me.

My hands started to shake and my mouth went dry. I begged my magic to transform me into a spider so I could crawl out of the alley, but my power wasn't responding.

"Explain," Blair demanded. She nudged the ball of lightning closer to me, and I flinched as it sent sparks into the air that burned holes in my shirt and flesh. "Who are you and how do you know where she is?"

"Uh, hi. I'm Z-Zulli—a military soldier just like you. You can call the Chitol military base to confirm it. I swear!"

Myra raised her hand. "I can confirm! I've met Zulli before."

There was a dark gleam in her turquoise eyes, one that reminded me that she hadn't forgotten about our brawl earlier, but she didn't bring it up.

"Blair," the tall female growled.

The male followed with another single word. "Eli."

There were no formal handshakes, no "nice to meet you." Just a firm nod in my direction acknowledging my existence.

"I have a ... contact," I said, gulping as I remembered the answer Ryker had always given me when I asked where he got his information. "She, um, saw Lizzy at a warehouse not too far from here. She was in pretty bad condition. But the people there are really dangerous. I don't know this Adrian guy, but he didn't seem like the kind of person who can handle heavy hitters. He's going to need your help."

Myra gave a questioning glance to each of her companions before she responded with a smile. "Oh, goodie! A team up!" She delicately clapped her fingertips together.

"Oh, no." I shook my head and waved my hands in front of me. "I said he needs *your* help. Not mine. I can tell you where she is but I'm not going with you."

The plan was to have Adrian draw the guards' attention while I snuck in unnoticed to search for Ryker. Having Myra and her team also present would only add to the distraction, but physically going to the warehouse with them would ruin my entire plan. Three sets of military eyes glued to me at all times wouldn't allow me to sneak away and find Ryker.

Myra didn't give in, insisting that I absolutely needed to go. Was this a part of her scheme? Maybe she had the same idea and planned on throwing me to the wolves while she went to rescue her sister.

"I'll go flag down a cab," Eli pivoted and jogged toward the curb.

"A cab?" I knitted my eyebrows and cocked my head.

"Well, yeah," Blair replied. "We're certainly not walking. How else are we going to get there?" She left the alley to follow Eli.

Transportation had never been an issue for me with Ryker's portal magic. Although I tried not to take advantage of his ability, I had never put much thought into how others had to rely on other ways to travel.

With Blair and Eli out of hearing range, I was left alone with Myra. My pulse spiked and I shoved my trembling hands into my pockets. Before she had a chance to join them, I had to ask her the question I was dreading the answer to.

"Why didn't you report me?"

Myra leaned in, a smile on her face but a warning in her words. "You felt it, didn't you? When you tasted my magic?"

"I felt … something. It was controlling me. I'm sorry I … I didn't mean to hurt you. What was your magic doing?"

"We all have our secrets, Zulli." Her sunny disposition turned into something cold and sinister. "I'll keep yours if you keep mine. But if you go snooping, make no mistake, you *will* become my enemy."

With that she joined Eli and Blair by the curb, where a white cab was parked and waiting for us to get inside. We piled in, Myra sitting in the front while I was sandwiched between Blair and Eli in the back. I gave the driver the address, and he pulled out.

The ride over was uncomfortable, elbows jamming into my sides and my body pitching sharply with each corner turned. It had been a long, exhausting day and as we entered into night I'd be running on fumes if it weren't for Adrian's magic boost. While I would have preferred to go back to the hotel and rest another night on that luxurious mattress, that wasn't an option. This could be the only opportunity I'd get to save Ryker and I wouldn't let it pass.

After a grueling forty minutes stuck in downtown traffic, we slid out of the cab and stood on the sidewalk in front of the barbed wire fence circling the industrial complex.

The entire area was eerily quiet, not a single person in sight. Except for the cab driver, no vehicles drove down the empty street either. It wasn't quite the flashy entrance I was hoping for, like those that Ryker, Kasra, and I had whenever we portaled somewhere and surprised our target. But I was here and that was all that mattered.

A sudden burst of emotions rose inside me, fluttering like a hummingbird with nervous excitement inside my chest. Everything was moving so fast, and I hadn't thought much about what I'd do once I got inside the building. What would happen if my father was waiting for me? I had little faith that Myra and her teammates would show him any compassion. My stomach surrendered to gravity, my heart sinking with it. What if something terrible had already happened to Ryker?

"Zulli, what are you waiting for?" Blair snapped her fingers at me. "Show us where to find Adrian and Lizzy."

Meow.

Circling around my feet on the sidewalk was a calico cat, her soft fur brushing against the bare skin of my ankles. Her whiskers tickled, the black patch on the left side of her face letting one of her striking blue eyes pop against the darkness.

"Is your informant a cat? I can sense her magic," Myra questioned with sparkling eyes, reaching down to give her a pat on the head. "She's so adorable!"

Catilda swatted her cat claws at Myra's wrist and hissed at her before jumping backward out of her reach. My best friend's magic swirled around her, a hint of that copper dust I had noticed earlier emanating from her skin and drifting up toward the evening sky. The smell of her magic wafted into the light breeze, except it wasn't just the earthy aroma of fresh cut grass. It was the whole front lawn: summertime embodied in a single scent—the sweetness of a freshly squeezed glass of lemonade, the floral fragrance of daisies blooming on the front porch. The air was warm sunshine caressing my face.

Her body took its human shape inches away from Myra, claws grazing her cheek. "Do not *ever* touch me again."

Blair launched a warning spear of lightning at Catilda's feet. While she leapt out of the way, her arm withdrew. Eli threw out his hands, a blue cloud of magic seemed to be pulling on Catilda's metal bracelets around her wrists.

"Oh, a cat shifter!" Myra gasped. Cold air swirled around her, somehow shimmering a faint pink color.

"Stop!" I cried out, pushing myself in front of Catilda and spreading my arms wide. "She's with me."

Catilda backed off, tightening the red bandana around her head and flattening some wrinkles from her tunic dress.

"Jerks," she muttered just loud enough for them to hear.

"Who is she?" Blair seethed.

"That's confi—"

"Catilda Harper. At your service." Catilda pinched the sides of her tunic dress and curtsied while I slapped a hand to my forehead. So much for keeping her identity a secret. "Your friend Adrian went inside about a half hour ago. What is up with that guy? He seemed to know I was a shifter but didn't say anything. There's something quite amusing about a grown man talking to himself while following a magical cat to a warehouse."

They gave each other pointed looks but didn't offer Catilda an answer.

"Okay. If you're the informant, then lead the way, Catilda." Eli fanned out his hand toward the industrial complex.

"Uh, right. Follow me. I watched Adrian go through a tear in the fence over here, but that's when I lost him. I didn't follow him inside." Catilda started walking down the sidewalk, littered with trash and weeds growing from uneven cracks. We wriggled our way through the opening.

The late evening sun had long been swallowed by the blanket of night. I peered up to see the sparkling stars in the sky, a rare treat since they weren't visible in the city.

Not much had changed inside the industrial park since this morning. Fewer cars were parked in the lot, the lamp posts surrounding them casting a soft ring of orange onto the asphalt. The flat, featureless building that was the warehouse was now dark and covered with shadows, but there was a flicker of life inside the building through a dull light in a window.

"What are you waiting for? Open the door," Eli commanded as we approached the side entrance of the warehouse.

Catilda pressed her lips together and stood in front of the keypad. Her fingers were trembling and her worried eyes darted in all directions.

"Um, actually, Catilda is more of an informant than a fighter. She shouldn't be the first inside, so why don't you just follow my lead?" Hoping no one had had a chance to change the key code, I punched the number into the keypad. A green light flashed and the door clicked open.

266

A frigid current of air left goosebumps on my skin, and I led them down the empty hallway. I needed to sneak away, but with three military soldiers and now Catilda tagging along it would be near impossible.

"Beyond those double doors is the main warehouse." I pointed to the end of the hallway. "The last time I saw Lizzy, she was locked away in a chemical storage closet secured with a key-pad. Be on the lookout for guards and be prepared for a fight."

Catilda scratched her arm, her gaze staring at the entrance to the warehouse.

"You should stay here, Catilda," I whispered to her. "You could get hurt, and I don't want anything happening to you, too."

She must have sensed the worry emanating from me because she responded with a reassuring smile and confidence in her voice. "Don't worry about me, hun. That overly generous fool has kinda grown on me. I want to help rescue him in any way I can."

A round of affirmative nods gave the go-ahead to storm into the warehouse. With Myra leading the pack, the double doors flung open. The team fell into place in a three-man formation, covering a three sixty view around them. Their determined faces promised pain to anyone in their way. Blair's electric ball of lightning intensified under her fury and a golden aura radiated from her skin. Eli had the boomerang in his hand, a dense magical cloud of navy-blue magic engulfing him. Then there was Myra, her slender frame giving her the advantage of speed and agility over her two taller teammates. A glossy pink sheen trailed off her hair as she whipped it side-to-side, searching for danger.

These were the powerful members of the Black Sheep, a group of elite soldiers consisting of the best the military had to offer, and I could only hope they'd live up to their reputation.

Unlike earlier, there were no employees skittering about the warehouse. It was well lit and oddly quiet, no forklifts being operated and no trucks being loaded. Tall rolling ladders reached upward toward the endless rows of sturdy industrial metal shelves, each one fully stocked with crates and barrels. A few pallets had been left on the floor that had yet to be placed. Across the side of every packaged item ready to be shipped were the stamped words "NightFly Technologies" in bright red letters.

Although I was supposed to be leading them to Lizzy, Catilda and I fell back, letting the team do what they did best while we waited for the opportunity to sneak off and search for Ryker. Suddenly, they ran for cover, their tight formation splitting as they crouched down behind empty bins and crates. Catilda and I scrambled behind them, slipping behind a forklift. My fingertips touched the cold concrete floor, and I let my magic search for the vibration of footsteps. My hands started pulsing with magic and my blood pumped uncontrollably through my veins. Nothing. Had my dad already taken Ryker and left? Was I too late?

I nudged Catilda with my elbow and nodded toward the end of the aisle. It wasn't very far, but in the cavernous space it seemed like it went on for miles. We had been about to slip past the others when a loud crash echoed from one of the aisles. The deafening noise rang in my ears, my sensitive hearing, even more sensitive than usual, picking up on every little detail.

"Nolan won't let you get away with this." It was Adrian's voice, an optimistic warning through a hissed breath.

There was no need to inform Myra and the others. They immediately leapt from their positions and were already heading in the direction of the noise.

"Zulli, what are you waiting for? Let's go." Catilda waved at me, but my feet didn't move.

"I think we should follow them. Adrian is over there with someone. Maybe that person knows where Ryker is being kept. Or maybe Ryker is with him."

Catilda let out an angry breath but followed me as I trailed behind Myra and the others, the clomp of their boots on the smooth concrete floor like a pack of wild bulls aggressively charging toward their target. They turned down an aisle at the far end of the warehouse, magic blazing and ready for action.

With a deep inhale, Myra expelled a cloud of her magical fog. It rolled down the aisle, the air so damp I could drink it. Everything became a haze, but I sensed the presence of two other unknown magic energies fleeing. As the fog lifted, Dr. Keller was left behind along with another man, baby-faced with the look of a pretty boy. He stood in front of a battered Adrian writhing in pain on the floor. A stack of broken crates, dented barrels, and splintered pallets surrounded him.

Eli and Blair covered Myra's back as she rushed over to her friend, dropping the black plastic case she was carrying to the floor next to him.

"Adrian, are you okay?"

"I'm fine," Adrian coughed as she helped him to his feet. "But Lizzy …"

The woman in question was unconscious, lying on a gurney right smack in the middle of the aisle. All the color had drained from her face, her long hair fanned out underneath her in mottled clumps. Her lids were shut, hiding those lethal turquoise eyes she had flashed me earlier.

Dr. Keller, wearing the same lab coat as before, had on a pair of headphones and was bobbing her head to a silent beat. She ignored the fight going on around her and continued working, sticking various needles into Lizzy's arm and filling a crate with plastic bags full of blood. The baby-faced man, severely outnumbered, viciously eyed us and waited for our next move.

Adrian turned in my direction, a glorious look of bewilderment twisting across his face and an unnaturally high pitch to his words. "Zulli? And … cat lady?"

"Catilda," she replied with her innocent giggle, her cheeks slightly reddening. "Pleasure to finally meet you. You're an odd one, but I think I like you!"

Adrian ignored her, dipping his chin to his chest and bringing his attention back to Myra.

"Look out!" Blair pointed behind Adrian. A blur of magic whizzed by, taking out Adrian's legs, followed by Myra's. The speedster, not the same one Ozcar had sent after me, was sporting a set of curly pigtails that fluttered behind her as she moved. The obnoxiously loud chewing of her bubble gum made me cringe. She stuck out her tongue at me, blowing a bubble that then popped.

Blair and Eli clasped their hands together, their combined magic abilities of lightning and magnetism creating an electromagnetic force. The beam of energy blasted a beam of energy directly at the speedster.

It missed their target, blowing up a pallet rack instead. A barrel of green liquid exploded, packets of colorful powders creating a rainbow of magic floating in the air. Thankfully, none of it activated.

I had no time to be amazed at their attack. The pretty boy, wearing an argyle sweater vest and bootcut jeans, raised his hands, and my feet began rising off the floor.

Catilda's magic swirled around her, and she bounded off in her cat form to avoid getting caught in the man's gravitational pull. She darted from shelf to shelf, trying to get closer to Adrian and Myra. Blair and Eli lost their footing and were thrown with tremendous force into a stack of wooden pallets. I called up my own magic, my two arms and legs transforming into those of an eight-legged spider. The vibration of the man's gravity magic tingled the hairs on my body, the sound rippling through me, thrumming along the way.

A silky thread shot out of my spider body, latching on to a nearby shelf. The struggle to pull myself out of this gravitational hold should have been draining, but, perhaps because of Adrian's magic, I had more strength than I normally would have had. I tugged on the thin webbing. Determined, I crawled my way out of the magic trying to drag me in the opposite direction and up toward the ceiling. Another thread fired off, attaching to a metal pole above me. This time, I ripped free from the gravitational hold and my tiny spider body soared through the air toward the man who had attacked me.

Halfway there something set off my magic inside me. The warmth had turned cold and vacant, all strength fleeing my muscles. My body fought against my own magic. The connection to my soul stretched and yanked on every strand, eventually forcing me to retake the shape of my human form.

The sudden release of my magic tore through me like termites eating their way through my flesh from the inside out. That familiar heaviness weighed down me as I tried to unleash my cat claws at the gravity user, the effort too much for me to handle while fighting. Instead, I opted for my fangs, hoping to steal a sliver of magic to boost the power that seemed to have faded.

The spiced smell of the pretty boy's aftershave overpowered his magical scent, but his magic tasted like rancid meat. The man struggled under my hold, grunting in frustration. His magic pressed into me, gravity crushing my feet into the floor, but I never backed down.

As I was extracting his magic, my eyes gazed up at Catilda, sitting in her cat form on top of a stack of pallets high up and away from trouble. She stood up and let out a meow, flicking her paw toward the end of the aisle.

My fangs ripped away, the man's magic replenishing a small fizzle of my energy. I gave him a solid punch to the jaw and shoved him away. Turning to make a run for it, I heard Myra call out in a compelling voice that sent a tingling shiver down my neck. "Everybody, stop!" She then blew out a haze of her fog magic that consumed the aisle.

For a split second, my feet obeyed her command. They refused to move, every limb locked in place. Every fiber of my being wanted to follow her orders like an obedient pet. But then the feeling suddenly faded, and I was on my way to find Ryker.

I whirled around, expecting Catilda to be following right behind me, but she was still locked in place high on her perch. She blinked her round blue eyes at me, giving me a wiggle of her ears and a flick of her tail, but her paws didn't budge. I shook my head at her, turning around and ready to climb up the two-story shelf because I refused to leave her behind. When she curled her feline lips and twitched her whiskers, I knew she was telling me I had to go.

With a quick glance back to Myra and the others, I saw that everyone else had been locked in place like stone statues except for me and Myra. She had the black plastic case in her hands and was walking over to Dr. Keller. Nodding back to Catilda, I mouthed her the words, "I'm coming back for you" and left her behind in the care of the Black Sheep, hoping they'd do a better job of protecting her than I had.

23

I BURST THROUGH THE DOUBLE doors and dashed down the hallway to where Lizzy had been kept, thinking that Ryker would
most likely be held in the chemical storage room.

Sooty ash from the burning fire I had set off in the hallway
earlier stuck to the beige walls, the pungent smell so intense I
could taste the bitterness on my tongue. The carpet had been
scorched, but not entirely incinerated. All the fire-proof doors
still remained intact.

My fist pounded on the thick metal door that led into the storage room. "Ryker? You in there?"

No answer.

A disappointed sigh escaped my lips as I threaded my fingers
through the short ends of my hair. I stared at the keypad, wishing
I had paid more attention to the code. I tried the same NightFly
Technologies phone number as the main entrance, but was re-
warded with a flash of red. I tried a few others, including several
street addresses and other phone numbers, but none gave me the
green light to move forward.

Rage fumed inside me, and my boot kicked the door in frustration. A tingling vibration shot up my leg, numbing it for a brief second before throbbing pain replaced it.

Searching my belt, I ripped off a yellow bullet and placed it on top of the electronic keypad. Backing away, I activated the magic. "*Fodio.*"

A series of pops and buzzes sounded as sparks flew and the circuits inside the keypad sizzled. Through the cloud of black smoke, I saw the red light flicker. When it deactivated, the lock clicked and I propelled the door open with both hands.

"Ryker?" My tongue went numb, my throat squeezing shut. My pulse beat in time with my ragged breath. Every muscle in my body quivered at the thought that I might be too late.

The room was shadowed in darkness, but I could never mistake the man sitting on the cold concrete floor, rocking back and forth as he clutched his knees to his chest.

"Ryker!" My body moved before my thoughts could catch up. As I stepped toward him, he slapped his palms to the ground, digging his heels into the floor and scuttling back against the wall.

My heart stopped beating, my legs weakening under my own weight as he spoke. "Who are you? How do you know my name?"

His clear tone was undercut with a choking heaviness that forced him to swallow several times. There was no lazy smile on his face to comfort me, just an infinitesimal twitch of his lips in my direction. Ryker's amber eyes that always burned with a fiery dedication now flashed with raw vulnerability. He gave me a look of agonizing emptiness that turned my soul inside out.

My knees gave out and I crumbled to the floor. "Ryker ... it's me, Zulli. We're friends. Don't you remember me?"

"Get away from me. I don't want to cause any trouble." Blackness crept over him, the smell of his cinnamon magic no longer a welcoming warmth. He thrust out his hand, punching

274

me in the chest. His weapons were long gone, but he jumped to his feet and waved his fists at me, ready to defend himself.

"I don't want any trouble either. I came to get you out of here. Can't you use your magic? Why didn't you just leave?" I used the metal shelf bracket to lift myself up from the floor.

Before he could answer, another shadow loomed in the doorway, the smell of the salty sea accompanying it. "Did you forget something when you left last time?"

Davian flicked on the light. He door stood with his hands buried in the pockets of his trench coat. Burn marks scorched the stubble on his chin and left side of his face, leaving his mottled skin covered with ugly red and purple blotches.

"What did you do to him?" My claws extended, my fingers shaking.

"Why do you always assume your mess has something to do with me? I told you, this was all your father's plan. He did this to him. I'm just along for the ride."

A growl of unendurable pain ripped from my throat, and I lunged at Davian with my claws engaged. With my magic returning, it steadily blazed through me, fueling my rage and giving me speed I never knew I was capable of. My hand came swiping down. Fabric ripped as my fingers cleanly dragged across Davian's chest and sliced through flesh. He lurched back, avoiding the full brunt of the attack, but four streaks of blood soaked into his patterned dress shirt.

Davian held up a hand, and I clenched it with every ounce of energy I had left in me. I squeezed tighter, the pointed tips of my nails penetrating deeper into his flesh. I heard grinding, bone rubbing against bone. A sharp popping sound followed Davian's growl, so guttural and filled with menace that it shook the metal shelving units around us.

"You won't get away with this, Davian. You're *done.*"

With each threat, my magic intensified. The spark caught in my core, detonating outward in shock waves. The gentle radiance of a campfire turned into a wildfire, searing every nerve ending in my body.

My claws felt sharper, longer, more deadly as they punctured Davian's wrist. But as I ripped them out, my magic powered down. I stared at my hand in disbelief. This couldn't be happening. Not now!

"I think you're the one who's done here." Davian caught the fear etched onto my face and knew something was wrong. With a pointed finger, he shot a magic spear into my stomach. The water was icy cold, the saltiness stinging the fresh wound as I collapsed to the ground.

Out of the corner of my eye, I noticed Ryker staring right at me. He had remained neutral this entire time, standing with a slight expression of bewilderment on his face. Now his eyes were now shaded with grit.

"Your father never wanted this. You should know that." Davian stepped over me, eyeing me like feral prey. He placed a hand over my nose and mouth, sending his water magic pouring through me.

I couldn't think, couldn't breathe. As his pressure intensified, it felt like I was being burned alive from the inside out. Every time I tried to take a breath, more water slipped down my throat and poured into my lungs, expanding until I felt like I was going to explode.

I kicked and screamed, but without magic at my disposal, I was powerless to fight back. The muscles in my throat and lungs spasmed, convulsing as my body struggled for oxygen. My hands shot up, reaching for Davian.

"Stay down!" He crushed my head into the concrete, and blackness crept in from the edges of my vision.

My life didn't flash before me. The only thing I thought about was my friends. Would Catilda ever break free from her family's shadow? Maybe Kasra could take my place as her best friend after I was gone. I gave up struggling when my mind wandered to Ryker. If he didn't remember me, would he even mourn my death?

"Leave her alone!" Ryker's words were like a jolt of electricity, jumpstarting my heart.

Through my glassy vision, Ryker's figure pummeled into Davian. The two of them tumbled into a shelving unit, the metal groaning as it came crashing down on top of them.

I rolled over onto my side, choking and coughing up water. The stale air in the room was a welcome rush into my lungs.

Ryker threw a punch at Davian's face, his expertly placed portal landing a hit on his side. Davian shot out streams of water like bullets. One went straight through Ryker's shoulder. Another grazed his thigh.

"Ryker ..." My voice was so low I couldn't hear myself.

With a bone crunching elbow to the jaw, Ryker finally knocked him unconscious.

"Are you okay?" There was a slight moment of hesitation before Ryker held out his hand to help me up.

"For now. Thanks for saving me. Ryker, you're hurt ..." I licked my lips, ready to heal his wound. My hand went to peel back the bloody fabric from his shirt when he twitched, pulling himself back and out of my reach.

"You really don't remember me, do you?" I tried to hide the tears filling my eyes and bit my bottom lip to stop it from trembling.

"I have no idea who you are, but he was going to kill you. I wasn't about to stand by and watch someone die."

A smile crept onto my face at the glimpse of the old Ryker I knew and loved. At least his sunny disposition hadn't changed.

"We should probably get out of here." Ryker took my hand and dragged me toward the exit. A swarm of butterflies elevated my stomach and caused a sudden wave of lightheadedness. The simple gesture may not have meant anything to him, but I was relieved that I could experience that gratifying feeling of his touch once again.

"Zulli, what's wrong?" The sound of my name from his mouth made my eyes swell with sorrow. Would I ever get him back?

"Nothing." I found a blue bullet on my belt and tossed it at Davian. "*Dormeo.*"

The dust cloud consumed Davian as he lay there unconscious, breathing in the sleep spell. "That should keep him out for a while. At least until the military can get here and take him in."

Ryker stared at my belt with a fascinating gleam in his eyes. "Are they all filled with magic?"

"Yes, but they won't be for much longer if we wait for his reinforcements to arrive. Let's go."

Now familiar with the layout of the warehouse, I easily led Ryker to the exit and into the parking lot, dodging a few guards along the way. Outside, night had settled over the city of Estine but offered no relief from the sweltering heat. A few street lights gave off a soft glow, enough that I could make out a flash of a red bandana and a woman in a leopard print tunic clutching something in her arms as she fled the scene of a crime.

"Catilda!" Raising my voice felt like coughing up needles inside my throat.

Thankfully, she heard me and waited for Ryker and me to catch up. "Zulli? Ryker! You're okay!"

Ryker said nothing, staring at Catilda with a stony expression.

"*Is* he okay?" Catilda raised an eyebrow at me.

"No. I think my father wiped his memory with Bliss." The words felt unreal coming off my tongue. "Where are the others?"

"Oh, I took the goods and ran. Some crazy stuff went down in there. That Adrian kid? He's got some really weird magic. Then this creepy shadowy guy showed up out of nowhere and Adrian, Myra, and Lizzy just … disappeared with him. Consumed by a shadow and vanished into thin air. They left Blair,

Eli, and me with the doctor and the people protecting her. That was when I snatched *this* and decided to make a run for it!"

I pointed to the black case Catilda was clutching in her arms—the same case Myra had been carrying around with her. "Great. What exactly did you steal from the military?"

The brightest smile beamed across her freckled face and her eyes lit up even in the darkness of the night surrounding us. She popped open the case and presented it to me. Inside was an unassuming baking utensil that had nearly cost me my life—a silver handled spatula with a purple silicone scraper lying on a foam insert.

"What? How? But ..." All I could do was stare at the magic object in shock.

"I can explain later, but I think we should bolt out of here before someone catches us. I know a safe place we can go."

"Okay, but we gotta stop at the hotel first. I left the bonding agent and blood sample in the safe before I left."

Catilda and I trotted over to a beat up blue pickup truck near the building entrance. The driver's side window was cracked open just enough for a spider to slip through.

"What's wrong?" Catilda asked.

"I ... I can't use my magic. I can't transform." That icy heaviness I'd felt after attacking Davian hadn't gone away. As much as I had tried to connect with my magic, the line was severed.

"Okay, guess you'll have to smash the window in, then." Catilda stepped back, ensuring she was out of my line of fire.

I reeled my hand back before Ryker stopped me. "The car alarm will go off if you do that." He checked around the seat, then pushed out his hand. It disappears through a portal and reaches for the sun visor inside the car. When his hand returned, a set of keys was in his palm. He tossed them over to me, taking a step away from me and Catilda.

"Ryker, you're coming with us. You can't stay here." I reached out, ready to grab him by his tattered shirt and take him by force. He stepped out of my reach and held up his hands like a shield between us.

"Look, ladies, I appreciate your help, but I don't know you. And right now, I don't know who I can trust. So, good luck."

He turned his back to me and began walking away when Catilda caught his wrist and pulled him back. "Wait!" She dug through her phone and flipped the screen around to show Ryker the awkward photo she had taken of the three of us in front of a sappy tourist sign by the beach. "Do you remember this photo? It was taken a couple of days ago when we arrived in Estine. *Together.* You may not remember us Ryker, but you *do* know us. You can trust us, more than you can trust anyone else inside that building. Plus, Zulli really likes you, so I'm not leaving without you."

The heat rushing to my cheeks felt like I had dunked my face into boiling water.

"See? She's not denying it. So, what do you say, Ryker? Will you come with us?"

Ryker took Catilda's phone and stared at the photo, the glow of the screen lighting up his face. She had taken the photo herself, and it was poorly positioned and off center. Half my face was missing from the frame, Ryker's expression looked like he had no idea what was happening, and Catilda had beamed a perfect radiant smile just as she had taken the photo. Some small part of me hoped that maybe seeing it would snap him out of the memory loss, like how being told the truth had snapped me out of mine. No such luck.

"Over there!" came the bark of a military commander. Reinforcements had arrived and we were out of time.

"Fine. But I'm driving." He snatched the keys from Catilda and jumped into the driver's seat of the truck.

The vehicle sputtered to life, no doubt audible to everyone in the area. As we drove through the parking lot, I saw Blair and Eli standing at the entrance of the warehouse talking with some other soldiers. I ducked in the seat to avoid being seen. Ryker

280

avoided making eye contact as he drove past them, and I directed him back toward our hotel.

24

"YOU REALLY DON'T REMEMBER ANYTHING?" I prodded Ryker while he took in the surroundings of our honeymoon suite. By now, the night was disappearing but the sun wasn't yet ready to wake up. My limbs already felt heavy without magic, but the exhaustion and fatigue crippling my muscles only made it worse. I had been up for nearly twenty-four hours straight and I wasn't going to last much longer.

"No. We really slept here? Together?"

My cheeks heated like someone had lit a flame under my skin, and Catilda laughed at me. "It wasn't like that … we just … you know … needed a place to stay. This was all they had available."

Ryker was surprised to see a duffle bag full of his clothes and equipment, and rummaged through it to find a pair of cargo shorts and a green striped polo. While he rinsed off in the shower, I took it upon myself to take a short nap. Missions were never predictable, and there had been several times I had to push through a full day without rest, but that didn't make the lack of sleep any easier to endure.

Once Ryker was finished, I hopped into the shower myself and changed into a pair of overall shorts and a crop top.

"Ugh. You really need a clothing makeover, hun." Catilda stuck up her nose at my outfit. "All you need is a straw hat and a pair of rubber boots, and you could go wrangle up some hogs."

"How is that any different from my current job?"

Catilda chuckled then crashed on the luxurious canopy bed while we finished packing. I was really going to miss that bed.

Before we left, I grabbed both the blood and bonding agent from the safe and made sure I still had the samples of Bliss given to me by my father. We hopped back into the truck, Ryker still in the driver's seat.

"Where are we going?" he asked Catilda, putting the truck into gear.

"The Rainbow Unicorn."

From the passenger's seat, I leaned over the console to address Catilda. "Um, excuse me? That sounds like some sketchy strip club bar."

"Of course it's not! It's my friend's shop. No one will look for us there."

"Catilda, we can't bring any more innocent people into this."

She clicked her tongue at me, curls bouncing as she turned her gaze out the window. "We can and we will. I trust Bailee with my life. Plus ... he kinda already knows about everything."

"Catilda!" I leaned into the back seat and punched her in the leg. "Ryker, say something!" He was rubbing the heel of his palm against his forehead. "Ryker? Maybe we should go back to the hotel and rest. If you—"

"I'm fine," he cut me off, keeping his gaze on the road. "What's the address?"

Catilda handed over a business card. The truck thankfully had a navigation system built into it, and so I entered the address and off we went.

The rest of the drive was quiet because Catilda and I drifted off into sleep. Now that the rush of survival had worn off, exhaustion overtook adrenaline. But Ryker powered on until we reached our destination about two hours later.

"Does Bailee know we're coming?" I questioned Catilda.

"I gave him a call before we left. He should be waiting for us."

As we exited the car, a rush of heat slapped me in the face. It was so early in the morning, the sun was just starting to ascend into the sky, but that didn't stop the sweltering heat from soaking into my skin. Crickets chirped in the open field that surrounded the magic shop, and even though we had left the coast behind, I could still get a whiff of that salty ocean breeze in the air.

The small cottage before us was located in one of the neighboring towns of Estine. The magic shop looked straight out of a fairytale, in perfect harmony with its surroundings, evocative and full of charm. The terracotta roof was a colorful array of oranges soaking up the early morning sun, vines of colorful flowers climbing up the teal shutters and clinging to the canary yellow siding. Lively green hedges with red berries lined the mosaic pathway that led up to the rustic wooden door elaborated with glass and wrought iron ornamentation. Right above it was a sign that read "The Rainbow Unicorn," each letter written in a different color.

I fully expected to see unicorns grazing in the large open field that surrounded the place.

"Catilda, sweetheart! Back already? Did you miss me?" A man leaned against the doorway, his exceptionally tight tie-dyed tank top showing off every muscle in his chest. Bleached blond curls coiled around his white ball cap, a friendly smile shining on his smooth face. His golf shorts stopped right above his knees. A colorful design of assorted tropical fruits was printed on the fabric.

His purple flip-flops clapped as he walked out to greet us.

"Twiggy!" Catilda hugged him, and he kissed her once on each cheek.

"It's like you never left, Cuddle Butt. Because you didn't. All your stuff is still upstairs in the guest room."

"How are you so full of energy this early in the morning?" Catilda asked.

He flipped a curl off his forehead. "Today is shipment day. I have to get up early to accept new shipments when they arrive."

I wasn't quite sure what was going on and quite frankly had no interest in getting involved. I stepped aside and waited for Catilda to introduce me.

"These are my friends, Zulli and Ryker."

"Zulli? As in *the* Zulli?" He removed his sunglasses to reveal honey-brown eyes, his gaze sweeping over me. Placing one hand on his hip, he circled his finger in the air suggesting I twirl around.

He grunted an approval at my short hair, complimenting the heavy green highlights, then frowned as he continued to make his way down my body. "What is *this*?" He spotted a mystery stain on my front breast pocket.

"Nice to meet you too, *Twiggy*. I'll have you know, I didn't exactly have time to coordinate my outfits while I was fleeing for my life." I crossed my arms over my chest to hide the stain and glowered at him.

He let out a hearty chuckle. "Such sass. I like her, Catilda."

Ryker stepped forward and held out his hand. "Hi, I'm Ryker."

"Bailee."

They clasped hands in a strong handshake, both offering a firm nod.

"Come on inside. It's too damn hot out here and my skin is shriveling."

The colorful exterior extended to the inside as well. Exposed chestnut beams lined the ceilings, while murals of gardens and mountain landscapes accented the walls. I felt like I had been transported to the countryside, the open windows making it a bit toasty but allowing the breeze to carry in the exotic scent of nature surrounding the house. Mismatched shelving and tables were scattered around the open space, the eclectic styles somehow tying everything together.

"You could take some style tips from this guy and clean up your shop." I poked Catilda in the arm.

"Oh, knock it off, hun. It's not *my* shop, anyway. Blame my parents for their poor style choices."

"Is this a Venus Fly Trap?" Ryker bent down to analyze a ceramic pot sitting on a wooden table. "I thought they were only found on Earth?"

"Yes, they are. I paid someone to acquire one and bring it back for me. They're one of the few carnivorous plants we know about. I feed it flies from time to time." Bailee closed the front door and locked it.

"Now *that* is my kind of plant!" I tickled the stalk of the plant, watching as its trap closed and its little prickly teeth clamped tight.

"Oh, yeah. It also likes spiders."

I yanked my finger away and ran to the opposite side of the room.

My phone buzzed in my pocket. I answered it, surprised it still even worked after getting drenched with Davian's water. "Kasra? I was just about to call you."

"Yeah, uh huh. I'm here in Estine. Where are you?" There was a sense of irritation to her voice.

"What? How did you get here?" I started pacing the shop, weaving around the tables and shelves. With my free hand, I scratched the fuzzy hairs on the side of my head.

"I managed to persuade one of the teams storming the warehouse to let me go with them. Told them I just wanted to work on my tan. They found Davian. He's locked away."

My shoulders sagged, my muscles loosened. "That's good. I dosed him with some sleep magic. I was hoping they'd make it in time before he woke up."

"That was you?" Kasra sounded surprised. "Because Myra is taking all the credit."

I bit the bottom of my lip, growling into the phone. While I was annoyed I wouldn't receive the credit for capturing him, I knew exactly why Myra had done it. I wasn't supposed to be at the warehouse, so her claim to have caught him covered me from having to explain what I was doing there in the first place.

"Whatever. It's done." I gave her the address to Bailee's shop and our call ended.

"You guys hungry?" Bailee addressed the room. "I make some *divine* chocolate chip pancakes."

He didn't have to ask twice.

Bailee took the stairs up to the second floor of the shop where he lived. Catilda, Ryker, and I shuffled outside to the patio with our freshly squeezed orange juice. A crafty rectangular shade sail was tied to the nearby trees, keeping the hot sun from setting us on fire. Potted plants lined the stonework border. Insects and birds buzzed about as I sat down at the glass table in one of the wicker chairs.

I removed a pack of gum from my pocket, unwrapped a piece, and started chewing. The magic dissolved on my tongue, unleashing a steady stream of energy that helped counteract the fact I was still groggy. I gave a piece to both Ryker and Catilda as well.

"What's the last thing you remember?" Catilda asked Ryker.

He threaded his hands through his hair, rubbing at the sides of his head. "I know I'm a military soldier. I remember training, going on missions. But I don't remember either of you being there."

"Catilda isn't a soldier," I reminded him. "She's my best friend. Works at Harper's Treasure Chest. But you and I have been teammates for the past six months. Does the name Kasra ring a bell? Tall, pretty, extremely impatient?"

Ryker shook his head, taking a long sip of his juice.

"Snickerdoodle cookies?" Another fail. I tried recounting a few of our missions together, none of which were familiar to him.

Hesitation crept into my voice. "Do you remember anything about … my father? Zavyr Taracula? Maybe doing a job for him at some point?"

"Why would I do that? Did he commission the military to do a job for him or something?"

Ryker was drawing a complete blank. My father had wiped all his memories of me, along with any connection he'd had to NightFly Technologies. My heart ached with misery, my chest clenched tight with grief that made it hard to breathe. Hearing those treacherous words from Ryker that he had been working for my father had shattered my world. The pain it instilled in me had become a tangible, living force that crept over me like some hungry beast clawing away at my soul. And Ryker didn't remember a damn thing about it.

Kasra came crashing through the shop, screaming my name. "Zulli! Where are you?"

I stood up from my chair and walked inside to greet her. "I'm over here."

"Where is he?" Kasra was wearing her military uniform, fitted khaki pants and a polo with her tactical vest hanging from her arm.

"He's out back, but Kasra—"

She shoved me aside and stormed past me out to the patio.

"Ryker! What the hell were you thinking?" She raised her hand like she wanted to slap him across the face, but instead wrapped her arms around him in a hug.

"You must be Kasra." A soft smile crept across his face, his dimples indenting his red cheeks.

"Excuse me? What's going on here?" Kasra turned to me with a scowl.

"My father erased Ryker's memories. He doesn't remember any of us and recalls very little of the past six months since we met." My gaze dropped, my foot rubbing against the intricate stonework of the patio.

We sat back down, and Kasra went over the same questions Catilda and I had drilled Ryker with earlier.

Ryker sighed, propping his elbow against the table, fiercely massaging his brows in circular motions.

"Something's wrong. You keep rubbing your head." My hand reached across the table to clasp his, but he pulled it away.

"It's just a headache."

The back door opened and Bailee came out with a plate piled about three feet high with pancakes and bacon. He placed the food on the table, introduced himself to Kasra, and joined us for breakfast.

For a while, we ate in silence until Catilda spoke up. "Bailee is a master in magic herbal spells and potions. I brought us here because I thought he might be able to help us."

Bailee blushed under the compliment. "I'm no Havana Harper, but I've been known to study some things here and there. Happy to help any way I can."

Catilda smirked. "Well, my mom is a super genius. I don't think anyone can rival her."

Once we'd eaten every pancake, Bailee's chair rumbled against the stone patio as he stood. Flapping his hand at us, he chided, "Come on, now. Don't dawdle around. Grab your shopping list and let's get working."

I quickly ran to my duffle bag that Bailee had offered to keep locked in his storage closet, grabbing what I needed. The four of us then followed Bailee down the stone pathway and past a flowing ceramic fountain, the mist spraying a magic-infused water that coated my face. The magic seeped into my pores, instantly hydrating my grubby, sweaty skin.

"It's my fountain of youth!" Bailee exclaimed, brushing a finger down his perfectly smooth, evenly complexed bronze skin.

Bailee's workspace was a converted barn, which had a warmer, more rustic feeling than the summertime cottage that was the main shop. The entire structure showcased its raw bones, oak beams exposing the curved ceiling. The timber siding had a natural weathered look, yet was strong and sturdy. Nature livened the barn with exotic flowers and plants in colorful pots scattered everywhere. Throughout the space were several tables and workbenches, some housing power tools and others fancy machines and glass beakers for magic experiments and testing.

Trusting Catilda's instincts about Bailee, I handed over my most prized possessions—the bonding agent, a syringe barrel filled with a sample of Lizzy's blood, and the spatula.

Bailee poked at the spatula with a single finger. "This thing really that dangerous? Does it mix deadly muffin batter or something?"

"I wish," I interjected. "It's a unique magical object that can perfect any spell, and I would appreciate it if you didn't mess around with it, tell anyone you have it, or experiment with anything other than what we need help with."

"And that would be?" Bailee cocked a curious blond eyebrow at me.

"Bliss. We need to find a way to … unmake it. Reverse the effects." I pulled out the pill bottle my father had given me after Ozcar's attack.

I peered over at Ryker, Kasra standing at his side. He slumped forward in a wooden sling chair, head in his hands. When he pushed himself back, he covered his mouth and dragged his fingertips down his face, closing his eyes. He placed a palm over his chest, taking deep but shaky breaths.

"Hmm. I see." Bailee followed my gaze over to Ryker, then cleared a table to begin his work. "I'm quite familiar with the drug business. May have indulged in a few of those designer magic drugs at various times in my life. Nothing serious, but I know a bad reaction when I see one."

I played with my fingers, scratching my palms and making my way up my arms. "Ryker didn't do this to himself. Someone forced him. I just want my friend back. Do you think you can help?"

Catilda stood beside me and Bailee, wrapping an arm around his neck.

"I have faith in you, Bailee. Between the two of us, we'll figure something out." She let go of him and squeezed my shoulder. "And if we can't, well, there's still my mom. But I worry we're fighting against the clock on this one. Whatever your dad dosed you with before, Zulli, this version of Bliss used on Ryker seems to be … much stronger and more permanent. It'll be harder for us to break through to the real memories."

"I'll do my best, Fuzzy Fangs." Bailee gave me a thumbs up.

My eyebrows scrunched and my head tilted to the side.

"Well, Cuddles here," his arm looped through Catilda's, "tells me you're a half-spider and half-cat shifter. So, you're officially Fuzzy Fangs."

"I can live with that. Better than Cuddle Butt or Twiggy."

He let out a snort then secured a pair of plastic goggles over his eyes, giving Catilda a pair of her own. He turned to me before starting his work. "There's not much you can do here. Why don't you go back inside the main shop and go upstairs to my bedroom? It's air conditioned on the second floor, and your friend looks like he could use a nap."

"Thanks." My feet shuffled over to Ryker. Kasra had pulled up a chair and was now sitting next to him, her legs crossed and feet bouncing impatiently.

"Well?" Kasra grumbled at me.

"I'm going back to the main house to take a shower and a nap. Bailee suggested Ryker should come too."

"Great," Kasra picked up her tactical vest that she had been carrying around with her. "I'll accompany you."

"Kasra, I'm not—"

"Gonna run off with Ryker and leave me behind again? I know. Because Ryker doesn't have any clue who we even are." She threw her head back, and her shrill laugh made me wince.

"What's so funny?"

"You lied to me, Zulli. I thought we were friends. But you didn't just jeopardize our friendship, you very well might have lost Ryker's too. You really screwed up this time, Zulli."

"I ... I never meant to. I just ... This is my mess. I wanted to deal with it on my own. What I was doing wasn't exactly approved by the military. I didn't want to get you involved." The tears spurted from my eyes, and Kasra left me standing in a pool of my own sorrow.

Ryker rose from his chair and staggered onto his feet using the edge of a table for support. Sweat was dripping off his face and his eyes glazed over. He slapped a hand to his shirt and gripped it tightly with his fingers.

"Guys ... I really ... I really don't feel ... so..."

My mind blocked out all my surroundings, focusing only on Ryker. His knees buckled and gave out from underneath him. He collapsed to the floor, taking the chair with him. It happened in a fraction of a second, but I felt like I was watching it all unravel in slow motion.

Ryker started convulsing, arching his back and bucking his limbs in short, jerking movements. Kasra rushed over, pushing him onto his side and slapping his back as he choked on his own vomit. Her mouth was moving, screaming something at me, but only a deafening silence reached my ears.

My heart beat furiously against my ribcage, my breath heavy with fear. Flashbacks of Briyan and his last moments flooded my memory. A terror screeched along my veins at the image of Shayne in the interrogation room collapsing under the effects of overdosing on Bliss. Blood pounded in my ears, the world around me completely lost except for Ryker. He was barely moving, his amber eyes lost to helpless vulnerability. White foam bubbled from his mouth as he gasped for air. I knew what would happen next if this continued, and dread crept down my spine knowing that there was only one thing I could do to stop it.

"Zulli!" Kasra's words finally reached me. "What are you doing? Help us!"

Having heard a crash, Catilda and Bailee came rushing over.

"What happened?" Bailee pushed Kasra aside, checking Ryker's pulse.

"He … he's had a headache ever since being drugged," I squeaked. My feet were cemented in place. If I tried to move with my shaking knees, I'd end up on the floor alongside Ryker.

I pulled out my phone, my thumb hovering over the keypad.

"Zulli, what are you doing? An ambulance won't get here in time."

"I know. But someone else can." I forced my finger to tap the screen and waited for someone to answer.

The man on the other line picked up, mockery fueling his words. "Well, hello there, little spider. What can I help you with?"

"Hello, *Dad*. We need to meet. Send your transporter right now."

25

---⬙---

BAILEE QUICKLY MIXED UP SOME herbal concoction and forced it down Ryker's throat. He then placed two hands on his chest and an earthy scent of wet rain permeated the air.

"This should help keep him calm, but it's not a cure. At this rate, the drug will kill him in … I don't know. A day? More likely hours."

He and Kasra helped Ryker back into the chair. Catilda used a wet washcloth to wipe the vomit and sweat from his face and clothes.

"You're a healer?" I asked Bailee.

He gave a cheerful laugh, his blond curls bouncing as he threw his head back. "Not by a long shot, Fuzzy Fangs. I have a connection to nature. I speak to the earth. I simply shoved a bunch of herbs down his throat and used my magic to amplify their effects on his body. He is *totally* tripping right now."

Ryker had calmed down but was mumbling and groaning incoherent words. His head rolled on his shoulders and his pupils were solid black and dilated.

A warm pocket of wind sucked in the air around me. Papers on a nearby desk and leaves on the floor swirled around in a cyclone.

My father's transporter was a well-dressed gentleman wearing creased black dress pants and a pale blue polo. His thinning hair had been combed to the side, his drab expression showing his boredom.

"Mr. Taracula has sent me to bring you and the boy back to his office," he said in a flat monotone voice. It was the first time I had ever heard the man speak.

"No way," Kasra stepped in front of the man, raising her finger to his nose. "You are not going without me."

"I'm sorry, Ms. Klein. Those are not my orders. Either the two of them come or none of you."

"Kasra." My hand delicately tapped her shoulder but she shrugged it off. "Let me make this right. If anyone can help Ryker now, it'll be my dad. I don't like it, but we need him. We don't have much of a choice."

"You really think Zavyr is just going to drop what he's doing to help you? If what you said is true, then he's the one who did this to Ryker in the first place! You're delusional, Zulli."

"He won't do it for Ryker, but he might do it for his daughter. I'm open to other ideas if you have them."

Kasra stepped aside and away from the transporter. Bailee assisted her in helping Ryker to his feet, Catilda making one last attempt to wipe away the sweat beading on his forehead. Ryker's arm draped around my neck, and I swung mine around his waist, his body radiating heat like a furnace.

"Don't you dare screw up again." There was a poisonous venom in Kasra's words that stung deep in my core, but there was also a worried twitch at the possibility of losing her teammate and friend.

Bailee handed me a water bottle, green herbs floating inside it. "If it happens again, you can use this to calm him down. But it's only a temporary solution. He needs help, and I hope you can get it before it's too late. Good luck."

"Thanks for your help, Bailee." He gave me a double kiss on the cheeks and backed up to make room for Catilda, who launched herself at me full force.

"I'll be back, Catilda." I squeezed her tight.

"I know. We'll be here continuing to work. Go save the world and your lover boy."

"I wi—wait, what? Ryker and I aren't … I told you it's not like that. We're friends." My face flushed as my lungs seized as I remembered him kissing my cheek. I had assumed his actions were a result of the magic talking, but he never took back his words. I glanced over to Ryker, thankful that he was too out of it to have heard her.

"Uh huh. Sure. Whatever you say, hun. Just go save him and bring him back alive." Her glittery eyeshadow sparked with her over-exaggerated wink.

Bailee gave a bouncing nod, while Kasra raised her eyebrows and tapped a finger to her lips like she wanted to add something to the conversation but decided against it.

The transporter didn't give me a chance to respond. He placed a hand on both me and Ryker. A slight heat enveloped me. There was a flash of black, and we ended up two hundred miles away in my father's office at NightFly Technologies.

Unable to keep himself steady, Ryker wobbled like a drunk and almost took me down with him as he pitched to the side. Together, we hobbled over to the imperious man sitting behind a sleek, modern desk.

"My little spider!" My father stood up and held out his hands like he was expecting me to run over and give him a hug. "I'm so glad to see you made it out of the warehouse okay."

"Yeah, unfortunately only one of us did. You can cut the crap, Dad. You know why I'm here. Fix him."

My father rounded the corner of his desk and casually leaned against the edge of it, rolling up the sleeves of his shirt and crossing his ankles. The black suit pants and vest he was wearing, along with a crimson button-down underneath, gave him the look of a well-polished mad man.

"I can't just *fix* him, little spider. The drug is experimental." He took a long look at Ryker, his silver eyes simply analyzing him like he was a lab rat. There was no concern or sympathy for his pain. "I think we may have gotten the dosage slightly incorrect. Too bad."

"I know you. You wouldn't experiment with something unless you had an antidote for it. You'd have a contingency plan in case it was used against you." My mouth went dry, the lag in my brain from exhaustion trying to keep up with my words. My heart beat uncomfortably under my ribs as my stomach churned. Exhaustion won the battle, and I dropped to the floor with Ryker still in my grip. I cradled his head in my arms and watched helplessly as his breathing labored and he gasped for air.

My father smiled and wagged his finger at me. "You think like me more than you'd like to believe. It looks like you need a nap, Zulli. Why don't you go back home and sleep this off?"

"Not until you fix him."

My father threw his head back, scoffing as he pushed off from the desk and stood over me on the rug. The late morning sun shone through his office windows, casting ominous shadows across his sharp features. "The boy betrayed you, sweetheart. He was spying on you. Let him go. Scum like that is not worth saving."

"How would you know how he really felt? I bet you were manipulating him right from the start. He had no choice!" My voice grew louder, a growl that was both harsh and judgmental. Inside my chest, my heart pounded, pumping boiling blood through my veins.

His dark laugh made my skin crawl, the hearty roar full of incomprehensible power that shook my bones. "Ryker never told you the whole truth, did he? He actually came to *me* requesting this job. I didn't push him to do anything."

"Liar!" A knot of tension twisted in my stomach and climbed upward, threatening to suffocate me.

"I guess we'll never find out." He shrugged and looped back around to his chair, sitting down to finish his work.

Ryker twitched, a small jerking motion like a shudder. Small, ragged breaths followed. His mouth fell open, silent screams trying to free themselves as he gasped for air. His chest spasmed, then his arms and legs flailed uncontrollably.

"Ryker! It's okay! You're okay." I poured Bailee's treatment into his mouth, but he couldn't swallow.

I sank further into despair as Ryker thrashed around while my father just sat there, going about this business. Tears flooded from my eyes, a hot spiral of heat clenching my chest. Desperation overcame me as he stopped moving. His breath slowed to a shallow whisper.

"Dad, please," I pleaded through choking sobs. "Help me. I'll do anything!"

He quirked an eyebrow. "Anything? That's a bold statement."

Relinquishing my hold on Ryker, I gently rested his head on the floor. Stiffening my shaking knees, I marched over to my dad and stared right into his predatory eyes. "Yes. I will do anything. What do you want? Confidential military information? Something from the vault?"

The look on his face, the way his resentful eyes pressed against me like frozen thorns, confirmed he had something more sinister in store for me.

"I have it on good authority that your next mission will be a search and rescue. Except … you will not be rescuing this person. I need you to kill him."

The words didn't immediately register as I stood there, frozen in place. My limbs tensed, no air making its way into my lungs. My mind went completely blank until I finally comprehended what he was saying.

"N-no. I am not a murderer. Pick something else."

"Davian has been captured. He is no longer of use to me. You will take his place. That is my price." Menace flavored his words. "A life for a life, Zulli. What's it going to be?"

Behind me, Ryker gave one last gasp, then went completely still. If working for my father was the price I had to pay for Ryker's life, then there was nothing to argue.

"I'll do it."

"Fantastic! Welcome to the family business, my little spider." My father picked up his desk phone and called for someone to come to his office immediately. He then casually strolled over to a bookcase, no haste in his step or sense of urgency in his movements. He pushed it aside to reveal a hidden compartment in the wall. He punched a few numbers into a safe, placed his finger on the scanner, and extracted a vial of black liquid.

"This is the only sample I've been able to develop, and I'm afraid this antidote is experimental. It requires a very rare ingredient we haven't been able to get our hands on. But everyone's magic is different, Zulli. I can't promise it will work or what will happen if it doesn't." He held out the syringe to me, then pulled it back. "I am doing this for you, Zulli. Not him. You are my daughter and I love you. Never forget that."

"Thank you." The words felt like a hot knife against my throat. This wasn't love and it felt wrong to be grateful.

"Step aside and out of the way. Give me room to work."

I took a few steps back, biting my fingernails as I watched my father bend down toward Ryker.

"In the hallway, Zulli. This process is extremely complex and I need to concentrate."

With a shaking step, I turned and scurried out into the hallway just as a female lab technician with thin wispy hair and a white lab coat appeared beside me.

"You needed me, sir?" The words squeaked out of her. The woman's hands were trembling uncontrollably, like she thought she might be in trouble.

"Yes, come in Dr. Aymes. I need your assistance. We're deploying the antidote on this young man."

"But sir, that's not—"

"Do *not* question my authority, Dr. Aymes. Now hurry up and let's get this over with." His silver eyes gleamed with something evil that terrified the poor woman even more. She didn't argue any further, rushing over to my father's side to assist him.

I stood right by the door, watching Dr. Aymes prick Ryker's arm with the needle and push down on the plunger to expel the liquid.

My father's lips moved almost silently as he concentrated. If I focused, I could have heard the what he was saying but all I could think about was getting my friend back.

I gripped the doorframe to steady my weak knees. My throat went dry and tightened. My heart beat so loudly it was the only thing I could hear. Ryker wasn't more than fifteen feet away from me, yet he was so far out of my reach. All I wanted was to see his cheery dimpled smile again, to hear the sound of his comforting voice telling me everything would be okay. I craved the smell of his cinnamon scent, to feel the tickle of his magic on my skin. He had become a much larger part of my life than I realized and living without him wasn't an option. The thought of it opened a deep, aching void in the center of my chest.

My father stood up and loomed over Ryker's body. Not so much as an infinitesimal twitch came from a finger or fluttering eyelid. I struggled to choke back the tears. The ticking of the clock in the hallway was a cruel reminder that time was slipping away, along with his life. With each fleeting second without movement, my hope that he might survive was replaced with a disturbing fear that I might never feel his warmth brush against my skin ever again.

The world was lost around me, my eyes focusing only on Ryker. My heart started racing when I thought I saw the faintest movement of his lips. Another spike of excitement came when

300

his shoulder twitched. He shot up, heaving in a deep breath to fill his empty lungs with fresh air.

I bolted over to him, pushing my dad and the doctor out of the way, and dropped to my knees. I pressed a hand to his back, rubbing it in circular motions as deep, hoarse coughs came out of his mouth. My other hand cupped his red cheek and turned his face toward me. "It's okay, Ryker. I'm here."

"Zulli?" His voice was barely a whisper. His familiar tone was charged with worry and concern not for himself but for me, and it warmed my heart. He remembered me.

"Yeah, Ryker. It's me." He struggled to keep his head straight. He rested it on my shoulder, then took my hand in his and squeezed. His eyes fluttered, and then he passed out.

"Ryker?" Panic shook me, my fingers pressing against his neck, checking for a pulse.

My father pulled me to my feet and away from Ryker. "He's fine. Just a little exhausted, and he needs some rest. Now, if you don't mind, I have a business to run. I'll be in touch." He picked up his cell phone, and his personal transporter appeared out of thin air with a pop of magic. "Rusl, can you please take them back to wherever they came from?"

Ryker, sluggish but awake, picked himself up off the floor and leaned against me while. A moment later, we were whisked away back to Bailee's shop.

Rusl didn't stick around, immediately leaving after dumping us off in the barn. Catilda was the first to rush over and greet me.

"You did it, Zulli!" Catilda squealed as she bounced up and down, the plastic goggles resting on her curly hair slipping down her face.

Kasra and Bailee weren't far behind, coming over to check on both me and Ryker.

"Good work, Fuzzy Fangs. I'm impressed." Bailee was about to give me a hug, but one of his machines made a chiming noise and he immediately went to check on it.

"Ryker?" Kasra pushed Catilda aside to see her teammate. Ryker's dimpled cheeks deepened with his smile. His glittering eyes radiated that magnetism we were all used to.

"Hey, Kasra." He massaged his temples, his forehead wrinkling between his fingertips. "Some things are still a little fuzzy, but I could never forget the best teammates ever."

"*Psh.* What about me?" Catilda whined. "I got you that damn spatula."

"You did?" His eyes were a smile that warmed her soul, made apparent by her rosy cheeks on display.

"Ah, it was nothing, hun."

"Glad to have you back, Ryker." I dug my fingertips into my scalp and scratched.

He turned to me and crushed me in his arms. I melted under his touch. I sniffed his shirt, wishing for the smell of his cinnamon magic but instead taking in the scent of dirt, blood, and sweat. Not the most pleasant of smells, but it was his.

"Aww. So cute."

My menacing glare could have sliced Catilda in half. Her eyes burned with a look harboring no regret.

"I need to go outside for a minute." I let go of Ryker and walked outside the barn, over to Bailee's fountain of youth.

I sat down on the edge of the fountain, letting the mist spray the back of my neck. The three-tiered fountain was decorated with wildlife, both with animals alive and ones made of stone. On top of the structure were colorful birds chirping and splashing their wings in the water. Below it the basin was surrounded with exquisite stone carvings of fish. The bottom was supported by three bears holding up a bowl. It seemed to attract a number of insects, including spotted butterflies and nightflies, the insects after which my father's company was named. My mother had always loved them, and I remembered sometimes sitting with her outside in the garden to watch them. During the day, the sunlight glistened off their two sets of iridescent wings, but at night, they glowed a vibrant rainbow in the moonlight.

302

"If you've never seen a field of them at dusk, it's quite a breathtaking sight."

My breath caught in my throat as I jumped up from the fountain at the sound of the sly voice. I curled my fingers, my claws appearing as quickly as they vanished. I shook out my hand, wishing for my magic to return.

A man with a black ballcap and tinted sunglasses stood before me. Even though he was wearing cargo shorts and a polo with his signature popped collar, he couldn't escape the dreaded heat. His short stubble of a beard glistened and a very visible sweat stain appeared just above his gut.

"Ozcar. What are you doing here? How did you find me?" With each step he took toward me, I took another one back.

"Zulli. Can I call you Zulli? I feel like we're on a first name basis now after all we've been through together."

I nodded, not really sure what to respond.

"I keep track of all the people who owe me something. You are no different. Plus, you made quite a mess at that warehouse. I believe you have something for me? I came to pick up my payment."

"It ... It's not here." My mouth went dry like I had swallowed a handful of cotton balls.

"Please. Don't try to fool me. We went through your hotel room already. It was clear you took everything and left. Now, if you don't mind, *give me the spatula.*" He emphasized the last words with sharp pronunciations, his demand promising pain if I didn't agree.

I gulped and turned around to head back to the barn, Ozcar following behind me. Instant reflexes kicked in. Ryker and Kasra assumed their attack stances, Catilda hid under a table, and Bailee, upon seeing everyone's panic, dropped a glass beaker on the floor and held up his hands.

"Relax, my friends. I'm just here to pick up what is mine." Ozcar strolled over to the table where Bailee was working.

"I think it's pretty obvious you are not a friend." I hid my anxiety behind a puffed-out chest and firm hands on my hips.

"Your words hurt me, Zulli," he said casually as he shook a vial of something Bailee was messing with, his calculating eyes analyzing the contents inside.

"Hey, don't touch—"

Ozcar dropped it on the floor before Bailee could stop him. "Oops. Hope that wasn't important."

He plucked another one from a test tube rack.

"Ah. Fascinating," he mused as he broke apart the magic in his mind. Again, it fell to the floor and he stomped on it with a leather boat shoe. "Bummer."

Down the table he went, destroying everything he lay his eyes on, except for one vial filled with a crimson liquid.

"Ah, the blood. I'll be taking this." He tucked it into a pocket and then eyed a black plastic case, the magic spatula still inside. He picked up the baking utensil, cradling it in his hands like he had found a lost child. "Oh, how I missed you."

"Get on with it, Ozcar," I snapped at him. The emotional rollercoaster ride of almost losing Ryker had left me mentally drained, and my body had really taken a beating trying to stop Davian.

"All right, all right. It was a pleasure doing business with you, Zulli. I have a feeling we'll be seeing each other again."

"I really hope not." The confidence in my voice wasn't as strong as I had hoped.

Ozcar made his way back to the front of the shop. The roar of an engine sent birds in the nearby trees scattering, and Ozcar drove off.

"Huh," I pondered as his truck faded from view. "He actually drove here. I figured a guy like him would have an easier way of getting around everywhere since his people always seem to always show up wherever I am."

"Don't flatter yourself, hun," Catilda said as she bopped me on the head and headed back inside the main shop. Over her

304

shoulder, she added, "Having a guy like that stalking you is definitely *not* a good thing."

By this point, the afternoon sun was hot enough to light my hair on fire. A loud yawn escaped me, and I nearly lost my balance trying to stay upright.

"Hey guys," Kasra came trotting over. "Just got a message from the colonel. He wants to see us tomorrow morning. We should get back to Chitol, clean up and get some rest."

"You're not sticking around for dinner? I make a mean pot roast." Bailee rubbed his hands together.

"Thanks, but I'm not sure I have enough energy left in me to even chew," I responded. "Maybe another time?"

"Just tell me when, Fuzzy Fangs." He flashed me a quick smile.

"Ryker? Are you okay taking us back home?" I squinted at him and bit the bottom of my lip.

"Yeah, no problem."

We said our goodbyes to Catilda and Bailee, insisting we'd be back to visit.

"Next time you can keep the trouble at home. I like my quiet life out here in the suburbs. But I had fun, Fuzzy Fangs. I hope everything works out for you …" He leaned in and whispered in my ear, "… and him."

His hands weren't quick enough for my reflexes, and I poked him playfully in the taut chest. My magic was coming and going, like it had taken a vacation and didn't want to go back to work. But right now, it seemed like it was eager to get back into action.

"Everyone ready?" Ryker grabbed his duffle bag, and I shrugged both of mine over each shoulder. Kasra, who had come empty handed, moved away from me and was the first to storm through Ryker's portal.

The spicy cinnamon smell was like a musical note in perfect harmony, that delightful aroma empowering my lungs to breathe. I followed Kasra, Ryker passing through last behind me. The portal closed, and we ended up back at my apartment.

26

"I GUESS YOU DIDN'T FORGET my apartment." The shock in my voice would have been more apparent had I not been about to fall asleep standing up.

"How could I?" Ryker sat down on my couch, his fingertips slowly scratching the sides of his scalp as his head dropped forward. "I come here so often, it's hard to forget."

Kasra let out a silent yawn. "I'm heading upstairs to my own place. The colonel wants to meet us first thing tomorrow morning. I'll see you then."

She stormed out of my apartment, slamming the door behind her.

I headed into the kitchen, dumping the remaining contents of a cereal box into a bowl. With no milk, I poured in a root beer soda. Ryker took my last remaining granola bar.

"That looks disgusting." Ryker wrinkled his nose up at my bowl.

"It is. But I'm hungry and I'm too tired to care."

He took a bite of his granola bar then put it down on the coffee table, continuing to massage his temples.

"Still have a headache?" I sat down next to him, giving him a comforting rub on the back.

"Yeah, it just won't go away."

Heaviness consumed me, an icy ball of doubt in my chest. My father had mentioned the antidote was only a prototype. How much of Ryker's memories would actually return? Would he still be the same man I've come to know over the past six month?

My throat was dry when I swallowed. Would he remember what he said to me in the hotel room?

"I know my couch isn't the most comfortable thing in the world, but you're welcome to sleep on it tonight if you don't want to go home. I can keep an eye on you until you get checked out and we're sure you're okay."

"Thanks. I'll be fine. But will you be okay, Zulli?"

His unexpected words sent my brain spiraling with thoughts. "Me? I've been drugged by my dad once before. Came out of it okay."

There was no humor in his serious expression. "You know what I mean. Most of the memories of this past week have been slowly coming back to me. Your father is the creator behind one of the most dangerous mind-warping drugs ever made."

"But you don't remember … anything else about my dad? Any specific jobs outside the military?"

Ryker scrunched his eyebrows at me. "That's the second time you've asked me that. Am I supposed to remember something?"

"Never mind. Forget I asked."

I sank deep into the couch and threw my head back. I had a hunch that my dad, the clever bastard, had used the antidote to restore the memories Ryker had lost, but only the ones he wanted to return. Any information Ryker had known about my father's operation was lost.

"Hey, what happened with Myra?" He gave me a wary look.

"We have a … um … mutual agreement. We're good for now."

Ryker rose from the couch on shaking legs. "I haven't forgotten my promise to you, Zulli. We'll work this out. Together."

His knee buckled under him. I darted to catch him before he fell, but it was he who caught me. A rush of dizziness left me disoriented and the room spinning. His arms embraced me, his amber eyes locked onto mine. We were stuck in that moment in time for only a few seconds, but I never wanted to let it go. That comforting feeling put me on top of the world and was a blazing fire burning in my soul. It had once been extinguished but now had sparked back to life. I pulled him in close, tears escaping my eyes and soaking into his ragged shirt.

Ryker offered no words, just held me in his arms and stroked my hair. He waited until I was ready to stand on my own, and with much reluctance, I stepped away from his warm embrace.

"I'll see you tomorrow?" He wiped away a tear streaming down my cheek.

"Yeah. See you tomorrow."

Ryker's cinnamon scent lingered in my apartment for a while after he left. I mustered up enough energy to take a quick shower, then changed into sweatpants and an old t-shirt before crashing on the bed.

Sleep had never been so welcome, my eyes so heavy I couldn't keep them open even if I wanted to. I snuggled under the comforter and didn't move until the next morning when someone shook me awake.

"Zulli? Wake up and get changed! We gotta go!" My brain rattled like a pinball machine under Kasra's violent shaking.

"I'm taking that key away," I mumbled to her, ignoring her and snuggling up in the blankets.

It was early morning, the apartment dark and cold. Heavy rain pounded on my windows, making it even more difficult to haul my ass out of bed to get ready.

"Ryker's waiting outside," Kasra said as she hovered over me, tapping her fingers against her forearms. "With food."

I shot up out of bed so fast that I fell onto the floor. Kasra waited impatiently as I changed into my uniform—tan khakis and an olive t-shirt, along with my tactical vest and belt, and locked the door behind me.

Ryker held out a coffee and something in a white paper bag. "I didn't want you resorting to eating moldy bread or something."

I snatched the bag from his hands. "You're the best."

The coffee burned as I chugged it down, the caffeine giving me a little extra punch to my morning. The egg sandwich had gooey, melted cheese and crispy, crunchy bacon. I managed to get about half of it down before Ryker said we had to get going.

A dark cloud suffocated the space in the hallway, Ryker's magic creating a swirling black hole that radiated intense heat. I dropped the sandwich, my heart jumping in my throat. Was that what Ryker's magic actually looked like? I had never been able to see it before. In fact, seeing raw magic was a rare skill and one I didn't have. So, how was I able to see it now?

"Zulli, what's wrong?" Kasra knitted her eyebrows at me.

I flexed my fingers, claws longer and sharper than ever before protruding from my fingertips. A neon green sheen glistened on my skin.

"Nothing's wrong. I'm good. Let's go."

Walking into the empty void was way more terrifying than the warm nothingness I was used to, but I focused on the spicy scent of cinnamon to get me through it.

"Could you maybe have portaled us to a less crowded place?" Kasra shimmied through the noisy crowd in the cafeteria, while I drooled over the smell of buttery pancakes.

"Sorry," Ryker apologized, shoving his hand out in front of a horde of hungry soldiers about to stampede over me on a race to the omelet station. "I can't remember where Colonel Buckner's office is, but I do remember the cafeteria no problem. We spend a lot of time here, don't we?"

We made it through the morning breakfast rush and out into the hallway, still heavily trafficked but much less chaotic. Kasra led the way to Colonel Buckner's office. As I passed the infirmary, I waved to my favorite doctor, Lana. She seemed to have her hands full with quite a few patients this morning, including a pale female with a jungle of black tattoos all over her body.

I only managed to catch a quick glimpse, but Lizzy seemed like she had made it out all right. A bit clumsy on her feet, some nasty cuts and bruises, but very much alive. An exasperated sigh whistled through my lips, relieved that Myra and Adrian had managed to rescue her.

Ryker knocked on the colonel's door, the grating voice behind it confirming that we could enter. "Come in."

The three of us filed into the colonel's office, standing in a straight line in front of his metal desk, black paint chipping off the sides. There was no glowing morning sun pouring in through his window, only the steady percussive rhythm of rain hitting the glass.

Colonel Buckner's chair rolled on the tile floor as he stood, his bulky body decked out in his military uniform and the hairs on his neatly trimmed mustache twitching along his upper lip. He pushed out the chair so forcefully from underneath him that it smacked into the wall and clattered.

"Explain yourselves." His magic was literally weighing down on me, and I could actually see it. Thick silver threads like fingers wrapped around my skin and constricted my movements. Combined with the fear swelling in my throat and lurching in my stomach, I felt like I was somehow suffocating on the air around me.

Kasra and Ryker both looked at me. Kasra hadn't been in on our secret side mission, and I wasn't sure Ryker remembered enough to craft a good lie. How much did Colonel Buckner actually know? What had Myra already told him?

I clasped my hands behind my back, hiding the shaking I couldn't control. "I'm not sure what you mean, sir?"

310

The colonel's magic intensified, and a crack sounded from my lower back.

"Just because you have been removed from your mission doesn't give you the right to slack off, Ms. Taracula. You haven't shown up once for training in the past week, and your blatant disregard for protocol is unacceptable. Soldiers are not allowed to just up and leave on vacation when there is work to do."

"Oh …" I scratched the side of my head. Myra must have kept her word and hadn't said a thing to the colonel about the spatula or our meeting in Estine.

"And you …" The colonel's glower trained on Ryker, who had been keeping himself calm and composed the entire time.

"Yes, sir?"

"You had requested some sick time because you were feeling unwell, yet you still managed to attend most of your training sessions. Perhaps you can teach Ms. Taracula here the meaning of responsibility."

A frown sagged on my face at the colonel's words. I had caught Ryker several times massaging his hands from overusing his magic. I had thought it was because he was always helping me, but he must have been sneaking off when I wasn't around to portal back to base and keep up appearances.

The colonel sat back down at his desk, steepling his fingers while he spoke in his haughty tone. "My niece, Captain Myra Llama, infiltrated Davian's compound and captured him. We will question him when he wakes up."

"Wakes up, sir?" Kasra questioned.

"Yes. It seems he was put under a pretty powerful sleep spell. He should be waking up any moment now." He twisted the hairs of his mustache between his fingers.

My stomach tightened and my fingers clenched tight. I tried to swallow, but there was no saliva in my mouth. I had hit Davian with a sleep spell before I left, but it should have been a light dose. Did my unreliable magic do something to the spell to cause this?

311

The colonel let out a grunting sigh. "Thanks to Myra and her team, hopefully Davian's capture will put a halt to the distribution of Bliss, but I don't think this mess is completely behind us yet. That warehouse was full of magic drugs and chemicals stolen from NightFly Technologies, and I'm not convinced Davian was working alone."

I bit the bottom of my lip and held my breath. The warehouse was off the books. He had no idea it actually *belonged* to Night-Fly Technologies, and therefore, my dad.

"Regardless, that is no longer your mission. I did, however, have a new assignment come across my desk yesterday. One that, for reasons unknown to me, has been passed down with the request for it to be specifically assigned to you three."

Kasra and Ryker straightened their spines, clapping their boots together and slapping their hands at their sides while staring straight ahead at the colonel.

"It's a search and rescue. A boy by the name of Colton Meyers. We have reason to believe his parents got mixed up with some bad people and fled Iradel for their safety, taking their son with them. You are to travel to Earth and secure his safe passage back here."

I locked my legs in place, digging my fingernails into my palms. I closed my eyes and counted the breaths in my head. *One. Two. Three.* My nostrils flared and my stomach clenched tight.

My father hadn't just asked me to kill anyone, he was asking me to kill a *kid*. A young, innocent kid.

"You're dismissed. I'll fill you in with more details when I have them."

My feet were moving, but my brain wasn't registering the motion.

"Well, that went better than expected," Kasra blurted out, flicking her blond braid behind her shoulder.

The three of us started walking, although I wasn't paying attention to where we were going. Ryker suddenly stopped in the middle of the hallway and I smacked into his back.

"What gives?" I barked at him.

He turned and faced me with a beaming smile on his face. "I just remembered something."

"Oh yeah?" A spark of hope blossomed outward from my chest.

"Yeah. I'll tell you over strawberry milkshakes and cheeseburgers later."

It never felt so good to smile. My magic was on the fritz. My best friend was struggling to remember who he was, and I had lost the trust of my other teammate, Kasra. Our friendship had a long way to go before it would be mended, but somehow, I knew that the four of us would get through this. We would fix this. Together.

Author's Note

Whoo! Congrats on making it to the end of the book. What's next? Zulli returns in Rise of a Rebel. You can also start reading about Adrian's adventure in the Black Sheep series.

Did you know that every time you leave a review, my dog gets to celebrate with a piece of cheese? Okay, sometimes I save some for myself, but you can help a pug out by leaving a review and supporting our cheese addiction.

Don't forget to follow me on social media so you can watch me make a fool of myself. You can also find a few free stories on my website, including Mixing Magic & Mayhem, a NightFly series prequel (and the origin of the magic spatula!). Scan the QR code below or visit www.christineschulzwrites.com.

Thanks for reading and stay magical!

Made in the USA
Middletown, DE
24 July 2023

35513716R00189